Spring Dawn

By Daphne C. Murrell

Mountain Paradise Publishers.
ISBN-13:
978-0615949963
ISBN-10:
0615949967

DEDICATION

This book is dedicated to Joy Berry and Herbert Trulove
for their unmeasured influence in the lives of my children through
the National FFA Organization.

ACKNOWLEDGMENTS

Thanks to Rick and Charis for their patience and cheerleading
as I worked through the processes of publishing.

Many thanks to Anita Hill for her willingness
to run through all this with me again and again and again,
and to Melody Murrell for that final read-through.

A big thanks to Dr. Victor Norman for his
missionary medical expertise,
and to Teresa Lesley for making sure
I got all those *nursey* terms correct.

Special thanks again goes to all of you who have read this series
and insisted I get it out there.
You can't know how much your support has meant.

PROLOGUE

Dropping her books to the floor, Angie saw no sense in bothering about the added clutter. Her room was its typical wreck. She was physically worn and emotionally exhausted from taking too many hours again, but at least she would be finished with seminary at the end of April. Maybe by then the mission board could sort through the mess concerning her appointment.

Kicking off her flip flops, she plopped onto the bed and dug beneath a pile of clothes for her laptop.

Maybe someone is online and feels like chatting for a while. I need to think about something other than the kings of Judah and Israel.

As the dated device crept to life, she removed her ponytail and shook out her long hair. This exhaustion was not only about today. Years of college, pre-med, medical school, internship, residency and now seminary had taken their toll. She was twenty-nine, still in school, and the promise of serving in the Pacific island nation of Padawin was looking dimmer each month.

She logged into Facebook and looked for the sign of a close friend online.

Yes! Michael Collins! I didn't think this would ever happen!

Michael was the agricultural missionary in Padawin. For over nine years he had served four tribal villages by himself. Great strides with two villages on the western coast had been accomplished, especially in the area of agriculture, but only eleven people had been converted. The natives struggled with the pull of the witch doctors and their intense tribal customs. The hope was that Angie could bring medical care and begin a process that would encourage more to trust Christ. The mission board, however, didn't appear to share this vision.

Angie clicked his name and quickly typed *hello*, hoping to catch him before he left.

Angie Wright: *Hello!*

Michael Collins: *Angie?*

Angie Wright: *Yes! Is this Michael of Padawin?*

Michael Collins: *Yes! I can't believe we're actually chatting! Where are you?*

Angie Wright: *In my dorm. Can you believe that? I'm 29 and still in school. I was just bemoaning that fact.*

Michael Collins: *Any luck with the board?*

Angie Wright: *Do you really want to hear about all that during our first*

1

official chat?

Michael Collins: *I guess not. Don't give up. I really believe that God wants you here. Things will happen. Remember, all things work out for the good.*

Angie Wright: *That's what my Dad keeps saying.*

Michael Collins: *I'd like to meet your dad some day. He sounds like a great guy.*

Angie Wright: *He is. Moms too. Did you know today is Valentine's Day?*

Michael Collins: *No. I don't keep up much with holidays anymore. We just celebrated Christmas here for the first time because I actually had enough Christians to warrant teaching them about it.*

Angie Wright: *So what did you get for Christmas?*

Michael Collins: *A monkey.*

Angie Wright: *LOL … You did not!*

Michael Collins: *They thought it would keep me company. They wanted me to bring it into the house and let it sleep with me and the whole bit. I just couldn't.*

Angie Wright: *So, where is it?*

Michael Collins: *On the back deck pacing the railing. It's a mean little thing.*

Angie Wright: *Save it for me. I want to see it when I get there.*

Michael Collins: *You'd better hurry. I have no intentions of keeping it around. It may "accidentally" run off to the jungle one day … I hope.*

Angie Wright: *LOL … I still think you're pulling my leg.*

Michael Collins: *I'm not that smart. Trust me, my sense of humor is lacking. Especially living over here. They don't get Western wit at all.*

Angie Wright: *Well, I do! I probably laugh more than I should. One of the professors here asked me if I took anything seriously.*

Michael Collins: *Life of the party type, I suppose.*

She typed several more sentences but got no response. She began to wonder if they had been disconnected.

Michael Collins: *Oh, man! Kita, a little guy here in the village, came running in to say that the pen for the cows broke again. I've got to go.*

Angie Wright: *Duty calls. It was great to finally chat with you!*

Michael Collins: *Yes! Maybe it'll happen again soon.*

Angie Wright: *Go get your cows.*

Michael Collins: *You hang in there, and don't give up. I've already told the villagers about Dr. Angie. If you don't come, they'll be highly disappointed.*

Angie Wright: *Keep praying, then. Take care.*

Michael Collins: *Bye, Angie. I am praying.*

She shut down the computer. Anything after talking with Michael would be a letdown. Picking up her Old Testament notes, she lay back in the bed to attempt memorizing the kings. Her mind wouldn't cooperate as it kept wandering to Padawin. She and Michael had exchanged e-mails for several months, but never had they been signed in online at the same time.

He was fun. I could work with that.

His e-mails had always been serious, but his chatting took a lighter turn. She was glad. Perhaps he was like her younger sister, Annie: an e-mail was often nothing more than a report of her day, to the point and just the facts please. In real life Annie was a ball of fire.

As she looked back at her notes and read the name *Rehoboam*, she became resigned that this wasn't going to be a fun night.

If I actually refuse to learn these names, will I blow my whole missionary career? It's not like the bones of the body or the major organs. Who cares who begat whom?

She forced herself to concentrate. Years of medical school had taught her that well.

Rehoboam. Jereboam. Abijah. Asa.

ONE

"Mr. Carson," Angie shot out quickly, having lost all semblance of patience, "I've waited my whole life for this. I'm a certified doctor! I know that God's called me to Padawin. The need there is great. I've talked with Michael Collins myself."

"We know, Dr. Wright. We've spoken with him also. There are a few circumstances we're uncomfortable with concerning this appointment. Please try and understand."

It was all she could do not to throw her phone against the wall. Had she been in his office talking to Fred Carson in person, she probably would have tossed something. May was approaching, and her year in seminary was almost over. She had studied hard to finish this last leg of education so she could leave for the mission field immediately. Yet after over a year of talking with the board, she was no closer to going than when she had finished her medical training last June.

"How can I understand?" she began to raise her voice. "There's a need there. I'm qualified to go. You have the power of decision; I have the funds for the supplies and the equipment. I'm ready to go. Where's the problem?"

"Dr. Wright, it's not as simple as all that."

"Is there someone higher than you I can talk to?"

"It's not a matter of politics. The board has discussed your case several times, and they always come up with the same issues. Padawin isn't the place for you at the moment."

"Have you discussed this with God?" she blurted out, then immediately winced in disgrace. Her temper combined with her mouth had struck again. She might as well hang up and attempt a more civil conversation later in the week.

"Dr. Wright, I assure you that we only want the best for everyone. Of course we've sought the Lord. There are many other places to serve, even in the Pacific. But we're not prepared to commission you to Padawin right now."

"Okay, thanks." She gave up and turned the phone off, perhaps too abruptly. Hurling it to her bed she tried to collect her thoughts without crying. She couldn't understand the problem. They obviously believed her to be capable and qualified for serving on the mission field, but they refused to send her to Padawin. It didn't make sense. Frankly, she was tired of negotiating. Maybe she should give up the idea altogether. She could open her own practice in the States, make loads of money, even drive a BMW if she wanted rather than cruise around in the beat up jalopy she'd had since college.

No. That's not who I am, and that's not my calling. God, give me wisdom! And please, give me the patience of Job!

She pulled out her notes and began to review for her last exam the following day. She was tired of school, tired of studying and tired of uncertainty. At least when the exam was finished, she could go home. Solace. But even there, changes kept it from being the place it had always been. Still, it was home, and home was wonderful.

She changed her mind. No more studying. She knew enough to easily pass with a *B*. Instead, she ambled to the sink and washed her face. Glancing in the mirror, she wondered if she had squandered her youth on false hopes. She was still young, but had only one dream in life: to be a doctor on the mission field. As she proceeded through medical training, she discovered the Pacific island nation of Padawin. As soon as she heard about it, she knew that was the place God wanted her. How? Hard to explain. She just knew, and she wouldn't bend or budge until her appointment there was finalized.

She pulled her sandy brown hair into its typical ponytail then tried to rub away the smeared mascara around her light green eyes. Dousing her full lips with a generous amount of Chap Stick, she put on a swimsuit and headed to the roof of the dorm to bask in the sun. All she needed was to get through tomorrow first; the rest of her life would develop afterward.

Carrying a folding chair to the top, she found a vacant spot among the girls who were anxious to take advantage of a warm, sunny day. Most of them were younger than she by several years with very little in common. As soon as someone discovered she was a doctor, an instant wall was erected. She really didn't mind. She wasn't here to socialize. At least she had Ed, a music major, who had become a good friend and someone with whom she could share her frustrations.

What a change. During medical school, when I was worn to a frazzle ninety percent of the time, the thing that kept me going was the dream of the mission field. I'd share that with anyone who asked. Here? I'm only frustrated. I've allowed myself to implode and I've almost locked my dream away out of fear. Irony is great in story books but can be an awful thing in real life.

*****

Thankful that her rattling vehicle had made the trip safely one last time, Angie pulled into the driveway of her childhood home in Dockrey. It was a small town in northwest Alabama where her father had served as pastor for twenty-five years. Her older sister, Andie, still lived here with her own family now. Annie and Alex, her younger sister and brother, lived in New York with their spouses. She beeped the pitiful horn and shook her head as the car sputtered and finally shut off. One thing was certain: if she didn't go to Padawin, a new car was in order.

Opening the front door, she basked in the familiar sights of the great room. Large and inviting, it held photographs and mementos of years gone by. She stepped in, dropped her luggage, and heaved a deep sigh of relief. For the first time in twenty years she had nothing left to do: no school to attend, no studies to complete, no applications to make. She was *free*!

"Anybody home?" she yelled as she headed to the kitchen.

"Back here," came her mother's voice from the master bedroom. "I'm getting dressed! Come on in!"

On her way to the bedroom, she noticed subtle changes. The fireplace mantle displayed new pictures of Annie and her husband Stephen, along with Alex and his wife, Megan. A new family photo of Andie and Doug with their four children sat on the coffee table. Above the mantle, however, hung the huge portrait that had been there the past five years. It had been a miserable sitting and she smiled as she thought of the uniqueness of her family.

"Wow, Moms," Angie said breathlessly, "you look beautiful. I hope I'm as gorgeous as you when I get *old*. Where're you headed?" The use of *old* was meant as a teasing jab, and she was waiting for the playful banter that usually followed.

"Oh, dear," Barbara Wright said sadly. "Sit down, Angie, please."

She sat on the edge of her parents' bed with a sense of dread rising. Normally hugs and kisses would have been the greeting, but she could tell by her mother's grim expression that something horrible had occurred. Her curly brown hair had been straightened and was perfectly styled for whatever the event was, but her brown eyes reflected sadness.

"What's going on, Moms?"

"James Marcum died Wednesday night."

Barbara said no more as she let the news register. James Marcum, the father of Angie's best high school friend, Cindy, and occasional boyfriend, Billy, was like a second father to her. She had spent a lot of time with that family during her childhood and teenage years. When struggling through her rebellious period in high school, James and Sue Marcum had been the adults she turned to for wisdom and advice.

"How?" was all she could manage to utter.

"He had a heart attack in the middle of the night. Sue called us around three thirty in the morning. She was hysterical. She had called 911 and they were on their way. Your father got there as soon as he could. We had Andie's boys; I had to stay here with them."

Tears welled in Barbara's eyes as she recounted the story. He was pronounced dead shortly after the paramedics arrived, even though they had worked hard to revive him. In a town as small as Dockrey, a man like James Marcum was known and loved by everyone, including the rescue team.

"I assume the viewing is tonight."

"At seven o' clock."

She got up to leave, but turned back and asked, "Why didn't you call and tell me?"

"Sweetie, you didn't need this your last two days of finals. All we wanted was for you to concentrate on finishing school … for good. We knew you'd be here soon enough; you could face it all then."

She left the room feeling her world crash down around her. She hated that she hadn't known so she could have contacted Cindy, but her parents probably knew best. As impulsive as she had become the last few months, it was highly possible she would have blown off Thursday's and Friday's exams and come home. Tears stung her eyes as she plodded up the stairs to her room.

*****

Angie hated funeral homes, funerals, viewings, eating because of them, and having to deal with death in any form. She often wondered if that was some of the reasoning behind her intense drive to become a doctor. She wanted to be in control, and somehow knowing medicine and being able to cure a few ills in life helped control some of the uncontrollable. Her desire had never been to practice medicine in the States. Right from the beginning she wanted to become a doctor and then hit the mission field. Unfortunately, reality wasn't as simple as dreams.

Once inside the funeral home, her initial thought was to find Cindy, but Jonathan Wright spotted his daughter first. She smiled a sigh of relief as he walked over and gently wrapped his arms around her. The familiar scent of his cologne held powerful comfort.

"You okay, honey?" he asked tenderly.

"Not really, Daddy. I'm still debating whether I'm mad at you and Moms for not telling me about this."

"We'll take our chances with the consequences." He pulled away to gaze into her face, his eyes full of empathy. "You look tired. Exams all over?"

"Every last one of them."

"You've done an exceptional job with your life, Angie. I want you to know that. We'd planned a special greeting for you; Andie and Doug were coming, and we were going to set up a conference call with Annie. As you can imagine, this took precedence."

"You know that's no problem."

He nodded and kissed her forehead. "Cindy's in the back room just down the hallway."

"Thanks, Daddy."

She straightened his typically disheveled tie and then gave him another glance. His hair was beginning to thin and gray, but he still stood like a hero in her eyes.

She waved a few greetings to some as she marched resolutely down the hall, but she wouldn't stop to chat. She needed to find Cindy. She stopped outside the small room where the body of James Marcum lay, dreading to go inside. Taking a deep breath, she forced herself to remain calm. It wasn't working. She clinched her fists, bit her lip, and willed herself into the room. Her first sight was that of Sue Marcum sitting in a chair a few feet from the open casket. Standing beside her was her daughter. As soon as Cindy saw Angie, tears began to pour forth from both of them.

"Angie," Cindy whispered in a cry. "I'm so glad you're here."

Angie put her arms around her friend and held her as tightly as she could. "I only just found out. I would've called you earlier, but I didn't know. I'm so sorry."

"What happened, Angie? You're a doctor," she sobbed. "We didn't even know he was sick! How could this have occurred with no warning?"

"Heart disease is often a silent killer. Some people have symptoms and find out early, but many are just like your dad."

Angie wished she could say more, something genuinely comforting, but there was nothing comforting in death. Even when people had suffered and death was the only option to end the pain, it still wasn't a true comfort. That only came with healing and restoration.

"I loved him very much, you know?" Angie told her.

"I know. He loved you too. He always said you were his second daughter. He enjoyed the visits we had last summer. He always thought a lot of you."

Tears were seeping from Angie's eyes. All she wanted was to run and hide rather than face the death of someone so dear. She went to Mrs. Marcum and offered her condolences, but when Cindy suggested they leave the room, she was relieved. She struggled with being in the same room with a lifeless, pale body just lying there.

The girls went outside, and Cindy immediately pulled out a cigarette.

"Are you crazy?" Angie asked her in disgust. "When did you start smoking?"

Cindy sighed, took a long drag, then slowly released a stream of smoke. "Oh, I don't know. It makes dealing with stress a little easier."

"Actually, it adds to the stress of your body in a major way."

"I don't need a sermon, Angie. I just need to get through tonight and tomorrow. Preach to me then."

"I thought life was going fairly well for you."

"Other than my father dying?" Cindy quipped with sarcasm.

Angie replied in the same sardonic attitude. "Well ... yeah. Even apart from his passing ... obviously all isn't at peace."

"Do you realize we're the only two girls in our class that haven't married? We're probably the only ones who haven't had kids either."

"One upside to that is we aren't divorced yet. So what? Is it really that big of a deal?"

"It is to me! It's like I have this mark on me that says *unwanted* or something."

"Please ... there's nothing about you that's *unwantable*. You're not married because you haven't found anyone you want to spend your life with."

"Hmph."

"Hmph? Now what on earth does that mean?"

"It could mean a number of things," was all she would say.

Cindy, a beautiful natural blond, was a striking woman with her blue eyes and petite figure, but the cigarette and fidgeting uneasiness were clues of deep struggles. Billy, her twin, walked up and immediately hugged Angie. Same blue eyes, same blond hair, but he lacked the positive qualities that drew her to his sister.

"Hey good-lookin'," he said with a smile. "What've you been up to?"

"You know me. School, school and more school." Angie tried to put some distance between them.

"How's Mama?" he asked.

"How do you think?" Cindy replied, puffing away.

"You got another one of those?"

"What is it with you two?" Angie asked disbelieving. "Your father just passed away from heart disease and you're out here preparing to join him!"

They both looked at her, surprised by the outburst, then went back to lighting up. Being with the twins brought back many memories. Their high school years had been spent together for the most part. They weren't the wildest teenagers in town, but they were a far cry from what her pastor father had considered acceptable. James was a deacon in the church, and Sue had always worked with preschoolers, but Billy and Cindy marched to their own drummers—and Angie found herself marching right along with them. She had dated Billy on and off during her last two years of high school. He was incredibly good looking, a notch above anyone else in Dockrey, but he was extremely cocky, a characteristic that grated on Angie to this day. He had been married and divorced twice already, and Angie knew to watch her guard with him. He always let her know he was ready for a repeat performance from high school if she ever felt the inclination.

"You still gonna do the missionary thing?" he asked as he dropped a couple of ashes.

"That's the plan."

"What a waste of beauty," he chuckled. "You'll be working with some African tribesmen and they won't even know how gorgeous you are."

"You never know," Cindy smiled, "maybe that's where her soul mate is."

"You guys are starting to irritate me," Angie told them. "I'm gonna mingle with the crowd inside and see if I can find more pleasant conversation. Besides, I hate smoke—and I'm *not* going to Africa."

TWO

"Angie's home," Jonathan said with a cheerful smile the following morning as he joined her in the kitchen.

"Was there some confusion about that?" she wondered.

"Sugar toast—you always make sugar toast."

"It's nice to be home. Do you realize that I'm through with institutionalized food forever? No more dorms, no more exams, no more reports, and no more cafeterias. I can eat wherever, whenever and whatever I want."

"Gee, I didn't realize sugar toast held such significance."

She placed a couple of pieces on her plate and headed to the back porch with her coffee. Her father did the same.

"How do you do funerals, Daddy? How do you just plunge through them without getting emotionally undone?"

"Death is a part of life on earth. It happens."

"Death is *not* a part of *life*," she said firmly. "It was a mistake of the fall. It wasn't supposed to happen—humanity wasn't created to deal with death."

"Maybe not, but it's here to stay, so you'd better get used to it. Now, sticking needles into people and sewing up their skin, *that* isn't natural. *That*, my dear, I would never dream of doing."

"God makes us all different, doesn't He?" she laughed gently.

"No kidding."

*****

Angie sat stone-faced through the entire funeral. The family had asked her to sit with them so she took her place with great uneasiness between a weeping Cindy and an unmoved Billy. Her father did a wonderful job managing to make the death of James Marcum truly seem like a homecoming in heaven. But as soon as the service was over, she went outside to rid herself of the dooming *funeralistic* atmosphere.

The ride to the graveside with her parents was quiet. As her father delivered the final words, she forced herself to listen. She wanted to tune out everything, pretend it wasn't happening, but the truth was this was the first funeral she had attended of someone who was dear to her. For years she would go out of respect for the families, but the people were never connected to her in an intimate way. She always felt sorry for them and wondered how they could face death so admirably. As she thought of the hole now left by Mr. Marcum, the lump in her throat lurched. She glanced at Cindy and Sue, both red-faced, make-up running, eyes swollen, as they realized this man who had dwelt at the center of their lives would no longer be there.

Why did you make death happen, God? Wasn't there some other way you could bring people home? I know You said the death of Your saints is precious in Your sight, but I have a hard time seeing anything precious about a situation like this.

With the graveside service over, many went to the Marcums to fellowship. Angie had no desire to *fellowship*, but after being raised in a pastor's home, she'd learned there were many things you did regardless of how you felt. She sat solemnly in the living room as memories began to pour through her mind. She and Cindy had spent uncountable nights sleeping on the floor while watching late movies. This was also the room where she had received her first kiss, compliments of Billy. This was the place where James Marcum told her the best thing she could ever do was listen to her parents who loved her more than anyone in the world. She had struggled to believe him because her parents didn't want to give her the freedom to do the things other teenagers did. She had trusted him and chosen to obey her parents even though everything within her shouted to rebel. She was glad now. If only Cindy and Billy would have chosen the same path and honored their parents as well.

"So, how's life, good-lookin'?" Billy asked as he sat down next to her with a large plate of food.

"Calm right now. I'm in the waiting stages of getting appointed to the mission field."

"I never pegged you for a bookworm."

"I never was. I'm still not that crazy about reading, but it's growing on me."

"Then why all the school?"

"It was required, you know, in order to become a doctor."

"Duh. I mean why didn't you pick some other profession? Man, a doctor? What a life."

"I didn't pick it; it picked me."

"Oh yeah, the God thing again. When did you get so religious anyway? Remember the church balcony? That wasn't very *God-honoring*, you know?"

Her face grew warm at the mention of the balcony. She and Billy had skipped discipleship training one evening to go make out there. Annie was sent by the teacher to find them, and she did. Her dear sister had held that over her head for many years. To Angie, that still was the most embarrassing memory in her life.

"We all grow up, Billy. I made quite a few mistakes in my youth, but I've made a lot of different choices since then."

"Yeah, but some of those mistakes were an awful lot of fun," he grinned at her.

"Maybe at the time, but now they're just humiliating reminders of a period I'd rather forget."

"You're so serious now. What happened to the *fun-loving-I'd-do-anything-for-a-laugh* girl?"

"Oh, she's still very much here," Angie told him as she stood. "Her idea of fun has changed a little."

She started to walk away, but Billy asked her, "Where are you going? I thought maybe we could get together sometime while you're waiting for the missionary thing to happen."

"Oh, I don't think so." She smiled cordially as she headed for a different place in the house.

*****

Back at her own home, Angie sprawled across the couch and flipped through the channels. She had no idea real life could be so boring. She also couldn't believe how senseless television had become.

We've got 180 channels and there's not anything worth watching.

She stopped for a moment on a local commercial playing one of her sister's songs. Annie had written jingles for local businesses before meeting up with Stephen and being whisked off to worldwide fame. She literally had become an overnight success. The Wrights had to install a large fence around the entire house and hire security for a time because of the press and fans gathering and often intruding. The fence was still there, and it was kept locked, but only one guard remained. There was always someone camped around the entrance, but no one had caused problems for several months. Most people knew Annie was in New York with Stephen and hadn't returned to Dockrey since January.

She decided to call her. Perhaps a talk with her sister would lighten the mood. She punched in the number and listened patiently to the rings.

"Hello, Dr. Sis," came Annie's familiar voice.

"Hey, baby girl." Angie smiled, happy to hear her again. "What on earth are you up to?"

"Thinking about putting up a Christmas tree."

"Are you serious?"

"We're doing this Christmas album, and for three months all I've done is sing and play holiday music. You'd think the hot weather would be a giveaway, but I still find myself in the Christmas spirit."

"Now *that* is funny. I'm glad I called. Give me a diversion, please."

"I guess you're pretty down after the funeral and all."

"Very down."

"I know you were close to Mr. Marcum. How's his family doing?"

"Sue and Cindy are pretty torn up; Billy, who knows? He actually brought up the balcony to me while we were eating today."

Annie laughed out loud then tried to stifle herself as she said, "Believe it when someone tells you your sins will find you out!"

"I'm just relieved that's the worst of it. It could've been more devastating. I'm thankful that I was level headed enough to make a few right decisions during that time."

"So, how does it feel to be finished with school?"

"Boring."

"No, that has nothing to do with school; that has to do with the fact that you're back home in Dockrey all by yourself."

"You're probably right. I've been thinking about getting some kind of menial job to pass the time. But please, let's change the subject. How's the pregnancy coming?"

"I'm finally showing. I didn't think I ever would. This fellow must be tiny."

"Sure he is right now. How many months along are you?"

"Just four. I haven't put on any maternity clothes yet, but I've had to stop wearing my jeans; they're too tight. That itty-bitty bulge down there pooches out a little too much for my comfort."

"That itty-bitty bulge is going to develop into a basketball very soon."

"I know. It's so exciting!"

"How's Megan," Angie asked about their sister-in-law.

"She's definitely got the basketball. It's adorable watching her waddle around. She's so short and tiny to begin with, and this extra weight makes her look utterly out of balance."

"What about Alex?"

"The doting husband. He waits on her hand and foot and is always leaning down to rub her tummy and talk to the baby. Megan says he sings to it every night."

"Growing another musician, I suppose? They still don't want to know the sex?"

"Nope. They're way more enduring than me. I couldn't stand not knowing. Stephen wanted to wait until the birth, but I told him I was gonna find out and it was unlikely that I'd keep it to myself. He caved. I'm not a very patient person, you know?"

"No! I had no idea," Angie laughed heartily. "You?"

"He's glad to know though."

"Picked out any names?"

"Now, what do you think?"

"Okay, he's already named."

"Stephen Jonathan Williams."

"Very fitting. I did think you'd be more creative though."

"Well, there's always the nickname possibilities. I wanted the baby to be named after Stephen. This is his flesh and blood, his first family in many years."

"You're a thoughtful wife. Married life has settled you down some, I guess."

"I guess," Annie agreed. There was a slight silence before she added, "Married life is wonderful, you know?"

"Glad to hear it. After spending an afternoon with twice-divorced Billy Marcum, I needed a reminder that there are still *good* things happening in the world for *good* people."

"God is very good, Angie."

"Yes He is," she agreed. "He's very good."

THREE

Angie hoped to melt away her anxieties while soaking in the hot tub on the back porch as her father sat nearby sipping his last cup of coffee for the evening. She shared her struggles with him, her inability to move the mission board, her frustration at having completed all the requirements necessary but not being allowed to go.

"Angie, you can be a bit forceful, you know?"

"Oh, please! I did my best to be compliant and sweet and understanding at the start, but after hitting one stone wall after another, it got a bit hard to just put on a smile and say, *Ya'll know best.*"

"Why won't they appoint you? What's the problem?"

"I have no idea! I've asked over and over and I get nothing. They say it isn't the right place for me at this time. No explanation."

He nodded slowly and ran his hand through his thinning hair. It did seem strange that no one was willing to consider it. However, he knew his daughter better than anyone, and it was quite possible that she had dug her own grave. She was insistent, opinionated and stubborn. If the board had any doubts about her before she showed her hard-headedness, she probably confirmed their biggest fears after her last outburst. He had taught her well to express herself. If only he had taught her tact in the process.

Angie dried off and slipped into a pair of sweats. Evenings in early May were often still chilly in northern Alabama. She wanted to spend a few minutes checking her e-mail before she snuggled down in the comfort of her own bed. *How pathetic that this has become my social life.* She started up the haggard computer only to be confronted with some kind of error message and a question as to whether she wanted to go into safe mode. *I don't even know what safe mode is.* She clicked *no* and leaned her head back to relax. Once the agonizingly slow process was complete, she maneuvered to her mail site and typed in her password. Thirteen messages.

"Yes," she said with a huge smile. Michael Collins had written again.

Dear Dr. Angie, I'm guessing that at this point in time you've probably finished your last exam and are sitting in the comfort of your wonderful Alabama home. I'm amazed at how committed you remain to the call even when the opposition is strong. I have to confess, when I mention you to the board, and I get their flat denials, I feel hopeless. But when you write and tell me of your burning conviction that God has called you here, my faith is rekindled. I've been meeting weekly with the Christians from two of the villages. I told them about you and your wisdom with healing. I've also told them about the struggles we're having getting you here. Sojay, one of the Christian men, told me we must pray for God to bring you, and that whatever the obstacles may be, we'd take every step necessary to defeat them.

You mentioned your sister and her husband sponsoring you. I don't feel like that would be the best plan. You wouldn't be under the protection of the board. Angie, even though the location where I serve is far from the cities where the turmoil always happens, I have to depend on the board for supplies, help, and if necessary, protection. If you were here without an official appointment, your life would be too vulnerable. I say let's continue to pray for God to work out a better way.

I'm so tired right now I can hardly keep my eyes open. We plowed and planted all day. My only acceptance is based on the fact that I can provide the knowledge for unlimited food and great varieties. You'd think after nine years I'd have more to show for my work than just eleven converts, but I'm confident this is where God wants me and that He'll bear His fruit in His season.

Have a good night back at home. I hope things work out soon. And remember what Sojay said: whatever the obstacles might be, we must take every step possible to defeat them.

In Him, Michael Collins, Missionary to the Padawin Islands

Angie smiled. He was so businesslike in his e-mails. She wondered what it was like for him to live there nine years with no contact other than tribesmen most of the time. Would she be too much for him? She was a bit of a free spirit—she liked to laugh, she liked to play, and she liked to enjoy life to the fullest. Would that be a problem in his serious-minded world? Would she be more like the fly in the ointment rather than a healing balm?

Dear Michael, My homecoming wasn't as wonderful as I'd hoped. My best friend's father passed away on Wednesday night so when I walked in the door I was hit with that news immediately. I dressed and went to the viewing. That wasn't my idea of a great night. Couple that with the fact that I'm NOT anywhere closer to going to Padawin, and it makes for one miserable girl.

Sorry to be so gloomy; I prefer cheery letters myself. One good thing is that I'm totally through with school. Do you have any idea what that means? I've gone to school as far back as I can remember. I've always had something in the wings that needed to be done, and now, suddenly, for the first time, I'm free! Whoopee! Except my best friend's father just died and my sister lives in New York and I'm not headed to Padawin. Ho hum.

My father advised me to spend my sudden allotment of free time praying and seeking God's direction for my life. He believes with me that Padawin is where I should be and can't understand the problem either. He said later this summer, if things haven't moved forward, he'll take a trip with me to visit the board in Richmond and see if we can get some answers. Tell Sojay I liked what he said. That's the way I feel too. If they'd tell us the obstacles, then we could set out to defeat them. I think that's going to be my prayer for the month of May: Lord, reveal the obstacles.

I'm tired too. Exams, driving back from New Orleans and the death of a dear person in my life have all added up to one very emotional letdown. I think I'll just sleep right on through to tomorrow afternoon.

Goodnight, farm-boy. Maybe in my next letter I'll be a bit more enthused.

Love, Angie

She hit the send button and read through the rest of her e-mails. She'd hoped there would be something from Annie, but as was the norm, nothing. Her sister had never been good about writing, and once she married Mr. Wonderful she seldom heard from her at all. They tried to call at least once every two weeks, but she still missed her Annie very much. Right now, she missed her immensely.

She turned off the computer and crept upstairs to her room. After brushing out her hair and slipping into her worn Atlanta Braves jersey, she picked up the guitar from the floor and began to strum through a couple of songs. She wasn't all that good and had only learned to play this past year. She was determined, however, to be able to sing and decently accompany herself for the islanders. She worked on translating simple hymns and choruses into Padawin and made sure she practiced at least fifteen minutes a day. She still struggled with some of her translating, not sure of all the words, but as her father would say, she got an "A" for effort.

She gently strummed a simple rhythm as she began to sing in Padawin:

Incredible grace how sweet it hears
That saved a bad like me
I before was lost but now I'm found
Could not see, but now I see.

She would die if any of her siblings could hear her. They were all incredibly talented in music. Her oldest sister, Andie, a Music Education major, had taught elementary music until this past year when she decided to stay home with her children. Annie had a Bachelor's in Music Composition with a Master's in Music Education. She was now married to a professional musician and they were completing a Christmas album to be released in the fall followed by a tour in the States. Alex, a Music major also, played amazing bass guitar for Stephen's band. Angie had never cared for music. She could sing okay, not a bad alto, and could read music fairly well, but she wasn't in the same league with the other Wright kids.

During her year at Seminary, she met Ed who was about as unique as her. Their connection happened easily. He was a music guy and taught her some basics on guitar, and they would sing together often. His beautiful voice and excellent playing backed by her mediocre harmony and gentle strumming made a nice match. He was non-pretentious, something hard to find among most ministerial students.

Blessed Assurance Jesus is mine
Oh what a coming of awesomeness of God
Child of salvation bought up by God
Born of His ghost and washed in His blood.

This is my story, this is my song
Adoring my Savior all the day long
This is my story, this is my song
Adoring my Savior all the day long.

It wasn't the full fifteen minutes, but at least it was something. She was drained and could easily let the guitar slide to the floor, but it was in bad enough shape already. She and Ed had found it at a garage sale in Picayune one weekend for only $25. It was that find that made her decide to take lessons from him. It was ugly, scarred, and didn't have the nicest sound, but as Ed said, it held its tune well and had *easy action* which was perfect for a beginner.

She laid it down gently and nestled beneath the covers. Reaching up to turn out the lamp, she closed her eyes and gave a deep sigh.

Lord, what do I do right now? I know You don't make mistakes. All that's going on in my life is to prepare me for something. You said that You give us more than we could ever ask or imagine. All I'm asking is to go to Padawin and live the rest of my life healing people and sharing Your Gospel. But apparently, this isn't Your plan for me at the moment. Why? What am I missing? Have I run ahead of You? I can't imagine! I've given myself to nearly 12 years of preparation. How much more time do You want before this call can be fulfilled? What step have I not yet taken? I'm going to ask You just like Sojay said, what are the obstacles? Please reveal them and then help me do whatever it takes to overcome them. Good night, Lord.

FOUR

"You'll have dinner with my sister, but not with me?" Angie wasn't sure if Billy Marcum was teasing her or propositioning her. Either way she refused to answer him. Hoping to appear uninterested but not outright rude, she checked her watch and then pilfered through her purse for a piece of gum.

"If I remember correctly," he continued, not getting her message, "there was a time when dinner with me was exciting."

He was still cocky, still annoying, and still incredibly handsome.

"We all regret things from our pasts," she said bluntly.

"So you're saying that I'm a *regret* for you?"

"Very big regret."

"Come, on Ang, you weren't complaining back then."

"I didn't know what else was out there."

"So, was I your *bad* boy?" He was definitely teasing now.

She rolled her eyes wishing Cindy would hurry. "Yes, I suppose so; you were my *bad* boy."

"Kind of sounds exciting, doesn't it? It didn't seem to bother you as a teenager."

"Actually, it did. My conscience gave me fits. I wish I would've listened to it a little better."

"You were never a *bad* girl, Angie."

"Hmm … I'm not sure how comforting that is coming from you. I'd guess our definitions of *bad* are probably drastically different."

"Ready?" asked Cindy as she rushed down the stairs.

"You have no idea how ready," Angie replied in relief.

"Are you bothering my friends again?" Cindy griped at her brother.

"It's not a friend; it's Angie!" he laughed. "She's practically family!"

"Then that makes you just a little sick, doesn't it … hitting on family? Let's go, Ang."

The girls squeezed themselves into the tiny sports car and then took off. Angie wondered how Cindy managed to travel in the thing. It was hard enough to get inside while dressed casually. How could someone manage with a tight dress and heels, Cindy's usual work attire? They drove to downtown Florence and pulled into their favorite little Italian restaurant of years gone by, Ricatoni's.

They ate and laughed, and Angie felt the trip was worth it to get their minds off of Mr. Marcum's unexpected death. The talk had been simple and casual until Cindy dropped the bomb she'd been holding onto all evening.

"You what?" Angie asked in total disbelief.

"I think you heard me clearly."

"You're having an affair with a married man?"

"I don't like to think of it as an *affair*. That sounds so sordid and ugly. It's a relationship, and it's mutual."

"The guy is married!"

"I know. But we're genuinely in love."

"That's *not* love! Love is when you're committed to someone for the duration. Love isn't a feeling, and love most certainly isn't defined by sexual attraction."

"All this from the expert?"

Angie shook her head not believing she was having this conversation. Her friend had always been far from perfect, but never blindingly ignorant of reality.

"It didn't start out with all the *attraction*. We were friends. His wife just had their second child, and she ignored him and his *needs* completely. I was only being a friend to him ... and then ..."

"For crying out loud! Do you have any clue what a woman goes through when she has a baby? Not only are there the intense physical changes, there's the lack of sleep and the often hormonal imbalances that accompany it. No woman is able to meet a man's every *need* after a baby comes."

"I'm telling you it's not like that," Cindy continued to defend. "He's a good man. He just needed someone to love him."

"You've set yourself up for some major kind of trouble here. If he loves you, why is he still with his wife? Plus, what happened to his love for her?"

"She's not the same person he married."

"I should hope not. We all change and grow—and two kids? Heavens! Then she has a husband who can't stay faithful? I bet she's changed!"

"He's just trying to do the right thing now. He wants to stay with her until the kids are a little older so she doesn't have to go through the early childhood years alone."

"How noble. I've never said this to you before, but it fits: you're stupid."

Cindy smiled and sighed. "I wish you'd be brutally honest with me. It's not good to hold things inside."

Angie ignored her sarcasm. "I can't believe you think this is okay. Does propriety mean anything to you?"

"This isn't something I planned. It just happened. I'm twenty-nine, Angie. I'm not getting any younger, and I want somebody to love."

"Cindy, you don't want this. You want the right one. You want a man who loves you wholeheartedly. You don't want someone with all this extra baggage in his life."

"Well, whoever or wherever this *right man* is, he hasn't shown up yet. I'm tired of waiting, and I'm tired of being alone."

"But that's just it; you're still alone. He doesn't come home with you every night. He's not with you every morning. He wasn't at your father's funeral with you."

"He *was* there."

"But was he *with* you?"

Cindy shook her head.

"Is this what you want? You want to settle for someone who's so selfish that when the woman he committed himself to is going through the hardest period of her life, he goes out and finds a convenient distraction rather than help her work through it?"

"Maybe this *is* what I want, Angie," Cindy shot back. "It's a great arrangement! In time, maybe things'll work out and we'll end up together, but for now, it all works."

"That's ridiculous! Love is more commitment than anything else. I doubt this man really knows how to love. He can't commit to his wife on one hand, but he stays with her. He claims to love you, but he can't commit to you either. I think he's just having his cake and eating it too. And you're serving it to him on a silver platter."

"Leave it to Angie to put me on a guilt trip."

"What did you expect me to do?"

"I guess be happy for me."

"I'll be happy for you when you find someone who is truly yours and loves you like you deserve to be loved. You're not second hand goods, Cindy. You're a beautiful, intelligent, and capable woman. Wait for someone who can really appreciate that and can treat you like you should be treated."

"I have waited, Angie, and I'm tired of it. I like what I have with Evan; I like being with him."

"But you're not *with* him. He's *with* someone else."

Cindy leaned back against the booth and closed her eyes. Angie knew how she felt and truly sympathized with her. The only thing worse than having nobody was having the wrong person, and there were many wrong people out there. Angie had come to the decision that there were things in her life to which she knew God had called her. Because of that, chances were slim of ever finding someone who could share that call. She decided to leave this part of her life totally up to the Lord. He was free to bring her someone if He had designed it. If not, she would live her days loving only the Lord, and would be honored to do so.

"Have you ever considered what God might have in store for you?" Angie asked cautiously.

"I prayed. I watched. I waited. I gave up."

"And so you just went out and had an affair."

"Stop calling it that! And *no*, I didn't go out and decide for things to happen like this. I was caught off guard, and before I knew what was happening, it was already a *thing*."

"Do you want advice, or do you just want to spill your guts out to someone?" Angie asked her seriously. It was hard to tell with Cindy.

"I guess maybe a little of both. I don't like the situation, but I like the man very much."

"No. You like the *attention* of the man very much."

Cindy half-nodded as if admitting it could be a possibility. This gave Angie a glimmer of hope and perhaps a window of opportunity.

"Step one: you have to end this relationship."

Cindy immediately began to protest, but Angie stuck her hand up to Cindy's face to indicate she wasn't through.

"Step two: get back in church so you can be around the kind of people who make right choices about relationships."

Cindy snickered. "What makes you think I'm not in church?"

"Puh-leeze. Step three: ask God to forgive you, cleanse you, and give you the desire to love Him more than any man."

"I don't know if I can go back to that kind of life again. It was … well … boring."

"It's boring because you've sold out to the lie that immediate gratification is all that matters, but every choice we make has consequences. Believe me, I know. When you give God your all, it's amazing how fulfilling a relationship with Him can be."

FIVE

Angie tried to enjoy Wednesday night church, but distractions were plaguing her heart. James Marcum's painfully obvious absence along with the knowledge of Cindy's ongoing affair managed to occupy her brain most of the service. She had spent a lot of time in prayer for her friend last night interceding that God would do a mighty work. She knew how hard it could be to make right choices after Satan had already dug his hooks into you deeply. Cindy wasn't a *horrid* person; she struggled with being fulfilled. She had never given herself to anything very long, and because of that, she never stuck with much: school, sports, clubs, or church. She now worked as a real estate agent, and thankfully, was wonderful at it. Angie was impressed that she had actually disciplined herself enough to get licensed. And real estate was a good option for her. Her clientele as well as her properties were always changing, and it was a lucrative job which was a necessity for her.

Angie spent the rest of the week lying around the house, sometimes the couch, other times the porch swing, and often times her own bed. She was hopelessly bored. Had Annie been there, they would've filled the time gleefully. But, of course, Annie was in New York, enjoying who knows what kind of pleasures with her new husband. She thought about writing Michael, or even better, perhaps he would be online and they could chat again like the one time last February. She glanced at the clock and roughly calculated the time difference. It would be five o'clock in the morning there. Bad idea.

God, what are You doing to me? Do you know how unbearable it is for me to sit around and do nothing? What is it that You're trying to teach me? I can't go to Padawin! Why? Are You not in control here? Well, okay, apologies. I know You're in control. I just don't know what You're doing with all that control! You also know that if I were in charge, I'd be doing things very differently. So, because things aren't happening like I think they should, I'm assuming that You're up to something beyond my imagination. Could you give me a hint? Please?

*****

The month of May poked by. It was almost impossible keeping her sanity. She spent a lot of time at Andie's and had a great time teaching the boys science. Her older sister was good medicine. She was more serious than Annie but had a lot of wisdom. They prayed together regularly seeking God's will and plan concerning Padawin. Angie enjoyed the relationship between Andie and Doug. As newlyweds barely out of high school, they had been exciting and impetuous. But now with four kids, a mortgage, a business, and a demanding life, it was comforting to see how they had settled into a stable and strong relationship.

If you ever find someone for me, Lord, this is what I want. Forget the passion and the excitement and all the goose bumps. I just want someone who can live life beside me.

As June began, she again called Fred Carson at the mission board. She tried to speak with confidence *and* humility, a very hard combination for anyone, but especially hard for her. She explained her deep sense of calling to Padawin. She reiterated its need for a medical doctor and explained how the tribes struggled with the dark bonds imposed by their witch doctors. She laid out a plan for reaching people for Christ using medicine. She told him of the money she had raised to purchase equipment needed to begin facilitating a small doctor's office. She was patient, she was kind, and she avoided any sarcasm or even humor for that matter. She was totally floored when he rejected her again.

At least I'm growing through all of this, she thought to herself. *Normally I would've taken someone's head off verbally. At least I just thanked him for the consideration and hung up. Tally one good point for me, 200 bad points for him.*

*****

"Did you know I'm a doctor, Daddy?" she asked one evening as they sat together on the back porch.

"I believe I recall some intense education bills the past few years."

"I am a genuine doctor, but I'm not doing a stinking thing."

"Frustrating, I bet."

"You have no idea. All the training, all the preparation, and for what? So I can sit here at home with you and Moms and get fat off of sugar toast and fried chicken."

"There are worse lots in life."

Angie looked over at him and rolled her eyes, a trait that she and Annie had perfected over the years.

"What's your biggest fear, Angie?"

"I don't know. Why?"

"No ... no explanations. Just tell me what your biggest fear is."

She leaned back on the swing and thought. Fear? There wasn't much she feared. She didn't like death, but that wasn't fear, just a healthy respect. She hated spiders, but that probably wasn't the category to which he was referring. Billy Marcum? She smiled. He would be a good fear, but no, that wasn't it either.

"I'm really not sure, Daddy."

"Well, when you *figure* it out, perhaps you'll *figure* out why you're not in Padawin yet."

"Now how do you *figure* that?"

"There's some reason why you're not there. I don't know why, you don't know why, but God does. There must be something He's trying to work out of you or into you before He's ready for you to go. Maybe if you could *figure* that out … well … I don't know."

"I've racked my brain trying to understand all of this. I can't make sense out of it either."

"That's why God's in it." Jonathan smiled. "You can't *figure* Him out."

After her father went to bed, she dragged out the laptop to see if there was anything interesting in the lives of her Facebook friends. She would settle for silly videos or controversial political issues at this point. After finally logging in, she checked her chat box. Michael was on again! She needed this. Immediately clicking on his name, she typed a greeting.

Angie Wright: *Hey!*

Michael Collins: *Is it actually the doc herself?*

Angie Wright: *How are things in the Pacific?*

Michael Collins: *Hot!*

Angie Wright: *I thought it was winter there. Aren't you in the Southern Hemisphere?*

Michael Collins: *Winter? What's that? I'm 30 miles from the Equator. There are some colder climates here, but you have to climb up to the top of the volcanic peaks to find them. I prefer to keep my distance.*

Angie Wright: *Have you ever seen a volcano go off?*

Michael Collins: *No! I don't want to either. We get a lot of rumblings here —earthquakes. At first, they bothered me like you wouldn't believe, but after a while, I just learned to roll with them.*

Angie Wright: *Was that a pun?*

Michael Collins: *What?*

Angie Wright: *Rolling with the earthquakes? You know, since earthquakes actually roll the earth?*

Michael Collins: *No, it wasn't an intentional pun. I told you I'm not that smart.*

Angie Wright: *How's the monkey?*

Michael Collins: *Horribly mean. I'm ready to shoot him. Forget the stupid monkey. I'm starving right now. Tell me what you ate for your last meal.*

Angie Wright: *Moms fried some chicken. We had rice and gravy and cooked a pot of cabbage.*

Michael Collins: *I'm salivating now.*

Angie Wright: *For the record, I'm a great cook.*

Michael Collins: *Really? How? When did you find time to learn to cook?*

Angie Wright: *Moms refused to let any of us leave home without having a good command of the kitchen. As teenagers we did a lot of cooking. I've enjoyed getting back into it since I've been out of school.*

Michael Collins: *Oh man, Angie! It would be so wonderful to have real food again! Forget the doctoring, just come over here and cook for me!*

Angie Wright: *I would in a minute if the mission board would get it together and send me over.*

Michael Collins: *I wonder how long this will go on? They can't put you off forever, can they?*

Angie Wright: *I'm tired of speculating.*

Michael Collins: *Sojay says it's because you and I aren't praying about it enough. He tends to see everything in black and white. I've tried to tell him it's not that simple, but he says it is. He says we need you, you want to come, God has called you, so what's the holdup?*

Angie Wright: *I can't wait to meet him. Shoot! I can't wait to meet you! Can you imagine sitting down and talking face to face?*

Michael Collins: *I can't imagine even talking with a Westerner face to face on a daily basis. I seldom speak English anymore. The computer is my only connection with the outside world and I'm pretty much illiterate where it's concerned. I've got the basics down, but that's about it.*

Dr. Angie Wright: *Ugh! Me too! I have no idea how to download or upload or anything. In fact, the one time I decided to try something I ended up getting a virus that wiped out my whole computer.*

Michael Collins: *Ha ... understood. I'm too afraid of messing something up to even try. I don't spend much time on it anyway.*

Angie Wright: *Just curious, how do you have electricity out there? Aren't you in some remote area hours away from civilization?*

Michael Collins: *Would you believe a water mill? I have quite a bit of knowledge of mechanical stuff, and I rigged this up shortly after I got here. It's been great! I have a refrigerator, a stove, and even an air-conditioner.*

Angie Wright: *Wow, I had no idea you had that kind of availability with electricity. I could bring more equipment. I was thinking I would have to opt for stuff that was totally run on battery power or generator. Do you have instant access all the time?*

Michael Collins: *Let me put it this way: in the nine years I've been here, the water has never been so low that the mill didn't turn.*

Angie Wright: *Unbelievable! This means I can actually set up a hospital there! I assumed a clinic, but now the possibilities are only limited by my abilities and knowledge. We're going to change the tribal lands of Padawin, Michael!*

Michael Collins: *We've got to get you here first.*

Angie Wright: *I'll get there. I WILL get there.*

SIX

Angie was getting used to riding around in the blue Bug. Annie decided against taking it to New York since it was pointless for them to drive. If they left the house or the apartment, they had to leave with security and a limo. They had thought about possibly selling it, but it had been the first car she'd bought with her own money, and bringing herself to get rid of it was depressing. She was thrilled knowing Angie was putting it to good use. In fact, she told her that if things didn't work out in Padawin for a while, the VW was hers.

It was nearing the end of June, and Angie was finally looking forward to something: July with the family. Annie and Stephen would be coming down for two weeks to celebrate Independence Day, along with Alex and Megan. The whole family would be together again for the first time since last summer, and possibly, she hoped beyond hope, for the last time before she left for Padawin.

Driving to the Post Office, she braced herself for whatever questions might be hurled concerning her future. It was hard to find strangers when you went into town. Everybody knew everybody. It had its positive points, but it also had a down side. Everyone in Dockrey knew that she wasn't in Padawin. That was good because there were many praying for God to make a way. It was bad because there was much speculation and talk as to *why* she couldn't go.

As she opened the box, the usual large bundle of mail came spilling out. She tossed a few pieces away immediately recognizing them as junk and stuck the rest under her arm. Glancing through the envelopes as she walked back to the car, a letter from the mission board caught her attention. She pulled it out and nervously ran her thumb through its seal. Back inside the VW, she closed her eyes, took a deep breath and then read the letter.

Dear Dr. Angela Wright,

We have reviewed your application to Padawin once again and regret to inform you that your request has been denied. There are circumstances surrounding this appointment that we feel are not in line with the standards that our mission board must follow. We understand and appreciate your passion to serve the Lord in the capacity of a Medical Missionary, but we cannot, in good conscience, send you to the tribal areas of Padawin. As we have told you often, there are many other places in desperate need of the services you have offered. If you would consider an appointment to another country, we could easily have you on your way before the summer has ended.

Dr. Wright, please make no more application for Padawin. We have reviewed your information time and again for over a year. We appreciate your courage and willingness to serve there, but we will not appoint you to this nation. Please reconsider your call to the mission field. If Padawin is the only place you are willing to go, then you need to begin looking in the States for a place to work. We have several medical positions available in areas here. The Native American clinics are good places to start. If, however, you are willing to take an appointment to a nation other than Padawin, please let us know. We can begin moving on that immediately.

Sincerely, Fred Carson, Chairmen of the International Mission Board

She crumpled the letter in her hand and leaned her head against the steering wheel. Tears burned her eyes and she didn't know if they were from mourning or anger. How could they do this? Her heart told her that she was destined for these islands! Why would she fight this long and hard to go if she weren't one hundred percent sure that God had called her?

Lord, what are you doing to me? I can't keep this up much longer! I have hope and I have faith, but I'm not unsinkable.

She looked at the crumpled wad in her hand and began to think that this indeed was the straw that was about to break her back. She wondered if she had any fight left. And whom was she fighting? What was she fighting? These were Godly people who sat on the board. Surely they sought the will and purpose of God when they considered their appointments. What was so impossible about sending her to Padawin?

She drove back to the house in silence. She couldn't even bring herself to pray. She thought of Sojay in Padawin and his simple faith. She wanted to do just as he had said, overcome the obstacles, but unfortunately no one would tell her what they were. All she knew was that her future was in the hands of a group of people who didn't agree with her life's mission. There was nothing she could do about it, and that final blow seemed to put the nail in the coffin. She actually felt the fight leave her body as she pulled through the gate and into the drive of her home.

*****

"Honey, I don't know what to say." Barbara tried to console her daughter as they sat in the great room later that evening. "I really believe that God has called you there."

Jonathan read over the words of the letter again, smoothing out the wrinkled paper. He shook his head in disbelief as he got to the words *Dr. Wright, please make no more application for Padawin.*

"I don't understand, Angie," he finally sighed. "This is so final and permanent."

"Tell me about it," she said with swollen eyes. "I guess it's over."

"Just like that?" he asked her. "You're giving up?"

"What do you expect me to do, Daddy? That made it pretty clear, don't you think? I'm not going to Padawin. I can't even apply anymore! What do I do now?"

He stood up and began to pace. He had learned patience through many years of ministry, along with raising four children. God had taught him much about waiting and trusting, but this situation was about to test those years of learning. He knew his daughter had struggled to overcome doubts and fears about Christianity more than any of his other children. She had risen above the reputation of a rebel and had given her life to intense education and preparation for one reason alone: Padawin. Did God intend for him to sit by and watch her dreams fall apart? He doubted it. Not Angie.

"Pack a bag," he said with sudden determination. "We're going to Richmond."

"What?" Barbara asked in surprise.

"If they're going to deny the appointment, and they keep claiming there are valid reasons, then it's time for us to find out why."

"They won't tell me, Daddy," she said flatly.

"I guarantee you they *will* tell me!"

*****

Angie and Jonathan left that afternoon for Virginia. They drove through the night and got a hotel room in the wee hours of the morning. All during the drive she still felt hopeless. She'd been struck down for the last time. He kept insisting the whole thing wasn't over, but she was already beginning to make different plans. Perhaps she could work with the local doctor in town. No, she did *not* want to stay in Dockrey if she had lost the mission field. Oh my, would people ever talk about that! Should she choose to work in a clinic somewhere? She could still help the underprivileged. The money wouldn't be all that great, but who cared? That was never her intention to begin with.

Rather than fall into bed, they prayed once more. They knew this was her absolute last chance to ever even *hope* for a future in Padawin.

*****

Michael Collins awoke with a strange need to pray. This had only happened to him twice before in his life. Both times had been due to intense demonic oppression from the witch doctors. He knew things had not been overtly evil for a while, so he didn't understand the sudden impression to battle intensely in prayer. Nevertheless, he immediately left his bed and fell with his knees to the floor.

Father, I don't know what I'm praying for. I don't know who I'm praying for.

Suddenly Angie's name was written at the front of his mind.

Angie? She's lost hope, hasn't she? Dear Father, give both Angie and myself the faith of Sojay. Show us the obstacles! Help us overcome! You know how desperately she needs to be here. Not just for the medicine, but for the women. I need her here! You need her here, Lord! For nine years I've struggled alone. I don't worry for myself, Father. I worry for Your work. There's so much to be done and so far to go, and I can't do it alone. Show us the obstacles. Give us wisdom and strength to overcome them.

*****

Late the following morning, Jonathan and Angie packed their few belongings, grabbed some donuts and coffee, and headed out to meet with someone from the mission board. After pulling up to the building, they offered one more prayer for confidence that the Lord would reveal to them the problems today, and that the people here would be open to negotiation.

"My name is Reverend Jonathan Wright, father of Dr. Angela Wright," he told the receptionist. "We would like to speak with someone on the mission board."

"I'm sorry, Reverend Wright, they're all in a meeting right now," she replied kindly.

"Well, that's perfect then. I'd rather see them all together anyway. Where are they?"

"You can't just go in, sir," she said nervously.

"Yes I can. Lives hang in the balance. They hold the key to these lives. I need to speak with the board ... now."

Angie smiled at her father's insistence.

"Sir, you don't understand how things operate. They have an agenda they must follow. They'll be busy all day. You should've made an appointment."

"Do you believe in God?" he asked her blankly.

Angie smiled bigger.

"Of course, sir."

"Then tell me where they're meeting, because God sent me here to speak with them."

"Sir ..."

"I don't need to hear any more excuses," he said resolutely. "I'll take my chances of reprimand with them."

The receptionist said nothing more, but held up her finger for a pause. She grabbed the receiver and pressed a small button on the telephone console. "A Reverend Jonathan Wright is here to speak with you."

"Tell them I'm the father of Dr. Angela Wright."

"He's the father of Dr. Angela Wright."

Jonathan smiled warmly at the receptionist, but she remained nervous. Apparently she didn't know the name, but she kept looking back and forth from one to the other.

"Yes, sir, I will." She smiled hesitantly at Jonathan and pointed down a hallway. "They'll see you. Down the corridor ... last door on the right."

"Thank you." He then turned to Angie. "I'll be back with an answer, I assure you."

"Thanks, Daddy."

Jonathan squared his shoulders and began to walk slowly down the hall. Angie watched as he faced the door, took a deep breath, and then walked in without knocking.

Please, God, do something here today, she whispered.

Jonathan entered the meeting room and confidently faced many surprised and tense people. He smiled a greeting and nodded his head.

"Have a seat, Mr. Wright. I'm Fred Carson," a middle-aged man said as he offered his hand. "I've spoken with your daughter several times."

"Yes," Jonathan said as he shook his hand. "You've written to her recently also."

"Yes, I have, Reverend Wright. How can we help you today?"

"Gentlemen, ladies," Jonathan began, "I really think you know why I'm here. You've repeatedly denied my daughter an appointment to Padawin. You continually say you can't send her there. You insist that there are valid *reasons* she can't go. I'm here today merely to discover those reasons."

"Reverend Wright, you have a persistent daughter," said one of the ladies.

"No ma'am. I have a daughter who persistently listens to the Lord. I wish I could explain to you the passion and discipline my daughter has shown in preparation for the mission field."

"You don't need to, sir," Fred Carson told him. "Believe me; we've seen it, read it, and felt it. There's nothing more we'd rather do than send her to Padawin, but we absolutely can't."

"Yes, you keep saying that, but you never say *why*. Whatever the problem is, has it occurred to you that there could possibly be a way to resolve it?"

"We've tried to come up with solutions, but frankly, there are no viable ones."

"Then, at least share with me why it is that Angie can't follow her dream and her calling. I feel like, if at the onset of all this, you would've told us what was happening we could've faced it a little better. As it is, my daughter, who's given her life for this, is sitting out there broken-hearted and defeated. I want an answer; I want the reason."

"Very well," Fred said as he stood up. "The bottom line, you see, is that for the past several years, Michael Collins has served the tribal region of Padawin."

"Yes, I know. He's been there for over nine years."

"Mr. Collins is a single, thirty-five year-old young man. He's healthy, active, and has brought a great ministry to Padawin. He lives in an extremely remote part of the island. It's many miles from the nearest city, taking him close to six hours to travel from the capital city, Taveren, to the tribal village where he makes his home. He is remote and isolated out there."

"So far you haven't told me anything I don't already know."

"Let me tell you more that you already know," Fred offered. "Your daughter is a single, twenty-nine year-old healthy young lady. Her desire is to go to this remote area and work side by side with him. Her aspirations are noble, but the fact remains that these two would be in a position that would compromise the standards of the board."

"I'm still not following you."

"You see, had either Michael or your daughter been married, this wouldn't be a problem. If they were working in a metropolitan area like Taveren, it wouldn't be a problem. But to have two young single people of the opposite sex working together in such a remote area, it would lack ... um ... *propriety*."

Suddenly Jonathan understood. His face flushed as his blood began to boil. "Of what are you accusing these two innocent people? Are you saying you don't trust them to be alone in this isolated region?"

"Actually," the lady who had spoken earlier stood to explain, "it isn't *them* that we don't trust. It's the view of the world. We believe in the commitment that both your daughter and Michael Collins have expressed toward the mission work in Padawin. We believe that we could expect nothing but the highest moral behavior from the two of them. *They* are not the problem. The problem is people who would review something like this and then begin to conjure up improper ideas that go against the very things we stand for."

"We would love nothing more than to send your daughter there to carry out the work that she's dreamed of. But we can't do it," Fred said with disappointment. "Believe me, Reverend Wright, with the persistence your daughter has shown, we've tried to come up with every possible solution to make this work, but there's no viable way to solve it. Your daughter and Michael cannot serve together in a remote area like that unless one of them is married."

Jonathan sighed deeply and ran his hand through his hair. They were right; there was no solution to this particular problem. *Propriety*, or the lack of it, had never crossed his mind. Yet he understood fully how an innocent situation could be twisted into something evil by way of gossip and insinuation. His heart began to break as he realized Angie's dreams were indeed about to be shattered.

"Well then," Jonathan said as he stood to his feet, "I agree with your decision. But I have one more request. My daughter is out there waiting. I would rather she hear this from you. Her heart will break, but she needs to know the truth. May I bring her in?"

The board looked at each other uncomfortably. Their impressions of Angie Wright had been passion and extreme impulsiveness. However, after a brief discussion, it was agreed they would tell her. Jonathan went down the hall and took her hand.

"They were right, Angie," he said sadly. "Their reasoning is sound. Come with me."

Angie entered the boardroom with her father, holding tightly to his arm.

"I'm Fred Carson," he said shaking her hand. "Would you like to have a seat?"

"No, I prefer to stand," she said frankly.

Jonathan smiled. No matter what she faced, she always did it with a sense of control. The board members looked around at each other and mumbled about her beauty. Fred Carson explained the situation to Angie. Her father watched carefully and could see the blood leave her face. He was prepared to help her if necessary, but she remained on her feet, and her expression never changed.

"I appreciate your candor ... at last," Angie said when the talk was finished. "I do wish that you would've mentioned this a year ago. I'm a big girl. Did I somehow seem so fragile that you didn't feel you could share this with me?"

"Actually," the same lady stood and came around to greet Angie herself, "you didn't seem fragile in the least. In fact, I think you scared some of the board members with your bluntness."

Angie didn't smile, but the lady did.

"I wish you knew how badly we want to send you there. You're a rare and precious jewel in this world. Our job is to appoint people with your kind of passion to places where there is great darkness. I'll be honest with you, Dr. Wright, if there were some possible way to get around this, I'd step on every head in here to get you there."

Some of the members chuckled at this statement, but her father took note that she never changed her stern expression. It may have seemed humorous to them, but her lifelong dream had just been stabbed and thrown into the ashes. She took time to look each member in the eye. The silence was long and uncomfortable. They would never forget Angie Wright.

"I'm glad to know the truth at last," she finally managed. Then turning to the door, she left.

Jonathan thanked them again for all their work and let them know how he appreciated their sharing the facts. He left to find his daughter. He knew her heart would be heavy with grief.

*****

Angie cried for a long time on the way back to Dockrey. There was no reason to try and cheer her. She would have to face this sooner or later, and the sooner she dealt with it, the sooner she could move on. Perhaps they had all presumed on God from the beginning. However, Jonathan had believed that God had called her there long ago; it had felt right the first moment she had shared her plans with him. How could everyone have so misread what they thought God was doing?

SEVEN

Angie sat late that evening with her decrepit computer on her lap wondering how to tell Michael. She scrambled her brain for anyone that might be willing to marry her so she could go to Padawin.

Billy Marcum's tried to sleep with me for years. Maybe he'd marry me and follow me over there. Okay, that's a sick thought. Think elsewhere. Ed? Yuck. No. Nice guy, great friend, but I couldn't marry him. This is hopeless. I need to give up. Just bite the bullet and explain it to Michael. Get it over with and move on.

She started a new letter and proceeded to put her thoughts down as clearly as possible. She wondered if he'd be anywhere near as devastated as her. Had he longed for her to come as much as she had longed to go?

Dear Michael,

I got another letter from the mission board; it was a flat denial again. In fact, they told me not to bother applying for Padawin anymore. They said it wasn't going to happen, they'd be more than glad to send me anywhere else in the world, but not Padawin. Daddy got frustrated, so he and I took off for Richmond to speak personally with the board.

They gave my dad an audience.

She went on to explain the situation. As she put all her thoughts down in black and white, she began fighting tears again. How could this be over? Were all those years of certainty for nothing? It was hard now to believe anything. It was hard to trust God, hard to validate dreaming, and hard to face the fact that she was a complete fool for giving herself to something so fully. How could she ever trust anything again in her life?

I can't tell you how tempted I am to say please never write again. It would be a taunt to hear of things in Padawin and know I couldn't go. But you've become a dear friend over the past year. If conversing with me has brought you any comfort or laughter or hope, then by all means, continue to do so. And when you get furlough, please come and spend a little time with me. Hopefully THAT won't be outside the bounds of propriety.

Love, Angie

Feeling defeated and empty, she sent the message, shut down the computer, and placed it on the floor of her room. She gazed at the beat-up guitar still lying in the midst of her mess, but the clutter went unnoticed. Leaning back on the bed, she tried to find comfort in something. She was home, she was healthy and alive, and she was still a doctor. The question was, what did she do now?

*****

As Michael read the letter from Angie on Saturday afternoon, his heart sank, not only for the situation, but also for the devastation he read in her words. He'd never known anyone with such certainty and hope in his life. He had longed for her to be here to encourage him in his work and his walk with the Lord; he had accepted it as a certainty. He left the house to meditate along the beach.

God, why would you do this? It's almost like the proverbial carrot on a stick. It had seemed so right and wonderful. I began to care for her and expect her in my life! Now it's been ripped away … all of it. The medical help, the ministry to the women, the ministry to me. I've been alone all my life, and Angie was a promise of someone to at least share my days with. How can I go on alone again?

Even Sojay, young in the faith, but strong in You, said that You were in control, not men. He said every barrier could be overcome, but not this. Lord, I'd almost be willing to marry a tribal woman just to get her here! Is there someone here I could marry?

He scrolled through a mental list of the young women in the four tribes he worked among. No, he couldn't bring himself to unite with any of them. It wouldn't be a marriage. He couldn't do it even for Angie. And imagine if by some miracle she did come; he would spend more time with her than his own wife. He would have more in common with her than a tribal woman. In fact, he would probably live his life with Angie, hanging on her every word. She was intelligent, full of spirit and committed to the Lord. There wasn't a single young woman in the tribe who had even heard the gospel yet; none of them were Christians. God wouldn't expect that from him. Maybe Angie could marry someone. No, she'd already gone through her list too. She couldn't do it.

Lord, is this an obstacle that can be overcome? I can't see it! I can't marry someone here. I've never even met Angie, but I care more for her than any of the people on this island whom I've known for years.

Suddenly the answer to the problem exploded as if a bolt of lightning had struck his heart. He nearly fell to the ground in delight. There was an answer! Just like Sojay said, God could do anything. He ran back to his house as fast as he could. He knew Angie wouldn't read her mail for hours, but he had to write it now.

Angie!

How badly do you want to come to Padawin? I can hardly breathe right now with excitement! Sojay was right! There's always an answer with God. I know how to fix this—I know how to get you here. First, hear me out. Don't judge my idea until you've had a chance to think about it fully. It can work; it will work.

The whole reason that you can't come is because neither of us is married. I'm not going to marry anyone here. There's no one on this island that I could ever unite myself

37

with ... even for a marriage of convenience. I just couldn't do it. I assume, from your letter, that you feel the same. You've tried to imagine anyone who could fill the bill, but you came up blank too.

How about this? We get married. I meet you in Hawaii. We find a local minister there, and we marry each other legally in the US. It could work. Don't discount this. It would solve many problems anyway. We can live together, work together, eat together, do everything together.

Now understand, I'm not expecting this to be a real marriage. In actuality, it'll be nothing more than a marriage of convenience. But it will solve the problem completely! I'll sleep on the couch. Whatever! I'll sleep in one of the clinic beds when we get it set up! I'll even build myself a hut if I have to!

Angie, don't you see? This is our answer. Please consider it. I'd do anything to get you here ... anything! I've never seen you, but I feel like I know you better than anyone in the world. I don't want to lose you or lose your work in Padawin. Think and pray about this, and please tell me I'm not crazy for believing it could work.

With Great Expectation, Michael Collins, Missionary to the Padawin Islands

He pressed *send* without re-reading the letter. He didn't want to give himself time to change his mind or reason through what he had just done. It was the only solution, and he was committed to getting her here no matter what.

*****

Angie got up slowly the following morning. She took her time getting dressed, stepping over various piles of disorder, and then trudged down the stairs. At the forefront of her mind was the dread to read Michael's reaction. She had come to grips with the fact that she wasn't going to Padawin and had no inkling of what to do next. *That* issue she was handling. But she had come to care for him and hated the thought of devastating him. They had dreamed of much together and this was almost like a divorce.

She ate some cold cheese toast and sipped on her coffee as she sat out on the back porch alone. When she felt awake enough to handle Michael's response, she put up her plate, filled her cup, and finally went to her computer. She turned it on and waited patiently for it to spring into what little life it had left. Sure enough, he'd written back. She clicked and read, but as she continued through the letter, her heart began to pound.

I can't believe this! Could it work? Could there still be a possibility that I could go to Padawin?

Yesterday she had come to believe she was the biggest fool in the world, yet Michael Collins was offering Padawin back to her!

Yes, I'd marry him! In a moment! I'm certainly not gonna marry anyone else!

She slammed the top down on her laptop possibly destroying whatever delicate piece was still keeping it running, and darted to her closet. She opened the door and began throwing things out onto the floor. There were several pairs of shoes, a shoe rack that was never used, an old tennis racket, and several shirts that had fallen off the hangers. She went inside, closed the door, and began to pray as she had never prayed in her life. Her call hadn't been wrong after all. It was simply that no one had seen the answer to the obstacle until now—until the obstacle had been revealed. Sojay was right after all.

*****

"Angie, this is too bizarre," Barbara said as she laid out the plan to her parents.

"Honey, I'm not sure about this," Jonathan agreed.

"Look, until the past two days, every one of us was certain about my going to Padawin," Angie explained forcefully. "We had no doubts. Then a group of people decided my fate and flushed my entire life down the toilet."

"Sweetie, that's a bit extreme," Barbara told her.

"I know, but that was the fact! Now, all of a sudden, there's a way! I'm not gonna marry anybody here! Sure, down the road I might meet someone, but it would be here, in the States. I don't want to be here! I want to be there! And if being there means I have to marry a total stranger … then here comes the bride!"

"Slow down, Angie," Jonathan tried to calm her. "All of this is coming off a hefty emotional rebound. You need to think and pray about this really hard."

"Daddy, that's what I've done all my life. If you tell me I can't do it, I'll honor you … but you know I'll probably hate you 'til the day I die."

He chuckled and stood up to embrace his daughter.

"Angie dear, I would never tell you *no* in this, but let me say something: this has to be *your* decision. I'm not going to say *do it* or *don't do it*. I trust your judgment. If you feel God would have you marry this man in order to carry out His work and plan for your life, then you have to make this choice all on your own."

"Yes!" she yelled as she jumped into the air. "I'm going to Padawin! I'm going! I am *actually* going!"

She hugged both of her parents and danced around the room. Barbara began to tear up as she realized indeed Angie was finally going. She would miss her daughter, but it was bittersweet knowing that her deepest dreams would come true. She also felt somewhat sad by the fact that Annie had married alone in New York with no family around, and now Angie would do the same. She had raised independent thinkers, but never realized how far their independence would one day pull them from her.

*****

Dear Michael,

Yes! Yes, yes, yes! Do you realize that 24 hours ago I thought I'd lost everything

I'd ever worked for? Then suddenly, with one simple letter, you gave it all back to me. I have no problem with this ... no problem whatsoever.

Don't worry about all the arrangements at the house in Padawin. If we can work through this, we can work through anything.

First, I have to call Fred Carson at the mission board. He needs to get things moving so we have an idea of when and where all this will take place.

Thank-you, Michael, with all my heart! I'm so full of joy right now that I feel I'll burst if I don't get out of this house and yell something.

Will Write Later w/ more Details!

Angie

She sent the letter, and then retrieved Fred Carson's number from the trash.

"Hello?"

"Mr. Carson, this is Angie Wright."

"Yes, Dr. Wright. How may I help you?"

"Michael Collins and I are gonna get married. How soon can I go to Padawin?"

There was a brief pause. Angie wished she could've seen his expression.

"Really?" he finally responded. "This was sudden."

"You said one of us had to be married. This way, we'll both be married. No one can bring any accusations about that."

"You're certainly right," he nearly laughed. "You're both okay with this?"

"He suggested it; it never crossed my mind. I was thrilled! All I've ever wanted is to go to Padawin."

"Yes, I know."

"Do I need to send in another application?"

"No ma'am ... no. I think we've got several here already. We'll start processing it immediately, and I'll most definitely call a meeting of the board. Now, there are several things you need to do while you're waiting."

"Just tell me," she said eagerly.

After a long list of mandated duties, he congratulated her again.

"Do you have any idea when I can leave?"

"Give us about a month to get it organized. You'll need at least that much time to pull *yourself* together. And Angie?"

"Yes sir?"

"I'm happy for you ... and Michael too."

"Thank-you, sir. You have no idea how excited I am."

After hanging up, Fred Carson looked over to his wife and grinned big. "There's a young missionary in Padawin who's about to get the thrill of his life."

After explaining the situation to his wife, who was already familiar with much of the story, he then give details of how unusually beautiful Angie was.

"He's never seen her; he has no idea," Fred laughed. "He thinks he's just done something noble in order to get a doctor out to his little tribes. I almost wish I could be there when they meet for the first time."

"What does he look like?" his wife wondered.

"*Cute as a button* I believe were the words used by the ladies on the board."

"Oh, my," she said slowly with a growing grin.

*****

Annie put down the phone and practically staggered into the upstairs studio at their house in the Adirondacks. Stephen stopped playing as soon as he saw her, concerned that something might be wrong with the baby because of her expression. He immediately stood and went to her.

"Is everything all right?" he asked in a panic.

"You're never gonna believe this. I need to sit down."

"Is something wrong?" He continued to probe as he led her to the couch.

"Angie's getting married."

The news registered unbelievable with Stephen too. "Angie? The doctor sister?"

"I can't believe it."

"To whom?"

"Michael, the missionary on the islands she's been planning to go to all these years.

"When did this happen? I didn't even know she'd been seeing anyone."

Annie laughed and told him, "They haven't been *seeing* each other. In fact, they've never seen each other!"

"What? How can they just decide to get married?"

"The mission board wouldn't let her go to Padawin because she and Michael were both single and of the opposite sex. So, Michael proposed ... and she accepted!"

"They've never seen each other?"

Annie shook her head and smiled, still stunned, as she said, "Not even a picture—you know Angie and her computer ineptness. She doesn't even have a picture on Facebook."

"Wo," Stephen grinned big. "Is he ever in for a surprise."

EIGHT

"I think you need to run that by me one more time," Andie said after Sunday dinner at her parents.

"Michael and I are getting married. It's the only way I can go to Padawin," Angie said excitedly. "I still can't believe it myself. I'm going to Padawin!"

"The Padawin part I believe." Andie was still in shock. "It's the sudden marriage part that's flying around my head in uncertainty. Daddy, are you just gonna let her do this?"

"I don't *let* or *not let* Angie do anything," Jonathan explained. "She's a big girl. I don't know if I totally agree with all of it yet, but I do know that for many, many years I've listened to her dreams of Padawin. If Michael Collins is the only ticket to get her there, then I guess I have to send my vote with him."

"Moms?" Andie turned elsewhere hoping to find some sensibility.

"Andie, all you ever dreamed about was marrying Doug and living happily ever after," Barbara said tenderly. "Your father and I thought you were too young, just out of high school, barely in college. But that was your only hope in life, the only thing you wanted. We understood how it felt to be in love, to be so desperately connected to someone that it hurt. So we let you marry with the understanding that you'd finish college. We weren't sure it was the best choice, but we knew it was what you wanted most. That's all we're doing with Angie. Her only dream has been Padawin. Her only hope to go is to marry Michael. What would you expect us to do?"

Andie looked between the three of them: Jonathan, Barbara and Angie. They all seemed settled and content with the decision. She was still reeling. "Am I the only one who thinks this whole thing is … well … for lack of a better word at the moment, *weird*?"

Angie looked at her and rolled her eyes. "Of course it's weird! It's practically an arranged marriage. But who cares? I sure don't! I'm walking on air!"

"Sounds like love to me," Doug threw out, at which Andie gave him a sharp and unappreciated glance.

"Hey," he continued, "don't knock this whole prearranged thing. It works really well in some cultures. Think about Isaac and Rebekah in the Old Testament."

"This is the 21st century!" Andie exclaimed.

"Yeah, but imagine this," Doug said with a grin, "this poor guy will be blown away when he gets a peek at his e-mail-order bride. He thinks he's getting some average Jill for a roommate, when in fact, he's getting one of the three hottest girls on the planet!"

Everyone looked at Doug with varied expressions.

"Is that how you describe my daughters?" Jonathan asked sharply.

"No sir. Excuse me, sir," he said quickly. "I meant to say one of the three most beautiful and intelligent girls on the planet."

*****

Dear Michael,

Everything is in motion now. My father and mother are with me on this ... thank goodness. Had they fought me, I would've seriously considered not going through with it. They trust the call I've had for many years, and they trust God's way in making the call a reality.

I still can't believe it. After talking with the board personally, I'd actually given up all hope. I'm now trying to get my mind back on track. Is it really happening? Am I really going?

By the way, perhaps you can get rid of the monkey now! You won't be alone anymore!

Love, Angie

Dear Angie,

I've told the people you're coming, and they're excited. You can't know what it means to them that someone else will be here to help them. When I showed them all the various aspects of agriculture and how it could benefit their lives, I immediately became a trusted friend. Getting them to let go of the superstitious ways they've lived with for hundreds of years is another story. I'll be so glad when you're here to begin teaching the women about Christ and the equality that He offers. Only two women are saved, and that was because of the salvation of their husbands. They had to break strongly with tradition to even bring their women into the Bible Studies. You, however, can begin your own.

As soon as we get some dates settled, I'll work with the board on making arrangements for Hawaii. There's a missionary family in Taveren, but getting it all done legally could be a problem. Besides, it'll be nice to always remember that we got married in Hawaii, don't you think? (smile)

I need to go. A child has fallen and cut his knee open. I get to perform stitches once again. I HATE that. I'll be glad when you get here!!!

Michael Collins, Missionary to the Padawin Islands

*****

Angie grinned at Fred Carson's name flashing across her phone's display.

"Hello?"

"Dr. Wright, this is Fred Carson! I hope you're packing."

Angie gave a scream of delight. "So I'm really going?"

"Yes, indeed. The vote was almost unanimous. One older lady, who seems to give us problems often, felt the whole thing sounded *tawdry*."

Angie laughed and said, "She's not the only one! One of my sisters is having a hard time swallowing the idea too."

"It's the most irregular situation we've ever encountered, but to be honest, Dr. Wright, I would've almost let my sixteen year-old son marry you just to get you over there!"

"I appreciate the offer. Do you have any time reference?"

"How about you depart from Nashville on July tenth?"

"No problem!"

"I wish you and Michael the best. I'm actually relieved that *something* finally worked out."

"Me, too, Mr. Carson."

*****

Angie's life took a sudden turnaround. From uncertainty and despair, to definite hope and a positive future, she found herself unable to stop smiling for the next week. July Fourth was around the corner, and she would be spending almost two whole weeks with Annie. The thought of leaving the place that had always been home, and the people who had always been family, to start a new life somewhere else should seem daunting, but she couldn't wait.

Angie and Cindy went out to dinner again later that week. Cindy lived in Tuscumbia, so Angie drove the blue Bug up to meet at her apartment. They crammed into the tiny sports car again and headed to an upper scale steak house. Angie waited until they ordered their drinks to share her news.

"I'm getting married to the missionary in Padawin, and I'm leaving July tenth."

"What?" Cindy blurted out in unbelief. "Are you in love with him?"

"No, but that's not the point. It's the only possible way right now that I can go over there."

"So now I *will* be the only single girl left in our class."

"Are you not going to chastise me too for making such a brash decision?"

"Are you kidding? It sounds hopelessly romantic to me. It's better than any of my prospects at the moment. You're going to a tropical Pacific island to marry a man you've never met who probably works hard in the sun all day long ... you know, bronzed and beautiful. What's to chastise?"

"I like your attitude, although I'm not necessarily expecting the bronzed and beautiful part."

"Why not?"

"Well ... he's a missionary. How many missionaries do you know that are ... well ... *bronzed and beautiful*?"

"So, he's ugly?"

"Not *ugly*. After your brother, I stopped looking on the outside."

"Billy is a jerk, isn't he?"

"I won't respond to that. Let's just say, I prefer to look at the heart when I look at a man. Michael is a wonderful person. He cares about the things I care about. The Lord is his first priority. He's given his life to work with the Padawin people just as I want to. That's all the matters to me."

"I know," Cindy smiled, "and that's why I think the whole thing is wonderful. You won't get any negative comments from me, except the fact that I'll miss you terribly. So, what does he look like?"

Angie laughed and threw her hands in the air. "I have no idea!"

"Isn't he on Facebook?"

"Well, yeah, but so am I, and I don't have any pictures either. I wouldn't even know where to start in getting them on there."

"This is pitiful. You're a doctor and he can build personal power plants but neither of you can upload a simple picture on Facebook."

"See, I don't even know the difference between uploading and downloading."

"Thank goodness you at least know how to turn the thing on so we can email and chat online."

Angie talked of everything under the sun, in fact, she was so wound up that Cindy didn't try to converse. Right now, her world had fallen apart. She was thankful at least one of them was happy.

"So what's the latest with the married man?" Angie finally asked, yet with tenderness, not judgment.

"I took your advice. I stopped the relationship. You can't imagine how hard it was. He begged and insisted he loved me, but you know what? He didn't seem sincere. I almost gave into him, but I began to realize that what you said was true. He didn't love me; I was just a wonderful convenience for him."

"Don't give up on what God has for you," Angie said with a warm smile as she reached across the table and took her hand. "He has a plan for each of us ... nothing is arbitrary. He's promised it. If you don't believe it, just look in front of you. I'm a living example!"

"I know," Cindy smiled. "Believe it or not, I've always trusted God in some small way simply because of your boundless faith. I may not show it by the stupid decisions I often make, but I somehow have always known it."

"Cindy, keep trusting God for everything you need in this life. Look, I have to confess, I almost gave up. I actually began to believe for the first time in my life that maybe God couldn't do all He promised. But He proved me wrong. No matter what happens next, I'll always trust Him to see me through it."

"And please pray that I'll develop that same kind of faith."

"I will, my friend, every morning as I watch that Pacific sunrise."

"I'm going to miss you, Angie."

"Then pray for me every day too. That way we'll always keep each other close."

Cindy nodded in agreement as a small tear begin to trail down her face.

*****

"Nervous?" Jonathan asked Angie as they relaxed on the back porch.

"About what?"

"Any of this?"

"Not a bit nervous, but I'm about to burst with excitement. I wish tomorrow was July tenth."

"Have you and Michael discussed your arrangements once you get there?"

"What kind of arrangements?"

He now put down his paper and stared at her above the rim of his reading glasses.

"Your living arrangements."

"We'll figure all that out when I get to Padawin," she said as bubbly as ever. "I'm not really concerned, Daddy."

He chuckled and picked his paper back up.

"What do you find funny about that?"

"You're marrying a total stranger and aren't the least bit concerned about where *you* will sleep and where *he* will sleep. Do I need to have that little talk with you again about the differences between men and women?"

"Please, Daddy, I don't *need* the talk again. I've studied human sexuality more than I ever cared to. I understand the differences."

"As long as you know."

"It's not like that anyway, you know. It's a marriage of convenience."

"Very convenient."

"What's *that* supposed to mean?"

"Angie," he looked up at her again, "for the record, you are unusually beautiful."

"Please ... don't make me blush."

"I'm just trying to state the facts. No matter how *convenient* this may all start out, at some point this boy is bound to feel attracted to you. You need to be prepared to deal with that."

"What if *I'm* attracted to him?"

"Well then, hallelujah," he said looking back down to his paper.

"You better not let Moms hear you say that. She'll accuse you of being sacrilegious."

"It's only sacrilegious if I don't mean it."

"Then exactly *what* are you insinuating, Daddy?"

"I'm just remembering the fact that you've always been pretty harsh with gentlemen in your life. It would be rather ironic if you suddenly met this total stranger and thought, *ooh-la-la*."

"Very funny," she said as she saw the grin growing on his face. "I might just surprise you all."

"It wouldn't be the first time."

NINE

"The next time we go to an airport, it'll be to send you off to Padawin," Jonathan said as they waited for Stephen and Annie to arrive.

"Don't think I haven't been considering that." Angie smiled.

He couldn't believe how at ease she was with the whole bizarre situation. Both of his other daughters would have stressed about the *what if's* associated with the circumstances, but not Angie. She was too excited to recognize any negatives at the moment.

"You've never flown before, have you?" he asked her.

"Never. Can you imagine how much fun that's gonna be?"

"Annie hates flying."

"I know, but that's sort of Annie-ish anyway, don't you think?"

He laughed. Annie was definitely the type to dread anything new and out of her control. Angie had elements that needed control, but leaned toward the fresh and unique. He hoped that her experience in Padawin would be one of continuous adventure. However, with Angie in the combination, there was bound to be adventure, created if not natural.

This would be the first time the sisters would be together since Annie's marriage in December. It had killed Angie, Andie and Barbara that Annie had gotten married without any of the family present. When she called with the news, Jonathan had to spend most of the holidays calming the disheartened women in his life.

Security began to close in around the doors where the passengers would enter. As soon as Annie and Stephen appeared, a large number of people, whom they had assumed were waiting for friends or family, began to crowd around them. Angie tried her best to get to her sister, but the group was persistent. Security began to peel people back, including her.

"Wait!" Annie called out. "The tall one with the long hair is my sister!"

Some people then turned to Angie and began to surround her. One security woman grabbed her by the arm and led her through the crowd. When she reached Annie, a line of guards let her through so that she could finally greet her.

"Come here! Come here!" Annie screamed as she reached out for her. They hugged tightly for a bit, not wanting to break the hold after the longest separation the two had ever known.

"Look at your little tummy! It's so cute!" Angie exclaimed as she put her hand on Annie's growing bulge. "Have you felt it move yet?"

"Have I ever! Where's Daddy?"

"Somewhere out there." Angie turned to see if she could spot him.

"There he is!" Annie shouted. She took a guard's arm and pointed toward her father while explaining, "That's my dad. Can you get him inside our little bubble here?"

"Yes, ma'am," he replied and immediately spoke into a small microphone on his lapel. Within 30 seconds Jonathan Wright was hugging his youngest daughter.

"You look absolutely radiant," he told her.

"Thank you, Daddy. It's good to be back home again."

Jonathan turned toward Stephen and gave him a hearty hug. "How you doing, son?" he asked warmly.

"To say *wonderful* wouldn't come close. I'm actually coming home somewhere for a holiday. It's hard to imagine."

"Welcome home, indeed."

*****

Stephen and Annie walked up the staircase to her old bedroom. Angie and Barbara had insisted they stay in the garage apartment, but Annie wouldn't hear of it. She wanted to stay in her own room with her husband for the first time. She sighed deeply as she made her way inside.

"Miss it?" Stephen asked her.

"Not really *miss* ... more like remembering."

Stephen glanced at his poster which was still hanging on the wall opposite her bed. "Love your decorations."

"I ought to pull it down," she said as she wrapped her arms around him. "I have the real thing now."

"Thank goodness! When I first came here I wondered if you'd ever warm up to me."

"Trust me; I was warm long before you ever realized it!"

Supper was chaotic. All three sisters were present, along with Andie's four children. Add Doug to any combination, and the result was bound to be glorious mayhem. Stephen had never considered himself an introvert, but after being around this family the few times he had, he realized that he wasn't the assertive man he had always assumed.

When Andie and Doug left, and things began to settle down, Annie and Angie found themselves sitting alone on the back porch.

"When's the last time you got in the hot tub?" Annie wondered.

"Hmmm, about eight or nine days ago. Too hot."

Annie nodded in understanding.

"Had any trouble with morning sickness?" Angie asked her.

"Not a bit, but I swear I could eat a horse at every sitting."

"You didn't do badly tonight."

"You were watching me eat?"

"I can't help it. I'm a doctor. You've never had a big appetite, you still look too skinny for your own good, and I just wanted to make sure the baby was getting plenty of nourishment."

"Thank you for caring, but trust me, Stephen keeps an eye on my every move."

"So, what's it like being married?"

"Wonderful," Annie sighed. "I never imagined life could be so sweet."

"This from the indelible single girl. I still can't believe you're married."

"You know what, neither would I if it weren't for this baby. Sometimes I can't fathom that all this happened to me so fast. This time last year, I had no idea what my future would hold. Occasionally I'll still wake up next to Stephen and think, *what on earth am I doing in bed with him*, then I'll remember everything."

"We always were sound sleepers, unless I moved onto your side of the bed," Angie laughed remembering the wrath of Annie's kicks, "but how do you forget that you're married?"

"Well, with the baby now, everything seems more concrete."

"Are you guys at all disappointed that you didn't *plan* the whole pregnancy thing for later?"

"Are you kidding? For Stephen, this baby is the *period*, the *completing point* of his life. He told me that he thought just having me work with him in the studio and on tour would be the most awesome thing that could've happened to him, but they pale compared to having his own child."

"Well, he has a real family now. I'm happy for both of you."

"And what about you? What about this whole marriage thing?"

"Uncanny, isn't it?" Angie laughed. "Who would've thought such a thing as this would happen?"

"Well, not in my wildest dreams! That's for sure! The thing I find funny is this time last year we were bemoaning the fact that neither of us would ever marry, and … well … here we are."

"Andie's ready to strangle me, you know? She thinks I'm totally out of my head and blinded by this whole missionary thing."

"I only have one concern about it."

"What's that?"

"I hope he's tall," Annie said seriously.

They sat silently for about five seconds, and then burst into laughter.

*****

"Grab a racket," Annie said as she walked by Stephen's lawn chair on the afternoon of the Fourth.

"What are we doing?"

"Playing Badminton."

"Should you play that while you're pregnant?"

"It'll be no problem if you stay on your feet and keep me from having to run too much."

"Wait a minute!" He scurried to catch up to her. "I don't think I've ever played this game."

She lifted herself on her tiptoes and gave him a peck on the lips. "It doesn't take a rocket scientist to whack the thing back across the net."

"I hope you're right," he said doubtfully.

It was decided the men would play the women. Between Stephen and Alex's constant concern for their wives, the game became pointless.

"What are you guys doing?" Doug yelled at the expectant fathers.

"My wife is nine months pregnant and she's out playing this stupid game in the heat of the day!" Alex defended.

"Isn't six months a very important developmental period for the baby?" Stephen asked with concern.

"Why do the pregnant ladies have to play?" Doug complained.

"Because it's July Fourth, and it's a family tradition," Annie yelled back at him. "Andie always played when she was pregnant!"

"Yeah, but she didn't stand there and whine every time she missed the birdie," Doug went on.

"Stop griping, Doug, and serve the shuttle!" Andie demanded.

"Why don't we let the pregnant husbands and wives play together?" Doug continued with suggestions.

"Because this is the last time we'll be able to play as a sister team with Angie." Annie silenced him at last and he threw his arms up in complete defeat.

TEN

"Okay, I think we can stop and get her out now," Angie said steering her father's pickup to the side of the road. "Just make sure no one else is pulling over too or sneaking up on us."

Andie looked carefully around the two-lane country road as Angie maneuvered to the edge. No cars appeared to be following. The two girls climbed out of the truck cab and quickly went to the topper over the back. They opened the hatch and pulled back the flaps to a huge appliance box. Annie climbed out looking slightly green.

"I hope you haven't been swerving around in my Bug like you just did this truck!" Annie complained as she worked to get herself out of the box.

"Well the last time we did this you weren't six months pregnant either," Angie said matter of fact as she and Andie helped their sister from the back of the truck onto solid ground.

"Are you all right?" Andie asked her. "You look a little pale."

"Besides being *slung* around back and forth," Annie glared at Angie, "it was unbearably hot."

"Are you gonna throw up?" Angie asked her.

"I doubt it. I don't feel *that* bad. Just make sure no one tells Stephen I didn't pull through this like a bed of roses. Agreed?"

"Agreed," Andie confirmed.

"My lips are sealed," Angie promised.

They climbed back into the cab still searching carefully for anyone who might not have fallen for the trick. All clear. Angie put the truck into first gear, and the girls headed to the mall in Tupelo for a day of shopping. The main reason was to help Angie acquire a durable wardrobe that could last her in Padawin until the first furlough. The other reasons revolved around simply having fun.

*****

"I love this store!" Angie said with excitement as she came out with another very safari looking outfit. "What's it called again?"

"American Eagle," Annie and Andie said in harmony.

"This stuff is great. A little expensive, but great." She glanced at the price tag.

"Angie," Annie reminded her, "we're not looking for bargains; we're looking for durability. Buy the shorts."

"Ooo," Andie said in awe. "Look at this shirt! Palm trees and coconuts all over it. And the green! It matches your eyes! Try this one on too!"

"Guys, I'm gonna go broke before I even get to the shoes!" Angie complained.

"Dear sister," Annie said with a warm smile as she placed both hands on Angie's shoulders looking her square in the eye, "surely you didn't think I'd let you spend a cent of your money on anything today."

"Well, I surely assumed that I would buy my own stuff just like I usually do."

"Assume differently," Annie smiled. "And when we've finished with all you need here, we're heading to an electronics store for a new laptop computer. Stephen insisted when he saw that rickety thing you've been using."

Angie just smiled with a confused look. She looked over at Andie who was also beaming.

"I was gonna get you a few things," Andie laughed, "but since Annie's married to a millionaire, what's the point?"

Annie pointed to the shirt Andie had discovered. "Try on the pretty green shirt with the palm trees."

"And this!" Andie said quickly as she handed her a skirt with the same print.

"When on earth am I gonna wear a skirt in the sand?" Angie complained.

"During all those romantic dinners you'll have while you're newlyweds," Annie grinned.

"Very funny." Angie grabbed the clothing and headed back to the dressing room.

When Angie was well inside, Andie tapped Annie on the shoulder and asked, "So what kind of chance do you give this marriage? You seem awfully optimistic about the whole thing."

"Why not be? This is all Angie's ever wanted. And you know how she pretty much gave up on marriage from the beginning thinking that it would be near impossible to find someone with the same call as her. Well, *bah-da-bing*! What do you know? There is someone out there with the same call. How could it go wrong?"

"Do you really think it's that simple?"

"Compared to what Stephen and I went through? Yes! To me, this seems as simple as it comes. Imagine, there's no dating process or rules to follow."

"Rules! I think the rules will be even more confusing. I mean, when you date, you know where you start and where you stop. You get picked up, you spend time together and then you say *good night*. But this? This is … unnatural!"

"To you," Annie said with a smile as she pointed toward Angie who was looking incredibly gorgeous in the outfit, "but not to her. To her this is the most natural thing that could've happened. And you know what, from what I've picked up, I think Missionary Mike feels the same way. As soon as he heard the dilemma, he knew how to fix it."

Angie walked out and mocked model poses, but several in the store were stunned by her beauty as she paraded around the room. Her sisters clapped and insisted she get it. Angie still wondered when she would actually find a time or occasion to wear them, but she acquiesced.

"Why are we here?" Angie wondered as they walked into the evening section of the most expensive dress store in the mall. "I most definitely will *not* be wearing anything from here on the beach."

"No," Annie agreed, "but you'll be getting married in Hawaii."

"I'm *not* getting a wedding dress!" Angie said resolutely. "That *would* be ridiculous!"

"Not a full length one," Andie tried to calm her. "But you need something exquisitely pretty for the grand event."

"What were you expecting to wear to your wedding?" Annie asked her.

"I hadn't really thought about it. Perhaps that cute little green thing with the coconuts that we bought?"

"No way," Annie said decisively. "Let's start looking through the white dresses."

"You will need white, won't you?" Andie teased.

"Of course," Angie said quickly. "What are you thinking?"

"Oh, the name *Billy Marcum* comes to mind immediately," Annie giggled.

"Sometimes I think you're pure evil."

"What *was* the deal with him anyway? Annie always acts like she's got something over you where he's concerned," Andie wondered.

"None of your business," Angie said quickly. "White, yes indeedy! Let's find the whitest white they've got."

*****

Dear Michael, I went shopping with my sisters today and had a glorious time! However, they made me buy a wedding dress. It's not long or super fancy, but it's definitely beautiful. I wanted to let you know so you wouldn't be caught off guard. I mean, personally I don't care what you wear, but I thought you might be a bit shocked if you showed up in your swimming trunks and I walked out decked in this white satin.

Also, Annie got me a new laptop! It's wonderful! I wish I would've had this one during all my schooling instead of that old beat-up, second-hand thing I dragged around all those years. It's incredible!

I can't believe I'm leaving in only four days. There seems to be so much to do before then. I know I'll forget something vitally important and live in misery for the next several weeks because of it! I've tried to be thorough, but I feel too scattered to have possibly done everything I need to do.

Let me know the final details about finding you at the airport. Kind of exciting, isn't it? We actually get to meet! Take care and see you soon.

Love, Angie

Dear Doctor Angie, Four days! It won't take you long to adjust to the easy-going lifestyle of the island. The people here will love you, but they'll think you're very sick for a while because of your white skin. Once they see that you've lived a week or two, they'll grow comfortable with your color. I've tried to explain the deal with different races, but some of them just won't buy it. Also, you'll work hard here. At the end of the day, if you have enough energy for anything, it'll generally be for reading or writing letters on that brand new laptop. Bring me a new one while you're at it! (Smile ... and please, just kidding) Of course, actually having someone around to talk with in the evenings will be a drastic change for me. At sundown, unless there's a tribal festival or celebration, everyone goes to their huts to be with their families. You may see fires outside with families gathered around them, and a lot of courting is done during this time, but generally families are strictly alone. That's why they gave me the monkey. I'm trying to help them understand that as Christians we're all a part of God's family, and we should welcome everyone, but to them it's still an infringement of precious time. So ... hey ... I'll now have a family!

Your flight will be in Honolulu around 4:40 pm. I'll be standing there, I guess with a sign that says Angie on it. I don't know what else to do. I thought about getting you to send me a picture via the Internet, but then it would only be fair to send you one in return, and I'm clueless as to how to go about it.

I'd better go. A storm is brewing something awful over here, and I don't want to take the chance of blowing up my sickly computer.

Crack and boom ... the lightning is downright scary. BYE!!!!

Michael Collins, Missionary to the Padawin Islands

ELEVEN

"What is this thing?" Annie asked as she helped organize the packing.

"Don't be sarcastic," Angie shot back. "It's my guitar. I know it's ugly, but it gets the job done."

"Ugly isn't a proper word for this … object."

"Stop criticizing my stuff."

"Play something for me," Annie asked eagerly.

"Don't even think about it."

"Oh, come on. Play something on your ugly little guitar. Prove to me that this thing is worth dragging thousands of miles halfway around the world."

"I won't play for you. Besides, I can't play without singing, and you don't want to hear that."

"You sing nicely," Annie said plopping down on the bed. "Just play one song. Please, please, please?"

"I'm not gonna play my guitar for you. I'm not gonna sing for you. Get off my bed."

"What are you carrying it in?"

"The guitar?"

Annie nodded.

"Nothing, I guess. I hadn't thought about it."

"I'll make a deal with you: you play and sing one little song for me, and I'll get you a gig bag."

"Gig bag?"

"Yeah, a carrying case."

"I don't need a *gig bag*. I need you to get off my bed. You're on my Atlanta Braves fleece blanket. It goes in the suitcase next."

Annie just shook her head and settled back farther on the blanket.

"Remember when I used to pin you on the floor when we were kids?" Angie asked her.

"Yes. And you did mean things to me."

"I would hold you down and let my spit dangle in your face—then suck it back up at the last second."

"That was so disgusting," Annie grimaced. "I should've told Billy Marcum about that. He may not have found you so appealing then."

"Could I have my fleece blanket, please?"

"Are you threatening to pin me down if I don't get up and give you the blanket? You do remember I'm six months pregnant, and the struggle I

56

would put up to keep the *spit* thing from happening might cause me great harm."

"Annie, I'm not singing for you!"

"Do you think I'd judge you or make fun of you or anything like that? I think what you're doing with your life is the most awesome thing in the world. Look at me! I'm living in the lap of luxury with every dream I could ever have imagined coming true on a daily basis. That's now what's happening to you. This guitar is just another part of all you're doing, and all I want is to touch that small part of you before you go. It's something that will connect us that never has before: our music."

Angie laughed. "My guitar playing and singing will never connect with your unbelievable musicianship!"

Annie gave a defeated look and got up from the bed. She folded the blanket as mournfully as possible and handed it to Angie. More pouting. Angie took the blanket and shook her head to indicate she wouldn't play her guitar. As she placed the blanket in one of the four open suitcases on the floor, Annie sighed heavily.

"I'm not going to do it," Angie said again.

"I know."

"Then why are you still pouting?"

"Because I'm truly hurt," Annie said as sadly as she could.

"I don't sing anything in English anyway."

"What? What language do you sing in?"

"Padawin, silly. What did you think, French?"

"How cool, Angie! Oh, come on! Just let me hear one little song. I've never even heard you *speak* in Padawin. Please, Angie, please?"

She closed her eyes and gave an exasperated breath. "If you didn't look so pitiful with that tiny bulge in your belly, this would never work." She picked up the guitar.

"Goody, goody!" Annie bubbled as she clapped her hands. "What's the name of the song?"

"If I can actually sing it on key, you should be able to figure it out."

She sat beside her on the bed, crossed her legs, and leaned the guitar on her right leg. Gently strumming she began to sing:

When the horn of the Lord will blow and time comes to an end
And the sunrise comes upon us bright and bright
When the ones who know the Lord go on to Heaven's special beach
And our names are called in Heaven I'll be there.

When our names are called in Heaven
When our names are called in Heaven
When our names are called in Heaven
When our names are called in Heaven I'll be there.

Annie clapped her hands again and hugged Angie tightly as tears pooled in her eyes. "That was incredible! You do wonderfully. And the language is beautiful. I couldn't understand a word of it, but I definitely recognized the tune, Daddy's favorite, 'When the Roll is Called up Yonder.'"

"Well, thanks for being kind," Angie said as she rolled her eyes slightly.

"I wasn't being kind. You know me, I don't *do kind* for the heck of it. I'm honest. I think your music is wonderful. You'll bless the Padawin people."

"Thank you, but if those tears actually fall from your eyes, I'm afraid I'll lose it. I don't want to cry yet. I want to wait until I leave."

"Then tell me something funny so I can dry them up quickly."

Angie thought for a moment. What would make Annie smile? Actually, just about anything.

"I considered asking Billy Marcum to marry me so I could go to Padawin."

Annie's eyes grew wide and her mouth dropped open.

"I was desperate!" Angie said in defense. "Trust me, the thought didn't last long. If I could've done it without him having to follow me over … maybe, but I dropped the idea right away."

Annie smiled and said, "Well, that cleared up the tears. Anything I can take down the stairs?"

"My ugly guitar."

"And I owe you a gig bag," Annie said as she picked up the guitar with new respect.

"And I'll hold you to it."

TWELVE

Michael awoke early on Saturday morning to prepare for the six-hour drive to Taveren. He glanced in the mirror as he finished brushing his teeth and admitted that he looked downright scraggly. His hair hadn't been cut since his last trip to the city four months ago. The beard was wild and too long for even his liking, but living alone and only seeing the tribesmen regularly, he found no reason to groom. Besides, he liked not shaving. He certainly hoped this woman coming into his life wouldn't insist that he change his comfortable, bachelor ways. If she did, she would have to learn a few things in the school of Michael Collins. He was who he was, and there would be no changes to accommodate her.

Where are these thoughts coming from? Until yesterday I was excited and living in great anticipation; now I fear for my life! What happened to the surety I've felt for the past year?

The drive to Taveren was long and bumpy. The path that was supposed to be the road was rutted out and washed through in many places. He hoped the civilized doctor wouldn't be scared away from the mission field by the drive in the Land Rover. *She may only last one month out here.* He then considered all the work he had put into creating a home with luxuries that most tribal missionaries would never have. He had made the mill that generated electricity so he could have air conditioning and refrigeration, computer access and electric lights. He had a bathroom with hot and cold running water and a covered deck over the river with an incredible view of Mount Podakind, the highest peak in the islands. He had even built a sewage and water filtration system at the Podakind tribe where he made his residence. No amoebas or bacteria here. He hoped she could appreciate the work he had done.

After the long, restless trip, he pulled into the sandy drive of Chet and Vicki Clarence, missionaries to Padawin in Taveren. They had been assigned to the islands the same time as Michael and had traveled over from the states together. They were the closest thing to family he had in the entire world. For the past nine years, he had watched their family grow by two children, James and Heather, and watched their ministry flourish. Every year they tried to make it out to his area for a week to visit and offer help. During these times Vicki tried to communicate with the women concerning salvation and their need to trust Christ. She had led Sojay's wife to Christ three years ago, and then Sojay's wife led another woman. Other than that, the women clung to superstitions.

Michael parked the dirty vehicle, grabbed his one overnight bag and headed for the front door. Vicki greeted him eagerly and gave him a warm hug. She was a shorter lady, slightly chubby, with light reddish hair and bright green eyes. Her welcoming smile and bubbly personality always made him feel at home. As soon as he walked through the door, James, five, and Heather, four, ran into his arms. He held them tightly for a moment and then produced two carved toys from the tribe as gifts. The children squealed in glee as their anticipation of presents was indeed, as always, met.

"You need a haircut," Vicki told him as she presented a glass of sweet iced tea.

He drank several large gulps and then said, "I know. Can you get to it sometime tonight?"

"Of course. You need to shave too."

He shook his head and grimaced.

"Michael, please! You look like a wild man with that thing. Besides, she needs to see that cute little baby face of yours."

"No," he said firmly. "I'll trim it, but I won't shave it off."

"Why? Your scar?"

She was referring to a large gash across his left cheek that he had never explained to Chet or Vicki.

"She's a doctor," he said plainly. "First thing she'd do is start questioning me about it. I'd rather avoid it right off the bat."

Vicki went for a towel, her scissors and the electric clippers, then sat Michael down outside.

That night at dinner Michael tried to relax and enjoy the evening, but both Chet and Vicki could tell he was nervous. He ate very little, even though Vicki had prepared his favorite meal of fried chicken. The conversation consisted mostly of their work in the city with hardly any mention of the doctor's pending arrival. While clearing the dishes from the table, Vicki took Chet to the side and suggested he try to pull Michael out of his shell to see what was wrong. As the men began to talk still at the table, Vicki strained to hear the conversation while washing the dishes and putting away the food.

"How far along are you on building the clinic?" Chet asked casually.

"Close to being finished. The floor and walls and roof are done. The plumbing is ready to be connected, but I still have to finish the wiring. I'm not sure where she wants all that equipment she had sent in, so I wanted to wait and see where the receptacles and lights needed to be."

"Smart." He glanced at the beard and asked, "Are you gonna shave that nasty thing off before you meet her?"

"No," Michael replied stubbornly.

"At least trim it."

"Maybe."

"Maybe? You're meeting this woman for the first time and *maybe* you'll look decent? Trust me on this: trim the beard, Michael. At least make a good first impression."

"I'm not out to make an impression. I am who I am."

"The woman's going to marry you. Please look halfway civilized when she first sees you."

"I'm *not* out to make an impression," Michael said firmly.

Vicki walked in and gave him a confused look. "Why?"

Michael sighed nervously and began to chew a fingernail. "This is a marriage of convenience. I don't want to give her the impression when I meet her that she can expect anything else other than that."

Vicki tried not to drop her jaw. "You don't even want to give this a chance? What if there's an attraction?"

"I'm not exactly planning on that," Michael said shyly. "Look, I never meant for this to be more than it is. I just need a lady out there to work with the women, and I desperately need a doctor. I don't *need* a wife. It's strictly convenience."

"Well, that's a change," Chet laughed. "When you first suggested this whole thing you were rather excited. What changed your mind? Cold feet?"

"Everybody gets cold feet," Vicki explained as she sat with them at the table. "Even Chet did, and look how ugly he is. He was lucky just to get married."

"What do you mean by *ugly*?" Chet asked quickly.

"Oh, come on. You're bald and tall and lanky. You weren't the catch of the year, you know?"

"Now you tell me. And I thought you married me only for my good looks."

Michael was suddenly quiet, staring into the other room where the children were playing as he started on another fingernail. Vicki nudged Chet.

"What's wrong, Michael?" Chet asked.

He just continued to stare and chew.

"What are you worried about all of sudden?" Vicki continued the questioning. "You were so excited and overwrought with joy, and now you're acting like your world has been turned upside down."

"'Fess up, buddy," Chet prodded. "What's the deal?"

Michael looked up to the ceiling squinting his eyes. "Okay, you're going to think I'm really shallow. Consider the situation."

They nodded.

"She's twenty-nine and single. She's smart and she's got a great sense of humor. She's very likable and easy to talk to, at least on the Internet. And the few times that we chatted, it was wonderful. I could talk to her with such ease."

"And this is a problem?" Chet wondered.

"*Why* is she single, then?" he asked the couple.

"Because she's going to the mission field and nobody would follow her here. You can relate to that!" Vicki offered.

"I doubt that," Michael retorted.

"What are you saying?" Chet asked him. "That she's going to be some kind of monster?"

Suddenly Vicki gasped and looked at Michael wide-eyed. "You're afraid she's going to *look* like a monster!"

The kids glanced up and James asked, "Where's a monster?"

Chet began to laugh slightly.

"You think it's funny?" Michael asked in surprise.

"Yeah," he said still laughing. "Maybe she won't be too skinny either so the tribe will at least think she's a *healthy* pale woman!"

Chet and Vicki drove Michael to the airport the next morning while leaving James and Heather with a trusted Christian neighbor. Michael said nothing during the trip. He still felt guilty and shallow. Who was he to judge anyone by anything other than a good heart and a love for God? He had communicated with Angie for over a year and had come to live for her e-mails, and now he was concerned that she would look like a gorilla and be his wife for life? He felt horrible, but he couldn't even bring himself to pray over it. He should have thought through this more carefully, but he impulsively assumed that it was from the Lord, and now he was having serious doubts. Yes, this was the only possible solution to the problem, but what if God never intended for her to be there in the first place? What if he had jumped ahead and would now pay for it the rest of his life?

*****

Angie hugged her mother, Alex, Megan, and then finally Annie as she prepared to leave for Nashville with her father. She was now crying as the reality that she was leaving home for good had hit her. She would be back for brief visits over the years, but for the most part, she would seldom see any of them again.

Stephen entered the room with a guitar case and a narrow Gateway computer box.

"What's this?" she asked through her tears. "A gig bag?"

"A little going away gift," Stephen told her. He placed the case on the table and opened it. Inside was a brand new, beautiful, green, thin-line Ibanez guitar.

Angie's mouth dropped open, and tears began to stream even more. "For me?" she choked out.

"For you," Annie smiled through her own tears. "You've worked hard to learn guitar so you can minister to these people on another level than just medicine. You deserve something better than that old clunker you planned to tote over there."

"And this," Stephen said as he lifted up the Gateway box, "is a new laptop for the guy. You mentioned his kept having problems. Tell him to enjoy the top of the line."

*****

The attitude in the waiting area at the Nashville airport was somber and silent. There was much Angie wanted to say, but she could no longer speak without crying. As she sat alone with the man she loved and respected most in the world, she remained silent.

When the final boarding call was announced, she tried to be strong and controlled, but she couldn't any longer. Her body began to shake and nearly convulse as she hugged her father one last time. Somehow, the idea of leaving them all behind had never been as much a reality as the joy of going to Padawin, but now she was wondering if she had made the wrong decision.

As though he could read her mind, Jonathan gently told her, "God will take care of you now. He planned this before you were born, and now you're fulfilling your destiny. We're all sad, but the grief will pass as each of us moves on to where God is leading. Be strong, Angie, and always remember that there are many who love you dearly and believe in what you're doing. We'll be praying for you every day."

THIRTEEN

Michael left the auto rental place from the Honolulu International Airport in a plain, white, non-descript car. He followed the map to the hotel, then sat in the car a long time after parking. *What on earth am I doing? I must have been crazy when I thought all this up.*

It was a beautiful resort area, and all the rooms claimed to overlook the ocean. The mission board had been wonderful to him since the decision to marry. They were even giving them three days in Hawaii to adjust to each other before leaving for Padawin. He was now dreading it.

"I have two reservations," he told the lovely young lady at the front desk. "One for Michael Collins and the other for Angie Wright."

"Just one minute," she smiled.

She's beautiful. Golden complexion, lovely brown eyes, petite.

He looked around and marveled at the crowd in the lobby. This was the middle of summer and a huge tourist season for the islands. It was a wonder they managed two rooms so late. Many of the people there were couples. He noted how each seemed to match. Two stood gazing contentedly, both medium height and handsome. He watched another, both heavy set and a bit demanding as they talked with the bellhop in animated tones. Another couple, both wearing glasses and of quiet demeanor, held hands as they stepped onto the elevator.

I always thought there was someone for everybody. I never imagined I'd end up marrying in this particular situation. How disheartening.

"Excuse me, sir," the receptionist said getting his attention. "I can only find one reservation, and it's for a Mr. and Mrs. Michael Collins."

"What?" he exclaimed as he leaned over the tall desk. "There's supposed to be two rooms! One for a Dr. Angie Wright and the other for Michael Collins."

"I'm sorry, sir, but the reservations were made so late. Are you and Dr. Wright not married?"

"Not yet. We need two rooms!"

"When are you to be married?

He weakly managed to say, "Tonight."

"Then there should be no problem," she said cheerfully.

"Is there any way you can get a second room? It doesn't matter if it's ocean view or not."

"Surely you're kidding? There are no rooms available for at least three weeks, and by way of information, every room here has an ocean view."

"Nothing? Can you at least check for a cancellation?"

"Mr. Collins, trust me, there's nothing available. You'll be married tonight anyway. There's no need for another room," she said with a knowing wink.

He nodded in defeat and sighed as she handed him two entry cards. His hands shook as he clumsily stuck the card into the slot. Maybe at least there would be two beds. He wondered if the mission board had done this deliberately or if they couldn't help it because of the tourist season. The least they could have done was notify him that two rooms were not available. He felt as though the rug had slipped out from beneath him—no, more like yanked out in a harsh jerk.

*****

Angie enjoyed the plane ride once she got over the emotions of leaving her family. She had a window seat and was thrilled that the sky was clear so she could look at the land, and now ocean, beneath her. She spent much time in prayer, mainly for herself, to have the strength and courage to leave her life behind and move forward in the life to which she knew God had called her. She prayed for Michael—that he would be able to handle someone new in his life and that they would forge a wonderful working relationship. She prayed they would have a true friendship develop right away so their work would always be a pleasure and a compliment to those who watched them for a testimony to God's love and greatness.

When the plane landed, and all were allowed to gather their things, she felt her nerves suddenly stand on end for the first time. In a matter of minutes, she would be meeting Michael Collins in person—at last. Her heart began to pound.

Amazing what adrenaline can do to a person.

She grabbed her large carry-on bag and began to move slowly down the aisle behind the many people ahead of her. She hoped her luggage had made it through the transfer at the airport in Los Angeles. If not, she had enough clothes in her bag to make it the next couple of days, but not her wedding dress. Oh well, that hadn't been her idea anyway. She hoped Michael didn't feel she had been presumptive by bringing a special dress in which to be married.

I bet that scared him to death, she laughed.

Michael tried to appear casual as he leaned against a post in the waiting area. He now felt silly about the big sign he had made with Angie's name. While making it, he had thought a huge sign would be cute; now he thought it was ridiculous. When the passengers began to appear, he stood slightly straighter and found his nervousness increasing a hundred-fold. His heart was hammering and his mouth was dry. He should have known to get a soft drink before coming into the area.

He tried to create a mental picture of what Angie would look like. She would most likely be smiling because she had such a winsome personality, but her eyes would likely be puffy from crying over leaving the family she loved. He needed to remember to be tenderhearted toward her because this had to be emotionally horrible. He imagined she would be wearing glasses as years of medical school and miserable hours would have worn her eyes down. She was bound to be slightly on the pudgy side, maybe a little like Vicki … or even more than pudgy.

The first few passengers entered the area, and he gazed toward each lady that looked close to thirty. No one responded. There was no way she could miss him with the massive sign. He was now glad he had gone ahead and trimmed his beard, but he still insisted on wearing his khaki cargo shorts, a t-shirt, and his hiking boots. He was *not* out to make an impression; he was who he was.

As people left, he continued to search. One young lady walked out and stared directly at him. She had to be the most beautiful woman he had ever seen in his life. In fact, he actually thought his heart stopped for a moment. When she made eye contact with him, she put her hand up slightly, waved a small wave, and then smiled at him. He immediately turned his gaze back toward the crowd to see if Angie had come out yet. No matter how hard he tried, though, he found himself looking back toward the gorgeous woman who had smiled at him. She was tall, long legs sticking out from beneath a lovely green skirt covered with palm trees and coconuts.

Turn your head, Collins! If you look at those legs again, you're gonna head straight back up to those incredible eyes … and those lips. I really should've left the villages more often.

He couldn't help himself. His eyes drifted back up to the woman's face. She was still smiling and looking at him. She waved slightly again. He gave a quick nod and averted his eyes back to the other passengers. Of all the times in his life for a strange woman to flirt with him, why now?

As soon as she stepped into the waiting area, she saw Michael with a large sign bearing her name. Yes, Angie Wright was actually nervous. She found herself smiling at his baby face hidden behind a trimmed beard. His sandy brown hair had obviously been recently cut because what had been underneath was considerably darker than the top which had been bleached from constant exposure to the sun. He had seen her as she stepped out. She smiled and waved, but he immediately looked behind her. She walked farther out into the area, still struggling behind the crowd of people, and he glanced over again. When she caught his eye, she waved and smiled a second time, but he quickly looked back at the passengers still unloading. Suddenly it dawned on her that he didn't realize she was the one.

She knew it might be cruel, but she wanted a chance to observe him for a moment, so she walked over to a large window and began to size him up. He was probably six feet, if that tall, and was dressed extremely casual. She liked that. His body was strong and toned, evidence of hard work. He squinted as he kept searching behind her, but his baby face intrigued her. He didn't look thirty-five. His beard was nicely groomed, and she could tell he had just trimmed it too because it was a darker brown than the top of his hair. He was definitely bronzed, but not brown. He must have been very light skinned before moving to Padawin. He kept glancing over toward her, but would always look back quickly to the unloading area.

She could stand it no longer. She knew she had to introduce herself, and began to smile even bigger when it seemed to dawn on him that she was walking toward him. She saw him swallow nervously and realized he was almost a panicking wreck. She had never seen anyone so nervous.

Michael tried to ignore the woman as she walked toward the window, but he knew she was staring at him. He suddenly felt the urge to run from the airport as quickly as possible and never return. He tried to concentrate on finding Angie among the passengers that continued to pour from the plane, but all the time he was aware of the beautiful brunette with the long flowing hair and incredible legs.

Look for Angie. Look for Angie.

Suddenly he realized the woman was walking toward him. Who was she? Why would she come over to him? He was obviously waiting for someone as he stood there with the inane sign. She continued her approach. He glanced at her and found himself locked in her stare. He swallowed hard as she came nearer, and then she smiled at him again. Every fiber in his body melted and he felt his knees growing weak. Suddenly he forgot all about Angie Wright. Things were not going well at all today. In fact, this was flat out disastrous.

"Hi," the woman said as she put out her hand in greeting.

"Hello," Michael nearly choked out. "I'm waiting for someone," he added quickly as he shook her hand.

"I can tell," she said as her smile grew bigger. "Angie?"

He nodded in embarrassment.

"I take it you haven't found her."

"No," he said trying not to look at her.

"Have you met her before?"

He shook his head and looked uneasily back at the other passengers.

"Then how do you know you haven't found her?"

He glanced at her for just a moment then averted his eyes again. "I guess I don't know."

"Michael Collins?" she asked gently.

He looked at her again and his eyes opened widely for the first time?

He was speechless.

"Are you Michael Collins?" she asked again.

He said nothing, but slowly nodded his head as the sign slipped from his hands and dropped to the floor. Angie reached down and picked it up. She then turned it toward her so she could examine it closely.

"Were you afraid I'd miss you?" she laughed as she turned it back around so he could see it. "Big sign."

"Uh …" he still couldn't speak.

"I take it you're a little shy about all this too," she said as she handed the sign back.

He took it and then turned his eyes to the ground. Shaking his head he finally looked back at her. His was utterly confused. "You're not Angie, are you?" he managed to say.

"The one and only," she said as her southern accent sounded even more pronounced.

He knees now did buckle, and he fell back into the column by which he had been standing.

"Are you okay?" she asked in concern.

"I'm sorry," he said as he took a deep breath. "I guess all this mystery and anticipation has finally gotten to me. I'm just a little overwhelmed by it all."

"I know what you mean," she said as she took his wrist and felt his forehead. "You're pulse is mighty fast. Do you need to sit down?"

"No," he said quickly trying to pull himself together. "We need to fight for one of those carts that carries luggage. I'm guessing we could never drag it all out by ourselves."

"You're right. Lead the way."

As Angie followed him, she took note of how determinedly he moved through the airport. He must have scoped it out before coming to meet her. She felt sorry for him though as he seemed extremely nervous and unsettled. Being Angie, she had to try and put him at ease.

"I don't know how many time changes I've been through today, but I can promise you, it doesn't feel at all like it's five o'clock in the afternoon."

"How's your energy holding up?" he asked.

"Well, I think I'm running more on adrenaline than actual available energy."

"It's probably dark in Alabama by now."

"I figured."

They nabbed a cart and found all eight pieces of luggage, the last being her new guitar.

"You play guitar?" he asked with excitement.

"That's debatable." She laughed. "And this," she lifted up a Gateway box, "is a gift for you. It's from my sister, Annie, and her husband."

"What is it? Something to do with cows?"

She laughed again. "It's a laptop computer."

"What?"

"You said your other one was pitiful and to bring you a new one."

"I was kidding," he said obviously embarrassed. "I never meant for you to actually bring me one!"

"I never meant to either," she said as she placed the computer on top of the other luggage. "And that guitar? I've never even played it. My family gave these to me as gifts before I left this morning."

"Wow, generous people."

"*Loving* people," she corrected him. "Incredibly loving people." Her demeanor changed immediately as her lip began to quiver and tears formed in her eyes.

"I'm sure it's hard to leave them," he said uncomfortably.

"Very," she forced a smile, "but I'm so ready to get on with what God has for me. Get used to it, Bucko—you're my family now."

Michael almost swooned as she smiled while reaching for his hand. He could have sworn electricity passed through his body at her touch. She squeezed and he squeezed back as they stood there silently staring into each other's eyes. Hers were still filled with tears, and he felt his heart could break. She had talked through e-mail often about her family, and she loved them as much as life itself. She left them behind to come be with him, and he couldn't imagine at this moment that he could ever tell her how grateful he was for that.

"Thank you for coming here," was all he could manage.

"No, thank you for being willing to marry me to make all this happen."

He chuckled as he said, "My pleasure," because she had no idea how euphorically happy he was at that decision right now.

His mind was currently plagued by the thought that rather than him being disappointed, what if she was. His irksome pride had even begun to doubt that God was in the thing at all. She was beautiful, vivacious and kind. In truth he had actually thought her to be a model because of her height and beauty. And here he'd greeted her looking like he'd just walked out of a cornfield. Thank goodness Chet and Vicki had insisted he trim that stupid beard.

FOURTEEN

After loading the car with all her things, Michael tried to concentrate on getting back to the hotel. Even though he had made the trip twice today already, he had been in near bereavement over the whole situation. He'd left the map at the room, and now he was struggling to keep his attention on driving. Gazing tiredly out the window she never realized he kept peeking down at her long, tanned legs. He would then glance up to see her incredible eyes trying to take in all the scenery of the island.

This cannot be happening. I know I'm dreaming. I'm at the hotel and I'm asleep, and I'm imagining all of this. This can't be Angie Wright. There cannot be a woman more beautiful in this entire world. How did this happen?

Suddenly he remembered the hotel situation. One room.

"Angie?"

"Yes," she said with a weary smile as she turned to him. He thought he would melt again when their eyes met. He quickly looked back to the road.

"The mission board had reserved us two rooms, or so I thought. But apparently because of the busy season, all they could get was one."

"That's no problem." She shrugged it off.

"With only one bed," he added.

She laughed this time. He found himself smiling with her. Apparently, she didn't consider any of this to be a dilemma. It compounded his guilt. Here was this beautiful woman willing to marry a total stranger, and she didn't seem to give a second thought as to what he might look like or how inconvenient this marriage might actually be. She was committed to the whole thing without any reservation. Yes, he would spend a lot of time in prayer tonight. God was good, and God was gracious, and he was thankful that God would forgive his doubts and fears … again.

He fumbled with the card as he tried to open the door to the room while she stood exhausted by the cart that held her luggage. Finally, he managed to get it unlocked and immediately felt embarrassed. He had more or less thrown his stuff around the space and hadn't bothered to straighten up before he left. He had still had the attitude that this *woman* would just have to accept him as he was. Now he was praying she would.

"It's kind of a mess," he attempted to apologize. "I was in a bit of a hurry to get to the airport after I settled in."

She just smiled warmly and said, "It looks like home."

Moving to the large drapes she pulled them open to reveal sliding glass doors leading to a balcony overlooking the ocean. She gasped. "Heavens," she said breathlessly. "This is beautiful."

He felt guilty again. He hadn't cared about the view when he'd unpacked. All he had done was imagine himself coming into this room with Godzilla's sister. He walked to the sliding doors and stood next to her.

"This is nothing," he said trying to pull out of his guilt yet again. "The view from our deck in Padawin is even better than this."

She turned to look at him. His eyes were shy, and she found that endearing. She was anything but shy, and she hoped that her boisterousness would never overwhelm him. His face was gentle and kind, and she could tell simply by looking at him that he wore a beard for one reason: to hide. She hoped that one day he would trust her enough to open up his life to her.

"Seriously?" she asked. "It's more beautiful than this?"

He nodded as he slid open the door. "Up there," he motioned toward his left, "sits the majestic Podakind, the tallest volcanic peak in all of the Padawin islands. Down here," he motioned below him, "is the Grentawoo River. And over there," he pointed to his right, "is the South Pacific. It's too awesome to describe."

Angie leaned against the rail and closed her eyes to the setting sun as her entire face smiled at his description. "You don't have to convince me; I can see it in your soul. I know I'll grow to love it just as you do."

"How can you not? It's more beautiful than words can describe. And a beautiful lady on a beautiful island are only deserving of each other."

She turned to look at him and could make out the blush this time.

"I'm sorry," he said quickly turning his head away.

"Don't be," she told him. "It's good you think I'm attractive. If you didn't, this whole thing could turn out to be quite a disaster."

He wouldn't look at her, but she reached up and turned his face toward hers. His shy eyes still tried to avoid looking, but she persisted until they did.

"Michael," she said gently, "you can always be honest with me. I'm a very ... open person. Our family is more or less like that. I'll always tell you how I feel; please feel free to do the same."

He simply stared into her eyes and gave a hesitant nod.

"When do we get married?" she asked lightly as she changed the subject in an attempt to rescue him.

"Tonight. Around seven o'clock," he said taking a deep breath. "I contacted the minister as soon as I got here."

"Thank goodness. At least we'll be married since we have to sleep together already!"

"Yeah," he said uncomfortably again.

"Where will it take place?"

71

"Wherever."

"Can we get married on the beach?" she asked excitedly.

"If you want. He's supposed to call us from the lobby when he gets here."

She clapped her hands in delight and said, "Wouldn't that be awesome to actually get married on the beach?"

"I suppose so. I never really thought about it."

"Is that okay with you?"

"Sure. I'll get married wherever you want."

*****

At six fifty the room phone rang.

"Hello?" Michael answered.

"Michael Collins?"

"Yes."

"Great! This is Pastor Akamu Maas. I'm down in the lobby with my wife and a deacon. Are you two ready to do this?"

"Yes, sir. Thank you for coming. We'll be right down."

He hung up the phone and went to knock on the bathroom door.

"The pastor's here," he said trying not to sound as excited as he was.

"Great!" Angie yelled back, clearly untroubled at showing her excitement. "I'll be right out."

He went to the mirror and straightened the tie as he glanced at the shoddy suit he had brought. He'd worn the suit through graduate school and seminary and never bothered to buy another one when he went to Padawin. He kept it for attending church when he stayed with Chet and Vicki, but other than that, it remained aging in his closet. He now wished he'd taken Vicki's advice and bought a whole new suit for the wedding. Angie had bought a dress; he could have at least gotten a new tie or something.

When she stepped out of the bathroom, he nearly lost his breath again. She had pulled her hair up with small wisps curled around her face. She looked like an angel. He knew his expression had to give away the adoration he felt at the moment. She smiled as she twirled for him, then looked to him for a reaction.

"You are truly beautiful," he managed to get out.

"That's what I was going for," she said perkily as she reached in to turn off the bathroom light. "Shall we go?"

After greeting the pastor, his wife and the deacon who would serve as witnesses, they walked down to the beach. Since everyone was dressed up, it was slightly uncomfortable, with the exception of Angie; she was basking in the moment.

"Would you please join hands," Pastor Akamu asked them.

Angie looked to Michael and smiled as she reached for his hand. It was cold and clammy. She leaned into him and whispered, "Nervous?"

"A little," he whispered back. "I hope I prove to be deserving of you."

"And I'm just hoping you can put up with me *'til death us do part*."

"I'll do my best." He smiled.

The pastor performed the ceremony, and they repeated their vows as sincerely as they could under the circumstances. Angie loved his shy eyes, and found herself smiling every time they faced each other to speak. He kept looking to the left or right, up or down to avoid her gaze, but when he would look at her, she would wink and whisper that all was okay.

"And now, I suppose, if you want to, you may kiss your bride," the pastor said uncertainly.

"Oh," was all Michael could say.

"Why not?" Angie giggled. "At least let's make it official. You don't have to kiss me for the rest of our lives if you don't want."

Michael blushed again and Angie tried to hold back a laugh. She leaned into him, face to face as they were equal in height, and gently kissed him.

"Well, this was rather different," the pastor laughed.

"Indeed," agreed his wife.

"I wish you both the best," he said as he shook Michael's hand.

"Thank you," Michael said weakly.

The pastor leaned in and whispered, "She's absolutely beautiful."

"I know."

*****

After finishing dinner in the hotel restaurant and changing clothes, Angie plopped down onto the bed. "So we have three full days here?"

"Yeah. We have the car, the room, and even some extra cash."

"All right!" Angie exclaimed. "We can live it up!"

Michael nodded again as he stood near the television. This was an odd and uncomfortable situation.

"Now, I'm totally exhausted. I'm sure it's way past my bedtime. Which side do you want?" she asked.

"Pardon?"

"Which side of the bed do you want?"

"I was going to sleep on the floor."

"You're kidding, right?" she smiled. "There's no way I'm gonna let you do that. It's a big bed and we *are* married. Pick your side. It doesn't matter to me."

Michael swallowed hard again and shrugged. She was really going to let him sleep with her?

"You're sitting on that side," he acknowledged. "We'll just call it fate and let you stay there."

"Sounds good to me," she said as she stretched and yawned. "Good night, then."

She turned back the covers and climbed into bed wearing socks, an Atlanta Braves jersey, and a pair of old boxer shorts. She smiled at him as she settled into her own pillow from home.

"You can watch TV as long as you like," she told him. "It won't faze me a bit. I'll be out like a light before you finish brushing your teeth."

"Okay," he said uncertain again, and probably blushing.

"Good night," she said as she closed her eyes. "Don't let the bed bugs bite."

"You too."

*****

Michael stayed in the bathroom much longer than he had intended. He spent most of the time on his knees. He hoped Angie didn't wake up and walk in on him and think he was sick. He prayed for forgiveness in not trusting God with his life and his future. He found it amazing that he could willingly give so many areas to the Lord with no reservation, yet fear to trust Him in others. Just this morning he'd convinced himself that he'd made the biggest mistake in his life, yet now he knelt in awe at the woman who was sleeping in the bed just on the other side of this door.

When he finally emerged, he was embarrassed that the television had been left on. He stole another glance at her and felt his heart would burst. He wouldn't expect anything more from her than what they had agreed on: a marriage of propriety so she could come and work in Padawin. However, she would be a wonderful face and spirit to wake up to for the rest of his life. His prayer now became for her not to detest him in the way he had detested her that morning. He couldn't wait to see the grins on Chet and Vicki's faces when they picked them up from the airport in Taveren.

FIFTEEN

When the sun began to shine through the glass, Michael rolled over to see if she had wakened. She was obviously a sound sleeper, but he doubted he slept a full thirty minutes last night. Carefully leaning up on one elbow, he studied her perfect face—her beautiful eyes, her pointed little nose, and those thick, warm lips which had touched his briefly the day before. They were one of the reasons he couldn't sleep as he replayed the kiss over and over again throughout the night. He had admired her lips the moment he saw her, even before he knew she was Angie. And when she had kissed him so willingly, she had stirred feelings in him he no longer thought existed. In fact, when he saw her that first moment at the airport, those feelings had awakened.

Slowly she began to stir, and then her eyes opened. He was embarrassed that he'd been caught staring.

"Good morning," she said sleepily. "What time is it?"

"Eight thirty-four."

"Hey, that's not too bad." She rolled to her back and stretched out her arms. "What do we do for breakfast here?"

He loved her southern accent. It was one more adorable thing about her. Surely there was something that was disagreeable. He watched as she climbed from the bed and shook out her long hair. No. Nothing disagreeable at all. Then he thought of himself. He was sure his hair was sticking up in several places, and his eyes were probably heavy from lack of sleep. Angie, however, looked like she had just stepped off a magazine cover. He couldn't help but stare again as she went to the bathroom and closed the door behind her. He just sat on the bed and shook his head in disbelief.

*****

They had their breakfast and then she insisted they see as much of the island as possible. They stopped by a supermarket to buy some things for a picnic and then began their journey. Michael was thankful for her constant chattering and how she read every piece of information on the tour map for every site they passed or visited. She laughed, she was awed, and she was excited over even the smallest details they discovered. She couldn't believe she was in Hawaii. He couldn't believe he was in Hawaii and married to her.

They finally stopped at a lushly wooded area to picnic. She pulled the lids from the deviled ham cans and then opened a pack of Saltines. He carried the small Styrofoam cooler to a rock next to where she was sitting and offered her a Coke. She smiled gracefully and told him thank-you as she reached up to take it.

"Okay, Michael," she said as she patted the ground next to her, "park it right here."

He complied easily and joined her on the ground. After a brief prayer, they began to eat.

"Did you picnic much growing up?" she asked him.

He shook his head. "No. Not really."

"We did often. In the summers when school was out, Moms would always pack up a picnic lunch once a week at least. Sometimes, if it just rained and rained, she'd spread the blanket on the great room floor and we'd eat it there."

"You seem to have a wonderful family."

"The best! It was a great way to grow up. I felt like I could do anything. Becoming a doctor was nothing. I was brought up to believe I could conquer the world if I wanted to."

He smiled shyly, wishing he had her candor and courage to say what was on his mind.

"What about your family?" she asked. "You've never mentioned them."

"I was an only child," he half shrugged. "My parents were killed when I was 16."

Angie didn't say anything, but merely looked at him again with that same expression of concern as when he had nearly passed out at the airport. He felt he could tell her almost everything when she looked at him like that.

"I'm so sorry," she said sincerely. "It's wonderful to see how God formed you into such an amazing person having experienced that kind of pain."

He waited for her questions concerning how they died, but she never asked. Could she be that perceptive, or was she just being kind? Usually when he told that fact, people immediately followed with how's and why's, to which he had never in his entire life told anyone, not even Jenna. The very thought of her made him nauseous.

"Are you okay?" she asked him gently.

"Yeah, I'm sorry. It seems that I'm all out of sorts since meeting you. You must think I'm a total jerk."

She laughed again. "Not at all. I think you're adorable!"

"Really?" he asked as he squinted and cocked his head to the side.

"Absolutely!"

*****

After an afternoon of seemingly endless sightseeing, they headed back to the hotel to clean up for supper. While Angie showered, Michael opened the laptop box and took it out on the balcony to study. He was so engrossed in figuring it out that he never noticed when she had left the shower.

She enjoyed the moment to watch him from afar. She liked him. He had finally relaxed enough to reveal more of his personality. He was reserved and not the kind of person who was ready to spill his life's story to just anyone, but she had enjoyed his humor as the day passed. She could still only find one word to describe him: adorable. His baby face, his scraggly hair, his thin beard, and his squinty gray eyes made him appear almost adolescent. She smiled watching him become animated over various discoveries on the computer.

"Enjoying your new toy?" she asked joining him on the balcony.

He jumped from surprise. "It's beyond anything I've ever seen before."

"I think yours is actually better than mine." She pulled over a chair and sat next to him.

"Well, I *am* the man, you know," he said with mock seriousness. "Everything I have should be better than yours. At least, in Padawin."

She gently slapped his arm and laughed. "Whatever you say, boss."

"Now wait, in Padawin, I'm not your boss. I'm more like your *lord*."

She loved his expression at that moment. His eyebrows were raised and his lips were pursed as he teased her about Padawin tradition. She couldn't help but smile. She knew at that moment she was going to enjoy life with Michael Collins.

"Well, my lord, Michael, you'd better wash off the grime and sweat so we can leave for one of those cute tiki beach eateries."

"Ahh, I like the sound of that. *Lord Michael.* I can see you're going to be very easy to get along with."

*****

Michael drove to a place suggested by the man at the front desk. When he pulled up to the entrance, a valet took the car and Michael escorted Angie inside.

"This place is magnificent," she said looking around at the decor. "I think I could get used to island living."

"That's good to hear. However, Padawin isn't a whole lot like this."

"No, I'm guessing it's a whole lot better." There was that gentle smile and those warm eyes of hers again.

The hostess asked if they would prefer to dine inside or on the beach.

"On the beach," Angie replied promptly.

He was relieved that she was decisive. There was nothing worse for him than being forced to make a decision when he honestly had no preference.

They followed the hostess out back to a wooden deck built onto the beach. Torches were lit, and a native band was playing a mixture of island

and pop music. They took their seats and began to look at the menu.

"It's expensive," she said sternly, used to scraping by on very little money for so many years.

"No, it's not. We have nothing else to spend our money on. Get anything you want. I'm paying, you know?"

She looked up at him and smiled that smile again, the one that absolutely hit his heart every time. "Because you're the lord?" she asked.

"No," he said sincerely. "Because I want you to have anything you want while you're in Hawaii. You deserve it."

"Why is that?"

"As hard as you've worked to get where you're going, you deserve these three days of Paradise."

She reached over and touched the top of his hand as she said, "Thank you. If you're not careful, you may lead me to believe that there's a real sweetheart lying beneath that baby face and beard."

After their meal they lingered at the table and basked in the continued process of getting to know each other. It was easy being with her. Appearing to sense that he wasn't assertive, she never forced anything from him. When she did ask questions they were never probing or uncomfortable. All was going well until suddenly her expression changed.

"What is it?" he asked.

"That song!" she exclaimed as the band began a new tune. "That's *Autumn Sunset!*"

"You like Stephen Williams?"

"Like him?" she laughed. "He's my brother-in-law!"

"Stephen Williams?"

"That's who bought your computer."

"Wait a minute," he said as he began to rewind all the information he knew concerning her sisters. "Then I've seen pictures of Annie all over the internet. Your sister, Annie, is Annie Wright, the girl who toured with him last fall?"

"Yeah!"

"Good heavens," he said nearly out of wind.

"Come on!" She jumped up and grabbed his hand. "We've got to dance to this song."

"I don't dance. I'm a missionary!"

"So am I, but nobody knows that here," she laughed. "Besides, dancing *is* in the Bible!"

"Not this kind of dancing."

"Yeah," she said as she wrapped her arms around his neck, "that never worked with my daddy either."

"I'm serious. I've never danced in my life."

"Then I'm gonna make a heathen out of you tonight!"

She moved his arms until they were around her waist and they began to sway with the music.

"You ought to hear my sister sing this," she said as she leaned into his ear.

"I've read that she has an awesome voice and can play piano beyond compare."

"You read right."

"Do you play guitar as well as she plays piano?"

Angie's only reply was another hearty laugh.

*****

Their last morning in Hawaii, Angie ordered up coffee, sweet bread, butter and jelly for breakfast rather than dressing to go downstairs. As they sat on the bed and ate, Michael still found himself completely taken by her beauty. But now, after spending three days with her, he discovered her attractiveness was an outer reflection of a deeper inner beauty. She was the most alive and vivacious individual he had ever met in his life. As he thought of Jenna again, he said a small prayer of thanks for the first time since she had broken up with him. He had always regretted losing her, but she refused to go to the mission field.

"There you go again," she said as she finished another slice of bread.

"What do you mean?"

"You get this look occasionally like you're somewhere else. I don't know whether to interrupt you or just let you stay there."

He raised his eyebrows in question.

"So, tell me Lord Michael, do I leave you there or do I try to bring you back? Sometimes reflection is good and necessary, but sometimes it's depressing and unfruitful. I'm not sure which yours is."

"Ah," he nodded. "It was a bit unfruitful."

"Do I bring that out in you? Bad memories?"

"No, oh no! It's just that being with you sort of makes me thankful that my life didn't take some turns in the past ... turns it could've taken that wouldn't have led me here."

He appreciated that she wasn't prying. "I was engaged in college. We started dating the end of our freshmen year. Her name was Jenna. I always told her I was going to the mission field. She said she couldn't imagine herself there, that she wasn't meant for third world living."

"She must have been beautiful."

"She was." *But nothing like you.* "She was cut out to be the perfect pastor's wife. She could play piano and had a pretty voice, very poised and articulate. I felt she would change her mind and go with me eventually. Yet all along, she was banking that I'd change and stay with her."

"Heading in different directions, huh?"

"Dreaming in different directions. I proposed during Christmas of our senior year. I'd saved up enough money to buy her a small ring, and she was thrilled when I asked. We made plans to marry in the summer. When I explained that I was going on to graduate school, she assumed I meant seminary, and she had all these plans to teach school and help put me through. We weren't even on the same page. When she realized I wanted to continue studying Agriculture, she was shocked. She wanted to know why. I said because I was going to be an agricultural missionary. She said she couldn't do it; she wasn't cut out for that kind of life."

"She wasn't called then," Angie inserted softly.

"Not at all. She told me if I didn't give up the idea, she wouldn't marry me."

Angie reached over and took his hand again. He was growing really fond of that simple gesture.

"I'm sorry," she said sincerely. "That had to be hard after losing your parents too. I don't understand how anyone could do that to you."

"Well, let's say it was my first and last experience with women. She was it, the only girl I was ever with."

"Until now," Angie smiled at him.

He blushed again and nodded. "Until now. I was just thinking that I was glad things didn't work with her."

"You should be. She wasn't the right woman for you."

"I know that now. In three days I've come to know more about you than I ever knew of her. She was just this beautiful stranger that wanted to be a part of my life. I didn't know any better."

"In three more days, you may know more about me than you ever cared to know," Angie said giggling again. "I tend to talk a lot ... senselessly sometimes."

"Never. Nothing you've said to me has ever been senseless. If it's in your heart, you just say it. That's not senseless, that's being honest."

"And *you* are being very kind."

SIXTEEN

"Have you got everything?" Michael asked as they tried to cram all her luggage onto the cart.

"I doubt it," she confessed frantically searching the room.

If it were possible, he believed Angie might be even messier than he. "What are you missing?"

"I don't know, maybe nothing. I always leave something somewhere when I go off like this. I'm just trying to make a final sweep."

He nodded nervously as he glanced at his watch. They had overslept from staying up too late on the last night of their Hawaii vacation / honeymoon. They hadn't wanted it to end. They agreed the mission board must have known what they were doing to put them up here for three days.

"If it's here, you'd better leave it," Michael said as he was getting impatient.

She looked up at him and smiled again. All concerns melted away. She could look all she wanted. If they missed their plane, another would be heading that way eventually.

"You're right," she said instead. "I'm giving up and following you out the door, never to return here again. Lead the way, Lord Michael."

He smiled as he pushed the cart out the door. Would life always be this fun?

*****

"You probably ought to wake up," said a gentle voice as Angie tried to rouse back to consciousness. When she managed to open her eyes, she smiled at the sight of the baby face leaning slightly over her.

"Padawin will be in sight in a moment," he told her.

"Wow, I must've slept nearly the whole trip."

"You did. You even missed the peanuts." He held up a small bag. "I saved yours for you."

"That was very thoughtful," she said as she gazed out the window. "Will we be able to see it from this side of the plane?"

"Oh yeah. It's rather large when you finally approach it. Look! There it is!"

She gasped. "I can't believe this." Her eyes were bright and her face full of excitement. "I'm actually about to step foot onto Padawin!"

"Yes, ma'am, you are. And I have the feeling that neither of you will ever be the same."

As they left the plane, Michael described Chet and Vicki. "He's really tall and bald with a great big trimmed mustache. She's rather short, a little on the pudgy side, with sort of reddish looking hair."

"Reddish looking? Is it red or not red?"

"It's *reddish*," he repeated with a grin.

Michael spotted them right away and began to wave, Angie following close behind. When they finally met, Angie stepped up and greeted them as though they were old friends. Chet and Vicki replied in like manner with full smiles and *I told you so* looks toward Michael.

"This is Dr. Angie Wright," he said proudly.

"No," she corrected him. "Dr. Angie *Collins*, new wife of Lord and Master Michael Collins."

"My, he's trained you well," Chet said as he shook her hand.

"He's taught me all about the Padawin culture."

"Don't let him fool you," Vicki stepped in quickly. "We may live here, but that does *not* make us Padawin."

"Now, now, Vicki," Michael cut in, "let's not confuse the nice doctor. I think she's doing just fine with her cultural education."

Angie enjoyed watching Michael give and take with the Clarences. This was the first time she'd seen him in a familiar environment. He was pleasant and talked easily. She hoped that one day he would be that free with her. She was honored that he had shared his story about Jenna, and hoped that as the years went by, he would eventually find the strength to talk about his parents.

*****

"The kids can sleep in the living room on the pull out couch," Vicki told them. "Angie, you can have Heather's room, and Michael, you can sleep in James'."

Neither Angie nor Michael moved, and both had uneasy looks on their faces.

"Or vice versa," Vicki said trying to read their expressions. "I promise I changed the sheets."

Angie realized quickly that Michael wouldn't say anything, so she stepped up.

"How about the kids keep their rooms," she suggested, "and Michael and I take the pullout couch?"

Chet and Vicki nodded, although somewhat stunned.

"They only gave us one room and one bed in Hawaii," Angie explained. "We've slept together every night. I think we're used to it already."

"Oh," was all Vicki said.

"That's fine. She changed the sheets on the sofa bed too," Chet said with a grin.

"It wouldn't matter if I had to sleep on dirt," Angie told them. "I've

82

been so tired today that I could probably just drop if someone pointed me to a bed."

"Dinner first," Vicki told her. "I've got something in the crock pot. I wasn't sure how quickly we'd get back from the airport."

"Can I give you a hand?" Angie offered.

"Legitimately, no. But if you want to offer some female company in the kitchen, I would gladly accept that."

"Done. Lead the way."

"We'll go get the kids down the street," Chet yelled to the ladies.

Once outside, Chet took a deep breath and then stopped Michael in his tracks.

"What a woman!" he exclaimed. "Man! Michael! This is practically comical! And you had no idea that she was drop-dead gorgeous?"

"None whatsoever, but that's not the half of it. She's the most spirited person I've ever come across. She's half dead right now from jet lag, but when she's awake, she makes you glad you're alive."

"And you're sleeping together?" Chet asked him with wide eyes.

"Yeah, but not ... you know," Michael tried to explain.

"Too bad."

"Well, we just only met ..."

"What happened to the marriage of convenience?"

"It's still that, I suppose. But after being around her for four days now, I'm almost willing to propose for real."

"That's a thought. Consider it, my boy. I mean, hey, if that's what you're waking up to every day for the rest of your life—wow!"

"I take it things are going well between you and Michael," Vicki said as she put a pot of rice on the stove.

"I don't think they could be any better. You'd think we belonged together."

"I believe you do belong together," Vicki said frankly. "From the day you first e-mailed him about coming to Padawin to work, I think a bond began. It's not the normal way most people meet and marry, but it sure looks like a positive thing to me."

Angie laughed. She liked Vicki very much; she spoke her mind. "I would say it's very positive."

"And so ... uh ... you just adjusted to sleeping together right away?"

"We didn't have a choice! But it turned out to be okay. In fact, it's been comforting to me to have him right there. It's hard to leave family behind like this."

"Tell me about it," Vicki agreed. "At least Chet and I had each other when we came here. It was so difficult watching Michael leave Taveren all by himself. It still is. Every time he visits our hearts ache for him. He's a good man, a kind and gentle man, but perhaps a little too shy for his own good."

"I noticed that, but as time rolls by, he seems more comfortable."

"Perhaps you'll be the one person that he can really open up to. He has a lot of wounds from his past but never talks about them … just keeps them bottled up."

"What kind of wounds?"

"I have no idea. Neither does Chet, and we're probably closer to him than anyone in the world."

Angie nodded in understanding. He'd lived alone for over nine years giving his life to minister to a strange people. Perhaps God had brought them together for more than just her calling. Perhaps the reason her call had been so strong was that she needed to minister to Michael Collins. Could she be the one to help chase the demons of his past away … whatever those demons were?

*****

"Michael," she whispered later that night as they lay in bed together. "Are you asleep?"

"No. Are you okay?"

"Not really," she said as she moved closer.

"What's wrong?"

"I don't know exactly. I'm a little homesick, I guess."

"I can understand," he said softly.

"The Clarences are great people. I'm going to enjoy getting to know them."

"They're easy to know."

There was silence as she tried to find a way to reach out to him. She needed more than conversation, but she didn't know what. Had he been any other man, she probably could have spoken frankly, but Michael was introverted and cautious. She could never let herself push him, even if it meant denying her own needs at times. She bit her lip as she felt tears begin to sting her eyes. She didn't want to cry right now and wanted to be strong during this transition, but her emotions were frazzled. She began to gently shake and sob.

"Angie," he said tenderly. "What's wrong? Please tell me."

"I'm sorry," she choked between sobs. "This is all so new to me. This is home to you, but it isn't to me yet. I know it will be in time, but right now it's just hard to feel this alone and be so far away from those I love."

"Please know that you're not alone."

For the first time since they had met, Michael reached out to her. He gently ran his finger down the side of her face and then touched her hand, holding it carefully in his own.

"Thank you," she said as she felt slightly comforted.

"What can I do to help?"

He had asked. He wouldn't have asked if he didn't mean it.

"Just hold me until I fall asleep?"

He moved closer to her and put his arm beneath her head.

"Thank you," she said softly as she felt the tension and fear begin to leave.

"Don't ever be afraid to ask me for anything, Angie. Never. Okay?"

"Okay."

SEVENTEEN

"Angie," Michael sang softly in her ear the following morning.

Before she even opened her eyes she smiled. Slowly she rolled over and forced herself to awaken. "Good morning. I feel like I only slept five minutes last night."

"You slept a full eight hours."

"Eight hours? You've gotta be kidding."

"Yep, and everyone's starting to stir around here. Chet's in the shower and Vicki's cooking breakfast. I didn't know if you wanted to get up before everyone came in, or, well, knowing you, it wouldn't bother you one bit to just lie around and sleep all day regardless of who did what."

She laughed. "You're exactly right."

"Anyway," he said as he pushed himself up, "we have a really big day today. Mega shopping trip this morning, and as soon as we finish we head to Podakind."

"Shopping?"

"The copter won't make a drop for another month. We need to make sure we have enough toothpaste, soaps, shampoo, sugar, flour, yadda-yadda-yadda to last us."

"That's sounds too hard today," she groaned. Her whole body was exhausted. "Maybe I can sleep in the car on the way home."

"Good luck," he laughed.

"Why would you say that?"

"You ever ridden a roller coaster?"

Vicki's breakfast was marvelous: eggs, bacon, sausage, and homemade biscuits. Michael encouraged Angie to eat well because it would be the best meal of the day. She tried, but her appetite was still several hours behind or ahead, she wasn't sure which.

"So Angie how is your Padawin? Perhaps we should practice some before you actually hit the tribes," Chet suggested as he started a conversation with her in the native tongue.

Angie smiled and replied, *"That idea would be good. I have never spoken much for anyone in this language. Much work I know I need. I hope it takes not too many bunnies for me to be good at talking."*

Everyone stared at her in confusion.

"Bunnies?" Chet asked her.

"What?" she was more confused than they. "What about bunnies?"

"I think she meant *days*," Michael guessed. "They sound close in Padawin. Is that what you meant? You hope it won't take many days for you to become fluent?"

She giggled and nodded. "This may be more adventure than you bargained for!"

"You're probably right!" Chet told her. "You do realize that many of your medical terms and such will have no word for them in Padawin. We've had the same situation with Christianity."

"I thought this may be so," Angie continued to talk, thrilled to put all her language lessons to use. *"I maybe just make up new words! I like to be creative when spirits attack me."*

"Attack?" Chet asked her again.

Michael admired her ability to keep on going without any concern that she was botching up the language. He smiled as they continued to talk, and she pressed forward as though this was the best thing she could do to learn. He would need to explain to the tribes that she hadn't spoken the language much and they would have to be patient with her in their communication. Actually, she was much better than he, Chet or Vicki had been when they first arrived. Very little was known about the language, and they were the ones who had created the study for Angie to use. The thing he looked forward to the most was hearing her try to translate her southern colloquialisms into Padawin.

"What are you laughing at?" Angie asked him as Chet left to answer the phone.

"Life is going to be fun with you around, Dr. Angie. I just hope the spirits and the bunnies don't attack us too often."

*****

As they loaded up the Land Rover, Angie was amazed at how much they could cram into it. Michael packed it full on the inside around all of her belongings and then began to tie things on top.

"I've never bought so much in my life," she exclaimed as she handed him another bungee.

"You'll be thankful for it as the month draws near its end. I doubled everything this time because you're here. I don't know if it'll be enough or too much. We'll just have to see. If it looks like we're running out, we'll have an early helicopter drop."

"So, you're just a *play it by ear* kind of guy?"

"You're in Padawin now. *Playing it by ear* is a way of life here."

He climbed down and pulled on the cord to make sure all was secure. When he was satisfied with the outside, he double-checked the inside.

"I now see why you only brought one little bag with you. No where to put anything."

"Yup."

*****

Michael had been right about the ride being a roller coaster, however Angie didn't complain. The countryside was breathtaking as they drove through forests and over mountains, into rivers and down steep hills. There were several volcanic peaks that she found awe-inspiring, and she tried to remind herself they were all dormant and that a team of volcanologists constantly monitored the Ring of Fire. Still, she couldn't help gazing at the top of each cone to see if smoke was rising.

Michael had also been right about not getting any sleep on the trip. Even if the road had been smooth and easy, she wouldn't have shut her eyes for anything. She wanted to soak in every ounce of the scenery. The terrain was varied; rain forests in some places and near deserts in others.

He parked near a river and announced it was lunchtime. Climbing out of the vehicle she found her legs wobbly from the ride.

"This place is beautiful," she said as she stared at the top of one of the peaks. "When's the last time one of these mountains blew?"

"There's one active right now about two hundred miles from here. It's making a brand new chunk of land as we speak."

She gulped and gave him a wide-eyed look.

"As for the populated islands," he continued, "nothing's blown here for close to three hundred years."

"Is that *good* as in we don't have to worry for a while, or is that *bad* as in we're due for another one sometime soon."

He laughed.

"That wasn't meant to be funny," she said soberly.

"I know," he laughed even harder. "I guess that's what makes it so humorous."

"What are we eating, by the way?"

"It's sort of like a fish jerky. I love it."

"Me too. Do we have a lot of this?"

"Oh yeah. We make a ton of it."

"Goody!" she said as she licked her lips. "Is it hard to make?"

"Everything's a little bit harder with tribal living. But it's a good hard. I think you'll enjoy it very much."

"You know what?" she grinned. "I think I will too."

After lunch, they drove on for several more hours. One thing Angie would remember: always get a good night's sleep before making this trip. Her body was stuck somewhere between jet lag and pure exhaustion, but she couldn't have slept for anything. She hoped there would never be a need to transport someone horribly ill to Taveren by means of the Land Rover. They would probably die from being beaten up.

"There's nothing we can do about the roads," he explained.

"I assumed. I wish I weren't so tired. I could probably have seen this whole trip as more of an adventure."

"The first time it's adventurous. After that it's more like a chore."

"Bite your tongue, Michael Collins!" she chastised him. "It's only a chore if we make it that! I promise you, as long as I'm along on a trip, it'll *never* be a chore again."

"And I'll hold you to that."

"You know what we should do next time? Camp!"

"Camp?"

"Yeah! We could break the trip up and stop somewhere to camp for the night."

"Turn a six hour trip into a two day affair?"

"I said nothing about affairs," she teased as she leaned her head over toward him for just a moment. He blushed again. "We wouldn't have to do it every time, but just on occasion to make it exciting."

"Did your family camp too?"

"Oh yeah," she said with a big smile.

She went on to discuss the phases of the family's camping evolution. They went from tent to pop-up, to small travel trailer. They had camped all over the US and seen most of the major geological and historical sites in the nation.

"You need to get ready for this," he told her with a huge smile. "Mt. Podakind is just over that hill."

"Really?" She sat higher in her seat.

"In just a minute, we'll cross this ridge and you should be able to see the mountain; I believe the clouds have finally broken."

Angie leaned against the front dash and waited expectantly as the Rover climbed what was to be the last steep hill before reaching their home. As they neared the top, Podakind blazed into view and Angie gasped in awe. "It has snow," she said breathlessly.

"The only place in Padawin."

"How high is it?"

"Just under 15,000 feet."

"I had no idea! Why didn't we see it earlier? Good lands! How do you miss *that*? You've got to be able to see it for hundreds of miles!"

"Hills, forestation, and the ever present thunderheads that make it play hide and seek. You can actually see it from Taveren, but it has to be a clear day." He pointed up toward the sky at the thick cloud cover. "We're very lucky to be seeing it right now. Notice all the clouds hanging around? God must be smiling on you."

"I'll have to remember to thank Him for that tonight," Angie whispered, still in awe of the mountain.

After several more miles, they drove past a huge garden, numerous acres wide and long.

"Is that your handiwork?" she asked him, taken back by the sheer size of it.

"Mine and the men of the village. This supplies an abundance of food as well as seeds for the next season."

"Seasons? How many seasons does Padawin actually have? This is winter and it's as warm as toast."

"Two seasons: summer and wetter," he smiled as he turned the final corner.

"A water tank," she said in delight as she spied one sticking up about a mile away. "You told me you had water, but I didn't expect that."

"It's filtered and clean too, probably my best contribution to the community."

"You're not kidding! Do you know how many health problems that alone solves?"

"Actually, yes," he said as he turned another corner, revealing a fenced in pasture of cattle. "In training they told me it didn't matter how well I fed them if the water and sewage were bad. They said I could come over here and plant vegetables and raise livestock until I was blue in the face, but the people wouldn't thrive without safe water and sanitary living conditions."

"You're right," she said as she reached over and touched his arm again. "Do you realize how much of the mortality rate you just threw out the window? You also made my job easier."

"Now if you can just override the witch doctors. Creating a sewage system was really hard. The other villages still have no sewage, but they all have water."

"Good for you. Oh my!" Angie exclaimed as they turned on a road next to a beautiful rushing river. "Is that the Grentawoo?"

"Yes … runs right behind our house. In fact, our deck stretches over it for about three feet."

"No way! It's gorgeous and so clear. I didn't expect that."

"It's one of our sources for water."

"And look!" she exclaimed again. "I can see the ocean out there! This place is almost surreal! Hawaii was nothing compared to this!"

"It's unspoiled. Nothing commercial."

"But water, electricity, sewage?" she leaned over to him and gave him a gentle hug. "You're amazing. Do these people know what you've done for them?"

Again he blushed.

She shaded her eyes trying to see what was ahead. At last she made out the beginning of several huts. "Is that it? Is that the village of Podakind?"

"That's it."

EIGHTEEN

As they approached, people began to line the edge of the path. Angie was immediately struck by the colors of their tribal clothing. Woven grass skirts had bits of reds, greens, yellows and purples mixed in, and their tops appeared to be rough-spun fabric dyed every color imaginable. They started waving as the Rover came closer. Michael rolled down his window and stuck out his arm to greet the villagers. They were very dark, much darker than she had anticipated. She now knew why they believed white people to be pale and sickly. She would make sure she appeared strong and capable from the get go.

As Michael veered to the left, she saw what she knew would be her house with the new clinic started on the side. It was made of concrete blocks that had been painted a brown color to match the huts of the village. People were now crowded around the vehicle and many were standing at the house awaiting them. They were yelling and cheering, laughing and smiling as Michael came to a stop.

Angie quickly grabbed his arm and asked, "Is there any cultural thing I need to know before I greet them. I would hate to make a faux-paus right off the bat."

"Not a thing," he reassured her. "Just be yourself. They'll love you."

"I hope you're right."

He stepped out and yelled a greeting while Angie reminded herself to appear strong. She swung open the door and jumped down from the seat. Immediately people began to shake her hand.

"Dr. Angie! You are here! We are glad you are here!"

"Let me touch you! You are the healer, Dr. Angie!"

"You are tall, and you are not as pale as Brother Mike!"

Angie looked at Michael who had come to stand next to her. "Did you know I'm not as pale as you are?"

He grinned and actually winked. He had a little spunk to him after all.

"Let me talk to all of you," Michael said as he waved his hand to quiet them. **"This is Dr. Angie. She has traveled all the way from the other side of the ball of the earth."**

"It's not a ball," yelled an older man.

"Yes it is," countered a teenager. **"Brother Mike has taught us this truth and we have seen the pictures from space. It is a ball!"**

"We are on one side; Dr. Angie is from another," Michael continued. **"She should be sleeping right now on her side of the ball."**

The people laughed at this and waved at Angie even more.

"She is also my wife now."

The people now cheered loudly. They waved their hands in the air and began to chant *Brother Mike, Brother Mike.*

"I would like to say," Michael continued, much louder than Angie had thought his voice could possibly get, *"that I'm giving back your stupid monkey!"*

At this the group nearly collapsed with laughter. Michael reached over and put his arm around her waist and gently hugged her. She didn't know if this was for his benefit or theirs, but one thing she did realize: Michael Collins was not as shy as she thought. He was a leader to these people, and he rose to the occasion of authority when necessary.

"That monkey stinks and I will never sleep with it!"

The crowd laughed even harder with a couple of younger boys actually rolling on the ground.

"Dr. Angie smells really delicious, and all the time! And I will sleep with her for the rest of my life!"

The villagers were wild with laughter and cheering. She could tell by their responses that they loved Michael and were proud for him to have a partner. She whispered a prayer quickly that God would indeed bond them together for each other ... and for these people.

"We have already had our honeymoon, but we are ready to unload our car. You will all get to meet Dr. Angie soon. Let us unpack and settle in before the sunset comes."

They nodded and began to start leaving when a middle-aged tribesman came forward and halted them. His face was gentle, not harsh as were some of the other men. He held up his arms and commanded the crowd to stop.

"Sojay," Michael smiled as he reached out and pulled the man to him in an embrace.

"My brother," Sojay spoke, and then he turned to Angie and added, *"my sister. We must kneel this moment and thank God for the blessing of wisdom to overcome the obstacles. I will pray."*

Sojay knelt and everyone followed. He prayed a prayer of power like Angie had never heard before. She was moved by his sincerity, but more moved at his thankfulness for her. When he finished, he embraced her also. She made sure she hugged him as firmly as Michael had so all could sense her strength. Then Michael took her hand and led her toward the house.

"We will unpack your car," Sojay told him as he called after Michael.

"Thank you," Michael said, then added, *"but be very careful with the two cow boxes. They are easily broken."*

Sojay nodded and began to direct the men and boys to carry in the items.

Michael opened the door to the house and Angie followed. It was a large room, measuring thirty-by-thirty, with a small kitchen and dining table in the far right corner, a bed in the far left corner, and sliding glass doors between them that led to the oft talked about deck. To her left was the door to the bathroom and to her right was another door which led to the clinic. The house wasn't decorated in any way, and books were stacked from floor to ceiling along much of the wall space. In the center of the room however, were three couches that formed the borders of a square, with a recliner forming the last line. Between each couch were small end tables having matching lamps that resembled palm trees. Along the wall to the right between the kitchen and the door to the clinic, was the only set of shelves in the room. Very few books were there; instead a huge stereo system occupied most of the space.

"I love what you've done with the place," Angie grinned at him.

"You're free to change anything you want," he said blushing yet again. "I never thought much about how it looked … until now. And I can tell you, I'm rather embarrassed."

She laughed and tousled the top of his hair. He was so adorable when he was self-conscious.

"Show me your deck, first," she insisted as she walked toward the glass doors.

"Gladly."

He opened one side and motioned her through. He had been right; it was breathtaking. Mount Podakind was beyond description although only sections of it were visible behind the clouds. The Grentawoo River was beautiful, and she immediately imagined hearing it as she drifted off to sleep each night. Over to the right was the Pacific Ocean, just down from the river. She could see the beginning of a white beach framed with palm trees.

Suddenly a piercing scream shattered the tranquility. She looked to her left toward the mountain, and there sat the monkey on the railing.

"Go away," Michael said sternly.

"No," she said with compassion. "He knows I'm a stranger." She walked slowly toward him with her hand barely outstretched. "Come here, little guy. I won't hurt you."

"Yeah, but he might hurt you."

"Come on, fellow. What's your name?"

"He doesn't have one."

She stopped and turned back to face Michael. "You never named him?"

"I never wanted him!"

"Poor thing," she said turning back and walking toward the monkey. "Did the big bad man treat you harshly? He told me ugly things about you. Are you really that horrible?"

As she got next to him, he only stared at her. She reached out her hand slowly to touch him. When she did, he jerked back slightly, but didn't run.

"Throw me a piece of food or something," she said quickly.

"Then he'll want to stay."

She turned around and raised her eyebrows at him.

"Okay," he said going back in to get a date. He tossed it to her.

"Here you go," she said as she held it out to the monkey.

It grabbed the date and jumped toward a tree nearby.

"There went your dinner," Michael said grimly.

"Not *my* dinner. Dates are a snack, Lord Michael, not a dinner."

When they walked back inside, the men were still bringing in items. She sat on the bed for a moment and was thankful it was queen-sized. A fan hung above it, and a large window was at the head.

She checked out the bathroom next. It was small, but very adequate. It even had a bathtub. She loved baths after a tiring day.

"This is unexpected," she said admiring the kitchen. "A double-sink, a four-burner stove and a full-sized refrigerator. The stove looks barely used."

"That's because it *is* barely used."

"Well, we'll certainly have to change *that*. Does this other door lead to the clinic?"

"Yes. I thought it might be easier for you if patients ever had to stay overnight. You could come in here to sleep, and then go back to the clinic to check on them as needed."

"You're a very thoughtful man, Michael Collins. You've worked hard to get this done in a month."

"It's not done yet," he told her as he opened the door.

The clinic was the same size as the house. The walls were still rough and bare. She could see pipes for plumbing and wires hanging all around the room. There were many boxes, and she could tell by the labels they were the equipment she had ordered.

"I wanted to wait and see where you needed outlets before I actually wired it," he explained.

She looked around and gave a sigh of wonder as she realized all that would come true in a matter of weeks. She then walked back to Michael and put her arms around his waist.

"You're an amazing man," she said as she looked him in the eyes. "You've done incredible things here. God's used you greatly. I'm honored to be your wife."

He blushed again and looked up to the left. She pulled him close and hugged him as a man came through the door.

"Can you not wait for the sunset?" he laughed as he carried the two computer boxes.

"We have been married but a few bunnies," Angie laughed back. **"Give us some time to adjust."**

"You will bear many children like bunnies during the rainy season if you continue on like this!" he said with a smile. *"Where would you like these, Brother Mike?"*

"You can drop them on one of the couches in the house," Michael said very distracted with Angie's arms around him.

"No!" she yelled startling them both. *"Don't drop them. Place them softly on the couch."*

*****

"You have eggs in here, at least I think that's what they are. They're mighty tiny," she said as she looked inside the refrigerator trying to decide what to cook. "Milk too! We didn't buy these today in Taveren."

"The villagers stocked it for us. We have our own cows and chickens," Michael told her as he hooked up his new laptop on the small dining table.

"Where's that chunk of cheese you bought today?"

"Look in the middle drawer in the fridge."

"Do you want an omelet for supper? Or should we ration the cheese? Or since we had eggs for breakfast, would you rather eat something else?"

He chuckled at her questions. "I'd only planned on eating dates and fish jerky tonight. If you want to cook real food, I promise I'll eat it and never complain one time."

"Can I make biscuits too then? I'll make enough to have biscuit toast for breakfast."

"Biscuit toast?"

"Sugar toast made from biscuits. Cut 'em in half, spread 'em with butter, top 'em with sugar, and toast them in the oven. One of my favorite breakfasts."

"I'm sure it'll be one of my favorites now too."

"You're awfully easy to please," she said as she removed the items from the refrigerator.

"When all you eat is fruit and cold meat, anything is a welcomed change."

"Do you like onions or peppers in your omelet?"

"Anything," he said getting hungrier each time she mentioned another item of food.

He got on the Internet via satellite, set up his system on the new laptop, and checked his e-mail. Sure enough, there was a message from the mission board concerning the rooms in Hawaii. They were highly embarrassed, but no matter where they tried, they could only find one room available in any hotel. They hoped this would not be a horrible start to what they anticipated being a wonderful working relationship.

Nothing horrible about it. Nothing at all.

"Supper's ready!" she announced as she brought two plates to the table already served. She placed a pan of huge hot biscuits in the middle with butter and jelly on the side.

"I made some iced tea," she told him. "Want a glass or would you prefer something else?"

"Iced tea? Is it sweet?"

"Very. That's how we make it back home."

"Wonderful," he grinned as he shut down the laptop and removed it from the table.

He couldn't imagine this was actually happening. For nearly ten years he had dined by himself because the Podakind people were guarded about family time. Occasionally he would be invited for dinner somewhere, but generally he ate alone, even at lunch. The men always went home to their families, and on days that he taught school, the children would leave for lunch also. It was a wonderful tradition if you happened to be a villager with a family. He, however, had no family, and mealtime had become one of his least favorite parts of the day.

"You're a hearty eater," she said with a smile as he reached for a third biscuit. "It'll be fun to cook for you."

"You can't imagine what my meal times have been like here. It's not just my lack of cooking ability either." He described the Podakind traditions and how the people held to them relentlessly. "I've tried to explain to Christians how we're all part of the family of God and we're all brothers and sisters, but they can't seem to relate that to meal time because that's strictly family time."

"Do they not have feasts or parties together?"

"No. They'll party and dance and sing and play games, but they don't eat together."

"No covered dish, huh?" she smiled.

"Nothing even close," he replied as he realized for the first time how truly tired he was. Since he had left on Saturday morning, he hadn't stopped to relax.

"Why don't you go shower and let me clean up the kitchen," she suggested.

"No way! You cooked all this; you shouldn't have to clean it up. You go shower and let me clean the kitchen."

"Well, you certainly weren't raised in my house, were you?" she laughed as she took his plate, stacked it on hers, and headed to the sink. "My brother never did dishes."

"I have no problem washing dishes."

"And I appreciate that, but I have an ulterior motive. If you shower now, by the time I get this cleaned up, you'll be through, and I can test out that bathtub."

"Oh."

"We'll see how things work out once we get into a regular routine. You may need to shower before supper sometimes, and we could trade up then."

"As long as you never expect me to cook," he said sternly. "I can barbecue in the pit at the side of the house, but I can't cook anything unless it's canned."

"I'll remember that. Go shower," she said shooing him toward the bathroom.

"By the way, exactly what meal is *supper*?" he wondered.

"The evening meal."

"Do we ever have dinner?"

"Depends. If it's a big noon meal, then it's dinner. If it's a sandwich or a bowl of soup, it's lunch."

"Is breakfast always breakfast?"

"Unless it's supper, like it was tonight."

He tried to process it as he walked toward the bathroom, but then he turned around to add, "I don't really care what any of it's called. If you cook it, I promise I'll eat it."

*****

When she finished her bath, she walked into the large room wearing her Braves jersey and boxers. Michael was on the computer again.

"Could I write my family?" she asked as she walked over to the table.

"Absolutely. We'll get your laptop going tomorrow; just use mine for now."

"Great," she said without much enthusiasm.

"How was your bath?" he wondered because she seemed so lethargic.

"Too wonderful," she said with a smile that again buckled his knees. Would he ever get used to that face, those eyes, her laugh, and that smile?

"It was all I could do to stay awake," she explained. "I do need to write my family, though. I'm sure by now they're either sick with worry or waiting on the edge of their seats for some information. I'll cure all the ills with one general letter tonight."

"Which side do you want?"

"I really don't care, Angie."

She sat down next to him on the bed. "Michael, are you disappointed?"

"About what? You?"

"Yeah, I mean, I'm not this normal type person. I know I talk a lot, and I'm taller than the average girl, and …"

"Stop," he said quickly. "You have no idea what having you here means. Not just anybody, but *you*. You belong here. I never, ever, want to imagine life here without you again."

"But you've only just met me …"

"Angie," he said as he closed his eyes and searched for words, "you have no idea how wonderful you are, do you?"

She just looked at him. Her green eyes were so tired that he knew trying to explain his feelings at this time would only be confusing. He couldn't even process them himself. All he knew was that she was the most magnificent creature he had ever met, and he wanted to grab her and hold on to her for the rest of his life. He had never believed in love at first sight, but Angie had changed all that in six days.

"Go to sleep," he said instead as he gave her a weak smile.

"I will, Lord Michael." She reached over and kissed his cheek, then giggled as she pulled back. "Your beard tickles."

Another blush.

"I'm gonna climb over next to the wall and hibernate," she yawned as she made her way to the far side of the bed. "Remember; just tell me to scoot over if I crowd you."

"You could shove me off the bed tonight, and I wouldn't even know it. I'm bushed."

He clicked the fan down to medium and then turned off the light. The moon was bright, and the mountain was literally glowing through the window. The rushing river sang a lullaby promising to lull them both to sleep. As he eased into bed and settled beneath the cover, he could see her face shining in the moonlight as she stared up through the window

"Sleep tight," she told him. "Don't let the bed bugs bite."

"Right," he said as he watched her close her eyes.

He gazed at her face in wonder until his own eyelids grew so heavy he could no longer keep them open. He glanced one last time then smiled as he drifted off to sleep.

NINETEEN

Angie awoke the next morning feeling refreshed for the first time in days. She smiled at the sound of the rushing river combined with the serenading of the birds and knew this place would soon feel like home. Turning over in bed, she discovered Michael was already gone. The smell of brewed coffee lured her to her knees where Mount Podakind came into full view through the window at the head of the bed, not a single cloud threatening its sight this morning.

We should sleep with our heads at the foot so we can see the moon shining on the mountain at night.

As she passed the sliding doors, she saw Michael sitting in the swing with his Bible open, eyes looking toward the mountain, and lips moving. She smiled at the thought of his praying, wondering if he prayed about her yet and if she would ever really fit into his life. There were many things she wanted to know, and it took a lot of control to patiently bide her time, but she knew what people like Michael were like: her brother Alex was one. Guarded people are protecting secrets. Alex had hidden things for many years and no one had a clue as to why or what. Because of that, he had been misjudged, mishandled, and misunderstood for the majority of his life. However, when the truth was revealed, he became a different person. She wondered what Michael could be hiding.

She pulled out a plastic container where she had placed the biscuits from the night before and began to make sugar biscuit toast. How many would Michael eat? Should she ask? She split open one biscuit for herself and two for him, buttered them generously, and then sprinkled sugar on top. She placed them to broil in the oven then began to make herself a cup of coffee.

When she opened the refrigerator to get milk for her coffee, she discovered a bouquet of freshly picked flowers sitting in a jar of water with a note saying "Welcome Home." *He must have put them in there this morning. What time did he get up, and how soundly did I sleep not to notice?*

When the toast was ready, she picked up a piece and went to the glass doors. Knocking lightly, she held up a biscuit to let him know they were ready. He looked over, smiled, and closed his Bible. He then said something obviously derogatory to the monkey as he shook his finger and came into the house.

"Were you being ugly to the monkey again?"

"Why don't you ask the monkey if he's been ugly to me? I was out there minding my own business when he starting pacing back and forth. It's unnerving, like he's plotting against me."

"He only does that because he doesn't feel like it's his home. Are you ready for breakfast?"

"It's *not* his home, and you have no idea how ready for breakfast I am. I'm anxious to taste this."

"More coffee?" she asked as she pulled out the pot.

"Yes, thank you."

"And thank you for the flowers," she said as she poured.

He blushed and nodded. She supposed that was his way of saying *you're welcome*. It didn't matter; he was still adorable.

They sat down and he asked her to return thanks. She thanked God for the beautiful day, the majestic mountain, a good night's sleep, and the food. Michael immediately reached for a piece of biscuit toast and took a large bite. He closed his eyes and sighed.

"Heavenly," he said with a full mouth and a smile. "Generally I have cereal or whatever was leftover from the night before. This is wonderful."

"This is my favorite breakfast," she confessed. "It beats anything: eggs, pancakes, whatever."

"It's my favorite breakfast too." He winked at her.

"Okay, explain our Sunday to me."

"First, we have a service here in the house for this village, Podakind. I hope that one day we'll have to move somewhere else and build a pavilion because of growth, but for now, our house will do."

She smiled when he called the house *ours*.

"When we finish, we take off in the Rover and travel about fifteen miles to the Baastu tribe. We meet in the hut of Kasteen and Mahlil. Kasteen is a Christian; his wife Mahlil has been borderline for several months. Her father is a chief, and she feels that to honor Christ would be to dishonor her father. We'll picnic there."

"By ourselves, I assume?" Angie wondered because of the family habits.

"Yes," he said with a sigh. "But we can picnic on the beach."

"Marvelous!"

"I wonder if you'll finally get tired of picnicking after you've done it here as long as I have?"

"I told you, nothing is boring unless you choose it to be. If it gets to the point that things are not all that great, then we opt for some changes to spice them up."

"Whatever you say."

"What happens after we picnic?"

"We then spend time playing games with the children and teenagers, well, the teenagers that'll let us. They grow up fast here, marry very young.

Some of the parents won't settle a marriage for their children quite as young as others, believing they lose their childhood too quickly that way."

"Good for them."

"Well, yes and no. Sometimes it becomes almost impossible for them to get married later because no one their age is available."

"Hmmm," Angie mused. "I bet you were quite the role model for those kids. Thirty-five and single?"

"Hey, you're not far behind me, you know?"

"But I'm twenty-nine, and I *am* married."

He smiled and shook his head. "Just play with the children, Dr. Angie. And, if possible, talk with some of the ladies. See if you can begin to build friendships. Mahlil is the only woman in the Baastu tribe that even attends meetings."

"Will they come here to the clinic if they're sick?" she wondered.

"I doubt it. You'll probably have to go there."

"Then I will. On Wednesday we go to the other two tribes?"

"Yes," he said grabbing another piece of biscuit toast.

Angie glanced out back to the monkey and watched as it stared into the house. She picked up another date from the bowl in the kitchen and took it out.

"You're going to spoil him," Michael griped as she slid the screened door behind her.

She slowly walked toward the creature holding out the date in her hand. He would alternate glances between her hand, her face, and the closest tree to the deck. As she got closer, he began to edge toward the tree.

"Come here, little fellow," she said softly in a high-pitched voice. "Come get some breakfast."

The monkey reached out slightly then pulled his arm back. She decided to make him come to her. She stood at the railing on the deck and lay the date in her palm as she continued to coax him closer.

"Come here, silly monkey. You need a name, don't you? What would be a good name for you?"

It began to inch closer. She kept smiling and talking, but wouldn't move her hand.

"How about *Cheetah*? "

The monkey pulled back.

"Okay, you don't like *Cheetah*. I don't know a whole lot of monkey names. Do you like *Bongo*?"

It merely stared.

"How about *MJ* for Michael Junior?"

"Watch it," Michael warned from inside the house. "It will *not* bear my name in any form."

"He's so mean to you, isn't he? Let me think of something more regal, perhaps, more worthy of such a noble creature. Let's see, my favorite books were Tolkien's *Lord of the Rings* series. How about Gandalf?"

"For mercy's sake," Michael complained again. "Please don't call him Gandalf. If you have to name him something, at least make it one of the inane little hobbits."

"Hey, the hobbits were noble creatures too!"

"Merri and Pippin?"

"Wonderful!" she exclaimed softly. "Pippin! That's perfect! There you go, little fellow. You are officially named now: Pippin."

Michael grumbled again. "You know you just ruined that whole series for me. I doubt I'll ever read it again."

"Come here, Pippin," she continued. "Does Pippin want some breakfast?"

The monkey began to crawl slowly trying to get to the date without getting too close to her.

"I know you want this," she went on. "That's right, Pippin. Get the date."

The monkey was finally close enough to reach the fruit. He looked up at Angie for a moment, then grabbed the date and darted back to the tree. Once safely on a branch, he glanced down at her and chattered something.

"You're welcome," she spoke back to it. "Now stop irritating Michael. If you don't, *you* may end up being breakfast one of these days."

TWENTY

When the time neared for people to arrive, Michael opened the front door so they would feel free to come on in. He was surprised to find many already gathered outside.

"They're eager to see *you* again. We haven't had this many here since the chief's son died. I can't believe it; even ladies and children have come."

"Come in, everyone," he said opening the screen door. *"Help me set up more chairs. I did not realize Dr. Angie would cause this many people to have such an interest in God."*

Sojay and a woman with four children came in first. Sojay greeted them both and then went to gather chairs from a storage shed outside.

The woman came up to Angie and said with excitement, *"I am Mosheed. I am Sojay's wife."*

Angie reached down to hug the short woman.

"I am nice to meet you," Angie told her. *"I have heard much about Sojay. His prayers are strong, and God would answer them ... no ... God did answer them."*

The woman's excitement couldn't be contained. She took Angie by the arm and led her to the kitchen where she could speak in secret.

"You will teach me about God, Dr. Angie? You will tell me the whole truth?"

"Yes, I want to," Angie answered a little confused. *"Do you not believe Michael teaches you all truth?"*

"He teaches all truth to the men, but he will not say these things to me. He tells the men they must be men of God and must stop bad things and they must live holy lives unto God. But all he says to the women is love your husbands and your families. Are we not to be women of God? Are we not to be holy too?"

"Yes, we are," Angie clarified. *"I will teach you to be women of God."*

"Yes! Yes!" Mosheed cried aloud. *"The women will listen to you, Dr. Angie. You are a healer, but you are a woman! They will listen to you when you speak about Christ!"*

"Why not Michael?"

"Because our women are proud and stubborn. They do not want one more man to tell them what to do. They want to have a freedom like those in the cities, but they cannot here."

"Why not? Why do they not say what they think?"

Mosheed laughed at the question. *"They would rather be enslaved and alive than freed and dead! Some of our people do leave Podakind. They go* to the city to live. They tell us there that women have work beside men. They even drive Rovers like Brother Mike. Here the women can do only three things. We cook, we take care of our homes, and we raise our children. We do nothing more. If women rise up, they are executed. They have a simple choice: to live."

"You do know that in Christ women and men are equal?"

Mosheed's eyes grew wide and her jaw dropped. "Brother Mike has said as much, but we have never seen this. You will show this to us?"

"Yes, and I will teach your women about Christ."

Michael walked by with a couple of chairs and asked, "Do you want to play something on your guitar?"

She was startled. She hadn't planned on it, but wasn't this why she had learned to play in the first place? If she started making excuses now, it would be easier to do the same each time an opportunity presented itself. After all, she had made excuses about music for many years. It was time to move past all that; this was Padawin.

"Sure," she said with a nervous smile. "If you think it would be appropriate."

"There's no such thing as *appropriate* in our worship meetings."

She went to the closet next to the bathroom and dug through her luggage until she found the guitar case. She had never even plunked a string on it. She pulled it out and laid it on the bed wondering if it were in tune.

"Dr. Angie is also a music maker!" said one of the children, very excited at the sight of her guitar.

"Look at its color!" cried another child. "It is like the ocean on a cloudy day!"

"Play for us, please, Dr. Angie," an even smaller child asked.

Angie smiled but she knew no children's songs. Then as she thought, she figured she could possibly pull one out with a little figuring. She sat at the edge of the bed, played a simple chord, adjusted two strings, and then started.

Jesus loves me this I know
And His Bible tells me so
Little children they are His
We are weak but He is strong
Yes, Jesus loves me
Yes, Jesus loves me
Yes, Jesus loves me
His Bible tells me so.

Angie didn't have the confidence of her sister, Annie, but she sang as though it were a concert crowd. One rule she had always followed: *if you're gonna do something, do it with all your heart.* The children applauded and laughed with delight at her singing. The adults had stopped and listened also.

"Dr. Angie is like a bird!" Sojay beamed. "She just opens her mouth and *out comes her music."*

"Sing us more!" a child pleaded.

"Later maybe we can all sing," Angie suggested as she felt her face flush slightly. That was literally her first public solo. Regardless of how talented the rest of her family might be, she would never claim to fit in among them musically. But this had been well received.

Michael walked over to the closet and dug through their mess until he pulled out a guitar case. Angie's face grew warm. Did he play too? She was now embarrassed. If he had a guitar, he'd probably played for years. He must have thought her few months of learning sounded pitiful.

"Why didn't you tell me you played?" she asked as he put his case on the bed and took out his guitar.

"You never asked," he smiled. "You did beautifully, you know?"

"Oh, I'm sure," she groaned, feeling more humiliated as the moments passed.

"Tonight, when everything is over, you and I will sit on the deck and play and sing together. I never thought something like this could happen. I am awed by you again."

"Not by my music!" she protested.

"Yes," he said simply. "You sing like an angel, you look like an angel, and you have a green Ibanez guitar."

"You've never heard my sisters sing," Angie said still trying to insist she was musically inferior.

"I don't want to hear your sisters sing," he said as he knelt down to tune his guitar. "Play your bottom E-string. I'll tune to you right now."

She complied, playing her string while trying to hide her insecurity.

The meeting was marvelous. Thirty-five gathered around the room, some on the couches, some in folding chairs, some at the dining table, and some on the floor. Angie sang two of her hymns, but Michael led in many songs. The people loved to sing! When they sang, it was loud and clear and strong. She couldn't remember the last time she had heard a worship meeting where the songs truly sounded like genuine praise. She followed Michael's chording easily and loved watching him play and sing. The thing that amazed her most was that not all these people were confessing Christians. Michael had explained to her that even though most of them believed in Christ and what he had taught, they were very slow to trust their lives to Him. They all agreed it was a decision that required great thought before commitment. When they sang, they sang to God in adoration, regardless of the condition of their hearts.

She was truly awed at his teaching. He spoke plainly and clearly to these people of great theological truths found in God's Word. He used everyday illustrations of things they could understand to drive his points home. He was a masterful storyteller, but he was also a man steeped in the Word of God. He constantly quoted Scripture from all over the Bible to support each point.

When the service was concluded, they prayed for quite a while. Everyone who wanted could pray. Angie marveled at the sincerity and trust these people displayed toward God. They gave Him credit for every good thing in their lives, and many of the prayers included special blessings for Angie. She was moved to tears several times.

"I was blessed today," she told Michael as they traveled to the Baastu tribe. "You're an amazing teacher."

He smiled his self-conscious smile. "But your singing capped the service."

"No way. The entire thing was meaningful. The singing, the praising, the teaching, and especially the praying; it was so heartfelt. We don't get that much back in the States. We have revival meetings hoping to spark that kind of sincerity, but it seldom happens."

"You followed me well on the songs. Next week, you and I will sing something special for them. Do you write songs too?"

"Oh, no!" she replied quickly. "I only decided to learn guitar so I could have music with me over here. I do *not* write music. That's Annie's department."

"Have you ever tried?" he asked.

"Well ... no."

"Imagine sitting on the deck with your guitar in hand watching the moon glow on the snowy peak of Podakind," he said almost dreamlike. "Then tell me you do *not* write music."

The Baastu people were as warm and welcoming as the Podakind. There were only twelve at the home of Kasteen and Mahlil, but the meeting was still wonderful. Michael preached an entirely different sermon. The singing was spirited, and the prayers at the end were as heartfelt and honest. Angie was again moved to tears as the people called out her name in prayer.

"Did you preach two different sermons to impress me?" she asked him, half teasing as they sat on a blanket beneath a palm tree on the beach.

He grinned. "No. I would never try to impress you." He bit into a biscuit and smiled in delight. "They're at two different stages. The Podakind need to understand holiness; the Baastu need to develop boldness."

"Will I hear two different sermons on Wednesday also?"

"Probably."

"Why would you not try to impress me?" she asked with a mischievous grin.

He leaned back against the tree and stared out at the ocean for a moment. She could tell he was trying to pull his words together carefully.

"Just spit it out," she told him. "That's what I do. I don't think too much when I talk; I just talk."

He chuckled then nodded in agreement. "You don't realize what you are," was all he said as he turned his eyes back toward the ocean.

She gazed at him in confusion. *What was that supposed to mean?* "And what exactly am I?"

He gave a deep sigh. "You're a breath of needed life here, not only to me, but to these people. You have so many things about you that make you stand out. You're beautiful and tall and strong. You have this spirit and life about you that's magnetic. These people can already sense something in you that draws them. And besides that, you have a great tan; you're not *pale* to them. How did you get like that anyway? How'd you get so dark?"

"Give me a moment." She was stunned. "Let me get past the other descriptions first."

"Do you really not know how wonderful you are?"

She looked into his face and gently smiled. He looked like a lost little boy who had finally made friends with someone for the first time in his life. She wanted to take him in her arms and swear to him that he was wonderful too, but she held back, offering her hand instead.

"You make me feel like a queen," she told him.

He was blushing again.

"I'm sorry that I'm such a touchy-feely person," she said as she squeezed his hand and let go. "My sisters always griped about it. It just seems to me that when you feel something for someone, it's much more intensified if you express it with something physical. Moms is the same way. I'm the only kid who got that."

"The people here will love you for it."

She nodded, then looked over at him and asked, "What about you? I do it so automatically that I never stop to think if I'm *invading* or something."

He smiled slightly and glanced back to the ocean.

"I make you uncomfortable, don't I?" she asked sadly.

"No. You make me ... wonderful."

He looked back at her and smiled again. She laughed slightly.

What happened to you that makes you hide behind such a huge wall? Thank you for at least letting down a few bricks now and then to let me see inside.

"Well, Dr. Angie, tonight we can talk to our heart's content, but right now, there are a group of children gathering who cannot wait to see the beautiful, new, tall woman play some games. Are you ready to go?"

"Ready and willing."

TWENTY-ONE

Angie enjoyed playing with the children and managed to coax some of the younger teenage girls to join in the games. After several hours, she was exhausted, and as much as she had enjoyed getting to know this tribe, she was ready to return home. She wanted to cook a good meal, take a hot bath, and relax for the rest of the evening.

After cleaning the kitchen with Michael's help, she headed for the bathroom. What luxury! She relaxed and lingered in the tub a long time. When she finally got out and managed to dry her long hair most of the way, she joined Michael on the deck.

"He's waiting for you," Michael told her as he pointed to the silhouette of the monkey on the railing.

"Hello, Pippin," she said softly. "Did you come back for another snack?"

She went inside for a date and then sat beside Michael in the swing. She waved it around so the monkey could see and smell it, then she opened her hand and lay the date in her palm.

"He won't come to the swing," Michael said firmly. "He hates me."

"If he really wants this date, he'll have to come to the swing."

Slowly it climbed to the floor and walked over toward the swing. He hesitated, but she wouldn't move her hand. She laid it on the armrest with her palm facing upward.

"You can have it, Pippin," she told him sweetly. "It's all yours, just jump up and get it."

The monkey would look at the date then up at Angie. His final look, however, was at Michael, which concluded with a scream and his running back to the tree for the night.

"He doesn't like you very much," she said disappointed.

"The feeling's mutual."

"That leaves me very torn. I'm afraid I like both of you quite a bit. I've never had a pet monkey before."

"You *still* don't have a pet monkey."

"Not yet," she said with determination, "but this is only my second night here."

They sat quietly in the swing and gently rocked back and forth. She was tired again, but this time it was a good tired. She had spent the day playing and sweating and talking and enjoying the life of Padawin. The bath had completely relaxed her, and now swinging on the deck while the river rushed by with the moon beginning to rise was heavenly.

"This is nice," she sighed.

"Yes, it is."

"Do you do this every night?"

"Not every night. Some nights I'll sit in the recliner and read. I was considering Tolkien again, but you sort of killed that. Why couldn't you have named him after someone from a Shakespearean story? I could've lived with that."

"I take it you don't like Shakespeare?"

"Not at all."

"The language or the stories?"

"Neither."

She smiled. He was sharing an opinion. That was good. "I don't care much for the language. When I read, I don't want to have to *think* too hard. Medical school did that for me. But I think his stories are full of irony—and *that* is the spice of life."

They were quiet again, just swinging gently as a slight breeze blew up from the ocean.

"Were you ever engaged?" he asked through the silence.

"Not even close. I dated now and then, but I never found anyone who had the same life's calling. The others in med school and training with me could never understand how I would go through all that just to leave the States and practice medicine somewhere for free. I think a lot of guys thought I was crazy."

He chuckled again.

"Are you laughing because you think I'm crazy?" she asked him.

"No, I'm laughing because they didn't know what they'd miss." He paused. "I sometimes wonder if I could ever live there again. I've been here so long and become so acclimated to this way of life, I don't think I'd ever fit in back there."

She stopped swinging and looked over at him. "You never did fit in back there, did you?"

He shook his head slightly. "Not really."

She took his hand, lacing her fingers in his, feeling the calluses as well as the strength. "You're an incredible man, Michael Collins. Fitting in is not what life is about. Fitting in means you follow the standards that others made. Fitting in is for people who have no imagination or vision for life. People like you and me were made to remind others that there's more to life than just following the last cow that went through the gate."

They sat quietly for several minutes, hand in hand, enjoying the river, the moon and the mountain, but mostly each other.

"I'm really tired," she said as she leaned her head back and let her hair fall behind the swing. "And as much as I hate to say it, I'm homesick again."

"I can't imagine how you've done this well. Your family means so much to you. I think you've fared admirably."

"I appreciate that," she managed through a wide yawn. "Can I go to bed now?"

"No problem."

She slowly rose and stretched, then reached her hand to pull him up from the swing. "I'm sorry about not playing guitars tonight. I was just too tired to do much of anything."

"You didn't hear me complaining."

"Except about the monkey," she teased as they went inside.

*****

After breakfast the following morning, they began to plan the placement of equipment in the clinic. Angie looked through the boxes to get the dimensions of everything she had ordered and began to sketch the layout for the large room.

"Is there any possible way to block off more rooms in here?" she asked Michael as she stared at the enormity of the thirty-by-thirty space.

"Sure. What would you like?"

"This room is massive, and it would be nice to divide it up so we could have one room for surgery and two more as examining rooms. This way, patients could be escorted to a room while they're waiting. Also, if there were ever any need for someone to stay overnight, they could have a private room, help eliminate some of the contamination."

"I could probably stud them off with what I've got around here already, but we'll need to order some plywood or sheetrock to actually make the walls. The helicopter won't be here for another month."

"That's no problem," she said as she leaned into him with a smile. "We can go ahead and get the wiring done and set up the equipment as though everything is ready to go. We'll just pretend we have walls."

They worked all morning, with several tribesmen stopping in to offer a helping hand, although it was probably more about their curiosity to see the new doctor again. Angie botched up her Padawin in the most humorous ways. The men laughed at her silly talk, and Michael enjoyed watching her complete lack of self-consciousness. He wished with all that was in him that he could be as free and open as she. The more he was around her however, the easier it was becoming to let down his guard.

They ate their lunch of fried egg sandwiches on the back deck as clouds began to gather. Mount Podakind was foreboding as the sun hid and thunder grumbled in the background.

"Have you ever been up to one of the volcanic cones?" she asked as she sipped her iced tea.

"Actually yes. About 40 miles away is an extinct cone. It's very beautiful. The vegetation around it is lush and thick, and even inside the cone it's green."

"You're kidding?" Angie gasped. "Can we go one day?"

"It's quite a steep climb."

"And you think that would stop me?"

"I doubt it. Does anything stop you?"

"I don't know yet."

Michael shook his head and smiled as she pulled the pencil from behind her ear and started adding rooms to her sketch.

TWENTY-TWO

"Dr. Angie!" came a lady's voice into the clinic for the first time that day.

It was Mosheed, Sojay's wife.

"Mosheed! I am so glad you have come to see me this bunny."

"And you are working in your healing house!" Mosheed was impressed. **"You have so many shiny things in here."**

"They are machines that help with the healing cycles. This is an X-ray machine. It will show me inside to your bones."

"That is hard to believe!" Mosheed said as she looked it over carefully. **"And what is this?"**

"It is a ... uh ... washer ... um ... it removes bad germs from all the machines so germs will not spread to others."

"That is good. Brother Mike explained to us long ago how horrible the germs are and that we must always be washing our hands and bodies to keep us strong and healthy. He showed us how to clean the germs from our water and from our houses. We now have latrines that keep nasty germs away from our homes."

"Brother Mike did nice things ... no ... incredible things by teaching you this," Angie said as she looked over to acknowledge him. **"He has made what I come to do an easier throw."**

"What will you be throwing?" Mosheed asked her in confusion.

"Nothing. Why?"

Michael laughed to himself but then cleared up the problem. **"Dr. Angie knows much about healing, but less about our language. She will not be throwing anything other than a ball when we play games with the children!"**

"Oh, man," Angie shook her head. "Will I ever get the hang of this language?"

I hope not, Michael thought to himself. *These little mistakes have become quite a bright spot in my day.*

*****

After dinner and baths, they spent the evening on the deck with their guitars. He taught her several of the songs they sang regularly and then insisted she teach him something too. With reluctance, she showed him *When the Roll is Called Up Yonder*.

"You do so well translating these songs," he told her. "The grammar in this language is all mixed up."

"Tell me about it. I hope I don't slaughter it too much when I'm talking."

"You do very well."

"Do you think it'll ever rain?" she asked as thunder continued to rumble on into the night. "I can't see the mountain tonight. It's like an old friend has left me."

"He'll be back soon. But there you go being poetic, yet you don't think you can write a song."

"That wasn't poetic. That was merely being ... personable toward the mountain."

"It *was* poetic. Now, let's write a song about the mountain being your friend."

"Not unless you sing me something you've already written," she said cautiously.

She couldn't see his expression, but he grew quiet. It was only fair; he was pushing her to do something she'd never done. She should be able to push back slightly.

"I can't. It's too intimidating. Your sister is Annie Wright and your brother-in-law is Stephen Williams."

"Touché'! That's what *I've* been trying to tell *you* every time you ask *me* to sing! Play me a song you wrote and I'll do anything you want," she offered weakly. It was probably useless, but worth a try.

"Anything?" he asked.

Although she couldn't see his expression, she knew there had to be a twinkle in his eye by the sound of his voice.

"Within reason," she said carefully.

"What do you consider to be reasonable?"

"No, it doesn't work that way. You tell me your offer, and then I'll tell you if it's a deal."

He clicked his tongue, and she could tell from the faint light in the kitchen he was shaking his head.

"You wouldn't do any different if the tables were turned," she insisted. "You'd never just agree to do anything I said without me telling you first."

"Sure I would. I trust you implicitly."

"Is that so?" she asked in unbelief. "You would tell me anything I wanted to know."

"That's not what I said. I said *I trust you implicitly*."

"Okay, you're gonna have to explain that one to me."

"What I mean is that you've never pushed me to go any farther than I've offered. Because of that, I don't feel like I have to ... well ... be concerned that you're going to force me to say something I'm not ready to say."

"I see," she nodded in understanding. "I'm assuming correctly then that there are many things about yourself you haven't shared often. And you don't intend to share them with me until you're good and ready?"

He breathed in deeply and leaned back in the swing. "I guess that's about the sum of it."

She smiled. At least he was showing some candor for a change. How long and how far would she have to go with him before he would let her inside his life?

"Okay," she finally gave in, "sing me your song, and I'll do *whatever* you want in return."

"Promise?"

"Yes!" she said exasperated. "I promise, cross my heart, hope to die, stick a needle in my eye!"

"A simple *yes* would have sufficed." He pulled up his guitar and began to gently pick the strings.

The bitter cold is painful
The winter seems so long
For all my life I've shivered
I've always been alone
But suddenly the sun has come and opened wide my heart
And suddenly the cold I've known is melting all apart

I can almost see the dawn as I watch the sun arise
And the mountain calls my name as this place makes me alive
And the winter that has chained my restless soul for much too long
Has suddenly begun to fade as I see the new spring dawn

My heart has always wanted
To simply just belong
But no one ever held me
I sang my songs alone
But suddenly the sun has come and warmed this side of life
And suddenly the cold I've known has vanished with the night

I can almost see the dawn as I watch the sun arise
And the mountain calls my name as this place makes me alive
And the winter that has chained my restless soul for much too long
Has suddenly begun to fade as I see the new spring dawn

He stopped suddenly and said, "That's as far as I've gotten. It needs something more, but I haven't been able to finish it."

Angie just stared into the darkness with her mouth open.

"That bad, huh?"

"Are you kidding me? It was, well, it was amazing. What a beautiful song. I had no idea ... well ... you expressed a lot in that song."

"I know," he said softly. "Too much too soon, I think."

"Oh, Michael," she said in a whisper as she looked toward him, wishing the moon were shining so he could know the sincerity in her eyes. "There's nothing you couldn't tell me. You do know that, don't you?"

She could see him nod. He seemed embarrassed. Somehow he had felt strength in the darkness and in their common bond with the music, but she knew he felt he had given too much. How did she convince him that he shouldn't be humiliated in any way?

"Michael," she said tenderly as she put her arm around his shoulder, "you have such a beautiful heart. Being with you has made my presence in Padawin perfect. You could've been this mean-hearted, hard to please man who could've started barking orders at me from the moment we met. Instead, you've done nothing but make me feel warm and welcomed, as though I've always belonged here right beside you. For you to sing me this song … it … well … it almost makes up for all the gabbing I do day in and day out. Don't ever feel like I couldn't appreciate something straight from your soul."

She could see a small silhouette of a smile as she gazed at his face. She breathed a sigh of relief. He understood.

"Now, what did you want in return?" she asked as she tried to change the subject to ease the moment.

He leaned his head back and actually laughed.

"What?" she wondered.

"The truth is, there were several options I had in mind, but suddenly now they all seem silly and embarrassing."

"Try me. I'm up to any challenge."

"Let me sleep on it," was all he would say at the moment.

"Don't wait too long. I'm sort of like a fairy godmother: if you don't put it in by midnight, the wish may just go *poof*."

As they climbed into bed that night, the rain began to fall at last. It started gently, but in only a few minutes, it became pounding.

"That's some storm," she said loudly over the sound.

"Welcome to Padawin. Wait until the rainy season."

"What does everyone do during the rainy season?"

"Stay in their huts and enjoy their families."

"What did you do?"

"Read. Play music. Eat a lot of fruit."

She giggled. "See, the monkey could have kept you great company if you would have just let him. He may have even liked Tolkien."

He only grunted in response.

She rolled over and bid him goodnight. "Sleep tight; don't let the bed bugs bite."

He grinned. Would she say that every night for the rest of their lives? He hoped so.

TWENTY-THREE

Because of the continuing rains, they were unable to make the Wednesday trip to the Gandushi and Bentahu tribes. The roads were either thick with mud or flooded altogether. However, by Thursday afternoon, Michael had completed the wiring and gone down to the river to hook everything into the generating mill.

"It all works perfectly!" Angie yelled to him out the window. "I can't believe you actually did this! You're a genius!"

He walked back up to the window and peeked in. "That surgery light is mega-bright," he said squinting toward the area that would be studded off soon as the operating room.

"The better to see you with, my dear," she teased. "I don't want to misplace any shiny objects inside an innocent tribesman."

"Yuck. I hate needles and any shiny object that has to do with doctors' offices."

"What? Are you saying you don't like doctors?"

"Personally, they're wonderful people, but I hate their methods ... too many needles and stuff."

"Hey, you told me you sewed up several yourself with stitches right here."

"Oh yeah," he said with displeasure, "as well as gave several immunizations against some of the more horrible diseases. That doesn't mean I liked it ... or that I could keep my lunch after doing it."

"Really? It would make you sick?"

"Anything with a needle was ten times worse for *me* than those receiving it."

"The needle is our friend, Michael," she said in a sing-song tone. "He helps us stay healthy."

He mumbled something she couldn't make out as he left the window to walk around to the front. Just as he was about to enter the door, a loud commotion at the road caught their attention.

"What's the excitement?" she asked as she joined him to see where the ruckus was coming from.

"I have no idea."

They watched as a crowd of seven people walked before a cattle drawn cart.

"That's Kasteen's wagon!" he said in surprise.

"From the Baastu?"

116

He nodded as he started toward the group. "I've never seen them come to this village in all the years I've been here. This must be important. I wonder why they didn't come by canoe?"

"There's his wife, Mahlil, riding in the back."

"Brother Mike," yelled Kasteen as he ran toward the couple, **"our young Joohenj has fallen! He needs the healing of Dr. Angie!"**

"I don't believe it," Michael said as he turned back to face her. "They brought their son, Joohenj, to you because he's hurt. They traveled this whole way to see you."

"I hope I can help him," she said with a hint of doubt.

"Of course you can. God would never send you a fatal case for your first assignment."

"Let's hope you're right."

They approached the cart, and Kasteen led the couple to the back. Joohenj looked pitiful. His face was swollen, and his right leg was obviously broken, possibly in several places. Angie immediately began to function in doctor mode.

"What has happen?" she asked.

"His vine broke during a fall," Kasteen told her.

"What?" she asked in total confusion.

Michael explained in English, "He was doing a type of bungee jump, and his vine broke."

"Are you kidding me? They bungee jump here? From how high?"

"It started here, well, actually in Vanuatu. It's a rite of passage. There's no telling from how high he jumped."

"Good lands!" she exclaimed as she looked back down to examine the boy.

"Can you help my son?" Mahlil asked with pleading eyes.

"I hope to. We must bring him inside. I will look at his bones and see where to start."

Angie had Michael and Kasteen bring him into the clinic on a stretcher and then lay him on a bed.

"Joohenj," she said to him as she leaned over and began to press against parts of his arm, **"can you feel my pushing your arm."**

He nodded.

"How about this?" she asked him as she gently poked his hurt leg.

"Yes!" he screamed in pain.

"Good," she said to the scared boy with one of her warming smiles.

"Good?" Michael asked her. "Some bedside manner."

"*Good* because that means his spinal cord is still intact. His leg I can help; a broken spine I can't."

She gently positioned the leg and then maneuvered the x-ray machine into place.

"Here are the breaks in Joohenj's leg," Angie explained as she showed the results to his parents. *"I will need to put a ... thing ... on all of these bad places in order for his leg to walk again. He will wear it for many bunnies."*

"Days, many days," Michael interrupted to correct her.

She rolled her eyes and sighed as she apologized first to Michael, "I just can't seem to get that word," then to the family, *"I am having hard times with your language."*

"We do not care how well you speak," Kasteen assured her. *"You see my son's bones. That is something no one else here can do."*

"He will wear the thing for as many bunnies as you insist," Mahlil teased Angie.

Angie laughed as she looked through a box of supplies for a splint that would fit his leg. She carefully set the leg and then offered him a set of crutches.

"You must not put leaning on this leg," she told him, then realized that may not be the best explanation. "Michael, let me tell you what to say and you can translate so we get this absolutely clear."

He nodded.

She continued in English, "You must not put any pressure on your leg for a long while. You must always lean on these crutches when you walk. I will give you small pills to help with the pain for a short time. You can only take three while the sun is up. Space out your time. Take one in the night."

She turned back to Michael and suggested, "We should take him back in the Rover. I still don't know how he made it in the cart here without intense pain."

"Oh, I imagine it was intense. We'll let Mahlil ride with us."

*****

Word of Angie's healing of Joohenj's leg spread quickly. Within the next week, people were lining up at the clinic each day, and several even traveled from the Baastu tribe. She asked that every one suggest any pregnant women come see her immediately. She had special vitamins that would help keep the babies healthy as they grew.

"I am Kartushah, Sojay's oldest son," a young man told Angie as he brought his pregnant wife into the clinic one day. *"This is my wife, Seendoo. She is having our first child. My father said we should come to you for help now."*

"Yes, you are a wise man for doing this," Angie smiled to them as she helped the young woman up on a clinic bed.

"My father says so," Kartushah told her, *"but Seendoo's father says the witch doctors are saying you are a demon."*

Angie whipped her head around in unbelief. "What?" she said aloud in English. *"They are saying I have evil powers when I help to heal people?"*

"My father," Seendoo spoke up, *"is a witch doctor. He lives out in the jungle and speaks to the gods daily. So do many others. They say you are cursing our people."*

Angie stood back in shock. Did the people believe them? She had only done good things so far. How could they trust the witch doctors still? Or worse, what if she made a mistake, or what if someone had a fatal problem she couldn't cure? Would they revert to trusting the witch doctors?

"I am not evil," she emphatically assured them. *"I speak with the only true God each bunny also. He is a good God, and He does not do evil things. I cannot heal everyone of every problem, but His wisdom gives me help to heal much."*

"We know," Seendoo said with a smile, *"and that is why we are here. The midwife says there is a problem with my baby. He is not heading right. We wondered if you might help."*

"Let me see how things are going first," Angie said as she tried to regain her composure from the witch doctor blow.

She smiled and chatted constantly as she checked Seendoo's vitals and then began the internal examination. The midwife was right: the baby was breech at the moment.

"Your midwife told you truth," Angie said calmly. *"Your baby needs to be upside down, but it is not. It may turn soon, though. You do not need to worry if this is what happens. When it is time for your baby to come, if it is not turning yet, we can maybe turn it. If not, I can maybe take the baby out another way."*

Seendoo smiled with relief as did Kartushah.

"These little balls have special foods in them that will help keep you and your baby healthy," Angie explained as she gave them a bottle of pre-natal vitamins. *"Take one little ball with your meal every morning."*

"Me too?" asked Kartushah.

Angie laughed. *"No, only Seendoo. Your job, Kartushah, is to make sure she eats plenty. Don't let her eat just one thing. She needs her meat and her grains, and she needs fruits and vegetables too."*

"She eats all the time!" he exclaimed.

"Then you are doing well," Angie told him confidently.

A nursing mother came in and bared her breasts to her. They were contaminated with a skin ailment and oozing. She gave her an ointment and explained that she needed to treat them regularly until the sores healed. She also gave her a bottle with several bags of formula to supplement the baby's feeding as the breasts healed since they weren't producing enough milk to keep it healthy.

"The witch doctors say the gods are punishing me," the woman told her. *"They say the gods want my baby to die."*

"There is only one God, and He loves your baby and you too," Angie

said with her gentle smile. **"He has sent me here. You use this cream, and you will be healed in several bunnies. Feed this milk to your baby, and he will be fat and happy soon also."**

"Thank you, Dr. Angie," the woman replied with a hopeful smile.

*****

"I'm sorry dinner isn't ready yet," Angie apologized as Michael peeked through the back door that evening.

"Are you kidding me?" He removed and then shook out his boots on the deck. "You haven't stopped all day. Did you even eat lunch?"

"I shared some dates and bananas with the monkey," she grinned.

"Be careful. If you don't make time for lunch, you'll start living off of those fruits. Do I need to leave someone here with you when I visit the Baastu to ensure you get proper nutrition, Doctor Angie?"

She shook her head and smiled. He was black from head to toe with the rich Padawin soil. "How did you get so filthy?"

"From playing in the dirt all day," he said as he slid open the screen door. "We did a lot of planting. The Baastu haven't been as open to receiving my suggestions as the Podakind. This is the first season they've allowed a full garden."

"Good for you! The people here live with you. They know you wouldn't steer them wrong."

"I suppose. The Baastu are a stubborn group. They don't want to copy the Podakind, even if it means their health and well-being. It's killing some of them that their people are walking 15 miles to your clinic."

"It's apparently upsetting the witch doctors also," she said as she turned with the plate of chicken to set it on the table.

"Oh, man!" he exclaimed. "Did you fry chicken?"

"Yes," she said proudly as she held up the plate. "I don't think I've ever seen such little chickens, though. I believe the two of us could eat the whole chicken alone."

"With no problem," he agreed eagerly. "Did you know that fried chicken is my favorite meal in the whole world?"

"No, I thought it was dates and bananas."

"Let me wash up and I'll devour that chicken for you. And don't even *think* about giving any to that stupid monkey!"

"His name is Pippin!" she called out to him as he went into the bathroom. "And he's not stupid!"

Michael ate piece after piece of chicken and helped himself to several servings of mashed potatoes and gravy. He even had seconds on the broccoli and cheese sauce.

"There's dessert also," she told him so he would save room. "Chocolate cake."

"Chocolate cake?" His eyes grew wide. "You made chocolate cake? How can you serve chocolate cake and fried chicken at the same time? I don't know which is best."

"Eat your chicken. We can have the cake out on the deck after you've showered."

He bathed while she insisted on cleaning the kitchen alone. As hard as she had worked, she knew he had physically put in a long, exhausting day. She cut him a large slice of cake and poured a glass of milk to have ready for him when he finished his shower. When he walked out of the bathroom, his face was beaming at the sight.

"I feel guilty, you know?" he said walking to the table. "You've worked all day too. You shouldn't be responsible for cooking and cleaning after all you've done."

"And what would we have had for supper had I left it up to you?"

"Dates and bananas," he said with a guilty grin.

"Exactly." She folded the dishtowel and grabbed her own cake and milk. "I'll continue to cook, thank you. Open the door for us."

He obliged immediately and followed her out. The monkey appeared as if on cue to investigate.

"Don't give a bite of this to that monkey," he warned her.

"I've heard chocolate isn't good for animals anyway."

"Then always make chocolate," he said with a smile. He took a bite and closed his eyes in delight. "How did I live without you? If you ever left me after this, I would follow you anywhere, you know?"

"So our marriage has kind of taken root, huh?"

He cocked his head to the side and looked up again as he thought on it. "I guess so. After three weeks of having you here with me in Padawin, I can't imagine losing you."

"That's nice to know. I have to confess that I was worried you might be this confirmed bachelor, and that you'd find my barging in on you and your life a bit unsettling."

He choked on his milk when she said this. "Are you kidding? It's almost like you're the best thing that's ever happened to me. Fried chicken? Chocolate cake?"

"So you only like me for my cooking." She gave a pouting frown.

"No way," he said, this time looking at her. "I like you for ... well ... everything about you. I lie in bed at night and listen to your breathing and find myself just thankful that you're there ... beside me. When I eat these incredible meals, and I look over at you, and there's this unbelievable woman sharing it all with me—I'm not alone anymore. I can hardly contain it. Your traveling with me to Baastu, Gandushi, and Bentahu is like a breath of fresh air. Everything you do and say is so enlivening. And to top it off, you like my songs even though your sister is a professional musician."

"I *love* your songs," she corrected him.

"See? How could I ever live without you again? I'd never have the nerve to sing to anyone else!"

Angie laughed at his statement, but inside she was actually honored. She had known him for almost a month now and he had opened up bits and pieces to her. He had still not said anything of his life before the mission field except for Jenna, but he had told her much about his life in Padawin. He would sing to her his songs on the deck at night, and they had even written one together. His songs were always deep and heartfelt. She believed he shared them with her to share himself in a small way—to share parts that he couldn't find the words to say, but could express in his music.

"I really do love your songs," she reiterated. "They tell me so much about you."

"And I really do love your chocolate cake and fried chicken."

"Maybe this would be a good time to talk about the books." She snuck in the statement.

He peeked up at her as he kept his head down.

"I don't want to get rid of them. I just want us to *place* them in a more pleasing way."

"How?"

"Could we build some shelves?"

"Absolutely," he said with relief. "I'll call Taveren and have them bring some materials when the copter brings the rest of our stuff next week."

"Great! As you've noticed, I'm not the tidiest person in the world, but getting your books off the floor might inspire me to do a little more with the house."

"I'm sure you've noticed," he grinned at her, "tidiness isn't high on my personal list of priorities either."'

They laughed together and finished their cake and milk as she described her ideas for the shelves.

TWENTY-FOUR

Sunday afternoon at Baastu, Michael and Angie played several traditional tribal games with the children. She enjoyed the attention she got both from the kids and from Michael. He was exceptionally playful with her that day, and she was able to get a deeper glimpse into his personality.

"Why don't we teach them baseball?" she suggested as they lay on the ground after some type of tackle. She wasn't sure about the point of the game they were playing, all she knew was that every time she ended up with the stick, she eventually wound up on the ground.

"Baseball? Are you going to try and Americanize these people?"

"I'm tired of their version of football," she groaned as she made her way up to her feet. "I don't know if my thirty year old body can take much more of this banging around."

"Thirty? Did you turn thirty?"

"Yeah," she said a little embarrassed. "Somehow it was hard to find the nerve to admit I was turning thirty."

"When was your birthday?" he wanted to know, the disappointment evident in his eyes.

"August second. It just sort of came and went, and I didn't know how to bring it up."

"You? Dr. Angie was at a loss for words?"

"It happens," she said as she tried to stretch out some of the tightness she knew would result in soreness tomorrow. "Not often, but it does happen. Now, what about baseball?"

"Later," he said with a sympathetic grin. "I think it's time we called it a day at Baastu. You look beat up."

"How generous of you. An hour ago would have been nicer."

"An hour ago I didn't realize you were such an old woman."

*****

The next morning, Michael asked Angie if she felt like packing a picnic; they were going to visit the extinct volcano. The trip to the mountain itself took two-hours, however, it was a beautiful drive. This was Angie's first time away from the oceanic tribes since her arrival at Podakind. She had forgotten how lush the forests were.

"Why does no one live out here?" she asked.

"There are a few here and there, but the tribes prefer settling near the ocean. Maybe it's the availability of the resources in the water, the ease of traveling on it. I don't know."

123

She sighed at the scenery and summed up her feelings. "I love these woods. They're so green and thick. This is how things look back home when it's early spring and we've had lots of rain. The different shades of green are always amazing to me. I never tire of life in any form."

Michael pointed up Mount Sheshney as he parked the Rover. "We have quite a climb from here. We'll go at your pace. We're in no hurry."

"Will we be able to eat at the top?"

"That depends on your speed."

The trail was steep and winding, with many huge rocks to climb around and over. She was glad for the exertion because it helped to loosen up the soreness and stiffness in her body from the day before. If she kept this up, she would look like an Olympian within the month! She stayed a steady pace and was rewarded with a breathtaking view when finally at the top.

"There's no possible way to describe this beauty," she said as she lay out on the ground in exhaustion after reaching the summit. "I need to get pictures of all of this to send home by e-mail. You really need to figure out how to do that."

"Me? You're the doctor."

"But the fancy shmancy camera thingy is yours."

"Well, I can get the pictures onto the computer; I just don't know what to do after that."

"I bet Chet and Vicki do—having kids a million miles away from grandparents. We'll take all your equipment next time we see them and let them show us."

He nodded and spread out a blanket on the thick, green grass.

"Can I step inside it?" she asked as she crawled toward the edge of the fifteen-foot diameter cone.

"Sure. As long as it's not smoking you should be fine."

She stopped crawling and looked back at him with raised eyebrows. "Smoking?"

"Just kidding," he winked. "Walk on in."

She stood to her feet and carefully made her way inside. He watched as she walked around the edge and then cautiously moved toward the middle. She smiled back at him as though she had accomplished a great feat.

"Take my picture!" she yelled. "This is too awesome to believe! I'm in a volcano!"

He reached into his pack and retrieved the digital camera. Standing back slightly he made sure he got the entire cone inside the viewfinder.

"Okay!" he shouted. "Smile!"

He took several shots of her posing, then several more when she was unaware. Afterward he held the camera down to his side and just gazed at his bride. When she looked up and found him starting she simply smiled and gave a wave, much like she had done at the airport in Hawaii.

"Come and eat!" he yelled.

"Good idea!" she yelled back while gently walking to the edge of the cone.

"I can't believe that you fried a chicken this morning just for the picnic," he said opening the container.

"Fried chicken is the best picnic meal ever. Didn't they tell you that back where you came from?"

"I don't recall anyone ever telling me that in Kansas."

"Kansas?" she said with a big smile. "You're from Kansas?"

"I never told you that?"

"No! You've never told me anything about life BP!"

"BP?"

"Before Padawin. Well, except about Jenna and your engagement."

He nodded quietly, and she knew that meant it was a memory he'd rather forget.

"Potato salad?" she asked as she handed him the common fork.

He took it, stuck it in the salad, and took a large bite.

"I never liked potato salad before yours," he told her. "It always had something weird in it that was just—well, nasty."

"This is Moms' personal recipe … directly from her mom. We all love it."

"Why do you call her *Moms* instead of *Mom* or *Mother* or even *Mama*?"

"Hmmm," Angie thought for a long while. "I have no idea. We've just always called her *Moms*. I guess Andie must have started it?"

"And what's with all the *A* names?"

"Moms came up with all the names before she and Daddy even married. She liked the name *Andie* because it was the nickname for her grandfather, Alexander. If Andie had been a boy, the name would have ended with a *Y* instead of the *IE*."

"Is her name still short for Alexander?"

"No, Alexandria. Moms made sure it still had a feminine ring to it. She's very girly, Moms is."

"I see," he said nodding. "Are any of your sisters very *girly*?"

"Are you insinuating that *I'm* not feminine?" she asked with a teasing grin.

"Oh, no! You, personally, are as feminine as they come. You're just not all that *girly*."

"Explain that one, farm boy."

"You're not a sissy," he said plainly.

"Oh. Thank you—I think."

"Trust me, it's a compliment."

"I'll take your word for it."

As they ate, she took in the scenery again. They were high up on Sheshney so she was able to see down into the forests and over to the other mountains. There were more volcanic peaks than she had been aware of.

"Are any of these active volcanoes?" she asked.

"Possibly."

"That's a great comfort."

"Did you ever stop to think that when you moved to the Ring of Fire it might be feasible that you would be living near some active volcanoes?"

"No," was all she would say.

The outing with Angie was like another vacation for him. Every day with her was like that. As she explored Sheshney's summit he stared in amazement again. He knew he had come to care for her and to need her more than he had wanted. Shortly after returning to Padawin, he had convinced himself that he must keep an emotional distance, but she had edged her way inside his heart. It scared him to think that he could become this attached to someone again, but everything about her captivated him. Her smile, her eyes, her beauty, her warmth, her compassion, her humor, and as much as he hated to admit it, even her body were things he found himself thinking about as he gardened in the middle of a field surrounded by numbers of Padawin tribesmen. He used to use his farming time for prayer, but now he found his thoughts preoccupied with her. He often told God it was His fault for bringing such a person into his life, but he always followed with sincere thanks for the gift. She was the picture of perfection, and even if she had been a horrible cook and he was still forced to live off fruit, he could have cared less. The fact that she made every meal a wonderful creation just reeled him in even more.

"Now *that* is a pleasant look," she said as she caught him smiling at her off guard. "What *are* you thinking?"

He squinted and blushed.

"Don't start blushing on me," she warned him. "Tell me what you were thinking."

He couldn't help it. She had caught him in deep thought about her and he had no alibi to pull out.

That's what I keep warning you about, Collins, he told himself. *Before you know it, she'll possess you, and you'll have no choice but to just give in to her.*

"Keep thinking," she told him a bit sarcastically, "and you'll eventually come up with something other than what's really in your heart right now. So, don't bother; I know it won't be the truth."

She turned her head away and stared back down toward the jungles and smaller mountains. He hated hurting her. Of all the people in the world he didn't want to hurt, she was the dearest, but he wasn't an open person. One thing he did know, he was finding it harder and harder to sleep at night with her next to him. When the moonlight was bright, it was exceptionally hard. It would shine on her face, her hair, her arms, and he couldn't close his eyes. All he could do was stare.

"Remember the night I first sang *Spring Dawn* for you?" he asked as he tried to pull things in a different direction.

"Of course. I'll never forget it. It was a wonderful night, a wonderful moment for us."

"I made you promise to do something for me," he reminded her.

"I know, and you never came up with anything. You kept insisting you would *think on it* and let me know."

"Well, it's been hard. Everything you do is so amazing. I couldn't imagine anything more."

"Pick up my wet towels off the floor?"

"They join mine while they're down there."

"I know. Perhaps we're not good for each other."

"Oh, no," he said without hesitation, "you're very good for me."

"Is that so? How?"

"In every way. But I have a favor for you now."

"Goody!" she said as she rubbed her hands together. "Anything."

"Remember Hawaii?"

"Everything about it," she smiled.

"Remember when we got married?"

She nodded.

"I didn't know anything about you at that time. You were just a face that I could finally put with a name."

"I understand. I felt the same way."

"And then down on the beach that night when we were married… and the pastor said we could kiss—do you remember that?"

"Are you kidding? Of course. It was our wedding and our first kiss."

"I was so nervous," he said with his blushing smile again. "I didn't think you would do it."

"Kiss you or marry you?"

"Either actually, especially after I saw you. You were so beautiful, and then when you stepped out in that wedding dress, I thought I was gonna pass out."

She giggled and gently ran her hand over his knee for a second.

"But that kiss," he went on, "it was so … oh, I don't know … tender? Heartfelt? Genuine? Yet I knew it couldn't be all those things because I didn't even know you."

"And why not? I felt all those things toward you. I wasn't *in love* with you then, but I felt them. I was committing myself to you for life, Michael … and I still am."

"I can't tell you how often I've thought of that kiss," he finally confessed. "I mean ... it's so hard sometimes because we're man and wife, yet at the same time, we're not. And I find myself feeling, perhaps, *too* familiar with you, when I shouldn't."

"I *am* your wife, Michael," she assured him. "I'm your wife in every way. Just because certain areas of our marriage have remained ... *undeveloped* ... doesn't mean that you should ever feel *too familiar* with me."

He was blushing again and embarrassed he had brought up the subject until she told him, "I think of that kiss often too."

He looked up at her instantly. "Really?"

"Of course. It was a special moment. I hope that sometime in the future, it'll be something that's as natural to us as singing with our guitars on the back deck."

"Do you really?"

"Sure. Did you think I didn't want anything more of this relationship? Did you think I just wanted us to be *good buddies* for the rest of our lives?"

"I didn't know. I hoped not—but I just didn't know."

They paused to think about the discussion. Neither said anything for a small while. But Angie finally interrupted the silence.

"So," she said mischievously, "was it *that* good of a kiss?"

He chuckled slightly and nodded. "Oh ... yeah."

"You thought so, huh? Was there any time period that you were looking toward for maybe a repeat performance?"

He rubbed his beard with his hand as he shook his head.

"What would happen if one of these peaks blew up on our way down the mountain here?" she asked.

He looked at her in confusion and answered, "I suppose we'd get covered in hot lava or ash."

"Wouldn't make it down, would we?"

"Highly unlikely ... if one actually blew."

She stared around at all the peaks surrounding them. "It'd be kind of sad, wouldn't it, if the only kiss we ever shared before being singed to death was that one on the beach in Hawaii, granted, it was very *sweet*, but, hey, our lives weren't hanging in the balance that day, you know?"

He laughed at her suggestion and shook his head again. He loved living life with this woman. She always knew what to say, how to say it, and exactly when to say it. "It would be very sad," he confessed.

"So, just for the sake of the surrounding volcanoes and the possibility of imminent death should we attempt a second one?"

He looked over at her and gazed for a moment before saying, "I honestly don't care a flit about the volcanoes. However ..."

She got up on her knees and crawled over next to him, her face next to his. "I don't know where to go with this," she admitted.

He nodded slightly as he looked deep into the green of her eyes. He could feel her warm breath on his face, and her lips were so close he could almost feel them too. He glanced down for a moment and saw that a slight smile, though somewhat uncertain, was formed on her mouth. He slowly leaned into her, refusing to close his eyes, and gently touched her lips with his. She didn't respond eagerly, but lightly, and he found himself feeling dizzy at the sensation. He pulled back for a second to see her eyes. They were open too. Then he kissed her again. This time her response was warmer, deeper, and stronger. He didn't want to let himself go for fear that anymore and he would totally give his heart away, but he couldn't help it. He kissed her again and again, trying to hold back his passion, but as she reached her hands up to his face, he felt himself falling.

"I love you, Angie," he whispered to her as he pulled back slightly. "I didn't mean to. It just happened."

"It's okay," she said as she looked into his eyes with complete kindness. "I've loved you for so long that I was beginning to get scared."

"Why?"

"Because I didn't know if you could love me back?"

"How could I not?"

"Because you won't share yourself with me. You give me bits and pieces of your life, Michael, but you refuse to give me *you*. If you love me, though, you'll show yourself to me ... eventually."

He nodded. "It's hard ... for me. My life ... it was nothing like yours. I can't just toss it out ... you know ... as though it were some normal event over the course of time."

"Believe me when I tell you that I totally understand that," she said as she ran her hand down the edge of his beard. "But I want to be able to give my whole self to you, Michael. I'm tired of holding back. But you possess the key to that."

He closed his eyes and nodded again. He knew indeed. "I can't believe I told you I loved you."

"I can't either. It must be a strong love for you to confess that."

"You have no idea."

"Yes, I do," she said as she leaned in to kiss him again.

He held her close and gently laid her back to the ground. He stopped briefly to gaze at her face, her eyes, her lips once again. He couldn't believe this was happening. He smiled and wondered if he could ever give her what she really wanted: his past. It would be hard, perhaps nearly impossible, but he would find a way. He loved this woman more than anyone ever in his life, and he would do whatever it took to seal the bond between them.

TWENTY-FIVE

As wonderful as Sheshney had been, neither Michael nor Angie spoke of it again—nor acted on it. Life between them went on as before, only now more stressed because of what had been said and done. The fact remained that she knew nothing more about him other than he had lived in Kansas, got engaged in college, and had been a missionary to Padawin for the past ten years. It killed her each night to simply lie down next to him and close her eyes as she pretended to go to sleep. This wasn't her nature, but she knew that whatever issues Michael held he must not be pushed. He was fragile; she could wait.

Michael felt the pressure. He knew the ball was in his court and that it was up to him to initiate the next move, but he couldn't imagine how to begin. It was easier to work hard all day, eat, shower and go to bed, than to face her questioning eyes. He loved her so much that it nearly tore him apart when he saw her or even thought about her, but just pulling things out of the hat that he had suppressed for so long was close to impossible.

"You need to get a flu shot," she said to him one morning in mid September as she set the biscuit toast on the table for breakfast.

"I don't do flu shots."

"This year's strain is really miserable. It's not a simple 48 hour thing. It lays you flat, they say. I've done a lot of research about it on the Web."

"I'll take my chances. I always do."

"I thought you gave flu shots here every year."

"I did," he said, barely glancing above the rim of his cup at her, "but I never took one myself."

"Have you ever had the flu?"

"Not yet."

"I guess I'll pray your luck holds out."

"Has Seendoo's baby turned yet?" He had seen a breech delivery once, and it was horrible.

"Not yet. There's still a chance it may in the last month or so."

"Have you ever done a c-section?"

"Assisted many, performed one. I can do it."

"I believe you," he said with a smile. "You can do anything."

"Anything except give you a flu shot."

The monkey appeared on the back deck, and Angie grabbed a piece of biscuit toast for him. She slid the screen door open and walked out to deliver the goods. Pippin was now comfortable with her, and he bounced down the deck right up to her so she could hand him the toast. He chattered at her as he took it and then bounded up to the railing to enjoy his bounty.

"Is sugar bad for animals too?" Michael asked as she came back inside.

"Probably. Processed sugar isn't really good for anyone."

"Good," he brooded as he got up to put on his boots.

*****

Angie spent the day giving out flu shots and seeing patients with mild cases of gastroenteritis and various arrays of respiratory infections. She put one child on an IV in hopes of equalizing the vicious cycle of vomiting and diarrhea, and gave an elderly lady a breathing treatment in order to try and avoid her bronchitis developing into pneumonia. The season had become very wet, and mosquitoes were out by the millions. The dampness also made the weather appear cooler and depressing, encouraging more indoor activity thus breeding and spreading more germs. She was thankful at least for the flu shots.

"Dr. Angie!" Kartushah yelled as he burst into the clinic. *"Brother Mike has been hurt very bad. He has blood everywhere?"*

Angie dropped what she was doing and jumped up to face Kartushah.

"Is he conscious?" was the first thing out of her mouth. She recomposed herself and asked again in Padawin, *"Is he awake?"*

"Yes, but there is blood everywhere!"

"Take me to him now," she said as she grabbed her medical bag.

She turned to Geechern, a young woman who had begun to help her in the clinic.

"Geechern, I must see to Brother Mike," she said quickly as she ran for the door. *"Clear the surgery room for him. Tell the others there will be no more healing today."*

Angie ran behind Kartushah as fast as she could. This was one time she was thankful for her long legs. She matched his stride step for step. As they approached the field, she could see the crowd of tribesmen gathered around him.

Please let him be okay. I can't do this without him. I can't be here without him.

As she neared the place where he lay on the ground, the group parted to let her through. She immediately began to assess the situation, trying hard to keep her emotions in check. She wasn't sure where the blood was coming from, so she began to question Michael about what had happened.

"Michael, what did you hit?" He was pale and his eyes were glassy.

"Plowing," he managed to say. "The mud was slippery."

She glanced at the plow. It was sharp, turned over, and extremely muddy.

"What did you cut?" she asked. "What part of your body is hurt?"

"My arm."

131

She quickly turned her attention to his right arm and took out a piece of gauze to try and wipe away some of the blood. He gasped as she touched the wound. It was a huge, gaping slice on his forearm measuring close to six inches long, and she had no idea how deep.

"Be glad it bled," she said to him as she continued to wipe the area around the wound.

"Love that bedside manner of yours."

"It helped to gush out some of that mud that's dripping all over the plow," she clarified.

"Kartushah," she said as she turned to face the tribesman, **"you must take someone with you and get the carrying bed. Bring it back here quickly as you can."**

Kartushah picked a man right away, and they both ran back to the clinic. She tried talking to Michael to keep him conscious. She wasn't sure how much blood he had lost, but it was more than she was comfortable with.

"You could've found an easier way to get my attention, you know," she told him lightly as she continued to wipe around the wound with fresh gauze.

"Are you gonna have to sew me up?"

"Only if you promise to be a good boy and not play hastily with the plow anymore."

"I'm serious." He was trembling now. She looked at his eyes and saw terror in them.

"Michael," she said softly as she placed her hand gently on his bearded cheek, "I'll have to sew this up. This gash is really bad. I'm hoping I can treat it here. We may have to transport you to Taveren. It's that serious. Do you understand?"

"I don't want to go to Taveren. I want you to do it. Please don't send me to anyone else."

She sensed his fear and leaned down to his face and smiled. "I'll take care of you, Sweetie. I'll do everything I can. Don't worry. Okay?"

He nodded, but wouldn't smile.

When Kartushah returned, the men helped her maneuver Michael onto the stretcher. As they walked back to the clinic, she held his wounded arm to keep it from moving. Once there, they took him to the surgery room so she could get a closer look at the gash beneath the bright lights.

"It's pretty deep. I need to deaden it first so I can clean it thoroughly before sewing it up."

He rolled his eyes back inside his head and closed them as his face grew greener.

"Michael, I have to do this."

She motioned for the two men to leave her alone with him. When they left, she leaned down over him and took his face in her hands. His beard was bloody, and his wavy hair that hadn't been cut since she had met him was matted with blood and mud.

"Michael," she said firmly, but softly, "you need to listen to me. Open your eyes."

He did. "I don't want any needles," he said groggily.

"I know, but there's no way you could stand the pain without them. I'll do it quickly."

"I'm really afraid of needles. Really afraid."

"Trust me when I say I believe you."

She stood up and went to a cabinet to get the syringes and medicine. She worked with her back to him so he couldn't see the needles as she prepared them. When she turned around, she hid them behind her.

"I'll do this quickly," she promised. "Once the medicine begins to work, you won't feel anything else."

He nodded and began to cringe. She raised the needle to his arm and made the first stick. He winced, but only slightly. As quickly as she could, she moved the needle to another section of his arm and injected more medicine. When she finished with the first, she started on a second one and glanced up at his face. His eyes were squeezed shut and tears were streaming down both sides. She felt her own eyes begin to pool as she finished the first step in what would be a long process that afternoon.

"That's all." She tossed the used syringes onto a tray. "You did well. The worst is over," she said with her compassionate smile as he opened his eyes again.

"You're not afraid of anything, are you?" he asked as she wiped the tears from his face.

"Yes, I am," she said soberly. "I'm so afraid that the passion we feel will never be realized. I'm afraid that one day we'll wake up and realize we lost everything before we ever took the chance to grab it."

"I still love you," he told her. "I still do."

"I know," she said as she gently kissed his forehead. "Lie back and relax. I have a long, messy job ahead of me."

"I do love you, Angie."

She cleaned the wound and realized it was as bad as she had thought. When everything looked clear, she began the process of sewing it. He would need a strong antibiotic to ensure no infection would set in. Even then she couldn't guarantee that all would go well. She would do her best to keep him here, but at the first sign of trouble, she would radio Taveren and have a helicopter out to get him immediately.

The longer she worked, the more relaxed he became. He actually seemed to doze off a couple of times throughout the procedure. When she finally finished, she gently touched his face to rouse him.

"All done," she said with a comforting smile.

He lifted his arm to see the wound. It was bandaged. "Good," he said closing his eyes again. "I don't want to have to look at it."

"You're gonna have to take a few days off, you know. Doctor's orders."

"No problem."

" Do you think you can get to your feet?"

"Probably," he said wearily, "but I may need to lean on you for a bit."

"That's fine. Let's get you home."

She cooked a light meal of chicken noodle soup, her mother's secret recipe for the ailing, and brought him a bowl in bed. She helped him sit up and placed it on a lap desk.

"Would you like a piece of buttered bread?" she asked.

"No thanks. This is plenty."

She smiled at his response. She had never known him to refuse food or claim that any amount was *plenty*. He obviously felt worse than he was claiming.

"You need to take these pills. One is for pain, and the other is an antibiotic."

"Thank you for the pills," he said as he looked at her gratefully. "You could've given me shots again."

"Not unless I absolutely have to. When was your last tetanus?"

"Two summers ago."

"Good," she smiled with relief. No need for that injection. "Mind if I join you?"

"Not at all."

She dipped herself a bowl and carefully maneuvered to the other side of the bed.

"You're a wonderful cook," he told her.

"Thank you," she said cheerfully, glad to see that he was pulling out of the trauma.

"I love chicken noodle soup."

"As far as I can tell, you seem to love just about anything. You're a hearty eater, farm boy. How's the pain?"

"It's beginning to throb more inside the wound now. The Novocain is wearing off."

"That's what I figured. It's a really bad gash," she wanted him to understand.

"How many stitches?"

"Thirty-three."

"Man," he said placing his spoon down on the desk. "That's a lot."

"Tell me about it. I tried to make it as clean as possible, but it's big …

134

and it's deep."

*****

After dinner, Angie guided him to the shower and got the water started. She wrapped his arm in plastic and helped him undress down to his pants.

"I'll let you take it from here," she grinned as she removed his belt.

"Don't stop now," he teased her back.

"You don't have that kind of energy, Brother Mike. I'll see you after the shower. Your hair is a mess. Do your best to clean it up. Here are some fresh clothes."

She laid a pair of boxers and a t-shirt on top of the toilet and waved goodbye as she walked out. Leaning against the door for a moment she let the memory of the last few hours take hold of her. She walked to the couch and collapsed as she began to cry.

Lord, don't let me lose him. This could've been so much worse. Something horrible could've happened and he would never know how deeply I love him or how much he means to me. I'm not trying to play games with him, Father; I'm just trying to be wise and patient.

*****

When he left the bathroom, he found her asleep on the couch. She looked tired and worn, much like she did when she had first come to Padawin. He debated whether he should wake her or not, but she was grimy and bloodied herself from working on him. She would want to bathe. He knelt down beside her, feeling groggy from the pain medicine he had taken at supper.

"Angie," he whispered as he gently moved the hair that had fallen over her face. "Why don't you take a shower?"

She slowly opened her eyes and smiled at a cleaned-up Michael. "Feel better?"

"Feel cleaner, but I'm pretty tired."

"Good. Why don't you go on to bed? I changed the sheets from the mud bath you gave them. I'll shower and join you later on."

He stood up and swooned a bit. She jumped up immediately to help steady him.

"You okay?" she asked concerned.

"Sort of. I'd better lie down."

She took his left arm and led him to the bed. She pulled back the cover and helped him ease onto the mattress.

"Are you chilled?" she asked.

He nodded, and she pulled the covers up to his neck.

"You lost quite a bit of blood," she explained. "Also, you'll be fighting infection for several days. I'm serious when I say you need to take it easy for a while." She placed her wrist to his forehead. "You might develop

135

some fever. Don't try to be superman, okay?"

"No problem. I'll be a good patient."

"I sure hope so," she said as she managed a smile. "I was scared for a bit there."

"I was too. I wasn't sure what had happened. All I know is that when I saw you, I felt like everything was gonna be okay."

"Go to sleep," she said as she tenderly ran her hand down the side of his face.

"*That* ... should be easy." He closed his eyes and let his thoughts drift to happy places.

TWENTY-SIX

When Angie awoke the next morning, she immediately looked to Michael's arm. She had barely slept. The bandage was slightly bloody; she needed to change it as soon as possible. She looked to his face and could tell he was sleeping peacefully. The pain medicine had worked. His hair was spread across his pillow, but at least it was clean. She tried to crawl out of bed gently so as not to wake him.

"Morning," he said sleepily when she reached the edge.

"I was hoping not to disturb you. How do you feel?"

"Not a hundred percent."

"I figured that. After breakfast I'll need to change your bandage."

"You can't imagine how bad it hurts right now."

"Yes, I can," she said smiling. "I'll get you some pain medicine as soon as I get the coffee made."

"Wonderful," he moaned slightly as he closed his eyes again.

"What would you like for breakfast?"

"That pain medicine sounds really delicious right now."

She laughed and gently ran her hand across his beard. As she gazed at his face, she noticed something she had never seen before: it appeared he had a long scar on his left cheek.

"What is it?" he asked, noticing her change of expression.

"You need a haircut."

"I know. Can you cut hair?"

"No," she replied firmly.

"I wonder where the monkey is," Angie mused as she stared out on the deck after breakfast.

"Maybe he drowned."

"He's always here for breakfast." She walked out back and called for him. "Pippin! Where are you? Are you hungry?"

Nothing. She gave up and walked back inside. Michael had made his way to the couch where he laid down waiting for the pain pill to kick in. She walked to the front door to see how many were lined up for the clinic already. She was shocked to see not a single person was there.

"Nobody's here today," she said in surprise as she turned back to him. "Do you think they're worried about you and feel they shouldn't come?"

"Maybe, but that does seem strange." He got up and walked slowly to the door with her. He glanced outside and shook his head in uncertainty. "I

137

don't get it. People would come. It's Friday. They know you don't work on Saturdays, Sundays and Wednesdays unless it's an emergency. They would be cramming for the weekend. They always do." He looked around for any sign of life. "How odd that no one's stirring at all."

"Maybe they're worried about you?"

"Possibly," he said as he looked out towards the rest of the village. "Everything is weird out there. Nobody's moving around. Where is everybody?"

"Should I go out and ask some questions?"

"I don't know."

"Let me get my shoes on," she said as she took his hand and led him back to the couch. "You lie down; I'll find out what's going on."

He relaxed back on the couch as she put on her shoes and walked out the front door. All was quiet for nearly a minute, then he heard her scream. His heart nearly stopped.

Angie! Oh, no, what happened? Don't let anyone hurt her!

Forgetting his own pain, he jumped up from the couch and quickly ran out the door. She was on her knees sobbing and heaving at the same time.

"What is it?" he asked as he knelt beside her. "What happened?"

"The clinic," was all she could choke out.

He turned to look and was appalled at the sight. The monkey had been slaughtered, skinned, and hung in front of the clinic door, his head removed and eyes poked out, hanging beside him. Michael turned his head away then reached out with his left arm to cradle her head to him.

"I'm so sorry," he whispered as she sobbed on his shoulder.

"Who would do this?" she asked overwhelmed by horror.

He knew, but he didn't want to tell her. In fact, he knew what the whole situation meant. He didn't want to tell her that either. He helped her up from the ground and took her back inside the house. Grabbing a dishtowel from the kitchen, he brought it to her so she could wipe her eyes.

"Do you know what this is about?" she asked as she began to gain control.

He closed his eyes tightly and nodded.

"What is it, Michael? Tell me."

His own pain had now returned, and he sat back next to her on the couch, dreading the explanation. "The witch doctors did this. It's their way of declaring an omen on you ... or me, actually."

"This is disgusting!" she exclaimed in anger. "Why did they do this to me? What is the omen about?"

"They're declaring death," he said soberly.

"What? Death of natural causes or death at their hands?"

"They aren't murderers," he assured her. "This generally happens when someone is so sick it's obvious they'll die."

"Are they bluffing the villagers ... trying to make them think they have some sort of control over life and death?"

"Probably. The people have begun to put their trust in you. Sojay told me last week that the witch doctors are angry at your medical abilities. You're not only curing the people of their illnesses, you're helping them to stay healthy. The witch doctors have pretty much been ignored. Seendoo's father is livid that she's trusting *you* to deliver this baby and not turning to him for his magic and mumbo-jumbo."

"What should we do?"

"I'm not sure. The timing is a bit too obvious."

"What do you mean?"

"My injury ... that much blood and all, and then your dismissing everyone from my room. It's possible they're thinking I'm worse off than I actually am. Maybe they're trying to gamble with this. They hate me because I teach of the true God which is against their entire philosophy. They kept the people in bondage with fear of their gods. They hate you because your medicine works. That was their last hold."

A knock on the door pulled their attention from the conversation.

"Brother Mike! Dr. Angie!" came Sojay's happy voice.

Angie jumped up and ran to the door to greet him. She opened the screen and embraced him.

"I saw Brother Mike come out to kneel with you!" he said with delight. *"They told us Brother Mike had been killed by the demons because he had taught us untruths!"*

"Brother Mike is very much alive," she told him with a gleaming smile.

She pulled Sojay into the house to see for himself. He walked slowly over to Michael, his face growing brighter with each step.

"I am a little tired and sore," Michael told him, *"but I am fine."*

Sojay breathed deeply and started to shake his head in amazement. He looked down at Michael's arm and furrowed his brow.

"Dr. Angie sewed me up," Michael displayed his right arm. *"It is a bit nasty, but God shows her how to heal people. You will always see where the blade cut me, but the blood and pain will eventually be gone."*

"Just like the scars of our Lord," Sojay smiled with confidence.

"Yes," Michael smiled back.

Suddenly Sojay ran from the room outside to the village and began to shout.

"He is alive! Brother Mike is alive! And he is very well! Dr. Angie has simply sewn up his wound! He is talking and laughing with me. They killed the monkey for nothing! There is no death in Podakind today! Come out and celebrate! God has granted us healing through Dr. Angie! Our people are well, and the witch doctors have lied! They still want us to fear their gods,

but who is like Jesus, the true and one Lord?"

Michael felt tears began to sting his eyes as he realized Sojay was simply proclaiming the Gospel. This was why he was here. This was why Angie had spent years in medical training, giving up so much of her life. This man understood the truth, and he was announcing it like a herald in the town square.

Slowly people began to emerge from their huts.

"Michael!" Angie yelled to him. "You need to be out here. The people need to see you."

He stood up and joined her just outside the door. She took his left hand and walked with him down the street to the center of the village, Sojay beside them, still beaming and yelling truth to the people.

"Tonight we will celebrate, not as our own families, but as the family of God," Sojay commanded the people. *"We will all prepare our foods and bring them together at the clinic at late afternoon. We will feed our friends and thank our God for bringing them to us."*

The people began to yell and celebrate as they came out to dance in the streets. Sojay laughed with glee, and Mosheed joined him. Michael put his arm around Angie's waist and pulled her to him in a tight embrace.

"Do you know what's just happened here?" he asked as he stood face to face with her.

"Not completely."

"The final straw that held them to the witch doctors has just been severed," he smiled. "Many will come to Christ tonight."

Angie leaned into him and touched her forehead to his. Her smile melted every part of him, and he forgot all about the pain in his right arm. He couldn't believe that ten years of work here had finally come to fruition, and he knew that he owed most of it to the conviction, call, and dedication of the woman who was now in his arms. He gently kissed her and then pulled back, embarrassed to show affection in public, but the villagers merely clapped at them.

TWENTY-SEVEN

The celebration turned into an all out revival. Many villagers prayed to receive Christ and denounced their faith in the gods of the witch doctors. Michael had always demanded that before they could proclaim Christ as Lord, they had to deny the religion that their tribe had followed for years. Many would have come to Christ earlier if they could have held to their former beliefs also, but he stressed they couldn't serve two lords. As the afternoon turned into evening, many brought torches to the clinic and lit them outside so the celebration could continue.

"Brother Mike," came a strange voice.

Michael turned around to see Kartushah, Seendoo, and her father, one of the prominent witch doctors. Kartushah offered his hand, and Michael shook it heartily. Pain seared through his wound, but he wouldn't flinch.

"I cannot compete with your God," the older man told him. **"I will leave my potions, swear allegiance to Jesus, and work with you in your fields and with your animals."**

"Then kneel with me now and declare your faith in Christ," Michael told him.

As the two knelt to the ground, the celebration came to a halt. Kartushah and Seendoo knelt also. Slowly the villagers followed on their knees. Seendoo's father boldly denounced his use of ungodly ways to sway the people with fear, and then loudly proclaimed his faith in the God of Truth and Love. When he stood, the people cheered and applauded. He held up his hand to silence them.

"I will no longer be known by the name Jankodend," he told them. **"That name meant great in the gods. Those gods were not great. I will now swear to become a teacher of the Truth. Brother Mike will name me now."**

Michael was startled at the idea. He would name the man something else? He looked over to Angie for help.

She came to his side and whispered in his ear, "The name *Joshua* means *the Lord is our Savior.*"

"But that's not Padawin," Michael whispered back.

The people watched in anticipation.

"He doesn't need a Padawin name. He needs a Godly name."

"We will speak of your old name no more," Michael told the man as he put his arms upon his shoulders. **"You will now and forevermore be known as Joshua which means the Lord is our Savior."**

"Joshua," the new man rolled the name around in his mouth. **"The Lord is our Savior. I am not worthy of this name. It is too great a name for a**

man who has deceived the people of the truth."

"No, it is a perfect name for anyone who has been bought by the blood of Christ," Angie stepped up to assure him. *"In the eyes of God we are all unworthy of the blood of His Son. But God makes us all like Him when we accept the sacrifice Jesus made. Jesus is our Savior, and your name will wear well with you."*

The new Joshua smiled at the doctor and shook Michael's hand again. Angie noticed his slight wince and marveled that he continued the firm handshake. She glanced at the bandage and noticed the wound had been bleeding again. When Joshua broke loose, Angie embraced him and then suggested the village welcome him into the family of God. As they moved toward Joshua in delight, Angie pulled Michael back from the crowd.

"Your arm is bleeding," she told him. "I need to get a look at it."

"I think I pulled something. I can't begin describe the pain right now."

"You don't have to; it's written all over your face. Can we excuse ourselves from this meeting without dampening the celebration?"

"Let's tell Sojay. He can take charge from here."

Angie walked over to Sojay and took him aside.

"Brother Mike's arm is bleeding a bit. I need to remove the bandage and clean it again. We do not want to offend the people. Can you take over?"

"Of course. You must take him to sleep also. He looks tired and pained."

"Thank you, Sojay," she said with a weary smile. *"You are a blessing to us, to God, and to your village."*

*****

After removing the bandage, Angie realized several stitches had popped. He still wouldn't look at the wound.

"I've got to sew up a few more places," she said softly. "I'm sorry."

"I thought so," he said as he kept his head turned.

"I'll need to deaden it again."

He merely nodded. She could see his face already turning pale.

"Want me to give you a flu shot while I'm at it?" she asked hopefully.

He shook his head. She gave up in defeat and went on with the job at hand.

When the wound was sewed back together and a new bandage in place, she helped him to the door that led from the clinic into the house. She took him to the bathroom and told him to get ready for bed. He didn't protest.

When she joined him in bed, his breathing was relaxed again; the medicine was taking over. She leaned up on her elbow and glanced at his face in the glowing moonlight.

"So much for taking it easy," he said with a slight grin as he turned his head to face her.

"I know. This *won't* happen tomorrow."

"No protest from me. I think I'll just sleep through the day."

"I may join you," she smiled tiredly as she reached up to move the hair from his forehead. She sighed as she lay back in the bed and closed her eyes in exhaustion.

"Ask me something," he requested. "Anything."

"Anything? Like anything at all? No boundaries or limits?"

"Absolutely anything."

He was offering to tell her something. There were so many things she wanted to know. Where did she start? It shouldn't be big. That would be too much. His parents' death could wait. What one thing from his past could she ask without draining him? She glanced at his face. His eyes were tired and his smile was weak. Something simple.

"Tell me how you learned to play guitar," she finally settled.

He chuckled. "You're too nice to me. The guitar, huh?"

She nodded as she snuggled next to him, careful not to nudge his arm.

"When I was in the seventh grade, I took Agriculture for the first time," he began. "My life up to that point had been purely miserable. My father was an alcoholic. As far as I know, he never worked a day in his life. He wasn't always at home, but he was never at work. Mama worked just about all the time. Some days, he would wait for her to walk in the door and he'd grab her by the hair and throw her to the floor, demanding money so he could get drunk. She would immediately pull out the wallet from her purse and give him everything she had. He'd curse and leave and then be gone for days. She was smart, though. She always had money hidden somewhere so that we could survive."

Angie stared at his moonlit face in unbelief as he relayed the details.

"In Ag, the teacher was impressed with me—I didn't know why. Mr. Lovejoy was just a really nice guy. All the students loved him. When we did a project, he always praised my work and said I showed a lot of promise. I didn't even know how to say *thank you*," Michael confessed. "I was too scared to say anything to anybody. My dad was a violent man. He said if I ever told about our home life, he'd kill my mother. Sometimes I thought she should die just to be released from the hell he put her through. On the rare occasions that he'd be so drunk he didn't come home for days, we'd be happy and relaxed. We played cards and Scrabble. She was a smart lady. She'd tell me to study hard and make something of my life. She said I had to work diligently to make straight *A's* so some college would pay me to go there and I could have a good job and be happy."

All Angie had asked was how he'd learned to play guitar. Apparently, he was bursting inside to share more.

"When Dad was gone, Mama would talk and talk and talk. It was like she had so much to tell me, but so little time to make it all known. I always listened. Because of her, I studied like crazy. The kids at school just thought I was this big weirdo, but they had no idea what my life was like.

"Our FFA had a string band, you know, sort of bluegrass type music that performed at various contests. Mr. Lovejoy had asked me to stay after school to help him build some shelves for the library. The band practiced in the Ag building. He saw that I was intrigued by the music and asked if I played anything. I told him no and got back to building quickly, afraid that my distraction might get me into trouble. He then asked me if I'd like to play an instrument. I said in passing that the guitar had always been something that interested me. I thought that would end it."

"We finished the shelves the next week, but he asked if I could stay after school the following day. He wanted to show me something."

She was now engrossed in the story. Apparently all this was connected to his guitar playing. How sad that something so wonderful held its roots in something so horrible.

"He brought out this brand new guitar," Michael said as his eyes lit up. "He said that he'd bought it a couple of years back with the intent of learning to play it for church, but he'd never gotten around to it. He asked if I would like it. I didn't know what to do or say, so I just sat there. I didn't know how to play the guitar, and I didn't know where to start. He told me to follow him, and we walked down to the band hall. The band director met us there and said, 'Michael, are you ready for your first guitar lesson?' I still couldn't speak."

She gently rubbed his arm as she felt the tension in the story.

"Mr. Lovejoy said someone might as well get some use out of the thing. So I went in and took a lesson. Every week I would go for a lesson. I didn't realize at the time, but Mr. Lovejoy was paying by the month for me to learn guitar."

"He was a wonderful man," Angie said gently, wondering what might have happened to Michael had this man not shown an interest in him.

"You have no idea how wonderful. By ninth grade, I was pretty good on guitar. I made the FFA band easily when I auditioned. Mr. Lovejoy kept right on encouraging me in shop class, and he was at every practice to hear me play. He invited me to church, and I began to go. Sometimes I'd go home with him and his wife on Sundays to spend the afternoon. It gave me a glimpse into what life could be. When my mom had told me to study so I could do something one day, I realized this was what she meant. People worked, played, paid bills, lived in nice houses, laughed, talked and loved together."

Angie couldn't imagine that anyone could actually have lived a life like this. It wasn't until he was in ninth grade that he had a taste of a normal lifestyle. "I'm glad Mr. Lovejoy knew how to live his faith out in a way that could touch the lives of others."

"Me too," he said sleepily.

"That was quite a story," she said as she sat up slowly so as not to jar the bed or his arm. "I loved hearing you play guitar before, but now I'll love it even more."

She leaned over and gently kissed his lips. He responded slowly. She knew the medicine and the exhaustion of the day had worn him out.

"Good night, Michael," she said softly as she took in his lazy smile. "Sweet dreams."

"Stay close?"

"Sure."

She snuggled nearer and carefully laid her arm across his chest. In no time he was out, but she stayed awake for a long while as she thought about all he had revealed to her that night. She hadn't anticipated how a simple request concerning his guitar playing would've ended up in a brief discourse about his miserable, dysfunctional upbringing.

Help me to heal him, Lord. How could a boy grow up like that and turn out to be so wonderful? I see now why he's withdrawn. Give me patience and wisdom to handle him with the care he needs to have his inner wounds healed as well.

TWENTY-EIGHT

Angie had Kartushah and Joshua bring in Michael's completed shelves. She shoved the books to the center of the room in preparation of organizing them at last. Smiling, she thought of how her family would be proud to know she was actually doing a little housekeeping. It had been nearly three weeks since Michael's accident, but he had almost had the shelves finished prior. He'd spent the last week staining them, promising her he would do nothing too strenuous to damage her handiwork on his arm. He was now walking around the fields and fences with Sojay to make sure all was being kept as it should.

She began with one pile of books and started sorting them by type and author. She would gather a sorted stack and take it to the shelves, trying to imagine how the room would look when everything was finally off the floor. It seemed an endless task until she finally came to the bottom of one pile. Lying on the floor was not a book, but a vinyl folder. She picked it up and read *University of Kansas* on the front.

This must be his diploma, she said as she opened it. Sure enough, but not a Bachelor's or a Master's; the diploma was a Ph.D. in Environmental Engineering. *Are you kidding me?* She stared in disbelief. She had known him for three months, and he had never mentioned this. He'd teased her often about the fact that she was a doctor, but he had never hinted at his own accomplishment. She took the diploma to the shelves, folded it back, and placed it for all to see. She knew it would mean nothing to the villagers, but it would be a reminder to him that he had fulfilled his mother's wishes by the highest degree possible.

When he returned after several hours, she had supper ready. He walked over to the shelves and nodded with approval at the order she had managed to create from his chaos. "Why didn't I think of this?"

"How was your afternoon, *Dr. Collins?*" she asked as he breathed in the aroma of fried chicken.

"Doctor? Have I been promoted?"

"You tell me," she said as she pointed toward the diploma. She smiled as he blushed for the first time in days.

"Where did you dig that up from?"

"From the bottom of the books. Why didn't you ever tell me you were a doctor?"

"You never asked." He gave his usual excuse for excluding information.

146

"Michael," she said in exasperation as she placed the chicken on the table, "I can't ask for information that I don't even know exists!"

"Would you like me to volunteer information to you on occasion?"

She just stared at him and sighed in frustration.

"I have some very interesting information for you, if you'd like," he said continuing the teasing.

"Do I have to beg you in order to hear it?"

"Maybe," he grinned. "It's big."

"How about you tell me your information or I throw the chicken in the river?"

He put his hands up in surrender. "I'll tell you! Save the chicken, please."

He leaned over to smell the food and announced, "I am thirty-six today."

"Today?" she asked wide-eyed.

"Today. October second."

"Your birthday's on the second too?"

"Ironic, isn't it?"

"Why didn't you tell me?"

"About both our birthdays being on seconds or about today being my birthday?"

"Either or both," she said with obvious annoyance. "I would've baked you a cake."

"I didn't think it would be fair. You didn't tell me yours, so I didn't know if I should tell you mine or not."

She rolled her eyes. "I was turning thirty. I didn't exactly want to proclaim my entrance into a new decade!"

"Well, I did tell *you*. I think I should get some credit for that."

"But you didn't tell me about the doctorate."

"So you've learned two big things about me in one day. Besides, it's my birthday. Don't chastise me. You have to be nice to me."

"Do I? Were you nice to me on my birthday?"

"Who knows? It came and went and I was never the wiser!"

"Well, happy birthday anyway. Let me see that arm."

He proudly produced the arm, now stitch free.

"Lovely scar you've got."

"I'm rather proud of it."

"I'm proud you survived the ordeal with nothing more than this scar," she said as she turned his arm in several directions. "How does it feel?"

"Nearly normal. It's still a little tender when I rub it or something, but other than that, it seems as good as new."

"Super. Go wash up for your cake-less birthday supper."

After supper, Angie insisted he go ahead and shower while she cleaned the kitchen alone. It was his birthday; he was released from kitchen duty. He stayed in longer than usual. She wondered if he'd decided to take a bath, but knew that wasn't the case as she heard the shower start.

She went out to the deck and sat in the swing. This had been a good Saturday, and she was proud of her accomplishment with the books. The mountain was beautiful and orange as the sun began to set, and the rushing river was a soothing serenade. She leaned her head next to the chain of the swing and closed her eyes as she thought of the tranquility this place offered her. It was truly her paradise. She didn't miss television one bit. She missed her family, but so many other things had filled her life that when she thought of them now, it was with a smile and not a frown. She had settled into Padawin, and this was now her home.

Michael's sliding of the screen door startled her. She glanced over to him quickly and was completely dumbfounded. He had shaved off his beard! She gazed at the face that had been hidden from her for months and smiled as she saw the blush appear on his newly exposed skin.

"What did you do, Dr. Collins?" she grinned in delight as she stood up to greet him.

"My hair is wild enough right now. The least I could do was get rid of the beard."

"You are so adorable," she said as she gently ran her hand across his clean face. "Did anyone ever tell you that you have the cutest little baby face?"

"Actually," he stammered, still self-conscious at the change and the attention, "I don't recall."

Angie traced the scar on his left cheek with her index finger. She assumed that if he had been willing to reveal it to her, he must be willing to let her notice it.

"That must have hurt. Nice job closing it up."

That was all she would say about it. She took his hand and led him to the swing. They sat and swung for a long while without saying anything. It was nice to be able to be together without all the tension that had plagued them for so many weeks. Things were far from perfect, but for her to just know a little bit about his past brought much understanding. If what he'd told her about his family was the tip of the iceberg, she almost dreaded knowing the iceberg. He'd given her enough to live on for a while.

"What can I do for your birthday?" she asked as she broke the silence.

"Stop asking me to get a flu shot."

"Can I ask you one more time and then promise to never do it again?"

"No, because if you ask, I'll say *no*. So why not just stop now."

"Okay, but if you get the flu, I'm not gonna tend to you. You'll be on your own with it, *Dr.* Collins. You'll bear the full brunt of your stubbornness."

"Agreed," he said with a sigh.

They relaxed quietly for a little while longer.

"Want to get out the guitars?" he asked her.

"Not tonight," she said as her eyes twinkled with just a spark of mischievousness as the sun began to fade.

"Okay. You look like you're up to something. What would you like to do?"

She sat up on one leg as she turned to him and began to stroke his clean face again. "I'm a little taken with this new man," she confessed. "This is really nice. You could've done this for me on my birthday."

"Then consider it a late birthday present."

"Considered," she said as she leaned in toward him and began to kiss his smooth cheek. She traced her lips across his scar and then gently kissed every spot where his beard had been.

He chuckled, "I should have shaved it off months ago."

"Agreed."

When she finally found his lips, she kissed him deeply. He placed his hands on her waist and within a few seconds she moved onto his lap.

"Happy birthday, Dr. Collins."

TWENTY-NINE

When Angie awoke the next morning, she smiled even before opening her eyes. Had last night been real? She peeked through one eye cautiously still fearing that it was all a wonderful dream; to wake up would be utterly disappointing. As she lay on her side, her face toward Michael, she focused first on his bare chest. It rose and fell with his deep breathing. She glanced up toward his face wishing she could study the scar on the other side and wondering what story it held. She began to look over his body to see if there were anymore unnoticed wounds. She had seldom seen him without a shirt; he even wore a t-shirt to bed.

He woke with a start as something he dreamed had caused him to jump. He took a moment to focus then smiled sleepily as he found Angie staring at him.

"Morning," he greeted as he reached over and took her hand.

"Good morning," she replied with a slightly shy smile. "Did you rest well?"

"I'm not sure yet," he said as he traced her hand with his fingers.

"Why not?"

"Well, I think I had this awesome dream, but then again, I wonder if it was ... well ..."

"Real?"

"Yeah," he sighed. "I wonder if it was perhaps ... real."

She lifted her bare arm above the cover and said, "I can't seem to find my jersey. Then as I thought about it, I realized, in *my* dream, that my jersey never made it to the bed."

He grinned and pulled her hand to his mouth. He gently kissed it and then held it to his heart. "I guess we either shared a dream, or it was indeed real."

"That leaves me in a slight dilemma either way."

"How's that?"

"One of us has to find my shirt, and it ain't gonna be me."

"I'm so tired this morning," he nearly groaned.

She giggled. "Did I wear you out?"

"I guess so. I feel like I've been hit with a ton of bricks."

"Are you ready for our Sunday?"

"Actually, no," he moaned as he rolled onto his back. "I would much rather just stay in bed all day."

"Well, if we're getting a chance to vote, I go with the bed too, however, in about forty-five minutes, an incredibly large group of people will be waiting for us at the new pavilion, and as much as they like me to help them with their illnesses, I doubt seriously they would enjoy hearing me butcher the Bible in the Padawin language."

"The ladies and children have never complained about your teaching."

"They're hungry for it," she said disappointed at the fact that she still bobbled communicating her points clearly.

"Trust me, Dr. Angie, no one has a problem with your Padawin."

"I'd love to lay here with you all day, Dr. Collins, but we really do have a service to conduct. Would you mind fetching me a shirt?"

He looked over at her and gazed up and down the sheet covering her body. "You didn't have a problem with the shirt last night," he grinned.

"Give me a break, will you?" she said with a self-conscious laugh. "The only light we had last night was the moon. For thirty years I've practiced intense modesty; it doesn't just end overnight."

*****

After services in Podakind, they loaded the Rover and began the journey to Baastu. The people greeted them with great excitement, dressed in their brightest colors. The children ran to embrace Dr. Angie as soon as the door was opened. Because of the struggles still between the men and women of this tribe, Michael suggested she begin to teach the women and children on Sundays after the singing as he kept the men with him. It had worked wonders. The women listened to her, the children loved her stories as well as her silly slip-ups with the language, and the men began to apply themselves to understanding and obeying the Word.

Michael's head was pounding as he got out of the vehicle, but he found himself smiling at the response the people gave to Angie. He whispered another *thank you* prayer as he wondered how he ever managed here without her. She had added so much to the ministry in Padawin that if she ever had to leave him, he doubted he could continue. Of course, it was about so much more than just the ministry now: he loved her. Last night had been the proof that all she had proclaimed to him about her feelings were true. It wasn't that he didn't trust her, or perhaps, maybe it was. He had hoped, and he had dreamed, but he could never bring himself to believe it, until now.

"Are you okay?" she asked him as they carried their guitars inside Kasteen's house.

"I have a hammering headache," he confessed, wishing he could drop the guitar, collapse to the ground, and sleep for several days.

"For how long?"

"A long time. Too long."

"Why didn't you say something?" she said as she rolled her eyes. "Take my guitar and I'll get you some Advil from my bag in the Rover."

*****

Michael wasn't hungry for lunch. He lay on the blanket while Angie munched and waded in the ocean. She would check on him occasionally but could tell that he probably needed to rest more than eat. She wondered indeed if last night had been too much for him. Maybe it had been too soon? What if he really wasn't feeling bad, but was feeling pressured? What if she had been too forward? That would be just like her: he shaves his beard to bear more of himself, and she practically seduces him. She closed her eyes in humiliation.

"Michael," she whispered gently as she woke him. "We need to get back to the village. I let you sleep for as long as I could, but time is winding down now."

"Yeah, thanks," he moaned as he sat up slowly. "I'm sorry about this, Angie. I never dreamed our first day after … you know … would leave me so … upside down."

She helped him to his feet. "It's okay. Why don't you let me drive back to the village?"

"No, I can do it. I need to do something to wake me up."

"That's not very reassuring."

*****

This Sunday Michael finally agreed to let her teach the children how to play baseball. He was glad she was in charge; he had no energy to think, much less play. He was now nauseous and would've accepted Mahlil's offer to nap in the hut except he wanted to watch Angie teach the children baseball.

"I have you all put into two groups," she started out. **"When we play, we have two places to play. Group one you are the infield."**

The children listened and watched as she demonstrated hitting the ball and then running the bases. She proceeded to explain how to get outs, and that three outs meant the other group came to the infield.

"Group two you are the outfield. You are trying to keep Group one from running around the bases."

The kids cheered at this. They loved competition. She continued to explain as many details of the game as possible. Then with great vigor, she proclaimed a loud *Play Ball*, and the game began. Because the children were so used to physical contact sports, it took a little coaching and coaxing to settle them down to simply play the game as it should be played. Michael laughed several times, despite his throbbing head, as she did her best to get them to play by American rules.

***

"How're you feeling?" she asked him while bringing the equipment to the Rover.

"On a scale of one to ten, about a negative five. My head hurts worse,

I think I'm gonna throw up at some point between here and there, and my whole body feels … yucky."

She gave him her most compassionate smile, but inside she was still wondering if he was making it all up. "Why don't you let me drive back. I know the road, just stay by the ocean."

"There's only one road."

"I know; that's my point. Let me drive. I'll clear off the back seat and you can lie down."

"Agreed."

As they rode back, she played the new Christmas CD of Annie and Stephen that she had received at yesterday's helicopter delivery; she hadn't even opened it yet. She was glad Michael was behind her so that he couldn't see the tears flowing down her face. As much as she loved Padawin, and now, as much as she had come to love Michael, she missed her family intensely. Hearing her sister sing was a reminder of how close they'd always been. For Annie, this had been her biggest dream: to become a music star. Now being married to Stephen, with a brand new baby boy, a joint album, and a tour coming up, she knew every dream Annie had ever expressed had come true.

She wished she could talk to her sister about all that was happening in her life. She was ministering to ladies in Padawin, and she was teaching children and teenagers to read. She was healing people of common diseases that had plagued them for years. She was functioning as an accepted member among the tribes, and Michael Collins had turned out to be the man of her dreams. Should she write Annie about last night? She had told her via e-mail weeks ago that she had fallen in love, but this next step wasn't something you just casually spilt out to someone.

She glanced back at Michael who seemed to be asleep on the seat. If he was able to actually sleep through this drive, then he indeed was sick. He didn't appear to be *faking* it, but she could never know. Once again she wished she hadn't been so forward last night, but something came over her out on the swing, and she found herself letting go of all inhibitions. He didn't appear to hold back either. It just seemed like the time was right. Now she was having doubts.

When they finally made it home, however, Angie's fears were put to rest. As she helped him out of the Rover, his face was flushed and his hand was hot. She immediately felt his forehead.

"Michael," she exclaimed. "You're burning up! Let's get you into the bed *now*."

He didn't resist, but followed obediently as she led him to their bed, removed his shoes and jeans, and tucked him in.

"Are you chilly?" she asked.

"A little."

"I'll get a blanket from the clinic ... and a thermometer."

When she returned, he was curled up into a ball and already asleep. She doubled the blanket and gently laid it over the sheet and comforter already covering him. She placed the thermometer just inside his ear and waited for the *beep*.

"One hundred three point nine!" she nearly cried out. She quickly got a glass of iced tea along with two more Advil and made him sit up in the bed long enough to take the medicine.

"I really want to sleep," he told her as he took the glass.

"I bet. Your biggest priority right now is to drink as many fluids as possible. You're gonna have to drink on and off for the next several hours. Get as much of this tea down as you can, then I'll let you rest for a while. But I'll get you up again in about 30 minutes for more."

"What's wrong with me? I don't ever recall being this sick in my entire life."

"Congratulations, Dr. Collins," she said as she pulled the covers up to his chin, "you've got the flu."

He glanced up at her and then rolled his eyes back into his head. "I've never gotten the flu before, not in the 10 years that I've been here. Are you sure it's not something else?"

"If I had money to bet with, I'd put it all on the flu. Just rest, for now, though. You've got several long, miserable days ahead of you."

THIRTY

As night began to fall, Angie continued to wake Michael every thirty minutes to force liquids down. He didn't protest. When a knock sounded on the door, she left his side to answer it. It was her assistant, Geechern.

"There are three very sick this afternoon," Geechern told her.

"Hot, sick to their stomachs with headaches?"

"Yes, exactly."

"The flu. Brother Mike's got it too. Should I tend to them, or can you handle it?"

"What must be done?"

"Advil tablets. You know how often to give them. And they have to drink lots of liquids a lot of times. They cannot be allowed to not drink."

Geechern looked over at Michael lying in bed and smiled as she said, *"He will be the first in line to receive his flu injection next season."*

"We'll see," Angie said with some doubt. *"He does not like the needle."*

"Who does? But those who have this flu this time will never want it again."

"I agree."

She continued to wake Michael to drink, and he always obliged. She took his temperature again; it had barely subsided to one hundred three point three. She gave him another dose of Advil and then changed into her jersey and boxers. She lay down next to him but didn't touch him. She knew his whole body had to be sensitive and aching. He rolled over to face her. The moon was bright again and high in the sky. He barely smiled.

"This wasn't how I'd wanted to spend this night," he said softly.

"Me either," she whispered as she reached up to move his hair from the sticky sweat on his forehead. "We'll get through this then there'll be many other nights for us."

"Yeah."

"Your fever's still very high. I'll wake you up throughout the night off and on to drink."

"I understand," he said as he took a deep breath and rolled onto his back again. "I feel as though every nerve in my body is on edge. I'm sleeping, but not sleeping at the same time."

"I can imagine."

He glanced over at her and asked, "Why are you taking care of me?"

"Because I'm your doctor," she grinned, "and your wife."

"You said you wouldn't tend to me if I got the flu."

"I lied."

"You don't have to do this. I brought it on myself; you warned me."

"I know, but it's just not my nature to let you lie around in misery."

"I'll be okay."

"Not for a while, you won't." She leaned over and gently kissed his cheek as she gave him her warmest smile. "I love you, Dr. Collins. Try to sleep. I'll wake you in a little while."

Sometime in the middle of the night, Michael woke up vomiting. Angie immediately ran for a plastic bowl in the kitchen cabinet. When he had finished, she wet a washcloth and cleaned up around his face first, then had him roll over in the bed so she could clean up the rest of the mess. Her jersey was splattered from the ordeal, but she didn't complain. Tears spilled from his eyes from the pressure of heaving, and his head was throbbing more than ever now.

"I need to get you to the couch so I can change the sheets," she told him as she gently helped him to sit.

"I'm sorry, Angie."

"I know. It's okay. I'm glad I can be here for you."

She removed the soiled sheets, replacing them with the only extra set they had, and then she changed from her jersey into an old t-shirt of Michael's. She got two more blankets from the clinic and spread them over the sheets, then helped him back to bed. She put the cleaned bowl down on the floor next to him.

"If you get sick again, here's the bowl. And please don't hesitate to wake me up if you feel bad. I can help. Okay?"

He merely nodded as he shivered from the fever and the weakness. This was going to be difficult now. As long as he could drink, the fluids and Advil could help. However, if he continued to vomit, he would get worse. If he couldn't keep anything down, she would have to give him an IV, probably along with many others who would be coming to the clinic.

He threw up twice more before morning, but he did wake her so she could help him with the bowl and avoid dirtying the sheets again. Each time she would take a wet cloth and wipe his face, then clean the bowl out to prepare for the next round. By morning, she was exhausted from lack of sleep, but when the first knock on the door came, she pulled herself from bed and braced for a long day. It would be like residency all over again, only this time she knew the reprieve would come as soon as the flu was over.

*****

Angie gave out much Advil and Tylenol the following morning. Very few had developed the vomiting as Michael had, but after a final count, it appeared that a total of sixteen were sick. She was pleased there were no more. Most of the villagers had taken the vaccine, so she didn't expect a high number, but as she visited the other fifteen, her mind stayed with

Michael back at the house. He needed an IV, but she didn't want to administer it until she could be with him the whole time.

"Geechern, I'm going back with Brother Mike. He will need an IV today," she said as they left the last hut of the fifteenth flu victim. *"Will you check on these throughout the day for me?"*

"I will. You get Brother Mike better with the IV. If any of these other foolish ones do not stop the vomiting, I will bring them to the clinic for you to needle them also."

Angie laughed at Geechern's assessment. She was a pleasure to work with. She was only nineteen but had aspirations to do more in her village than just marry and have children. Her father had arranged three marriages for her by the time she was sixteen, but she had refused. She had come to Angie shortly after she began the clinic and asked if she could work with her. Realizing right away that Geechern was exceptionally bright, she began to show her the basics of the clinic and then started teaching her to read and write. She learned fast and applied herself to perfecting each skill she was taught. Angie knew she could trust her to care for the other patients while she devoted herself to Michael.

When she walked back inside the house, she was relieved to see that he hadn't thrown up again since she had left him two hours prior. Of course, he hadn't drank anything either. She knelt down beside the bed and felt his forehead. He was still burning up.

"Michael," she said softly.

He rolled to his side and slowly opened his eyes.

"Do you think you can drink anything?" she asked.

"I'm afraid to. I'm so nauseous."

"I'm going to need to give you an IV."

He just closed his eyes and sighed.

"It'll only hurt slightly as it goes in. Once the medicine starts, you won't feel anything."

He nodded.

"I'll put some Phenergan in it also. It'll ease the nausea and help you to sleep."

"I won't fight it," he said, eyes still closed.

"Thank you," she said as she gently kissed his forehead. "I'll be right back."

She collected the equipment and walked in to find him dry heaving again into an empty bowl. She ran to him, threw the stuff on the bed, and held his head until he finished. When he lay back, she wet another washcloth and wiped his face.

"You'll be over this part soon—I hope. I'm setting up the IV now. You should sleep and rest well for the next few hours, and your body will be receiving plenty of fluids."

She hung the bag on an IV pole, attached the tubing and prepared his arm. "Michael, I'm about to stick you. It won't last long. Are you ready?"

He nodded, and she immediately began the process. His vein was large even though he had started to dehydrate. She was thankful. He flinched and moaned, but it didn't last long. She stuck the piping to the needle and started the fluid.

Once she had cleaned up the items used, she crawled into bed next to him and gently ran her fingers through his wiry, tangled hair. She cradled his head next to hers and gently kissed his forehead. "You'll be over some of it soon," she whispered.

"Thank you, Angie," he said as he nuzzled his head next to her. "Thank you."

*****

They both slept peacefully for two hours until a knock awoke her. She carefully left the bed so as not to disturb Michael, and answered the door. It was Geechern again.

"I am sorry, Dr. Angie," the young woman said as she held up a man she had seen earlier. *"He will need one of your IV's also. He was too stupid to take one needle for a little moment, and now he must bear one for a day."*

"Come on through this way," Angie said with a slight smile.

They went through the door that led from the house to the clinic and then helped the man into one of the rooms and up on the bed. She followed the same procedure as she had with Michael and got the fluids and Phenergan running through his system.

"How are the others?" Angie asked wondering if she would need to prepare more beds for administering IV's.

"They are very sick, but they are keeping down their fluids."

"Have any others developed the flu?"

"Not so far," Geechern sighed. *"How are you feeling?"*

"Tired," she confessed as she released a deep breath.

"From what you have said, it would seem that Brother Mike is sicker than all the rest."

"I'm getting that feeling too. I should have known he was sick yesterday morning and made him stay home. At that time he only complained about being tired. I just assumed it was ..." Angie stopped her explanation short.

"What were you thinking?"

"We had a long night," she blushed slightly. *"I just thought he was tired."*

"It must have been a very long night! Go be with your husband. I will watch this fool for you."

"Thank you, Geechern. You are a wonderful helper for me."

"This I know." Geechern chuckled and waved.

She grabbed another bag of fluids to take in for Michael. He was resting well, and some of his color had returned. She felt his forehead; it was slightly cooler. After taking his temperature she breathed a small sigh of relief. It was down to one hundred two point one. The worst was over, but the flu was far from gone.

She realized she hadn't eaten anything since last night. *Just like residency. No time to think or live, just react and move on.*

She made herself a sandwich of roasted pork and found some leftover potato salad. She was so tired that she had to make herself finish her food before dropping into bed next to Michael. When she did, he didn't stir. The Phenergan was working on both counts: no vomiting with restful sleeping. She curled up next to him and dozed off instantly.

*****

The beeping of the IV pump woke her this time. She was vaguely aware of the sound and what it meant: she needed to change the bag. She opened her eyes slowly, got her bearings, and edged her way off the bed hoping not to wake Michael. He continued to sleep peacefully. She changed the bags, injected another dose of Phenergan, and then went into the clinic to see how the other patient was doing.

Geechern was reading over the last lessons Angie had given her. She looked up and smiled confidently when she came into the room.

"My patient is sleeping and not vomiting. How about yours?" Geechern asked.

"Same with mine," she said while assessing the patient on the bed. She smiled at the thought that Geechern was considering this patient *hers*. What possibilities could this young woman's future have held had she not been born and raised in Podakind?

That's not the attitude to have about this, Angie, she told herself. *God placed her here for a reason. Her temperament, her drive, all these are here in Podakind for some purpose. Don't begrudge God in His decisions. She's here working with you. Maybe she'll become much more than a willing assistant in the years ahead. Train her and trust her.*

"Your patient looks well," Angie said wanting to encourage her. **"He does not seem as bad as Brother Mike."**

Deciding to make her mother's chicken noodle soup, she prepared a large pot so she could give some to all those sick with the flu. Hopefully Michael could stomach a few spoonfuls. She contacted Sojay and asked him to find some volunteers with containers to carry soup to the ill. It wasn't long before she was ladling out soup and sending it off to encourage the sickly. Michael slept through it all.

"Brother Mike will learn from this I hope?" Mosheed chuckled as she prepared to take her container of soup to someone.

"I hope so. He hates needles. To him, the pain is not bearable."

"And the pain of having babies is not bearable either, yet I have five!" Mosheed laughed. **"Let Brother Mike have all your babies! He will think your needles are nothing after that!"**

Angie smiled as Mosheed waved goodbye, but something fell in the pit of her stomach. Pregnancy. She hadn't even thought about that on Saturday night with Michael! How could she not? She was a doctor, for heaven's sake! She had counseled numerous women over the years about thinking clearly in the heat of passion, yet she hadn't thought one bit about the possibility of becoming pregnant herself. She knew her cycle and was fairly regular. It shouldn't be an issue at this time.

How could I do this? And I chastised Annie for not using birth control after her whirlwind marriage.

She glanced down to her stomach and gently rubbed her belly. This would be bad timing. Her attention was diverted as Michael began to stir on the bed.

"Hey, Sweetie," she said as she knelt beside the bed again and waited for him to open his eyes.

"Good morning," he said sleepily.

"Not morning. It's just about nightfall. How are you feeling?"

"I've got to go to the bathroom really bad."

"Good," she said as she stood to help him up.

"Good? You and your crazy bedside manner. I'm miserably about to pop."

"Yes, *good.* This means your body has absorbed and processed all the fluids I've been pumping into you."

She rolled the IV pole behind him to the bathroom and waited outside the door. After helping him back to the bed she took his temperature again. One hundred one point nine.

"You're still very sick, but not as sick as you have been. Do you feel like trying some chicken soup?"

"Really?" he asked with a weak smile. "You have chicken soup?"

"What's left of it. There are fifteen others in the village with the flu also. I sent some out to all of them earlier."

"You're not a doctor; you're an angel," he said admiringly.

"Well, that was a generous compliment. Does that mean you're willing to try some soup?"

"I would love to try some soup."

"Just a little." She knew his stomach would still be queasy.

After supper, Angie cleaned up the kitchen and then checked back with Geechern and her patient. He was doing well and had eaten the entire bowl of soup. They discussed his case together but she let Geechern make the decision to send him home. She then took a hot shower and dried as much of her long hair as she could handle before giving in to exhaustion. When she returned, Michael was making himself a glass of iced tea.

"I'll get that for you," she said at once as she came rushing to the refrigerator.

"It's okay. I think I can manage this much. Besides, you look wiped out. Why don't you lie down?"

"After you get into bed, I will."

"I see you got your jersey cleaned up. I'm sorry about last night."

"Michael," she said rolling her eyes, "you didn't throw up all over everything on purpose."

"No, but I chose not to take the flu shot on purpose."

She climbed onto the bed and patted his spot beside her. "Come on to bed, Dr. Collins. At least let me snuggle up next to you tonight."

He swallowed several large gulps of tea and turned out the light. Placing his glass on the floor next to him, he eased into bed. She wrapped her arm over his body and placed her head right next to his. He put his arm around her so she could lie on his chest, her hair still damp from the shower.

"Your wet hair feels soothing on my skin."

"Good. I love you, Dr. Collins," she whispered, totally deplete of energy.

"I adore you, Dr. Angie," he replied as he gently stroked her hair. "I'll make this up to you. I promise."

"You'd better."

THIRTY-ONE

Angie slept soundly that night, with no one waking her the next morning for any needs. When she opened her eyes she felt refreshed. Michael was still sleeping peacefully, so she gently felt his forehead for fever hoping not to disturb him. He was still very warm. She eased herself out of bed and found the thermometer. As she placed it in his ear, he awoke.

"Checking for mites?" he teased.

"Maybe. One hundred two point zero—not bad, but not good. How do you feel this morning?"

"Like I need desperately to brush my teeth."

"That's a good sign. Grooming was the least of your concerns yesterday."

"How does my hair look?"

"Ha! You don't want to know."

"That bad?" he groaned as he sat up in bed. He was dizzy and closed his eyes to steady his spinning."

"Wo, farm boy, you still need to take it easy. Compared to yesterday, how do you feel?"

"Much better than yesterday, but nowhere close to normal."

"I understand," she said as she offered her hand. "Let me help you to the bathroom. Brush your teeth, wash your face, and see if you can rid yourself of a few tangles. I'll make some buttered toast for breakfast."

"I can't believe this, but plain buttered toast sounds really good."

After breakfast and getting down two more Advil, Michael fell back asleep. Angie had wanted to listen to the Christmas CD again but had been so busy with the sick there had been no chance. She placed *Winter Passion* in the stereo and sat back on one of the couches as she read the liner notes from the cover. It was wonderful to hear Annie's full, passionate voice singing out her favorite Christmas songs even though it was the beginning of October. Christmas was a hugely celebrated holiday at the Wright home, and this would be her first year to miss it. She wondered if she and Michael would find a tree to decorate here in Padawin.

"What are you listening to?" Michael asked several songs later as he came to join her on the couch.

"What are *you* doing up?"

"I am so tired of lying around," he moaned as he plopped down beside her.

"That's good," she smiled then quickly added remembering his criticisms of her bedside manner, "because it means you're not as sick as you have been."

"You got that right. Now, what on earth are you listening to? What an awesome voice."

"That's Annie," she said proudly as she handed the CD cover to Michael. "It came in last week's helicopter delivery. See, here she is with Stephen. I played it in the Rover on the way back from the Baastu, but you were completely zonked."

"So that's why I was dreaming of Christmas. She is one beautiful girl," he said as he stared at the cover. "Mr. Williams did almost as well as I did. I do think I got the better of the two sisters, however."

"You *are* feeling better. Wait! Here is the song they wrote together on the tour last year. You won't believe this song! *Winter Passion*. They wrote it even before they fell in love."

She grabbed back the CD cover and he lay against the couch to give the song his full attention. As he sat and listened, he believed it to be the most amazing voice he had ever heard. As much as he hated to admit it, Annie's voice was in a whole other league from Angie's, just as she had tried to explain. He loved to hear Angie's sweet melodies, and she was a wonderful singer, but this was beyond description. When Stephen joined in, it made a very impressive duo. However, as the music went on, he simply became impressed with the song itself. *Passion* was definitely the word to describe it.

"I never thought I would hear a *hot* Christmas song," he whispered.

"That's nothing; wait for the bridge."

As the song played on, he then became fascinated by the piano playing. "That Stephen Williams is some pianist."

"That's not Stephen; that's Annie!"

"No way. That has to be Stephen Williams!"

"Trust me, I've personally watched her play this. That is my sister doing the arpeggios."

When the song finished, he just stared at the stereo in disbelief. "That will definitely become my favorite Christmas song. I'm sure glad I heard that *after* I was married. Does your pastor/father approve of your sister singing something so ... uh ... provocative?"

"She's married too, you know?"

"Yeah, but not when she wrote that."

"True, but you should hear the song she wrote shortly after she met Stephen. It was called *Unlit Passion*. *That* song was the definition of provocative. She'd never admit to me that it was about her feelings for him until after they married. She just didn't trust him."

"Really? Why not?"

"Annie's not a trusting person at all. She's honest and opinionated like I am, but nowhere near as trusting."

Michael took the CD and looked at the picture of Annie. She and Angie shared the same long, dark hair, and the same incredible lips, but their eyes were definitely different. Angie's were light and happy with always a hint of a smile forming inside them, whereas Annie's were dark and carried a sense of brooding melancholy.

"You really are a trusting person," Michael admitted. "Do you just trust everybody?"

"Sort of. My idea is that you trust everyone until they prove themselves untrustworthy."

"That's a switch. I don't believe I've ever known anyone with that philosophy. I've sort of always felt that you shouldn't trust anyone until they've proven themselves trustworthy."

"With that attitude, I'm guessing you've trusted very few people in your life."

He didn't have to think long to agree. In fact, the people he had trusted his entire life could be counted on one hand. "What happens when people disappoint you, prove themselves to be untrustworthy?"

"I feel sorry for them mostly."

"You're kidding? You feel sorry for them even though they betrayed you?"

"Why not? In order to deliberately hurt someone, it means that something has to dwell inside of you that is dead and ugly. That should be pitied."

"You're an incredible person. I find it nearly impossible to just take someone at face value and trust them with … well … whatever. I just can't do it."

"Why?"

"Why doesn't your sister trust people?" he asked as he tried to avert the attention from himself.

"Because my sister is a genius and people have always envied that or been intimidated by it. Their way of dealing with her was to belittle and humiliate her in order to elevate themselves. Of course, she never helped by being such a smart-alecky-know-it-all. What about you? Why don't you trust people?"

He didn't want to get started on this conversation. He had thought earlier in the week that maybe he was ready to tell her everything, but as the moment presented itself, he felt uncomfortable and claustrophobic. He sat silently. He couldn't open his mouth.

"Do you trust *me*, Dr. Collins?" she asked as she looked him in the eye.

"More than anyone," he said, wishing he could tell her more.

"Then that's all that matters," she said cheerfully as she gave him a quick kiss and hopped up from the couch to take the finished CD from the stereo.

Michael stared at her in unbelief. How could she be so understanding all the time? She was drastically different from Jenna. Jenna had pressed and prodded constantly. She had made him feel guilty anytime he was silent. She had constantly pushed him to communicate about any and everything. If he liked a meal at the cafeteria, he had to say so. If he didn't, he had to complain. If he liked her outfit, he had to comment. If he didn't, he should tell her so she could dress better for him next time. She was always pushing him to discuss his past, his present and his future. She said a relationship was built on communication, so she intimidated him to communicate every moment they were together. If he ever was silent while around her, she accused him of closing himself off. No matter how much she prodded, however, he could never bring himself to tell her about his past. Even when she used the ultimate tool, her body, he still couldn't tell her. His willingness to marry her had come more out of guilt than of love. After sleeping with her several times at her parents' house on weekends away from school, he was convinced that God would never use him if he didn't marry her.

Now here he was with Angie, a gift from God, who had chosen to love him without knowing much of anything. As talkative and fun loving as she was, she never made him feel self-conscious in the silences. In fact, the thing that had endeared her to him the most was how they could sit on the back deck or in the house together, yet never utter a word. They might be reading or listening to the sounds from the jungle, the river or the ocean, and never say anything. If their eyes happened to meet, she would always smile warmly, but never felt the need to break the mood they were in. She knew his past was harsh, but she didn't pry. She had seen the scar on his cheek, made obvious note of it, but never asked him point blank what had happened.

Then there was Saturday night. She had started out flirting with him on the swing then before either of them knew what was happening, the evening had become more and more passionate. He didn't mean for things to go as far as they did, but she intoxicated him. He could never get enough of her, and when she didn't protest, all he wanted was to be with her.

He glanced behind the couch and saw that she was busying herself in the kitchen. He knew she had to be disappointed. All she had asked him was why he didn't trust people. He could have at least given her some kind of reply. Instead, he clammed up, bottled up and closed up, and her generous response was to kiss him and make him lunch. This guilt was much different from the guilt Jenna had put him through. Jenna made him feel guilty for being who he was. Angie made him feel guilty because he *should* be a better man.

He got up from the couch and walked into the kitchen where she was preparing grilled cheese sandwiches and tomato soup. Coming up behind her he put his arms on her waist startling her. She jumped and squealed then giggled as she turned around to face him.

"Wo there, farm boy," she grinned.

How could he explain all that he felt for her? Simple: he would open his mouth and just say whatever he thought. That's how she did it. She didn't manipulate nor did she bait him. She simply gave him everything she possibly could without demanding anything in return.

"I wish I felt one hundred percent, or even ninety or eighty," he told her honestly.

"Me too," she said as she put her arms up around his neck.

"You've become my life. I never lived until I met you. Did you know that?"

"No," she whispered as her expression changed from teasing to serious.

"When we finish lunch, I'll share my life with you. I'll lay it all on the line."

"You don't have to," she said with her typical compassion.

"Yes, I do. I owe everything I've become to you. It's time for you to know all that I am and all that I've come from."

"Michael, Sweetie, when you're ready, I'll be here."

"Angie, I'll never be ready to tell this," he said sincerely, "but I'm ready for you. I never thought I'd have someone in my life that I treasured as much as I do you. You're my life, my soul, my very breath. I know it hurts you that I hold back, but you never show it. You're too good to me. I'm not testing you. I just ... I just ... I've never talked of it."

"What about with Jenna?"

"No!" he reacted quickly. "I never told her anything. Nothing."

She smoothed his hair and touched her head to his. Giving him that smile again, she gently kissed his cheek, his scar.

"Michael, I can't give any more of myself to you than I already have," she said softly. "I love you with all my heart. I'm committed to living the rest of my life with you. I'd be lying to say I'm not curious, but it's not because I'm simply dying to know. I want to know *you*; I want to know what makes you who you are. I want to know why you left everything behind to come out here and give your life to these people. I mean, Michael, you haven't returned to the mainland once. What makes a man do that? You've treated me with such respect and kindness, giving me the freedom to live with you and change your home, shoot, change your life. You've made me fall in love with you so much that I ache for you when I'm not with you. I don't want to pry inside your life; I just want to know your life because that helps me know you better—more completely."

"I know," was all he could answer.

As sick as he still felt, just being with her like this ran warmth through his whole body. All he could think of at that moment was being with her again. He kissed her hesitantly, not wanting to stir anything deeper inside, but to let her know how he felt. She didn't respond with hesitancy, however, but eagerly and passionately. As she pressed her body tightly into his, he began to feel himself losing control, just like on the swing.

"No," he said as he slowly moved her away. "Like I said, I'm not one hundred percent yet."

"I'm sorry," she said as she turned away in humiliation. "I don't mean to push you, Michael."

"Wait. Don't ever think I don't want this. I still feel like warmed over mashed potatoes from this stupid flu ... plus ... I need to tell you everything about me first. Let's eat then let me get it out. Afterward," he chuckled, "you'll probably have to let me sleep again before I'm up to anything."

She smiled and nodded, then ran her hand down his face before turning back to finish the sandwiches.

THIRTY-TWO

When lunch was over, Michael went to the bed and laid down. His head was hurting again, and his body was still weak. He had tried too much too soon, but when he had joined her on the couch it was simply because he wanted to be near her. As she finished washing out the lunch plates and glasses, he gazed at her in amazement again. Would he ever get used to having her around? She swore to him that she would be with him for the rest of her life. Could she really make that promise, knowing him so little?

When she finished the kitchen, she poured him another glass of iced tea and brought him two more Advil.

"Take these and rest for a while," she said smiling. "I'm going to check on the other patients for a bit and see if everyone is fairing as well as you."

"Please, don't go." He took her hand. "I know you're trying to be polite and give me a way out of this. I don't want any more excuses—please stay."

She smiled again. She always smiled. She climbed over him and laid down so she could rest her head on her hand as she watched him.

"I told you about Mr. Lovejoy," he began, "and how he took an interest in me and got me the guitar and all."

She nodded.

"Well, I started going to church with him. There were three kids there who really walked with God, and their hearts broke for me. They took me right in. They sat with me in Sunday School and church, they invited me to their homes after church to spend Sunday afternoons—they basically became my friends. Mr. Lovejoy continued to encourage me in every way possible. He had his own little ranch, kind of appropriate for an Ag teacher, and he gave me a piglet and a calf to raise on my own to enter in the fair. The FFA string band was doing wonders, and I was at the top of my class in every subject. During my freshmen and sophomore years, my mom got off work for both awards ceremonies to watch me take top honors. I suddenly had hope.

"The only problem, though, was that the more I got involved at school and in church and with string band, the less I was home. Mama swore it was wonderful and that she was proud that I had these great opportunities, but I spent very little time with her anymore. I dreaded going home.

"On my sixteenth birthday, Mama had asked that I come home after school because she had something special planned. I had band practice, and told her I'd be home some time after four-thirty. When I walked in, the house smelled wonderful. All we ever ate was hamburger something. We couldn't afford anything else. But that night she had cooked sausages with mashed potatoes and a tossed salad. I came in and she wished me a happy birthday and sat me down to dinner right away. She talked so much that night. She obviously thought Dad was gone for the evening. It was wonderful.

"She told me how proud she was of me that I'd worked so hard to do something with my life. She begged me to never give up, but to go after my dreams. Then she handed me a little gift box. She explained that she had saved money for months to be able to give me the dinner and a gift for my sixteenth birthday. She wanted it to be special.

"I opened it and was amazed." Tears began to form in his eyes and he reached up to keep them from falling. "She had gotten me a golden chain with a little gold guitar charm hanging from it. I couldn't believe it."

He choked up for a moment. Angie said nothing but gently rubbed his arm and waited.

"I hugged her and thanked her so much. Then I asked her why she stayed with Dad. Why wouldn't she move on? We could pick up and go anywhere we wanted. We didn't have to stay. She just told me that there were some things she loved too much to risk losing by leaving. I had no idea what she meant.

"As the clock neared six-thirty, I knew she would have to be at work at seven, so I just enjoyed lingering in the conversation. It was rare that she and I got to talk like normal people. Dad despised anything she ever did for me. Suddenly the door burst open, and he came barreling in. He was drunk, and he was mad. He started yelling at her about why she had bribed him. Apparently she had saved enough money to give him something to go out and get drunk on. She'd never offered him money before, so in the midst of drinking, it occurred to him that she was up to something.

"He started ranting about the food and threw our dishes, smashing them against the wall. He took her by the hair and wanted to know what the celebration was about. She said 'It's our boy's sixteenth birthday. I just wanted to give him a special night.' He then starts yelling about where all his special nights went when I came along. That's when he saw the necklace. I had put it on and was proudly wearing it for Mama. He reached up and ripped it off. He then started cursing at her. He knew she'd gotten it for me.

"I'd had enough. He was so drunk and angry that he was gonna hurt someone if he wasn't stopped. I told him to leave her alone and get out of the house. I said he could come back when he sobered up. He laughed like I was the biggest fool in the world. Mama began to plead with me to leave him alone. She said not to push him.

"He let go of her hair and grabbed mine and dragged me to my bedroom. He threw me against the wall and took my guitar out of the case. He said he'd show me what happened to little boys who didn't honor their dads. He slammed the guitar against the wall over and over and over again. I just watched in silent horror. I couldn't believe this was happening."

Angie's hand went up to her mouth then she reached over and gently squeezed his.

"Mama couldn't stand it. She came running in yelling for him to stop and to leave me alone. She said he could do whatever he wanted with her just not to hurt me. He walked out of the room. We both thought he was leaving. We sighed with relief for a moment, until he came back in with a pistol."

"Michael," Angie gasped, but she said nothing more.

"He pointed the gun at my head and said I had ruined their lives. He said if I hated my life, it was my own fault."

"You were a child, for heaven's sake!" she exclaimed. "How could it be your fault?"

"He was crazy and drunk," Michael spat out. "He then said he would do anything to get rid of me. Mom started screaming, 'You promised you wouldn't hurt him! You promised me!' He said, 'That's right, and I certainly don't want to be a promise breaker.' So he turned the pistol toward her. I screamed and jumped on his back. He threw me against the wall and picked up the neck of my broken guitar. He came at me swinging it like crazy and gashed my cheek here."

Michael pointed to the scar across the left side of his face. Angie nodded in understanding as tears streamed down her face.

"He then went over to my mom and grabbed her by the hair again. She was so small and petite, only 5'1". He just held her there, laughing at me and telling her what a wimp I was. He then put the gun to her head and asked me what I was gonna do next. I just froze. The look on Mom's face told me to not push him, so I just sat there against the wall. I just sat there." Tears began to fall as he repeated again, "I just sat there."

"Michael," Angie said through wide, red eyes as she moved up on the bed and scooted over next to him. "He didn't ..."

"He pulled the trigger," Michael said with control. "She went limp immediately."

"No!"

"He then turned the gun on me. I knew I was dead. I knew there was no hope. I was already about to faint from the blood that was pouring from the gash in my cheek. I knew if I tried to get up or even move, he would nail me—so I continued to sit there.

"He told me he'd promised Mama he wouldn't harm me as long as she stayed with him and supported him, no questions. But if she ever left, he would hunt us down and kill me right in front of her eyes."

"I don't believe this," she said in anger. "There are agencies that could have protected you both!"

"You didn't know my father," he said shaking his head. "See, he wanted to ruin my life from the beginning. He never wanted a child. He told me he had forced her to have three abortions before I was born. She had pleaded to keep me. He agreed, but with huge reluctance. So, he told me I'd have to live forever with the guilt of her death. Had I not been born, everything would've been fine."

"You know that's not your fault, Michael," she assured him.

"At thirty-six? Yes. At sixteen with my mother lying on the floor having half her brain splattered on the wall behind her? No."

He closed his eyes and wiped the tears as he tried to find the strength to finish his story.

"You don't have to go on," she told him.

"See, I do. That's only half," Michael said shaking his head now. "He told me that I needed to live with the guilt of all of it, and he didn't want to kill me because all that would do would be to put me out of my misery. He wanted me to be miserable for the rest of my life. So he put the gun to his head and … bang."

Angie actually cried out this time. She sobbed as she fell over Michael's chest and grieved for him.

"I crawled over to my mother and put her head in my lap," he said as he now began to cry. "I didn't know what to do. I just sat there holding her bleeding head and crying.

"A neighbor had heard the gun shots and called the police. Her name was Miss Annabelle. She came running into the house and found me there with my mother. She knew I was close to Mr. Lovejoy, so she ran back and called him too. Mr. Lovejoy and Officer Roberts got there first. They kept asking me what happened. I couldn't speak. I couldn't say a word. Mr. Lovejoy explained that it was vitally important I make a statement or they would have to investigate me."

Angie leaned up again so she could see his face.

"I told them, 'I'm sixteen today. My mom gave me a party. My dad was mad. He killed her, then killed himself.' That was enough. Mr. Lovejoy took me to the hospital then he took me to his home where he and his wife helped get me cleaned up.

"At my mother's funeral, I put the necklace in her coffin. It was the dearest thing I had, so I wanted it to be with her forever. Mr. Lovejoy offered his home if I wanted. I had nowhere else to go, so I agreed. The following month I accepted Christ. It didn't ease the hurt, and it took years to ease the guilt of all my father had put on me, but I went on. There was a small consolation at the fact that my mother's misery was indeed over, and that I no longer had to go home to that house and that situation anymore—

but life was ... hard. Very hard.

"During my senior year, I decided to give my life to missions. I was good at agriculture and designing and building stuff. I decided I'd go somewhere far away and give my life to helping others find a good life as well as life in Christ, just like Mr. Lovejoy did for me."

Angie formed a weak smile through quivering lips as she picked up his hand and cradled it in her chest.

"But there's more."

"How?"

"When Jenna started giving me attention, I was floored," he went on to the next stage of his life. "I was at this small Christian college preparing for the ministry, and she was this gorgeous preacher's daughter with stars in her eyes of marrying a great minister. When she found out how committed I was to the ministry, she latched on to me and began to try and mold me into the man she wanted. She did everything she could to change my heart, but I kept insisting I was going to the mission field.

"During the fall semester of our senior year, we went to her parents' house for a weekend. They were out for the afternoon. They trusted us explicitly."

"She seduced you," Angie said as she closed her eyes. "Just like I did."

"No!" he said quickly, sitting up in the bed for the first time. "You did not! You are my wife! You've done nothing but love and care for me in the deepest ways since I first met you. She did nothing but try and manipulate me from the very beginning. She sensed I was weak. She thought she could change me, but she didn't know from where my convictions radiated. She couldn't understand that I was committed to something more than just an ideal."

"Why didn't you tell her about your past?"

"I couldn't!" he exclaimed. "As much as I wanted to trust her, I never could. And then after that first weekend together at her house, she began to pressure me about making a big mistake, and that it would be wrong for either of us to ever marry anyone else."

"She seduced you and she tricked you," Angie said disgusted.

"Yes. When she finally realized I wasn't budging on my plans after I told her I was going to Kansas for my graduate degree, she dropped me flat. She told me good luck on ever finding anyone who would want me."

"I want you, Michael," Angie said sincerely as she looked hard into his eyes.

He smiled through his tears, his hurt and his anger. He reached up and cradled her face with his hand. She kissed it as a few more tears ran down her cheeks.

"I wish, more than anything in my life, even more than I wished my mother had lived, that you had been my ... well ... my first. Jenna was this horrible mistake."

"Michael, don't wish anything about me. I'm just thankful that you made it here in one piece with your head and life intact. How did you get through all that? Your mother? Jenna? How can you be sane right now? I don't think I could've handled it."

Michael pulled her down next him and held her tightly in his arms. "There were a lot of factors. The biggest, I guess, was choosing to never go back again. My life has been one of running from something horrible toward something good. I worked like a dog in school because my mother told me it was the only thing to guarantee a good life. I went as far as I could go with the doctorate so that I'd know everything I needed to know to live well myself and to educate the tribes when I left the States. Coming to Padawin wasn't only about ministering to them; it was about starting over and leaving everything behind."

"I can understand that now," she said softly, starting to gain some control.

He rolled over and turned toward her, his eyes puffy both from crying and from sickness. He had allowed her to see inside his soul. They stared at each other as she smiled and gently traced his scar with the tip of her finger.

"I'm so happy to have you here with me, to have you in my life," he told her. "I don't know if I can ever tell you what you've meant to me. As for Saturday night ..."

Angie rolled her eyes and blushed as she interrupted him saying, "I shouldn't have pushed you there."

"Did it appear that you were pushing me?"

"At the time, no, but I really didn't mean for that to happen."

"Are you sorry it happened?"

"No," she confessed. "Not at all. What about you?"

"My only regret," he said soberly as he continued to gaze at her, "is that I hadn't told you all this before. I never dreamed you would ... want me ... in any way ... especially in *that* way as long as there was all this unsettled stuff between us. I also felt like you should know, well ... that you weren't the first. I hate that more than anything, Angie."

She simply sighed and smiled, then leaned over to softly kiss him. "Michael, the only thing I care about with us is that there are no walls any longer. I was so afraid that you would never let me love you fully because you would never fully reveal yourself to me. But now ... how could I hold anything against you."

He kissed her back then pulled her closer. "When I get over this stupid flu, life will be unbelievable for us," he sighed. "All I ever want is to be with you. Who knows, we might even raise a family someday. I don't know, Angie, you've changed everything about me. I stopped dreaming when I was sixteen ... even with Jenna. But you—you brought me back to life."

Angie snickered a bit and pulled back to look at him again. "You'd really like a family?"

"Only if you would," he said right away. "I'd never force anything like that on you if you weren't ready."

"You do realize that on Saturday night we didn't even think about the possibility of a family?"

He stared at her confused for a moment, then the reality of what she said sunk in. "You could be pregnant?" he asked wide eyed.

"I doubt it. But we weren't thinking. It *could* happen."

"Would you be okay with it?"

"I suppose. I'm not against it. If we have a choice, I'd prefer us to be settled here and figure out our own life first. I want to know you, live with you, and love you all to myself for a little while at least."

"I'm still … I don't know … amazed by all of this. I never told you this, but as long as we're confessing things …"

He paused and she gave him a questioning look.

He blushed slightly. "When I first saw you at the airport in Hawaii, I had no idea you were *the* Dr. Angie. I actually thought you were this model, and I was … uh … feeling these things about you and feeling really guilty because I knew my future wife was somewhere behind you."

She laughed.

"By the end of that first week, I was so dazzled by you I didn't know where my head was, but more so my heart. It was like a dream. Yet … here you are."

"And here I'll stay."

THIRTY-THREE

When Angie awoke Wednesday morning, she had already determined she and Michael would not be traveling to the Gandushi or the Bentahu. Michael's fever was still lingering around one hundred two, and she didn't want him up and about yet. As it was still early, she slipped on her bathing suit before breakfast and walked down to the ocean for a morning swim.

The water was just cool enough to be refreshing, but warm enough to not be uncomfortable. She loved the ocean and its vastness and how it reminded her of the hugeness of God who simply spoke it all into existence. Since coming to Padawin, she often felt like there was too much to be done and that she could never accomplish it all. The ocean would remind her that God never intended for her to do it all. Her job was to obey Him moment-by-moment, day-by-day, and then He would lead her to do what He had set out for her.

Just as a ship can't be over the entire ocean at one time, neither can I do everything that needs to be done all at once. Father, teach me to trust your timing in my life. I would've never believed that Michael would share with me what he did yesterday so soon. Although, and I confess this to You because You knew my heart anyway, I was getting rather exasperated with him for never offering anything. Thank You for helping me bide my time, keep my mouth shut, and love him anyway. God, help me to be what he needs to complete his life. I feel so inadequate to be the one that binds up his heart, but I know You'll give me the wisdom and strength required. After all, You're the one who brought us together.

She continued to pray as she swam and let the joy of being here and belonging here envelop her. Padawin had become her home nation and Podakind her village. She loved the people, the work she did, singing and playing with Michael, reading, teaching, and mentoring the ladies in the four tribes. She loved the climate, always warm and humid, but just enough breeze to make it wonderful. She loved the ocean, the banana trees, and the river that rushed by her house and provided electricity. She loved the deck where she and Michael spent many evenings laughing and singing together, and she even loved volcanic Mount Podakind that stood majestically behind their house. She understood how this place had captured Michael's heart, and how easy it was to never want to leave.

*****

"Good morning," Angie said in her typical cheery fashion as Michael began to stir. She had already showered, washed and dried her hair,

175

and was now making sugar toast.

"What have you been up to today?" he asked as he slowly rose from the bed.

"I went for a swim in the ocean. How are you feeling?"

"A little better."

"You still have a fever," she told him as she placed the plate of toast on the table. "Come have some breakfast and I'll get you a couple more Advil."

He was thankful that she hadn't kept her promise to ignore him if he developed the flu. He had never been this sick in his life. He took a bite of the toast and relished the initial crunch followed by the melting of the sugar and butter together from the warmth of his mouth. He had never heard of such a thing until she came, and he was thankful right now that this was what he was eating rather than some fruit or leftovers. The very thought of it turned his stomach.

"What are your plans today?" he wondered as he watched her hurriedly eat breakfast and drink down her coffee.

"People are lined up around the clinic. I guess they assumed we're not heading to the other two tribes because you're so sick."

"Well, while you heal the world, I think I'll listen to that Christmas CD again. I still can't believe that was your sister's voice I heard yesterday."

"She's awesome, isn't she? If you need anything, I should be right here in the clinic. Make sure you get plenty to drink today, okay?"

"Okay."

He sat in quiet contentment as he finished his breakfast and listened to the music. Life had never seemed so heavenly to him, even in Padawin. He had believed this was his paradise, but when Angie moved in, it somehow improved one more notch.

He walked by the stereo and picked up the CD case on his way to the couch. Annie was almost as beautiful as Angie. It made him wonder what the oldest sister looked like. Angie kept a photo of her parents on the kitchen counter, but he had never seen any of the other family until the CD.

He lay back on the couch and opened up the cover to read the liner notes. Annie had written something special to Angie.

Special thanks to Angie, my soul sister, who always made me believe I was better than the rest. I miss you.

Michael ran his fingers over the simple, yet deeply meaningful message. He wondered what it would have been like to grow up with a *real* family. How would it have felt to have a father play catch with him, to encourage his guitar playing, and to have gone to work? What would family vacations have been like? What kind of woman would his mother have been had she been able to relax and be a wife and mother? What would it have been like to have had brothers and sisters to have played with through the years?

Michael thought about all the things Angie had said about her father. He was a kind man, but a strong man. He was wise but always careful to let his children make their own decisions and even their own mistakes. He had been, and still was, actively involved in their lives. As a man of God, not just a minister, he had always been careful to take any simple occurrence in life and turn it into an opportunity to teach about how amazing God was. Michael could imagine the man in the photograph on the kitchen counter putting his arms around his children and telling them they could conquer the world if they wanted. A part of Michael wished he could have had the opportunity to know Jonathan Wright, to have had him touch his life in some way, yet another part feared him—felt intimidated by him. Would Jonathan have thought Michael a suitable man to wed his daughter? Angie, beautiful beyond compare, intelligent, cheerful, as perfect as anyone could be, married to a brooding hermit who had the most dysfunctional childhood imaginable. What did he have to offer her? She had offered him the world.

*****

Chet Clarence walked into his house in Taveren to find Vicki sitting on the couch watching the television with furrowed brow. He pulled off his coat, loosened his tie, and joined her, taking her hand as he tried to interpret the events unfolding on the screen.

"Anything concrete?" he asked her.

"Not yet," she said concerned. "No one seems to know what's going on exactly. Have you contacted the mission board?"

"Yes. They're on standby."

"What about Michael and Angie?"

"I haven't tried to contact them yet. I wanted to wait until we knew for sure what was going on." Suddenly panic overwhelmed him. "Oh man! This is Wednesday; they're off at the other two tribes today!"

*****

Angie talked and laughed with her many patients who came through the clinic that morning. They had learned to trust and appreciate her as more than just a healer, but as a friend and as one who could teach them the truth alongside Michael. They didn't hesitate to correct her Padawin language anymore, but only after laughing at her mistakes first.

Geechern had become a big help. She was a fast learner and avidly asked questions to help further her knowledge. Angie even talked her through putting in an IV for another flu patient that morning. She explained the constant importance of maintaining a germ free environment, of always washing her hands, and how the sterilizing machine worked to thoroughly decontaminate all the instruments. Angie would ask Geechern to diagnose some of the simpler illnesses and suggest the proper treatment.

She hit each one on the nose.

After a light lunch, Angie took some time to teach school since they had missed it the past two days. She was pleased when Joshua and Sojay showed up again. They were hungry to read the Word for themselves and be able to teach and understand truth like she and Michael. Between Michael, Chet and Vicki, the entire New Testament, except for Revelation, had been translated into Padawin, along with Genesis, Psalms and Proverbs. Presently, Michael was working on Exodus, Chet on Deuteronomy, Vicki on Joshua and Angie had started Judges. They hoped to have the entire Bible translated within the next three years.

When she had finished the brief session with school early that afternoon, she looked in on Michael. He was asleep. Rather than disturb him, she took her Bible and walked down to the ocean again to read and pray. Her heart felt heavy for some reason. She sat in the sand beneath a palm tree and began to pour out her thoughts to the Lord. She prayed for Sojay to continue in his boldness with the faith and that he would persist in sharing the true God with all he knew. She prayed for Joshua who had embraced his walk with Christ with the same tenacity he had once had as a witch doctor. She prayed that his desire to teach the Word and guide others would come to fruition. She prayed for Mosheed and Seendoo that they would continue to be examples of Godly women who had found freedom in relationships with Christ. She prayed for Kartushah, who as a young man formerly filled with pride and arrogance, had now released his mother and wife from tribal traditions that had enslaved women for many years. She asked God to give him the strength to be an example to others who could not imagine relinquishing such control. And she prayed for Geechern, that God would grant her a supernatural understanding of medicine so she could begin to carry out certain duties in the clinic without having to be under Angie's watchful eye.

After spending much time on the beach, she began to grow hungry again. She should have eaten a real lunch. She brushed off the sand and headed back for the house. Michael was awake and reading.

"Where have you been?" he asked as she walked in the door.

"Back at the beach."

"Spending a lot of time down there today, aren't you?"

"Yeah, it's like I just can't get enough of it. I wonder how I ever lived without it all these years."

"You belong here, you know?"

"Yes, I do," she said with a smile as she opened the refrigerator. "How about some eggs and biscuits? I'm starving. My lunch was pitiful."

"That actually sounds good, but it's only three thirty. Will it ruin our supper?"

"Who cares? We live in Paradise! We can do whatever we want.

Have you poured down the liquids today?"

"Yes, Dr. Angie."

"Very good, Dr. Collins."

*****

"This is it," Vicki said mournfully as she jumped up from the couch. "You give Fred Carson the final call and I'll get in touch with the helicopter pilot to get Michael and Angie. Six hours isn't very long. You'd better try to touch base with Michael next. Hopefully they'll be back from the other tribes by now."

"I'm on it," he said as he immediately punched Fred Carson's name on his phone.

THIRTY-FOUR

Mid-way through dinner, a banging knock made them both jump.

"What on earth?" Michael yelped from the startle. He cupped his hands to his mouth and yelled, **"Come in! It's open!"**

It was Kita, Sojay's eleven-year old son.

"What is it?" Angie asked immediately realizing he was in distress.

"Seendoo's baby won't come!"

"It's not time!" Angie panicked.

"Tell that to the baby! You must come soon! I can't hear that crying out any more!"

Angie jumped up and ran to the clinic for her bag. She stuck her head back inside the house before she left and said, "Don't clean up the dishes! I'll do it when I get back!"

"Did her baby ever turn?" Michael asked.

"Not as of last week. This may be a C-section."

She ran to Kartushah's hut next to Sojay's. They both met her immediately.

"This is not the normal scream," Sojay said with great concern.

"I should think not," Angie said wide-eyed. **"The baby is still not upside down I think."**

"Can you turn it around?"

"No, but there are other choices. Let me see her and I will decide." She pushed her way inside the hut.

A quick examination of Seendoo revealed that the baby was still breech. Angie commanded Sojay and Kita to bring the stretcher so they could move her to the clinic. Within ten minutes Seendoo was on the surgery table, and Angie had Geechern put in an IV needle while she prepared the epidural. Fifteen minutes later Seendoo's pain was relieved.

"You may sit with her at her head," Angie told Kartushah. **"Seendoo will be fine right now."**

"How did you stop her screaming?" He asked in relief.

"By stopping her pain for the little bit. Geechern, are you ready for this?"

She nodded with excitement. This would be her first surgery. Angie smiled. She was blessed to have such an eager helper.

*****

Michael vaguely heard the radio call. "Michael Collins, come in! Michael Collins, are you there? This is Chet. Come on, partner, you'd better be there. Pick up the mic, Michael! Over!"

He was slightly groggy from having fallen back asleep, so it took a few more calls to register what was happening.

"Michael! This is Chet! Are you in, partner? Come on and pick up the mic! God, let them be back, please."

Chet was in a panic. Michael collected his senses and stumbled from the bed to the radio transmitter. He picked up the mic and pressed the button to talk.

"This is Michael, Chet. What's going on?"

"Thank God!" Chet said with a gasp of relief. "Michael, a helicopter is about to head out to get you and Angie! There's been a coup in the government!"

"Are you kidding me?" Michael asked with half of a laugh. Chet was good for jokes.

"Michael, I am *not* kidding! I wouldn't dare jest about something like this! It's been brewing all day. We don't know who the rebels are, but they've captured President Arisha. They're saying they haven't executed him yet, but they're threatening to. You and Angie need to be ready to leave in thirty minutes."

"I'm not going anywhere," Michael said determinedly.

"You don't understand!" Chet was panicking again. "They hate democracy and they especially hate Americans who brought it here. They're giving all Americans six hours to leave the country. Any who don't will be rounded up and …," he paused, "and killed."

"They're not coming out here," Michael insisted.

"They have your names. They said they'll hunt you down. They specifically mentioned missionaries because we're teaching our culture to their people. You've *got* to leave, Michael. There isn't a choice in this!"

"Listen, I'm not leaving the island. They can shoot me dead, but I'm not going."

Chet paused. "You will be shot, if you don't leave."

"Bring them on!"

"Don't be an idiot! What about Angie? What if she refuses to go because you won't go? Are you prepared to watch them put a bullet through her head too?"

That statement grabbed his attention. No. He had seen it with his mother; he couldn't watch that with his sweet wife. He was more than willing to die himself in Padawin, but he couldn't let that happen to her.

"Are you understanding me, Michael?" His voice was so loud it was distorting through the transmitter. "Look, man, I've got to get going. Vicki and the kids are waiting in the car right now. The copter will take you to Port Moresby. We'll meet you there at the airport."

Michael said nothing. He was trying to fight the confusion that was reeling through him. He couldn't leave Padawin; it was his only home. But

Angie…

"Michael!" he yelled again. "I don't have time to hash this out with you! The mission board will pull their support! You know that. You can't do this work on your own, partner. And you can't stay there with Angie. You've *got* to leave!"

Michael's hand shook as he pressed the button on the mic and said, "I'll see you at Port Moresby."

"Yes!" Chet yelled back. "Michael, this is the right thing to do. You know that?"

"It's the right thing for Angie."

"Yes, and you're her husband. It's the right thing for you too."

"Get going, Chet."

"See you, partner!"

Michael sat quietly for a moment trying to still his shaking body. How could he leave Padawin? This was his home. Angie. He knew her; she wouldn't go if he wouldn't go. If they stayed, the possibility was high they would be executed. He slowly got up to tell her. He knew she was in the clinic performing surgery on Seendoo. Could she be finished by the time the helicopter arrived?

Just as he was about to open the door, she burst through.

"They have a boy!" she exclaimed. "An adorable little boy!" The look on Michael's face alarmed her. "What's wrong?"

"We have to leave Padawin," he said with no expression.

"Your fever is still fairly high. You must've had an awful dream."

"Chet just radioed me. Some rebel group has invaded the capitol and overthrown the government, at least for the moment. They've captured President Arisha. No one is sure if they're going to kill him or not. We have to leave. The helicopter will be here shortly to take us to Port Moresby in New Guinea."

"I'm not going," Angie said without hesitation. "I just performed a section on Seendoo. I can't walk away."

"You don't understand," he found himself repeating Chet's warning. "One of their first duties is to rid the country of freedom loving Americans. Their plan is to hunt us down and execute us. They've given us six hours to evacuate the country."

"Like they're actually going to come way out here!" Angie laughed. "You can go if you want; I'm not going anywhere. I've waited ten years to get here, and I'm not leaving after only three months."

"The mission board has mandated it, Angie. We can't get any support or supplies from them if we disobey this order. Your clinic and medical work here is null and void if you can't get supplies."

"I'll find a way," she said resolutely.

"Angie!" he yelled as he grabbed her arm. "We *have* to leave! We don't have an option. They know who we are. They will specifically search us out because they resent our teaching another culture to their people. I won't watch you killed! I can't do it, Angie! I can't lose you like I lost my mother!"

She closed her eyes. "But Seendoo ..." she said weakly.

"You must show Geechern how to treat her from here on out. God knew what was gonna happen, Angie. Think on His timing. She could've gone into labor tomorrow ... or an hour from now. You preserved her life and the baby's."

She nodded and turned back to the clinic.

When the helicopter landed, villagers gathered around to see Michael and Angie off. They had thrown as much of their stuff together as possible, and the pilots loaded it while they said their goodbyes.

"The inside sewing will fade away," Angie reminded Geechern again. *"The outside you must cut away in seven bunnies."*

Geechern smiled and nodded at her teacher. She was eager and excited and exuding with confidence. Angie hugged her tightly as Michael grabbed her arm to go.

"God be with you all!" Michael shouted to the people. *"Sojay and Joshua have copies of your Bible! The children may have to help them read some times!"*

The children smiled and clapped at this statement.

"Trust these men to lead you into truth!" he exhorted them.

"As Paul followed Christ and told his believers to live as he did, so will we live as you and Dr. Angie did," Sojay said warmly as he reached out his hand to Michael.

Michael grabbed his hand and then pulled him toward him. *"God will guide you, Sojay. Just trust Him."*

"Yes, and you do the same."

Michael nodded and waved goodbye to the rest of the crowd. He helped Angie into the chopper and followed. As it lifted off the ground, the tribe below waved furiously. Neither knew when they would see each other again, but in his heart, Michael was determined he would return.

As the helicopter zipped across the ocean, he put his face in his hands and shook his head. How could this be happening? And it was indefinite as to when they could return. He knew had Angie not been here, he would never have left. He would have hidden out somewhere until the search was past, and then returned, always keeping a watchful eye for more rebels. He glanced over at Angie. She was peering out the window and sobbing. He hadn't even thought of her through this. He had been here for ten years, but she had dreamed of coming for ten years.

He leaned over and put his arm on her shoulder. She turned back to look at him, and her eyes were so red and swollen with devastation that he immediately pulled her to him. She sobbed even harder. He held her for a long time and was actually thankful for the distraction from his own grief. As he comforted her, he found it easier to believe that leaving Padawin was the right thing to do.

THIRTY-FIVE

Michael pushed the luggage cart through the airport as he and Angie searched for the Clarence family. He tried not to be alarmed, but he couldn't help wondering if they had made it out of Taveren. The whole city of Port Moresby looked like a war zone from a recent monsoon that had blown through. Power lines were down and streets were blocked with fallen trees. It was possible that the other missionaries just hadn't made it to the airport yet. They walked to each gate and looked through the groups hoping to catch a glimpse of their friends. As they approached another gate near the end of the airport, they heard a shout.

"Michael!" yelled Chet's voice. "You had us worried!" Chet came over to him and helped him wheel the cart to the sitting area. Vicki smiled with relief.

"Ditto," Michael told him as he reached out his hand in greeting. "We were afraid you guys hadn't made it."

"How are you doing, Angie?" Chet asked, noting her swollen eyes and grave expression.

"I can't believe this," was all she could say.

Vicki came over and put her arms around her and just held her for a moment. Angie cried again.

"I was finally beginning to feel like things were falling into place," Angie said between sobs. "How could this happen?"

"I don't have the answer to that," Vicki confessed. "If I did, I'd feel a lot better about this myself."

"We need a phone so Angie can call her parents," Michael said as he looked around for a booth.

Chet just shook his head. "All lines are down from the storm, but my cell is working fine. First thing we did was call our families when we made it to safety. We knew they'd be worried."

"I'm sure mine is," Angie mumbled.

Michael felt a sting of regret as he realized no one in the world was watching or caring about his fate in Padawin.

"Michael, man, we really need to get you a satellite phone," Chet practically scolded. "That was ridiculous trying to contact you on the radio. I know before you didn't really want to have immediate access from the outside world ..."

Michael finished his thought, "but things are different now. I agree."

"I was scared," Chet confessed.

"Understood. So what's the plan for now?" he asked as they all sat down.

"Fred Carson got tickets for us; we'll fly out at three this morning. The rebels are still holding Arisha, or so they claim. We saw three Americans executed already on television."

"I thought they were giving us six hours!" Michael exclaimed in unbelief.

"I told you they weren't very nice," Chet said with raised eyebrows. "That's why I was so insistent that we leave as soon as possible."

"Did you have any trouble getting out?"

"No. The locals were more than helpful to see to it we got to our plane *undisturbed*."

Michael nodded as he glanced around the airport. He looked at his watch, only eight thirty-five. It was going to be a long wait for the three o'clock flight. Angie was sitting next to Vicki, still looking devastated. James and Heather were putting together a puzzle on the floor. These kids knew nothing of life in the States. He wondered how well they would adjust.

Then suddenly a thought hit him: where would he go? He hadn't been to the mainland in ten years. To the Lovejoys? To Kansas? Surely Angie didn't expect him to follow her back to Alabama. He ran his fingers through his shoulder length, bushy bleached hair. He needed a haircut and a shave. He still had a fever and he still felt downright miserable.

"We were afraid you'd be out at the other far away tribes," Chet told him. "I was scared to death I wouldn't get a hold of you in time."

"Funny thing," Michael smiled slightly. "I have the flu. If I hadn't, we might not have even been back to our house by now."

For the first time Angie's expression changed from devastation. "I never thought of that. Your flu was a gift of God, Michael."

He smiled at her and asked, "Does this mean you won't beg me to get a flu shot again?"

She jumped up from her seat and ran over to him, dropping down in the chair beside him and throwing her arms around his neck. When she pulled back, she said to everyone, "That Scripture that speaks of everything working out for the good, that even applies to the flu! I was so furious at him for not taking the shot!"

Vicki asked Michael in disbelief, "You didn't take a flu shot?"

"I never take a flu shot!" he exclaimed. "I hate needles!"

"It was a miracle that I didn't force him to," Angie told them, "but I figured he was a big boy. I thought this flu was God's judgment on him for being so hard-headed. I realize now God had a plan for it all along."

"Angie, go ahead and call your family and then we'll see if we can rustle up some food." Chet suggested as he glanced at his watch.

Heather and James responded right away as they claimed near

starvation. The men and the kids went to grab something to eat while Angie called home.

She dialed the number as though she had just called yesterday. It would still be morning in Dockrey so they should be home. She hoped they hadn't heard about the upheaval in Padawin; they would be worried sick.

"Hello?" came her father's voice.

"Daddy! It's Angie!"

"Angie! Where are you?"

"Port Moresby, New Guinea. We fly out of here in a few hours."

She could hear him yelling for her mother in the background.

"Are you all right?" he continued asking. "Is everything okay? Were you affected at all by the uprising?"

"We're fine," she told him as the tiredness and emotions of the day began to catch up with her. "We got out quickly."

"Where are you headed now?"

"It looks like we're coming to Dockrey for a while."

Her father whooped and then relayed the news to her mother. She could hear her scream in delight.

"Your mother says she'll get your room ready."

"Tell her to forget it. If no one's in the garage apartment, we'll just stay there."

"We'll?" he asked.

"Michael and I. He's coming with me."

"Oh. You won't need your room?"

"No, Daddy." She could feel herself beginning to blush. "We're married, remember?"

"Yes. I just didn't realize that ... well ... I didn't realize *how* married you were."

"Very married," she said slowly and deliberately.

"I see." There was a long, uncomfortable pause. "Well, we'll get the apartment ready. It'll be yours for as long as you need it."

"Thank you, Daddy," she said as she felt tears begin to form again. "I love you and Moms very much ... and I very much love Michael also. You'll fall in love with him too. He's a wonderful man."

After hanging up the phone, Jonathan looked over at his wife. "She wants to stay in the apartment ... *with* him."

"*With* him?" Barbara asked in unbelief. "Are you sure?"

"Oh yeah," he said with a big nod. "She claims she loves him, rather emphatically I might add."

"Oh, my. I didn't quite expect this."

"Well, I thought about it, but never imagined it would ... well ...

never mind."

"I understand, dear. She did describe him as rather handsome and kindhearted."

"Yes," was all Jonathan could say as he stood to go back to the church.

"Be thankful that she's alive and well and coming home," Barbara reminded him as he went for the door.

"I will," he said with a slight irritation in his voice.

"Jonathan Wright!" Barbara said a bit louder than she normally spoke. "Before you decide to judge *anyone* or *anything*, I want you to remember the two of us sitting on the couch trembling in horror this morning as we listened to the news that Padawin had been taken over by hostile rebels whose first plan of action was to execute all Americans. We sat here dumbfounded because we knew there was no way in heaven or earth that our daughter would leave that island! They could've put a rifle to her head and she would've defiantly told them to pull the trigger! You know that! I can guarantee you that the only reason she's heading home is because Michael Collins talked her out of staying. You can't deny that."

"I'll keep it in mind," was all he said as he went out the door.

"How are things in Podakind?" Vicki asked Angie after she settled down from the emotions of the phone call.

"Wonderful actually." She pictured the paradise in her mind. "I had just finished a C-section when Michael told me the news of the overthrow. The people were astounded that such a thing could be done … removing a baby like that. So many have come to Christ and are being discipled. How will they carry on with our being gone?"

"You know what's so wonderful about all of this?"

Angie shook her head. She saw nothing wonderful in any of it.

"God knew all along," Vicki explained. "Our whole purpose in being here was never to become a crutch on which the Padawin people must always lean. We were there to show them how to lean on God themselves. Michael has taught those tribes for many years, and we've pastored and discipled in Taveren all these years. Maybe God is ready to test them on their own for a change."

"Maybe." Angie didn't want to agree; she wanted to still be there. "But what about the medical end? I was just getting started."

"Who knows?" she said warmly. "I can't answer for God, but one thing I do know: He never makes mistakes. He has a purpose even in this."

Angie nodded as she thought, *Daddy would say that God is up to something.*

*****

The men brought back some sandwiches for the ladies, and they talked and ate as the hours slipped away. Heather and James became increasingly cranky while trying to fight sleep. Vicki held Heather in her arms, and she finally gave in. Chet picked up James after a crying fit about being ready to go home, and he fell asleep within minutes. Michael checked his watch: eleven forty-two.

He stood up and went to the window to gaze out at the lights of the airport. He still was unsure about what to do. Maybe now that he had gotten Angie out of Padawin, he could send her on to the States, and then he could go back to Podakind. However, the thought of being there without her was hollow. Padawin would never be the same for him. He pressed his forehead against the cool glass; it felt good to his fever.

"Here's some Advil," Angie said as she came up behind him.

He took it and leaned back against the window again.

"What are you thinking about?" she asked him.

"What to do now. I have nowhere to go, you know? I have nothing on the mainland ... no one."

"What do you mean *what do you do* or *where do you go*? You go with me. I thought that was a given."

"I can't go with you," he said through a regretful sigh. "I'm this guy that your family only knows as the *arranged marriage husband*. You can't bring me home."

"Are you kidding me? I've already told them you're coming! Are you saying you have no intention of going home with me?"

"Right," he said flatly.

She grabbed his arm and turned him around harshly as she glared at him in unbelief. "You'd better have a good reason ... a better one than the lame statement you just offered."

"Angie, I can't go with you. I'm not a part of your family," he tried to explain. "They would never accept me as ... as ... as anything. I'm this nobody kid with a dysfunctional background that's managed to sneak my way inside the life of their daughter. I can't do it."

Angie took a deep breath and nodded slightly, not actually in understanding, but in accepting his resolve. "Okay, then I guess we can stay at one of those furnished places the mission board holds for missionaries on furlough."

"What? I didn't mean you couldn't go! By all means, go be with your family!"

"*You* are my family now, Michael," she said soberly. "You are my husband. Did you think all those promises I made in Padawin were for Padawin alone? Did you think that when we stepped off the island everything we had shared suddenly became null and void?"

He kept staring out the window.

"Did you think Saturday was just a one night stand?"

He turned back at her and his eyes were desperate. "No, you know I didn't think that."

"Then why are you ready to ditch me and everybody that made me who I am simply because we're not on your turf anymore?"

He closed his eyes. His head was throbbing again and his palms were sweating. All he wanted was to fall into her arms and plead with her to never leave him, but he felt too unworthy. She was right: he could handle her on his turf, but he couldn't go back with her to hers.

"My parents have an apartment over their garage," she said as she tried a new tactic. "We can stay there for a while, until we decide what we need to do."

He shook his head and reiterated, "I'm *not* going home with you."

"Then you'd better call Fred Carson and find some place for us to stay, because I'm not going without you. I'm your wife, Michael Collins, and for all I know I could be carrying your child. I will *not* leave you. Is that understood?"

He looked into her eyes and saw she was unmovable. Her face was still streaked from the tears, her eyes still puffy, but she was still the most beautiful woman he'd ever seen. He hated that when he looked at her all he could think of was desire. Her lips, though somewhat dried and slightly cracked from the sun, were still as inviting as ever, just as they had been the moment he first saw her at the Honolulu airport. He reached out for her and she readily pulled herself into his arms. He held her close, breathing in the scent of her hair, relishing the feel of her body against his, and he wondered if he could let her go as easily as he was trying to right now.

"Michael," she said gently, "my family will adore you simply because I do. They don't need any other reason. They never have to know about your past. Don't be so quick to judge how they'll treat you. However," and she pulled back to look him in the eyes, "if you refuse to go with me, then I'll stay with you wherever you are. I won't leave you."

He nodded at her and pulled her to him again. "Are you sure?" he asked, needing to know that he wouldn't be an outcast.

"Absolutely and positively. The next best thing to having you meet me would be having you meet my family."

"You do know that you're the best thing that's ever happened to me?"

She looked at him and smiled as she said, "You've mentioned that. My family will embrace you, Michael."

"Even as your husband?"

She didn't answer. She only smiled and then leaned in to kiss him fully. As he felt her lips press against his, he lost himself in the passion that she could stir so easily. How could he have ever doubted anything? How could he ever imagine a life without her next to him?

Alabama, here I come, he thought as he put his arms around her waist and pulled her closer.

Chet and Vicki tried not to stare, but the kiss took them by surprise.

"Well, okay," she said as she tried to avert her eyes from the passionate couple. "I guess that answers our question about how the marriage was working out."

Chet chuckled and nodded as he said, "I told you he could never keep his hands off of her."

"That's not your everyday *good buddy* kiss they're sharing there. In fact, I can't remember the last time you kissed me like that."

"Well, watching them sure kind of gives you the desire, doesn't it?"

They laughed as each held a sleeping child in their arms.

"Time does change things for a while," she smiled at him. "We couldn't get that close right now if we tried. We'd have to pry these kids away."

He agreed. One thing that would happen for sure after arriving at his parents' house in Memphis: the grandparents would keep the kids for a few days while he and his bride took a second honeymoon. It would be nice to rekindle some of the fire that Michael and Angie shared as newlyweds.

*****

When the six finally boarded the plane, they collapsed into the comfortable seats after hours in the hard chairs at the airport. Chet and Vicki settled the children as well as they could, then at last reclined themselves.

Michael was still struggling with his agreement to go home with Angie. She seemed certain that her family would ignore their awkward marriage arrangement and simply welcome him with open arms.

"Go to sleep," she said to him as she gently kissed his cheek before lying back in her own seat. "You can mull over all your insecurities after resting."

He grinned as she felt his forehead. She was beginning to know him too well.

"Ugh! Will you ever get over this flu? Let me get you some more Advil."

She stopped a flight attendant and explained that her husband was very sick and needed some water to take his medicine with. The lady brought something to drink immediately. Michael smiled as he took the pills. It was comforting to know that someone was taking care of him, someone wonderful, beautiful, and incredible. *Angie.*

THIRTY-SIX

Jonathan Wright tried not to pace, tried not to wring his hands, and tried not to look as frustrated as he felt inside. He stood next to the large window in the waiting area of the Memphis airport and watched for Angie's plane to land. Barbara sat happily in one of the seats, eager to see her daughter again and thrilled that she was simply alive at this point. Jonathan, however, couldn't erase the words from his mind that Angie had said yesterday on the phone:

"We're married, remember?"

"Yes. I just didn't realize that ... well ... I didn't realize how married you were."

"Very married," she had said slowly and deliberately.

He gazed toward the sky and tried to be as thankful as his wife, but he could feel the sweat forming around his collar as his thoughts drifted to a tropical island, his beautiful daughter, and some strange man who had managed to weasel his way inside her life in a matter of three months.

He must be some character. How on earth could Angie be so foolish to just give herself to him and this marriage without a second thought? What if they can't go back to Padawin? What are their options now? You can't annul a marriage that's been ...

"Jonathan," Barbara called out to him, "would you sit down and relax?"

"I'm trying to relax but honestly, it's impossible. How in heaven's name do I greet this character? *Welcome, weasel!*"

"Jonathan!" she exclaimed this time. "I can't believe how much you distrust Angie in all of this!"

"Angie? This has nothing to do with Angie! This has to do with a man who's lived on an island for ten years and suddenly winds up with a mail-order bride—a beautiful one at that! I trusted him when I agreed to let her carry out this whole ridiculous marriage ordeal, never thinking that he'd take advantage of her this way! I thought he was a man of God who would respect and treat her with ..."

"Didn't she tell you that she was in love with him?"

"And you can just leave it at that, huh?"

"I *know* Angie. She's not impulsive, nor is she stupid."

"Her heart is bigger than her head," he said flatly.

"Not when it matters. I can promise you that if she fell in love with him, it wasn't out of stupidity or coercion or circumstance, but because she saw something in him that completed her. And has it occurred to you at all that perhaps God was in this from the beginning?"

"Hmph," was all Jonathan would say to that.

*****

The trip to Memphis had been nearly unbearable. Because of the quick scheduling, there had been long layovers everywhere. They were parked at Honolulu for three and a half hours. They had to wait five hours in Los Angeles, but that allowed them plenty of time to get Michael a haircut and a shave. They stayed four hours in Denver, and then had to linger another three hours in Houston. Compounded with all of it were the many time zone changes. Michael's temperature was flaring, and his body ached from the fever as well as lack of sleep. Angie kept him hydrated and medicated as often as possible.

Michael wasn't sure if it was the fever or his nervousness that kept his dreams in a tizzy every time he closed his eyes. One dream had Jonathan Wright greeting him at the airport with a shotgun. Another had them back at the house in Padawin on Saturday night. It started out wonderful as he relived the swing and the final move to the bed, but suddenly Jonathan appeared from the bathroom. He was appalled at the sight and began to chastise them both for such behavior when he had come all this way to visit. When Angie awoke him for the final descent, he was covered in sweat and his heart was beating in overtime.

"How do you feel?" she asked him as they prepared for the landing.

"I don't know which is worse: my body from exhaustion or my emotions from tension. I can't imagine your dad just extending his hand and saying, *Welcome to my family*."

"My daddy's a good man. He might protest a little, but he doesn't know you yet. He's a good judge of character. I promise you he'll be polite at first, but as the days pass by, he'll begin to see you as I do: a man with a heart of gold and a deep love for God."

"You won't leave me alone with anybody, will you?"

"No way, besides, I still have to get you past this flu."

If being sick would keep her next to him for the present, he was thankful to have it.

*****

Barbara jumped up excitedly as passengers began to appear. Jonathan stood behind her, his skin crawling at the thought of meeting the *weasel*. Then there was the whole ordeal of having to greet his daughter. She wasn't the same Angie; she was ... different. She was married to a complete stranger, she had been in a tribal village for months, and—for crying out loud, she was married to a complete stranger, *very* married, and that was the bottom line! His jaw tensed while passengers began to unload.

As the people made their way out, Barbara spotted Angie first. She immediately yelled her name, threw her hands up into the air, and started to cry synonymously. She then covered her mouth as her daughter smiled and waved back. Breaking from the line, she ran to her mother and embraced her frantically.

"Moms," she whispered as she held her for a few seconds.

"Sweetie, it's so good to have you back. I'm so thankful you're alive."

Angie gazed up at her father who was standing behind Barbara. "Hey, Daddy," she said warmly. "It's good to be back home for a little while."

She pulled back from her mother and then went around to greet her father. He pulled her close and held her tightly.

"Welcome home, baby," he said as tears began to form in his eyes also.

Barbara had no problem discovering Michael even though she had never seen a picture. He just stood there, arms by his side, looking lost and alone as he stared at Angie. Obviously this was he. He appeared tired, almost ragged, and completely out of his element. Barbara smiled at him, walked over and held out her arms. His eyes had the expression of defeat as she came nearer. She put her arms around him and hugged him gently. "Welcome, Michael. It's so wonderful to finally meet you."

"You too, Mrs. Wright."

"You look worn out."

"I am," he replied. "I've been a little bit sick, too."

"Oh, my," Barbara said quickly as she reached up to feel his forehead. "Michael, you have fever!"

"I know. Angie's made sure I've had plenty to drink."

"Good for her! Let me get you some Advil right away."

"I just had some about an hour ago."

"Well it's not working. I probably have some Tylenol in the van. We can double dose you and knock this thing out.""

Angie came over to Michael, pulling her father by the hand behind her. When she got to him, she gave her wonderfully reassuring smile.

"Daddy, this is Michael," she said with great respect. "Michael, my father."

Jonathan stared briefly at the man he had come to despise within the last forty-eight hours. He was a bit shocked at the humility that dominated his expression. In fact, Michael could barely meet his eyes. Jonathan wanted to believe that the weasel was expressing guilt, but when Michael did manage to finally look up at him, there was no hint of pride, arrogance or deceit. Jonathan forced a smile as he extended his hand.

"You look like you've had a rough few days," he said as Michael shook it.

"You have no idea," Michael replied avoiding eye contact again.

"Let's get you both to the van as soon as possible."

Michael looked over to where Chet, Vicki and the kids had been greeted by Chet's parents. He waved toward the family.

"We'll keep in touch!" Chet yelled at him as he threw his long arm into the air.

Michael nodded and waved back, looking as though he had lost his only friend.

*****

In the van on the way home, Angie talked non-stop. She explained Padawin in much detail to her parents, from the people to the places to their ministry together. She went to great lengths to describe all the work Michael had done over the years to create the environment at Podakind that allowed her to work with ease and proficiency. She talked of the revival and of Michael's teaching, of their singing together and playing with the children. She spoke of the different tribes and how Michael was careful to present the Word to each in ways that would benefit them most. She described the shelves he had built and how she had come to discover his doctorate. She detailed the visit to Mount Sheshney and how she walked inside the volcanic cone. She talked about how much she loved the ocean and how settling and spiritual it had become for her.

Jonathan listened with delight as Angie described every detail imaginable of her life in Padawin. It was hard to believe she'd been there only three months. All that had been accomplished in that short amount of time was phenomenal. He would glance in his mirror occasionally at Michael who either smiled at Angie in admiration or leaned his head back with closed eyes. When Angie had disclosed that he was coming off a bout with the flu, Jonathan actually found himself feeling pity for weasel. This wasn't the man he had built up in his mind. In fact, he was floored by Michael's humble nature. He had somehow envisioned him an aggressive man with strong opinions. Instead, he had discovered that Michael merely lived with the people and had shown them how to grow food, raise cattle, clean up their water, and develop a sewage system before he ever attempted to share Christ. When they saw his love and concern for them, they asked him why, and then he shared his mandate.

"How long did it take them to ask you why you were there?" Jonathan wondered.

"Nearly two years. I suppose I could've said something earlier, but I really wanted them to hunger for Christ. I only wanted to be salt for a while."

Jonathan nodded. It was a wonderful approach. *You are the salt of the earth*, Christ had said. Perhaps if Americans tried to be salt more, there would be less confusion about Christianity in this country. People would thirst to know what made believers so wonderfully different. Instead, many Christians had lost their saltiness and conformed more to the world than to the Word.

"That's a great concept," he commented. "I admire someone with the patience and fortitude to persevere in that. We Americans tend to want instant results so we don't take the time to build those kinds of bridges. Unfortunately, our converts often have shallow roots."

Angie jumped in to say, "The Padawin people never have shallow roots. Michael insists that if they commit to Christ, they must do it whole-heartedly and denounce their former gods."

"We should all have that kind of commitment," Barbara acknowledged.

THIRTY-SEVEN

When they finally reached Dockrey, Alabama, Michael was taken by the quaintness of the town. The buildings along Main Street were old but refurbished. The people weren't in a hurry to get anywhere, and dotted along the street he noticed folks chatting away as they lingered at storefronts. Angie knew the name of every person they passed. As he thought about how bubbly and friendly she was, he imagined everyone in this town loved her dearly. He wondered how well they would take to her new husband, the hermit from the South Pacific.

As the white minivan pulled into the driveway, Michael remembered Angie telling him about the security fence surrounding the property. Around fifteen people stood outside hoping to get an exclusive glance at Stephen and Annie Williams. No such luck today.

The house itself was impressive but homey. Jonathan had done most of the work himself. Michael could easily imagine three little girls and a younger brother growing up in the warmth of this place; his heart longed for his own mother. He hadn't felt that in a long time.

Driving up to the house, Angie's smile grew wider. She was home, and for the first time he felt that perhaps this might not be a miserable experience after all. Her father hadn't belittled him or even stared him down for that matter. Barbara Wright had been as sweet and gentle as anyone could be. Michael's body was chilled, tired, and his head was killing him. He tried to act as though he felt on top of the world, but no one was buying it. Barbara rushed him into the house while Jonathan insisted on getting the entire load of luggage.

Michael sensed pure emotional warmth when he entered the great room. Large exposed beams ran from the roof, and a balcony overlooked from the left. To his right were a brown leather couch and two shabby, matching recliners along with a television and a meager stereo system. The kitchen was off to his left along with a dining area presenting the largest table he had ever seen in an actual house. To the back he saw the door that must lead to the back porch, the place where he knew the family spent many hours together.

"Michael," Barbara said sweetly as she motioned him toward a recliner, "just have a seat over there and I'll get you something to drink. Is iced tea all right?"

"Perfect," he said wearily as he eased himself back into one of the chairs. From the creak it moaned out when he sat, he knew it had seen many years and much action from the Wright family.

Angie walked in and stopped to consider the sight of her house again. Her whole face lit up as she surveyed each area of the room. She came up to Michael and gently felt his forehead. "It's time for some more Advil," she said as she turned to the kitchen to join her mother.

When Jonathan came in with the first of the bags, Michael jumped up immediately to help.

"I've got it, son," Jonathan told him quickly. "I'm thinking your best bet for now is to stay still."

"I can't let you do all this alone. It wouldn't be right."

Jonathan laughed. "Those two women in the kitchen would heartily disagree with you! If they come out here and see you carrying in luggage, I'll be tarred and feathered. For the sake of peace in the household, just let me handle it."

Michael smiled and sat back in the chair, but he wouldn't recline. He couldn't fully relax while Mr. Wright carried in his things. Barbara came out with a glass of tea followed by Angie bringing the Advil. He had lived away from women for so long that he didn't take any of this attention lightly. Just being with Angie and having her take care of him had been unimaginable after years of being alone, but now to have her mother immediately join in was too much. He stood in respect but was met with protests and arms pushing him back down into the chair.

"Here's the last of it," Jonathan said as he carried in a few more pieces. "Should I take them on up to the room?"

"Let me help you," Michael said as he stood up from the chair.

"I've got it," Jonathan insisted. "Just relax."

"Impossible," Michael said as he handed the glass of tea to Angie and walked over to Jonathan. "It goes against everything I am to just sit here and let another man carry my stuff."

"But you have the flu!" Barbara exclaimed.

"Yes, ma'am," he acknowledged, "but I'm not paralyzed. Lead the way, Mr. Wright."

"If you insist," Jonathan said picking up an armload.

Angie placed the tea on an end table and grabbed a few things herself, followed by Barbara doing the same. Jonathan led the way up the stairs and to the left to a door near the end of the balcony. He nudged it open and moved inside. When Michael went through the door, he marveled at the room. It was wonderfully furnished for a garage apartment. To the left was a sitting area with a television. Straight across from the door was a small kitchen and dining table. To the right were the bathroom and bed. The thing he loved most, however, was the carpeting. He couldn't carpet the house in Podakind because of frequent flooding from sudden torrential rains or monsoons. He desperately wanted to remove his shoes and run his bare feet across the flooring.

"Welcome home," Angie said softly in his ear as she came up behind him.

"I hope you'll find this place comfortable," Jonathan said awkwardly. "You both know you're welcome to stay here as long as you like."

"Thank you, Daddy," Angie said as she dropped her things and walked over to kiss his cheek. "We have no idea what kind of time frame we're talking about. In fact, we don't even know how to plan our lives for the moment."

"Then don't," Barbara said cheerfully. "Just relax and enjoy yourselves. I think you both deserve that for a while."

Michael smiled at the warmth that exuded from Barbara. He knew now that Angie got her ability to be so personable from her mother, while her straight hair, green eyes and height came from her father.

He loved the Native-American motif around the room and couldn't wait for a chance to examine the many framed photos and books lining all the shelves. For now, however, his only wish was to drop into bed and sleep for the next three days if possible. But this plaguing question kept creeping to the front of his mind: were Jonathan Wright's eyes starting to brood? He reached up attempting to loosen the collar on his t-shirt.

"You both look so tired," Barbara said with deep sympathy as she rubbed her hand along Michael's back. "Why don't you rest for a while, and I'll get started on supper in a little bit? I'll let you know when it's ready."

"Thanks, Moms," Angie said as exhaustion began overrule her excitement. "The truth is we could probably sleep through supper and right on 'til morning."

"I'm sure you could," Barbara smiled, "but I'm willing to bet you haven't had a decent meal in a couple of days."

Jonathan tried not to be frustrated about the fact that he was leaving his little girl alone in that apartment with a man, but reason reminded him that she was thirty, she was married to that man, and that man didn't appear to be too horrible a weasel ... at least not yet.

"Told you," was all Barbara said as she smiled teasingly at him while passing him on the balcony.

"Told me what?" he asked a bit annoyed because he knew to what she was referring.

"He's not quite the monster you'd created in your mind, is he now, Dr. Frankenstein?"

*****

Barbara had made fried chicken, mashed potatoes with gravy, green beans and homemade yeast rolls. Michael now knew exactly where Angie had picked up her culinary skills. She and her father carried on most of the conversation with Barbara adding a comment or question now and then. Michael's only words were to compliment Barbara on the meal and to thank Jonathan for having him in his home. They were both gracious, but Michael agreed with Angie's previous prophetic assessment of her father: he was being polite.

After supper, Angie insisted she help her mother in the kitchen. Michael wasn't sure what to do. Normally he would either help Angie or shower. His questions were quickly answered when Jonathan motioned him toward the back porch door. He had no desire to be alone with Angie's father, but he had no desire to be disrespectful either. He went out with some hesitation, but was pleasantly surprised by the atmosphere of the porch. It was covered with cushioned chairs and potted plants, along with a bench swing, a couple of short, round tables, and a hot tub. So this was Angie's hot tub. He began to inspect the connections and wiring and nodded in admiration at the handiwork.

"Very nice," Michael said with approval. "You do fine work, Mr. Wright." He was forgetting his insecurity for the moment as he got caught up in the various aspects of the porch. It was wonderfully inviting and he once again imagined the family spending limitless hours back here over the years.

"It's a room that sort of evolved over time," Jonathan said as he took a seat.

"Oh, I doubt that. This took the caring hand of a creator."

Jonathan laughed. "Good assessment! I like the way your mind works."

Suddenly Michael was brought back into the reality of where he was and who he was with. His nerves returned as he took a seat on the porch opposite Jonathan.

"Wait until you see the back yard; it's a work of art. Barbara loves tinkering with flowers and landscaping. Now me, I'm a fruit and vegetable man myself."

"You garden?" Michael asked with a bit of enthusiasm at the possibility of finding something in common with Angie's dad.

"Every spring, every fall ... have quite a bit growing out there now. Got a lot of collard greens, mustards, turnips, as well as some broccoli and such. Typical fall garden."

"I can't put in a fall garden in Padawin. It never cools off enough."

"I can imagine," Jonathan said as he propped up his feet on the closest short table. "I'll bet the soil is incredibly rich over there."

"You wouldn't believe how rich. The volcanic area is bursting with nutrients. I always test the soil before planting, and it's overflowing with so much natural enrichment that I seldom add anything. I did teach the people to compost, so that's all we ever need."

"I've always wanted a compost pile, but Barbara thinks it'll attract rats and every other varmint in the area."

"Not if you do it right. Just build a nice metal box. Even dig it into the ground if you want. That's the richest fertilizer you can make. If you start now, by the time your spring garden is planted, you'll be ready to go."

"Really? Have you ever made one of these metal boxes?"

"More times than I can remember."

"That's right," Jonathan nodded. "You have a doctorate in Agriculture. I just might have several little projects for you to help me with while you're vacationing."

"My bachelor's was Agriculture," Michael started to explain, but then stopped short. Who was he to appear boasting to this man by spouting off his degrees? "There's nothing I'd like better than taking on some projects."

The minutes began to pass quickly as Jonathan carried the conversation away dreaming up various things he'd always wanted to do around the house. When he learned of Michael's carpentry skills, he became more animated. He listed several tasks he'd wanted to undertake, but really lacked the time and skills to do properly. With Michael at the helm, he believed he could do just about everything he'd planned to get to *one of these days*.

"So what are we discussing?" Angie asked as she brought Michael a glass of fresh tea and two Tylenol.

"A few little projects here and there," Jonathan replied.

"What are these?" Michael asked as he took the capsules.

"Tylenol," Angie explained sitting down in a chair beside him. "It's too soon to take anymore Advil, and I assumed you'd be ready for a shower and then on to bed."

"You assumed correctly, Dr. Angie."

""Then I suggest, Dr. Collins, you swallow those pills and head on up the stairs.''

"Gladly."

Michael took the Tylenol, managed several gulps of tea, and then let Angie pull him to his feet. He told Jonathan goodnight as she led him through the door into the great room where Barbara was just leaving the kitchen.

"Michael's gonna shower in the apartment, and I'll use my old bathroom," Angie told her mother as they started up the stairs. "After that, we're out for the night."

"I understand," Barbara said warmly. "Are you feeling better, Michael?"

"Yes, ma'am. How could I not after a meal like that?"

Barbara giggled. "Sleep tight; don't let the bed bugs bite," she called out to the couple as they reached the top of the stairs.

Michael smiled. How many times had Angie said that to him?

Barbara dried her hands after wiping off the table, her final task. She hung the towel on the stove handle and joined her husband on the back porch. He was sitting quietly with his elbows propped on the chair arms, his chin resting on what looked like praying hands. Barbara sat down beside him, piling her feet up on the table.

"So, how was your visit with the weasel?" she asked him.

"Let's just say he's made a better first impression than I anticipated."

"Admit it, he's a nice guy."

"I won't admit anything yet," Jonathan said stubbornly. "He's sick. All this niceness may be nothing more than an inability to be obnoxious because of his intense illness."

Barbara laughed and reached over to take his hand. "You're one hard-headed man. Your daughters get that from you, you know?"

"I know," he said without changing his stern expression. "Apparently, they're not all as hard-headed as they ought to be."

"You know what would be really funny?" Barbara chuckled as she squeezed his hand.

He looked over at her but refused to smile as he asked, "What?"

"If it turns out you really like him."

"I believe you're counting your chickens already, Mrs. Wright."

"Hard-headed."

*****

When Angie finished her shower, she went to her old room to find something clean to wear to bed. The bedroom was still stacked with boxes of books she had lugged back over the years of her education. She had taken a few with her to Padawin, ones she thought would be beneficial as reference books. They were still there, sitting on shelves in the clinic and in the house. She hoped the day would come when she and Michael could return and carry on the work that God had allowed them to start. Just the thought of Padawin caused her to whisper prayers again for those who would hopefully keep the torch burning while they were away.

She rummaged through her drawers hoping to find a large t-shirt or an old pair of scrubs to wear to bed. Apparently her mother had gone through her things when she left and only let the nicer ones remain in the drawers. She pulled out a legitimate gown, a Christmas gift from her mother several years back that had never made it on her body. It was a silky purple gown with purple lace on the sleeves and hem that landed near her middle thigh.

"Why not?" she mumbled as she slid it on. She smiled at the image: very feminine and girly. It wasn't a look she wore often.

Her old green robe was still stuffed inside her luggage somewhere in the apartment, so she snuck out of the room and tiptoed across the balcony. She opened the door quickly and shut it behind her, hoping she had made the tromp undetected by her father. Modesty had always been stressed in their house. When she turned around from shutting the door, however, Michael was sitting on the bed staring at her wide-eyed. She felt her face grow hot. She was modest toward her father, but hadn't considered Michael.

"Well, that's certainly a new look for you," he grinned.

She laughed and nodded, feeling extremely self-conscious at her skimpy attire.

"Where has this been all these months?" he asked, obviously enjoying the fact that she was the one feeling awkward for a change.

"Tucked away in my drawer for many, many years," she said as she moved quickly to her side of the bed. "It was a Christmas gift from Moms."

"I see," he smiled, his eyes following her. "Your mother has lovely taste."

"Whatever," she grumbled as she tucked herself beneath the covers. "This thing has lace and is silky. It'll probably make me itchy all night, not to mention cause me to sweat and then stick to my body."

"Feel free to remove it if it becomes unbearable," he chuckled as he reached up to turn out the light.

"In your dreams," she said softly, not really meaning for him to hear.

"Exactly."

"Feeling a little better, are we?"

"That Tylenol seems to have worked miracles tonight."

"I'll say."

THIRTY-EIGHT

When Michael managed to open his eyes the next morning, he felt warm again. His hands were cold and clammy, but his face was hot and sweaty.

"I swear I'll take that shot next year," he groaned as he looked over to Angie. She wasn't there.

He slowly sat up in bed and glanced around the room. Her gown was lying in the middle of the floor next to their luggage, and her suitcase was opened with clothes strewn around the area where it lay. He laughed at her messiness. He was thankful she wasn't one of those obsessively neat women. He could never have handled that pressure.

You knew just what I needed, he whispered in prayer. *How could I have ever picked anyone more perfect for me than Angie? How did You manage that?*

He took a few moments to examine all the framed photographs in the room. Most of them appeared to be from vacations throughout the years. The girls always seemed to love the moment, whereas the younger brother always appeared detached. He looked to be quiet and shy next to the energetic sisters.

He took in several more of the photos, noticing the changes that had taken place over the years and the ways each girl began to develop her own uniqueness. He was still puzzled by Alex and his ability to almost disappear in each picture. He was a good-looking boy, but the bubbly girls seemed to overwhelm every shot. He hoped that perhaps he would have the opportunity to meet Alex at some point during this *furlough* to the states. Maybe they would have something in common. Of course, what could he possibly have in common with a man who grew up in a family filled with love, excitement, adventure and support like the Wrights? If he had ever been in a situation where he was totally out of place, this was it. He, raised in complete dysfunction, was now living with the picture perfect family. He hoped that he would somehow manage to fit in.

After viewing the last of the pictures, he dressed and combed down his short hair, wetting it quite a bit to get the frizz and cowlicks under control. He then decided to go ahead and shave. His first complete shave last Saturday had impressed Angie beyond anything he could have imagined. Apparently a clean-shaven face was something she admired.

When Michael made it to the bottom of the stairs, he heard laughter from the back porch. He went over to glance through the small glass pane and discovered Angie and her parents all rearing their heads back in hysterics. He tried to imagine what could be so funny. His first thought was himself; were they laughing about him? No, why would they be laughing, much less even talking about him? At this moment, Angie practically being back from the dead, he was probably not the priority of conversation. He couldn't help but remember what it was like to be laughed at all those years growing up. Kids would point and giggle, make up degrading names, and then say derogatory comments about his parents, his home, or his clothes. He couldn't believe he actually developed a numbness toward it all at such a young age. He knew however that he could never change his lot in life, and his only hope was to live through school, go to college, and fulfill his mother's hopes.

What if Mr. Lovejoy had never given me that guitar or paid for lessons? What if I'd never been in the string band? Mother may have never felt the need to celebrate my sixteenth birthday so elaborately. She would've never bought me that necklace. What if Dad had not walked in that night? Would they still be alive? Would his mother finally have had the courage to leave him if Michael was out of danger?

Enough of the "what if's!"

Michael had been through two years of intensive counseling after the death of his parents. The state paid for the counseling, but Mr. Lovejoy had picked the counselor, a former pastor who was extremely sensitive, very intuitive, and had a keen sense of discernment when it came to spiritual and psychological matters. He had reminded Michael during every session to never dwell on the *what if's*. He explained how they were wasteful and unproductive. To always wonder what *might have happened* had one thing never occurred was a useless effort. The fact would always remain that it happened, and every chain of event that occurred as a result also happened. The best step was to stop the negative series by making choices that were positive and helpful. The results for Michael were miraculous. He graduated from high school with honors, went on to get a doctorate, and ended up on the mission field doing exactly what he had wanted to do. But suddenly things were very different ... incredibly and wonderfully different.

He walked over to the kitchen and found a hot pot of coffee and two pieces of sugar toast lying on top of a cookie sheet. He smiled; Angie had made breakfast. He poured his coffee, put his toast on a paper towel, and then stood bewildered for a moment in the kitchen. Did he join them on the back porch or did he sit alone at the long dining table? Was he really a part of this family? Was he really married to Angie in their opinion? She had captured his heart from day one, and somewhere along the way, she had fallen for him too, but how did the family feel about all of this?

He sat at the table and had his toast and coffee alone.

*****

Angie enjoyed spending the morning with her parents on the

porch. If she closed her eyes, she could transport herself back to a time when life was uncomplicated. As children, they had played, laughed, cried, and delighted themselves in growing up in this house with this family. She and her sisters had felt they truly were the luckiest people alive. Their parents loved them and encouraged them to do and be all they desired. It wasn't until last winter that Alex had revealed to the family why he had always been withdrawn, distant, and incommunicative: he had been repeatedly abused by an uncle under the impression that the uncle would murder his sister if things ever changed. That blot had changed her whole vision of reality.

How could that have been going on beneath all our noses and no one ever have a clue?

She immediately thought of Michael. He hadn't been sexually abused, but his abuse was just as horrendous. She had always thought Alex to be merely a wimp without an opinion, but after last Christmas, she realized that judging others because they are vastly different from yourself can be a dangerous mistake. Who knows what kind of child, teenager, or man Alex would have been had his life been as carefree and simple as his sisters'? Even though Michael had a rough beginning, at least someone stepped in during the last of his formative years and rescued what might have been a lost cause.

"I suppose Michael is sleeping in," Angie said as she glanced at the clock on the back wall.

"I wonder if he's feeling any better," Barbara added. "He looked so pitiful at the airport yesterday."

"He looked better then than he has all week. I'm gonna go check on him. It seemed like his fever was beginning to break last night."

She retrieved her cup and plate and opened the back door. She was floored to find him sitting alone at the table drinking his coffee.

"Good morning," he said with a small smile.

"What are you doing in here?"

"Eating breakfast."

"Why?" she asked more sternly. "You had to know we were on the back porch."

"I heard you," he said as he avoided her eyes by gazing into his cup. "I didn't want to interrupt. I wanted to give you some time to visit without me being the white elephant in the room."

"Michael Collins," she exclaimed softly as she rolled her eyes. "You are *not* a white elephant at this house. You're a part of this family. You belong here now just as we do. Things like *sitting on the back porch* while we have breakfast are very traditional family things to do. It'll be too cold in a couple of weeks. You need to experience these things with us. This is the kind of stuff that'll make you feel like you belong here."

He still wouldn't look at her. He stood as he crumpled his paper towel and headed back into the kitchen.

She wouldn't let him get away with it. Following behind she insisted, "You do belong here, Michael. You're my husband."

"To us, I am—in Padawin. Here, I'm just this strange man you brought back with you."

Angie turned him around and forced him to look at her. Her first thought was to sail into him, but when she saw the lost-ness in his eyes she melted. She smiled instead, eliciting a sigh of relief.

"How are you feeling?" she asked him tenderly.

"Better, but still fevered."

She placed her wrist to his forehead and wrinkled her brow. "Will you ever get over this?" she wondered aloud. "Let me get some Advil." She turned toward the cabinet, but he reached for her arm and pulled her back to him.

"You *are* feeling better," she said now with a mischievous smile.

He didn't answer her but simply pulled her closer. When his lips lightly touched hers, she could feel his smile against her own. It felt heavenly. He only kissed her lightly but she responded with her own agenda. By the time her mother walked in and cleared her throat, they had forgotten where they were.

"Well," Barbara said with an awkward smile, "I take it the missionaries are feeling all better this morning."

THIRTY-NINE

After giving Michael an official tour of the grounds, they walked into the house to find the phone ringing. Angie rushed to get it and squealed in delight at the name written on the display.

"Annie!" she answered.

"Angie?"

"Yes! Oh, my gosh! Are we actually talking right now?"

"I can't tell you how relieved I was when Daddy called and said you were coming home. I nearly made myself sick over the news of the overthrow. Stephen and I were watching TV when the announcement was made; I literally almost threw up."

"Well, that's about the size of it for me too. I didn't want to leave; Michael made me."

"Angie!" Annie exclaimed in horror. "Don't tell me that! They would have killed you!"

"I spent ten years of my life preparing to go there and can only manage to stay for three months! It was a bit abrupt, don't you think?"

"Don't ever tell me that again. When I see that Michael of yours, I'm gonna give him a big kiss of thanks for bringing you home."

Angie giggled and looked over at Michael. "Annie says she's gonna kiss you when she sees you."

He blushed.

She pulled the phone back to her ear and asked, "Any chance you'll be coming home soon?"

"You better believe it! With my sister back from the Pacific, you know I'll be there! The band is almost finished with tour rehearsals. Stephen said if everyone worked hard these next few days, we should be able to wrap up for a couple of weeks and then come back again at the beginning of November."

"Annie, that would be so wonderful. Being away from you has been the hardest part about all of this."

"I know. Before ... we could just pick up the phone and talk any time we wanted. Now, I actually *have* to write an e-mail if I want to communicate with you. Do you know how taxing that is on me?"

"I do now. It's hard to find time to sit and write anymore."

"You really loved your work there, didn't you?"

"More than I can say. I promise you, if Michael hadn't insisted I leave, I would still be there."

"I said don't tell me that again! Big kiss for Michael," Annie repeated. "He must hold a lot of sway with you to have talked you out of staying."

"Oh, he does.

*****

After lunch, Michael went upstairs to watch television while Angie took off for her *alone time* as she had always called it in Padawin. He appreciated the fact that even though she was very physical and emotional with people, she also needed time to herself. He had known people in life that were unbearably clingy; Jenna had been one of them.

As he flipped through various channels, he struggled to find one thing to watch. After nearly an hour of senseless switching, he landed on a show where a woman confessed to her husband she'd had an affair with his sister. Enough. He turned off the television and decided to find a good book to read or just find Angie. She had become better than any book.

He looked around the house, but found no sign of her. He did notice another hot pot of coffee, so he proceeded to fix himself a cup. Jonathan came walking into the kitchen just as he finished.

"You're looking better," Jonathan said as he went for a cup also.

"I'm feeling much better, at last."

"So tell me, what are the chances of you getting a flu shot next year?"

"Extremely high. I don't ever care to feel like this again."

"I wanted to ask you about something, but I didn't want to push you. I know you've had a rough week and all. Between the flu and the overthrow, you're worn to a frazzle. But, I would love for you to preach one or so Sundays while you're here."

Michael nodded and smiled at the thought. He hadn't taught nor preached in English for over ten years. "I'd be honored."

"Angie tells us you are quite a gifted teacher."

Michael laughed nervously "She only thinks that because I speak Padawin so fluently. She's impressed with my delivery."

"Oh, I doubt that. It takes a lot more than good language skills to impress her."

"By the way, have you seen her around anywhere?"

"Oh yeah," Jonathan said in a cautious manner. "She was brooding in the swing out beneath the big hickory tree,"

"Brooding?" Michael wondered. Angie didn't brood. "About what?"

"Padawin. I know I owe her life to you and doubt I could ever thank you enough. I'm sure you had to do some major coaxing to get her out of there."

"I have to confess to you, if it hadn't been for her, I would've stayed myself."

At this statement Jonathan looked over at him in confusion. "You would've been killed."

"Probably, but it's hard to explain what life is like there. It's my home. They are now my people."

"I can understand ... I suppose," Jonathan nodded as he took a sip of his coffee. "I still owe you a huge thanks. When Barbara and I watched the news that morning, we stared in horror. We knew she'd never leave; it's not her nature. She would stay to the bitter end and give her life for that cause."

"I could've given my own life easily, but I couldn't bear to see Angie give hers." He closed his eyes and tried to shake out the thought. After seeing his father shoot his mother, it was easy to visualize someone shooting Angie. He never wanted to see that image again.

"She says she loves you," Jonathan said without looking at Michael.

"Yes," Michael nodded, not looking either. "And I love her. I know that may be hard for everyone to understand ... but ... well ... I actually can't explain it. She's very easy to love."

"I know," Jonathan agreed with no emotion in his voice. "I look forward to getting to know the only man who ever managed to capture her heart."

Michael nodded nervously. He still wasn't sure whether he was comfortable getting to know anyone in Angie's family. She was incredible; he was a dud. He hoped that whatever it was that Angie adored about him could be embraced by the rest of the family as well. If not, he would be like a lone fox on a hillside of hounds. He already felt a little cornered, but then, he always did, everywhere but Padawin.

He walked out to the back porch and spotted Angie sitting beneath the large hickory in the bench swing. As he watched he noticed she appeared to be wiping tears. Was she crying? He wavered as to whether he should join her or go back into the house. He finally opted to walk on out. He knew she would hear the screen door creak when it opened. She could invite him to sit with her, or she could ignore him. He would take his cue from her response.

As soon as the door sounded, she looked over and motioned him to come sit. He was glad. He was still feeling out of sorts and out of place. She was his only beacon of security here. He walked over slowly, sipping his coffee, and taking in the beautiful view of the faintly colored hills in the distance. When he reached the swing, he could tell from her red eyes that she had indeed been crying. She reached out her hand and pulled him down next to her.

"Having a rough afternoon?" he asked as the autumn breeze blew wisps of hair around her face.

"Very," she replied as she reached up to wipe her eyes again. "It's still hard for me to grasp that I'm back in Dockrey. I was only in Padawin for three meager months."

"You did an awful lot during those meager months."

"But what if that's it? What if the coup is never settled and we can't go back? What if we have to make different plans? What if things don't change?"

"That's way too many *what if's*?" he said as he tried to shake the thoughts from his tired brain. "We can't live in the *what if's* right now. If we do, we'll drive ourselves crazy."

"I'm already there," she moaned as she leaned her head on his shoulder. "How can you be so strong and sure right now?"

"Half of it's because I'm sick, the other half is because I'm faking it."

She chuckled. "I appreciate your honesty, however, it doesn't give me a whole lot of security about this. You should've told me that in no time we'll be flying right back and all will be well in our little world."

"There are some things that I'm sure about. I'm sure of my call to Padawin, but I'm even more sure of *your* call there. You had to jump a lot of obstacles to get to there, and I can't help but believe it was for more than three months. I don't have any answers or explanations, but I do have the gut feeling that our lives there aren't finished."

She nodded and stared out to the hills. "That was a nice bit of reassurance. I think that'll get me through the rest of the day. If I were you, though, I'd start working on tomorrow's reasoning."

"Hmmm," he mused. "I'm a one day at a time kind of guy."

*****

By suppertime, Michael and Angie were exhausted again, still recovering from jet lag. Angie had put on a DVD to watch, but they both fell asleep somewhere near the beginning. She had promised him she would borrow Andie's *Lord of the Rings* series when she returned from the mini-vacation with her family to see the autumn leaves, but as tired as they both were, she doubted even Frodo or Gollum could have kept them awake.

Barbara came in and gently roused them for the meal, spaghetti and meatballs. Since meeting Angie, so many things had changed in Michael's life, beginning with eating. He had for the most part just existed when it came to food since college, but Angie insisted on every meal being wonderful. He now knew why. Meals at the Wright house were not just for the purpose of nourishment; they were a major part of family life. Michael couldn't remember a time that his family actually sat at the table together to eat. He and his mother often did, but his father always took his plate to the television.

"Is there anything you ladies can't cook?" Michael asked as he helped himself to another piece of garlic bread.

"Duck," Angie replied at once.

"Duck?"

"We've never cooked duck," she reiterated.

"The girls always wanted us to have a duck at Christmas because of some movie they used to watch growing up," Barbara explained. "I have never cooked a duck in my life! My only experience with ducks is watching them swim around in the pond. I can't cook a duck! That would be like boiling the family cat."

"Moms!" Angie exclaimed. "That's disgusting!"

"Exactly! I will *not* cook a duck in my lifetime."

"Have you ever eaten duck?" Angie asked him.

"Quite often. We would hunt them during duck season."

"What about Cornish hens?" Barbara wanted to know.

"Never."

Angie laughed as she said, "He might as well have! Those chickens in Padawin are about the size of Cornish hens."

"That little?" Jonathan asked.

"Tiny," Angie informed him.

"You can't fatten them up, Michael?" Jonathan wondered.

"It's their breed," he explained. "The Padawin chicken is just a small bird. I considered introducing some new ones, but what's the point? These people are used to their little chickens, so let them continue raising them. Also, since the little ones are native to the island, you stand the chance of having newer, bigger ones killing off the little ones. That would sort of be a travesty."

"Good point," Jonathan agreed. "However, as long as you eat here, we'll serve our chickens big."

"We have to have Cornish hens some night," Angie insisted. "Moms, cook them that special way when you put the butter all over them and then baste them with apricot jam."

"Absolutely," Barbara agreed. "Maybe Monday night."

After supper, Michael insisted on helping the ladies in the kitchen. He washed the pots and Angie dried and put them away. Jonathan had gone to his room to look over his sermon one final time. The idea of preaching to a congregation in the States was both exciting and terrifying to Michael. He had never been much of a communicator here; Padawin had been a different story.

Angie was headed upstairs for a shower, so he decided to try the television in the apartment again. He turned it on and began the ritual of flipping through the channels with the remote. He discovered a station that majored in woodworking and carpentry. Now *this* was interesting. He was amazed at the tools and equipment available. The builders were creating some incredibly obscure pieces of furniture and shelving. They were obviously more interested in the decorating end than the useful. He became so engrossed in the program that he didn't notice when Angie came in.

"This must be exciting television," she said as she joined him on the couch.

"It's amazing what these guys are building. Look at those shelves! I should've done that for you in Padawin."

"I think your shelves are just fine. They serve a wonderful purpose."

"I glanced in your parents' bedroom today. They look as though they could use a few shelves, not to mention *your* bedroom too."

Angie leaned back on the couch and giggled. "We have lots of books. The truth is, we don't need shelves, we need to go through our books and ferret out the ones we should keep and the ones we should get rid of."

"You should never get rid of books! A book is never useless."

"When you have as many as we do, trust me, some are useless."

He looked over at her and raised an eyebrow as he asked, "Did you want to get rid of any of my books while you were going through them?"

"Of course not. They were all *useful* books. Let's see, if I remember right, there was one called *How to Write a Readable Paper*. I'm sure that'll come in handy on your next doctorate. And what about *The 2002 Farmer's Almanac*? That one was of particular interest to me."

"You never know when you may need one for research."

"I'm sure," she said rolling her eyes again.

He turned back to the TV to watch the finishing touches on the shelving. He was so taken by the program that it took a long while to realize she was staring at him and smiling.

"What are you smiling at?" he asked when she finally caught his attention.

"I find it rather weird to see you getting caught up in Western culture. You are so *non all of this*."

"I know. I find it weird too. Did you have any trouble giving all of this up to come to Padawin?"

"Are you kidding? I was ready to head to Padawin 10 years ago! There was the simple problem of needing an education that kept me from going. I wanted to be a doctor, remember?"

"And a fine one you turned out to be," he said as he turned off the television at the show's end.

"Which reminds me," she said abruptly, reaching her wrist up to his forehead. "Your fever seems much better. Let me go get a thermometer."

She started to get up, but Michael pulled her back down to the couch. "Trust me on this," he whispered. "I'm feeling *fine* at the moment."

He leaned in and kissed her neck just below her ear. Her entire body wiggled in response.

"My goodness," she grinned as she looked him in the eye. "That was rather invigorating."

"How about this?" He kissed below the other ear.

Her body wiggled again. "You're doing strange things to me, Dr. Collins." She sighed. "I don't believe I have a medical explanation for this."

"And here?" he smiled as he went for her lips this time.

"This, I understand," she giggled as she lay down on the couch and pulled him back with her.

"We are married, aren't we?" he asked as he began to kiss down the front of her neck.

"I sure hope so."

FORTY

Sunday morning found Angie and Michael slow to get out of bed. They were still dealing with jet lag, and the prospect of getting dressed up for church was somewhat daunting. She tried to sit up and gain her wits about her, but he pulled her back down.

"Let's pretend we're both sick and play hooky," he suggested.

"You're being a little bit wicked this morning." She laughed as she gently kissed him.

"And you're not complaining about where your jersey is," he said as he pushed the hair from her face.

"What's the point?"

"I rather liked that little purple deal you wore the other night."

"I didn't. It scratched."

"Well, it didn't bother me for one minute."

"I'll keep that in mind," she grumbled as she sat up in bed again. "Come on, let's get up. I don't feel like explaining *hooky* to my father."

He found that thought more than sobering and began to immediately move from the bed.

*****

During Sunday School, the teacher never got to the lesson. The entire class time was spent asking Michael and Angie about their life and ministry in Padawin. She was as lively and animated as ever and answered most of the questions which didn't bother Michael one bit. Occasionally she would ask him to clarify something or explain something that had occurred before her arrival. He would answer quickly and then let her get back to the talking.

"Weren't you worried about the volcanoes?" a lady asked them.

"At first, I worried all the time, especially with Podakind practically sitting in my back yard! The clincher, I guess, was when Michael took me to the cone of Mount Sheshney."

"You actually went up to a volcanic cone?"

"Yes, and it was beautiful! It's extinct, meaning it's not *supposed* to erupt anymore."

"How do they know that?"

"Michael?" Angie asked as she looked over at him.

"No seismic activity occurs beneath its surface. Apparently it closed up and moved on to some other section of land."

"But it's lush and green up there, and the coolest spot I had been to on the island … temperature-wise, that is."

"Did you go inside the cone?"

"All around the inside. Then we picnicked next to it."

The bell rang and everyone shook Michael's hand and hugged Angie on the way out. When they had left, she reached up to feel his forehead.

"You seem only a little warm," she said with minor concern. "You still should've taken some Advil."

"I'm *nervous*," he corrected her. "Any warmth I feel this morning comes only from being under the scrutinizing eyes of your church family."

In the sanctuary, it seemed as though the entire church greeted Angie. He had figured right: the people here adored her too. She always graciously introduced him, and people gave different reactions to the meeting.

So, you're the lucky guy.

We never thought old Angie would get married.

How did you manage to nab her?

I guess it took the possibility of getting stranded on a tropical island to make her start thinking about marriage, huh?

What's it like being banished with Hitler's sister?

Apparently people had different opinions of her temperament.

He enjoyed the service. Even though it was very planned and organized, he found it refreshing to be on the receiving end of ministry for a change. For the past ten years, every move he made, every decision he considered, and every word that came from his mouth was always weighed in the context of ministry. His only reprieve had been the few times each year he spent with Chet and Vicki. To simply sit in a worship service as part of the congregation had become foreign.

When Jonathan began his sermon, Michael was highly impressed. He was the kind of preacher that sought to make every lesson practical, something Michael had always aspired to himself. No part of the passage was left without something applicable to put with it. Michael wished he had brought a notepad so he could remember the points and apply them to the Padawin people one day. He and Angie *would* return to their islands. He knew they would.

*****

Angie tried to concentrate on her father's preaching; he really was excellent, but she found herself feeling more like a silly school girl sitting next to a new boyfriend in church. Her father would read the next section of Scripture and then begin to elaborate, and she would insist to herself that she would hear this point out, but Michael was right within her field of vision, so his clean shaven face, long scar, and absorbed expression would grab her attention. So many things would go through her mind without her realizing it until her father would move on to the next passage and Michael would move his gaze down to his Bible.

She thought of how precise in doctrine Michael's teaching was. If her father and Michael were to ever have a discussion about theology, they would impress each other. Michael's teaching was every bit as impeccable as her father's and just as easy in delivery. For a man who had such an atrocious start in life, he had accomplished much. She thought of his coming in from the fields with his long, wild hair dripping with sweat, yet a content smile on his face from a hard day's work with the village men. And she knew it was much more than just the physical labor that made him smile. He used every opportunity to minister to these people. It was remarkable how he could care for them so deeply, be real and open with them, teach them and love them, yet never let down his guard enough to breach any chance to be a witness. He had explained to her once that just as Paul told his followers to imitate his own life because basically he imitated Christ, Michael wanted to be able to point to his own life as an example of true Christianity for the tribes. And he had succeeded.

She thought of how appreciative he always was of every little thing she did. She never imagined someone could be so thrilled to have coffee and sugar toast ready when awakened each morning. When she made desserts, he acted as though she had hung the moon. If she dished him some and brought it out on the deck, he nearly bowed in thankfulness. For simply washing his clothes with her own, he made her feel as though she had lifted the biggest burden in his life. When she offered to help him teach school to the children, it was as if an angel of mercy had come in and shed some glorious light upon his world.

But the one thing that moved her more than any other was how he loved to hear her sing. That was wonderful to her because she was *not* the musical talent in the family. Each of her other siblings had careers in music, but Angie had always been lacking in that area. She had been forced to take piano as a child, but when it became obvious that she didn't have proficiency there, her father insisted that she not be made to continue. But Michael loved to hear her sing and play her guitar and had shown her much more since her move to Padawin.

Then there was the way he looked at her. Anytime she would catch him staring her way, it would appear that he adored her. She had longed all her life to have someone see her like that. Men had made many passes at her over the years, and she understood that she had an attractiveness that encouraged it, but she had always tried to dress modestly and act discreetly. It never seemed to matter, though. Year after year some med student or intern, and later on even a couple of doctors, would suggest some illicit activity. It never failed to sicken her. She kept thinking she would get used to it and be able to laugh at it all one day, but when a doctor with three kids made an overt pass toward her, she literally went to the bathroom and threw up. Why would God bless her with an appeal like this yet never give her anyone whom she could love? Then she married Michael.

Her father began another passage and she looked down at her own Bible. When she did, Michael glanced back at her and gave a quick wink. There she went again. All the events of last night began to replay in her mind. The couch, his kisses, and then finally a wonderful time of intimacy. Since last Saturday night in Padawin, she had longed to be with him, but the flu, the coup and the trip to the States had taken everything out of them. Last night had been a wonderful reassurance that even if they never could step foot in Padawin again, she would be fine. She had found the love of her life.

*****

Sunday dinner was obviously the biggest meal of the week at the Wright house. Angie explained that normally Andie and her family would come eat after church and spend most of the afternoon there. It was also common for them to randomly invite a family from church if the mood hit them. This weekly ritual of fellowship and fun had been around many years. Michael was thankful Andie's family was away for the moment and that Annie and Alex were bound up in rehearsals for the Christmas concert tour. He doubted he could have handled the entire entourage at once. He was having a hard enough time trying to find his way around Barbara and Jonathan Wright. Barbara, of course, had been wonderful from the beginning, but Jonathan had been for the most part exactly as Angie had described: polite.

When dinner was finished, the family moved to the back porch. Here the conversation took a more serious turn. Jonathan began to probe deeper into Michael's life. With nearly each question Michael would turn to Angie for support, and she would always smile and nod as if to tell him this piece of information was safe to disclose.

"What did your father do?" Jonathan asked nonchalantly, having no idea this was a loaded question.

"He was an alcoholic," Michael said trying to keep his nerves under control. "I never really remember him working. My mother was a hard worker, though ... at a beef processing plant."

Jonathan quietly absorbed the information. Michael looked at Angie; she simply smiled and nodded.

"What made you decide to go into missions?" Jonathan rerouted the questioning, not pursuing the family matter any deeper.

"My parents were killed when I was sixteen. My Ag teacher took me in and mentored me. He influenced me toward agriculture, but in my heart I wanted to reach out to others and be that same kind of influence. This man was the *salt of God* in my life, and I wanted to be that to people who needed the Lord also ... people like me."

"Why missions?" Jonathan continued.

"My interests in Agriculture and building things kind of prompted me in that direction. I believed God was leading me to use that knowledge to benefit those who didn't have it, those outside of US influence. I knew God could take the gifts of growing food and raising farm stock to use as an opportunity to bring His life to those in spiritual darkness. The more I learned the stronger that call felt."

"Why Padawin?"

"I was reading a nature magazine one day while in the dentist's office. It talked of Padawin and its history and culture. It spoke of the volcanoes and the spiritism that had risen from their fiery showers. I looked at the pictures and fell in love with the islands. I began to research them and discovered that no missionaries had ever gone there. It was like *wham*! The Spirit of God hit my heart like a lightning bolt, and I knew that was where I needed to go. I had everything these people needed to improve their lives, and the greatest need was Christ."

"Was this before or after your doctorate?"

"Before. The reason I decided to go ahead and complete my doctorate was that I wanted as much knowledge and information to take with me when I went. My advanced degrees actually weren't in Agriculture but in Environmental Engineering. I knew there would be many more needs than just growing and raising food, so I felt the longer I could stay in school, the more questions I could ask, the more problems and needs I could anticipate, the better prepared I'd be to bring light to these people."

"When did you know you were in love with Angie?" Jonathan shot out with no warning.

Michael's eyes grew wide immediately, and he looked over at her. She still gave him that warm, reassuring smile, and her eyes glowed with support.

"When she stepped off the plane in Hawaii," Michael stated.

"What? You knew you loved her at that moment?" There was an alarming change in Jonathan's tone.

"No, I didn't *know* at that moment that I loved her then, but when I look back at it now, I can easily see how I immediately was drawn to her. By the time we said *I do* that night, I was already smitten."

"I see," Jonathan mumbled out as he ran his hand through his graying hair. "Why?"

"Sir?"

"Why were you *smitten* with her?"

That was easy; there was no reason to even consider that answer. "Because she was the most caring, tender-hearted, vivacious, gentle, fun-loving, and giving person I'd ever known. Because when she looked at me as we repeated our vows, I knew she was saying it forever; it wasn't just for convenience. And when she stepped into the Podakind village, she stepped into it with the idea that we were a team, and she made sure everyone knew it. When I look back now, I realize that ... that ... somehow I was incomplete ... before her."

Michael looked over to Angie. He was flushed from feeling under the microscope. He needed to know that she agreed, that she was behind him, and perhaps that she even felt the same. He got the reassurance, not only by her smile, but also when she stood up and came over next to him. She knelt on the floor beside his chair and reached up to take his hand.

"I know it seems odd," she began to tell her parents, "how all of this came about, but if you want to know how I feel about it, I believe God was in the whole setup. It's easy to write it all off as coincidence. Michael was a single young man called to Padawin who went through a lot of things in his life to get there. I was a single young doctor who had one goal in life: to go to Padawin and minister healing and Christ to the tribes. When we met, it was much more than just the common call or common age that melded us together."

She stood up as though she were lecturing a class. "I knew nothing about Michael except his name and what he did, yet my heart fell for him almost immediately. His gentle eyes," she looked down at him and smiled, "his tender manner, his humble nature, all these things drew me to him like no man I'd ever known before. Daddy, you told me from the very beginning to not even think about a man who wasn't considering the mission field, so that's exactly what I did. Do you remember telling me that if God intended for me to marry, He'd bring someone into my life that would perfectly fit the calling He had given me?"

Angie stared at her father waiting for a response. After a long, uncomfortable pause he finally nodded.

"There's no other man on the entire planet that fits more perfectly into the calling God has placed on my life."

"But what about that call now?" Jonathan asked defensively. "You're no longer in Padawin."

"But our hearts are," Angie replied quickly, "and our calling is still there. God could've allowed the uprising to take place four months ago. Had that happened, Michael and I would've never met. Quite possibly, I may have even given up on the whole thing and just turned my heart elsewhere, but that's not how it happened.

"Instead, God gave us three wonderful months together. We worked side by side, ministered Christ together, laughed together, sweated together, taught together, sang together, played together, cried together, and," she looked to Michael as she finished, "we loved together, Daddy. None of this was an accident. Michael is the man of my heart and the man of my dreams, and God led me to him step by step by step."

Michael wanted to stand and applaud her, but instead he sat still and waited for Jonathan's response. He knew the man had to be suspicious of some island hermit seducing his daughter, but it hadn't happened like that … not at all.

"I think it's wonderful," Barbara said with tears tracing her face. "So many people search long and hard to find a soul mate, but the two of you trusted God to find each other, and He lived up to the faith you displayed."

"Just how married are you?" Jonathan blurted out. "I mean, exactly how far has this thing gone? Are we beyond annulment here?"

"Jonathan!" Barbara exclaimed in disgust.

"Daddy!" Angie yelled out. "I don't want an annulment! Haven't you heard what I've said? What Michael and I have is for keeps; I'm not seeking any annulment!"

"Enough," Michael said calmly as he stood and put his hands up for the conversation to halt. "Mr. Wright, I'm sorry if you're disappointed in me. I know that Angie is way out of my league, and had we met at college or seminary, she wouldn't have given me a second thought."

"Michael!" Angie screamed in frustration. "That is *not* true! I would've been drawn to you immediately!"

"You can't *know* that," Michael said almost sadly. "You might think that because of how you feel for me now … but you really can't know that."

He walked toward the door to leave.

"Michael," Angie went after him, "my heart doesn't tell me that."

Jonathan stood and said, "How do you know what your heart is telling you? This whole situation is completely unrealistic!"

"Fine, Daddy!" she yelled back. "What if I'm carrying your grandchild right now? What does *your* heart tell *you* about that? Michael is the love of my life … in every way possible! I've given my heart, soul, and yes, Daddy, my body to him, not because I'm deluded, but because I've found someone who completes me! Why are you so against that?"

Michael walked out, and Jonathan sat back down, sighing deeply as he closed his eyes.

"So you've really slept with him?" Jonathan asked her after Michael walked out.

She stared at him in disbelief. "I've shared a bed with him since our first night together in Hawaii."

Jonathan opened his eyes and glared at her.

"There was nothing sexual about that," she explained. "But as time went by, and every day I grew closer to him and found myself falling more deeply in love with him, sharing his bed in every way became something I *desperately* wanted, Daddy. I love Michael. I adore him with all my heart. If you can't accept that, then we'll find somewhere else to go. It's wrong of you to make me choose between you or him."

"Wait just a second," he said soberly. "I never said anything about making choices."

"Then what *are* you saying?" she asked through tears. "I've tried to convince you I'm in love with a wonderful man of God, and you've systematically shot down every reason."

"I just feel like the whole thing was rushed! You leave for three months and come back to tell me you might be pregnant from a man I just met two days ago! How am I supposed to take all of this?"

"You say *hurrah! My Angie found the only man she could ever truly love!* You say you're proud for me and that you hope our life turns out for the best. You don't start asking about the possibilities of an annulment!"

"It's my job to take care of you!" he defended. "I need to know that this *decision* you've made is the right one! I can't just stand by and accept all of this blindly without knowing all the facts!"

"And that, therein, is where the bottom line lies," Angie said as she reached for the doorknob. "You don't know all the facts. You don't even know Michael, nothing about him. You can't know all the reasons why my heart is in his hands. And perhaps it never occurred to you that maybe God had a purpose for bringing *me* into *his* life. Perhaps Michael has wounds and hurts that God knew I could bind up and heal. This marriage is *not* all about me, you know? It's about the both of us, and I'm committed to it."

She opened the door and walked out, heading immediately to the stairs. She didn't want to imagine what kind of state Michael would be in when she found him. She was embarrassed and irate at her father. She never thought he could be so insensitive and bull-headed. He had practically pushed Annie toward Stephen, even so much as sending her to stay alone with him during the holidays last year. Yet here was Michael, a man committed to the work of the Lord, and he was trying to sabotage him.

Angie walked into the apartment and began to look for Michael. She half expected to find him packing his things and preparing to leave, but instead she saw him lying on the bed curled up in a tight ball. She could hear him crying. She ran over to the bed and immediately took him in her arms.

"Sweetie," she said gently, "none of this changes anything. I love you, Michael. Please know that I love you."

She could feel him nod, but his sobs wouldn't allow him to speak.

"I'm sorry my home wasn't a safe place for you. I never dreamed my father would act this way. He's never been an unreasonable man before. If you want us to leave, I understand. Fred Carson mentioned some furnished housing for missionary couples on furlough. We can go there."

Michael wouldn't speak, but he shook his head *no*.

"Okay, we don't have to. I'll do whatever it is you want me to do. We can go to Kansas … wherever … I'll go to Africa with you if that's what you want."

When he finally gained control of his emotions, he sat up on the bed and looked at her in complete despair. Angie knew how hard it was for him to express himself, so she gave him time to gather courage.

"I'm going back to Padawin," he finally said. "I belong there. I've never belonged anywhere else in my life, and I *don't* belong here."

Angie closed her eyes tightly as tears began to fall again. She nodded in understanding. "I'm going with you," she said weakly.

"No," he replied quickly. "Angie, I can't let you go back with me. They'll kill you."

"They'll kill you, too."

"I don't care," he mourned. "I'd rather die there, where I belong, than try to live my life proving to people that I deserve you when in fact, I really don't."

"Michael, it has nothing to do with deserving anything. God gives grace to us all. If you go back to Padawin, I'm going with you."

"Please don't. I can't lose you like that, Angie. I just can't do it. Please let me go alone."

"Never. 'Til death do us part, Michael. I made that promise, not only to you, but to my God."

FORTY-ONE

"What time is church tonight?" Michael asked groggily after waking from an unsettling nap.

"You're not going, are you?"

"Sure, I am. I'd never forsake the *assembling together of believers* with the exception of the flu and major monsoon rains."

"What about all the mess with my father this afternoon?"

He sighed deeply and shook his head. It wasn't that he *wanted* to go; it was that he *must*. "As much as I don't care to face your father, even less sit under his preaching at the moment, the right thing to do as a child of God is to go. So I'll go," he said plainly.

"You don't have to."

"I know that, but God can speak in some of the most unexpected circumstances. A couple of hours ago we decided jointly to most probably give up our lives in Padawin. If that's *not* what God wants, we need to be listening for any word He might have for us, regardless of who the vessel is."

"But my father?" she said in near disgust.

"Your father is a man of God," he stated quickly. "He may not understand our marriage or our love, but that doesn't make him any less the man he was before we returned. He spoke a mighty message this morning; we need to hear what he says tonight."

She nodded, not in agreement, but in willingness to follow his lead.

"I do have one request," she said as she stood and stretched, feeling tired and drained from the whole week coupled with the stressful afternoon.

"Anything."

"I want to see my sisters before I go."

"Is that possible? Annie's in New York."

"She'll fly us up; trust me on that."

"Wow, does this mean I might get to meet Stephen Williams?"

"No *mights* about it. He doesn't leave her side."

"And when does Andie return?"

"Supposedly tomorrow afternoon. She still doesn't know we're here."

"Andie doesn't like me either, right? Only Annie?"

Angie chuckled. "I don't know. She wasn't *for* the whole situation. She may change her mind when she meets you."

"Here we go again," he sighed as he finally stood. "But Annie *does* like me?"

"Annie will love you," she said with a wink as she put her arms around his neck. "Besides, she's still very much a newlywed. She likes the whole idea of being in love. She's happy for us."

He touched his forehead to hers and closed his eyes. "I wish I could've met Annie first. It might have made the rest of this more bearable."

*****

As Jonathan prepared to leave the house, Barbara called out to him from the couch in the living room. She wouldn't face him; she merely spoke … loudly and perturbed.

"I just want to say six names for you," she yelled out. "Adam and Eve, Isaac and Rebekah, Jacob and Rachel. I'll let you do the math since you're the theological genius."

Jonathan grunted and walked out the door headed for the church. He had been totally baffled by Angie's response. He had only tried to reason out this ridiculous situation, and she had gone to pieces emotionally.

What was she thinking? Okay, his parents died when he was sixteen! Tough break, but that doesn't mean that my daughter has to pick up the pieces twenty years later. They don't even know each other! It must've been the sun, or too much fruit—heavens, I don't know! But how do two people, Christian people, just … well … do what they did? I don't like it!

And what is Barbara trying to pull? Adam and Eve? Who are they in light of all this? Isaac and Rebekah? Jacob and Rachel? All of these have a connection to my Angie somehow? I hope she came to her senses after this mess. Fat chance they'll even be in church. Some missionary he is! He's brainwashed my daughter against me! My Angie…

*****

When Michael and Angie left for church, her parents were already gone. She tried to talk him out of going again, but he insisted they were to never forsake God's people, even if it meant the pastor was at odds with them. They were to always obey God ahead of man.

When they walked into the church, many greeted them. Rather than sit up near the front on the second or third rows, as was Angie's usual custom, she and Michael chose the very back. They sat quietly and soberly. The decision they had made that afternoon had been perilous, and they knew their lives were on the line. Michael thought they might try to create some type of hiding place to where they could escape if terrorists ever invaded the camp, but there would be evidence they were living there. That might possibly put the tribe in danger. Many things were on the line with this decision, and even though they were committed to it, he knew he had to listen for God's possible take on the situation. He couldn't forget what Chet had told him: if they were killed, their ministry to Padawin was over. If they waited, they could possibly return someday and finish what they had started.

When the song service was over, Jonathan Wright stood to preach. His head and heart were a mess of jumbled chaos. Nothing he had wanted to say seemed like the right thing. When he took his place behind the pulpit, he was shocked to see Michael and Angie sitting in the back. He tried not to stare, but it floored him. He hadn't seen them come in, and he had assumed they wouldn't show. *He* wouldn't have come had the tables been turned.

He looked over the crowd and spied Barbara whose eyes were still puffy from an afternoon of crying. She had made it clear to him that she believed Michael was a Godsend to Angie, and that Angie had found the love of her life. She had spent close to an hour arguing that point, but Jonathan wouldn't agree. He glanced back to the couple. Their faces were grave and resolute; he assumed he could count on their leaving tomorrow.

"It's amazing, isn't it," he began, "how some things can drive us to our knees so quickly? Wednesday morning, Barbara and I were watching the news when we heard that Padawin had been overtaken by rebels. When they reported that all Americans had only six hours to leave, our hearts failed us, and we *fell* to our knees."

He paused. He honestly didn't know where he was going with this. All he knew was that this was the first thought that had popped into his head.

"However, somewhere on Friday afternoon, after seeing my little girl safe and sound back home, I left my knees. I was thankful to God, yes, but I became conditional with Him. *Thank you God for bringing her back, but now that she's here and alive, I have a few demands of You concerning her situation.*"

He paused then said, "Have you ever done that with God? Plead for Him in desperation to work a miracle, and then when He does, you just sort of pull the lifeline back and begin to think you can take matters into your own hands … as though there never was anything you needed from Him in the first place?"

He placed his Bible on the pulpit and waited for whatever was next. He had no idea what he was saying, and even worse, he wasn't sure if this was God or guilt talking. But whenever he looked back at Michael and Angie, a twinge would knot up inside him.

"When you called me to pastor here, oh, over twenty-five years ago, I promised you I'd always be honest. I've confessed a lot of things from this pulpit, a lot of failures, a lot of mistakes, a lot of misjudgments. Wednesday morning, I hit my knees in desperation, and Friday afternoon I got up and took matters into my own hands—mistake … failure … misjudgment."

He paused, gazed down at Barbara who was now looking expectantly, and then glanced back at Angie and Michael. Their expressions hadn't changed. He continued, secretly praying that God would give him some direction. If not, he would look like the biggest buffoon in all of Alabama that night.

"Most of you know Angie really well," he said with a smile. "She's a lot like my other two daughters: bull-headed, stubborn and opinionated."

Gentle laughter rolled around the congregation.

"When Angie told us she felt called to the mission field as a senior in high school, most of us welcomed the commitment. In junior high, missions had fascinated her, while in high school, *other* things did."

Several laughed at this. It was true. Angie had been very mission-minded in her younger years, but then went through quite a wild streak as a teenager. Michael glanced over at her with a questioned look.

Jonathan went on. "When Angie came home from college, pre-med, and said she was going to some obscure Pacific island nation called *Padawin,* most of us just smiled and said *that's nice, dear,* while we were actually thinking, *time will tell.* Time did tell. After many obstacles, Angie saw her dream and calling fulfilled: she went to Padawin. Not without a fight though. The mission board wouldn't allow her at first because she was single and Michael Collins was single."

Understanding began to register across a few faces in the congregation. People tried not to look shocked, but several exchanged wide-eyed glances.

"So, I'll just let all of you put two and two together on that statement," Jonathan said with a grin. "Yes, Angie married Michael simply for the reason that she couldn't go to Padawin if neither of them were married."

He let the confession sink in.

"I had no problem with it when I thought it was all … simple. Then something really bizarre happened, well, let me classify that. Something that *I* thought was bizarre happened. My wife actually predicted it. I scoffed at her. But somewhere down the road, Angie and Michael … well … decided they *liked* each other."

People began to look around the building for the couple. When they were spotted, there were smiles of acknowledgment and gentle nods. Angie smiled back, but Michael kept his gaze on the preacher.

"As I've already said tonight, I hit my knees on Wednesday because I needed God to intervene. I knew Angie's commitment to Padawin, and I knew her stubbornness. I wasn't concerned that she *couldn't* get out in six hours; I was scared to death that she *wouldn't* get out in six hours. I honestly didn't think she'd leave."

He looked back at Angie who was still staring with a slight scowl. Michael's expression was not of repugnance, but of intensity. Jonathan now knew what he needed to say, but he wondered if he had the humility to carry it out—Michael would.

"When Angie called me some time that day, I don't even remember when, I was still on my knees. And when she told me that Michael had insisted they leave, at that moment in time, Michael Collins was a miraculous answer to a desperate prayer. But as soon as my miraculous answer stepped off that plane in Memphis, I got off my knees and onto my high horse. I forgot about God's workings and began to work on some things myself, and the beginning of those things was to judge a man I'd never met."

Angie leaned over to Michael and whispered, "I think you're about to get a public apology."

"It's not an apology I want," Michael whispered back. "I need a clear word from the Lord."

"Then listen up, Dr. Collins. I think you're about to get one."

Jonathan looked down to Barbara again who was now smiling. It warmed his heart and gave him courage to continue. God had given her to him thirty-six years ago, and she was indeed a precious gift. Did *he* deserve *her*? Probably not, but God had granted him her love and her life regardless of his flaws and stubbornness, and he was eternally grateful.

"Marriage is an odd thing when you start to think about it," he continued as he casually leaned against the pulpit. "Two people commit themselves to each other for life, at least that's the way it's supposed to be. And you know what constantly amazes me about marriage? Almost everybody marries an exact opposite! Have you noticed that? I've married countless couples in my time, and during premarital counseling some remarkable things are revealed, the most remarkable being that the couples actually believe they'll break the mold; they'll have the perfect marriage. Hmmm. I married an opposite."

He looked down and winked at Barbara. She smiled and nodded in agreement.

"My wife is a wonderful, cheerful, personable lady. She trusts everyone and makes it her job to please everyone. Are you uncomfortable, ill at ease? Then call Barbara and expect some results immediately. Me?" He shook his head and dropped his arms down in exasperation. The congregation laughed again. "I'm opinionated, stubborn and hard-headed, pure and simple. Now remember, I hit my knees on Wednesday, but I got up on Friday. It was almost as if I drew a line in the sand and said, *God, You can go so far and then I'll take over.*"

He paused. He had confessed, but there was no point, no message, in this little sermon. He knew there had to be more. He thought of Barbara's six names she had called out when he left.

"God brought Eve to Adam ... just sent her there out of the blue ... and Adam was awed at the gift. Abraham sent for a wife for Isaac, and Rebekah met the requirements. When she was given to Isaac, he was awed at the gift and loved her right away. When Jacob first met Rachel at the well, he was awed and agreed to work for seven years in order to marry her."

He looked back toward Angie and said tenderly, "God gives wonderful gifts. Over the years God has granted me five inexplicable gifts. The first was Barbara. When she came into my life, I knew completeness like I'd never known before. Then came my three beautiful daughters. What more could a man ask for? Three girls with minds of their own and drives that pushed them to succeed, each in their own area. Then God gave me a son, a sensitive, talented young man who's now a wonderful father and an accomplished musician. Yes, I hit my knees on Wednesday, but I got up quickly, almost stubbornly, on Friday."

He ran his fingers through his hair and struggled to go on.

"Michael, would you come up here for a moment, please?" he suddenly asked.

Michael's face went pale right away. He tightly squeezed Angie's hand, stood up and walked to the front of the sanctuary.

"During Michael's reprieve from Padawin, I hope we all get the opportunity to hear him speak," Jonathan said as he went down from the platform and extended his hand. Michael shook it and looked at him in confusion.

"All I heard concerning Michael Collins before I ever laid eyes on him had to do with his commitment to his ministry, his commitment to missions, and his commitment to the Master." Jonathan chuckled and added, "That'd make a good sermon, wouldn't it?" At this point, however, the congregation was utterly perplexed.

"If Michael Collins had a flaw, it was that he'd sacrificed everything to stay in Padawin and carry on the work he began ten years ago. He was a man with a heart that was strong in all the right places. I'm sure you can see why I was so concerned about God's choice for my daughter," he added, mocking himself.

He placed his arm around Michael's shoulder and gave him a strong hug.

"As I look back, I remember that feeling when I hit my knees on Wednesday ... that desperation and hopelessness. What I don't remember is when that feeling left and the sense of *I'm in control now* took over. It's baffling how our flesh can be so conniving and convincing at the same time."

He now looked at Michael and asked, "How many years did you say it was before you ever began to actually share Christ with the tribesmen?"

"Two years before they asked why I was there. That's when I began to tell them about the great love of God."

"Imagine that kind of perseverance!" Jonathan exclaimed. "As a preacher, I find that rather intimidating. I mean ... I consider it my job to share the Gospel with my mouth. Isn't that why you hired me in the first place? Yet Michael understood something that most ministers in America never grasp: you have to live the thing before you can speak it. For two years Michael brought health and food to these people in a way they'd never known before. It took them two years to finally ask him, *Why?* It took me one day to tell you why I was here, and that was without you ever seeing anything in my life lived out.

"I have to wonder why I left my knees. How could I go so quickly from abject anxiety to complete arrogance? Listen to me now, people. I left my knees because on that three hour drive back from Memphis, Angie talked non-stop ... I know you may find that hard to believe."

There was gentle laughter again; everyone knew the Wright girls were famous for talking.

"During that ride all I heard about was the incredible work that Michael had done, the incredible man that Michael was, and the incredible husband that he'd become. I wanted to believe that I felt *protective* of my daughter, but that was hogwash! What I felt was embarrassment at my lack of perseverance and planning. I'm very comfortable here in Dockrey. Too comfortable! I'm so comfortable that I believe way too often that when souls aren't being saved or people aren't committing themselves to discipleship, it isn't my fault. You folks are just going through a dry period. Y'all need to get it together!

"Ah, beloved, what a deceitful web the heart does weave," he said with soft conviction. "I'm the shepherd, and you're the flock entrusted to me. When my heart grows dry, so does yours. When my commitment wanes, so does yours. When I leave my knees, there's no one to intercede ... no one to stand in the gap."

He went back to Michael and put his arm around him again.

"I hit my knees on Wednesday because I knew only God could help. I left my knees on Friday because my pride got the best of me. You know what this church needs? A missionary. We need someone to come here with the sole purpose of bringing us to the feet of Jesus so that we may look up and gaze around the throne. How pitiful that I could grow so complacent and comfortable when God has given me a mandate to fan the flame of His presence in your lives. I haven't even tried to light the flame lately, much less fan it!"

Now he looked toward Angie and motioned for her to join them at the front.

"God has blessed us with two people who have a burning desire for missions," he said as she came forward. "Our church needs them; I need them. For as long as God keeps them here, I want to go to them as a resource. Where they see a need, I want their insight. Where they see a weakness, I want their strength. And where they do not see Christ, I want their faith."

Angie took Michael's hand at the front, unashamedly, as though she truly belonged in this partnership. Michael squeezed it hard.

"I've confessed a weakness to you tonight," Jonathan began to wind it down. "I've had it really good here, and you've all been pleased with my complacency. That means that the attitude that *I'm all right doing as little as possible* is very infectious. I know that I need to kneel at this altar for quite a while. Perhaps I'm not the only one who feels convicted tonight. This invitation is for others who have hit their knees and then stood up in arrogance when all was well. This invitation is for anyone who's guilty of thinking that faith boils down to showing up at church a few times a week and putting in our time. Perhaps you can pray with each other and encourage each other to become missionaries here, in Dockrey, in our part of the world, and to attack that mission with the same fervor and zeal that the Dr's. Collins have."

As the piano started, Jonathan went over to Michael and Angie and embraced them both. He asked that they forgive his arrogance first, then kneel and pray for him. As they knelt, Jonathan began to feel the burden lifted that he had held for a long time, the burden of falling into a rut and being completely content to lay there.

FORTY-TWO

There was a chilly bite in the air when Angie and Michael left the church. She felt him shiver as she took his arm to walk back down to the house.

"Cold?" she asked.

"Yes. I haven't felt this kind of weather in a long time."

"It's only the beginning. By the end of the month, we should have a fire in the fireplace most evenings."

"That reminds me of another regret I have."

"Regret? About what?"

"I always meant to take you down to the ocean one night and build a fire on the beach to roast clams." There was a bit of homesickness in his voice. "It's wonderful ... one of those things about Padawin that I love. I imagined us bringing our guitars down there and playing for awhile."

"We'll do it someday," she said as she leaned her head on his shoulder.

He was quiet as they walked. The night was cool, the sky was clear, and the moon was dazzling.

"Do you feel more ... uh ... comfortable about being here now?" she asked.

"Yes," he said simply.

She didn't need to ask more. He was a man of deep thoughts, but few words. She had learned from the beginning not to push him. His *yes* was backed by many emotions and much contemplation, and she understood they were there even if he didn't express them. She was merely glad to know that he could say *yes* with heartfelt conviction, and that she was there for him to say *yes* to.

When they got inside the house, he rubbed his arms to warm up. "Does that hot tub work?" he asked raising his eyebrows.

"Last I knew. You wanna go in?"

"Only if you join me."

"I better pass. Until I know for certain whether I'm pregnant or not, it wouldn't be the best idea. The high heat would raise my body temperature—not good for developing babies."

He turned and stared with a strange expression. "Do you really think you might be?" he asked with a tiny smile.

"Not really. I'm late, but since being in Padawin, everything has been off schedule for me. Last week was really stressful. I don't actually think I could've gotten pregnant at that time, but you never know."

He nodded. She couldn't tell if he was disappointed or relieved.

"How would you feel if I were?"

He shrugged his shoulders and squinted toward the ceiling. "Happy. I think having a family with you would be the greatest thing in the world. But then, it's like you said, we're just starting out. Being alone together for a while would be nice too."

She went over and wrapped her arms around his waist, smiling and gently kissing the tip of his nose. "How would you feel if I weren't pregnant?"

"Happy," he said with a chuckle. "Either way I end up with you."

"True. I'm torn at the moment myself. Part of me hopes all this is just my imagination and stress. I'd like to build a life with you before we start adding anybody else, but the thought of carrying a child is something I never believed I would experience—it elates me. Then also there's the fact that if I were pregnant, we would possibly have the baby here, a much better alternative to Padawin. However, I don't intend to stop with one child unless there are severe complications, so having them all in Padawin is just as good as anywhere else."

He laughed. "Your brain never stops! For the record, we'll probably travel to Taveren when the babies are due. I would feel better having them there. They have a good hospital. Both of Vicki's were born there—C-sections."

"What? You wouldn't trust Geechern to give me a section?"

After changing clothes, Michael stared out the back window beside the bed. The moon was nearly full, and he began to identify craters that were clearly visible. He loved to lie on the beach at night and name all the constellations. That was another thing he hoped to do with Angie someday. Perhaps he would take his own children down there in the middle of the night to watch meteor showers.

She left the bathroom and came next to him, gently putting one arm around his waist. Her eyes were teary.

"Are you all right?" he asked in concern.

She nodded barely and reached up to wipe a small tear.

"What's happened?" he asked this time. Something was wrong.

"I'm not pregnant." She tried to smile through her disappointment.

"That's okay," he said as he put his arms around her and pulled her close. "You said you shouldn't be anyway."

"I know, but it was still hard not to hope."

"Oh, we can still hope. Besides, we've just started all of this, and I'll have to confess that I've rather enjoyed the process."

She laughed as she nuzzled her face into his neck. "So have I.

Interesting process God created there, wouldn't you say?"

They stood quietly while he cradled her head in his hand and gently rubbed her back with the other. He would never tell her how disappointed he was by the news. The thought of having a child with her had thrilled him, and her announcement just now had hit his stomach with a heavy thud. But like he told her, they were just beginning. Time was on their side. Besides, after the gash on his arm and the flu, he was glad to be the one comforting for a change.

"We could do the hot tub now," she suggested.

"Maybe another time," he said, hoping to hide his disappointment.

*****

The next morning breakfast on the porch was just as Angie had described. They sat with Barbara and Jonathan, everyone dressed in sweats and wrapped in blankets, eating their toast, drinking their coffee, talking and laughing about any and everything. It was like a breath of fresh air for Michael to not sense the tension anymore. He still struggled with disappointment when Angie told her parents she wasn't pregnant, but the conversation quickly switched in another direction.

When Angie and her mother left the porch, he sat quietly with Jonathan for a time. Michael loved the colors on the trees. Although there was still plenty of green, the bright yellows of the hickories, mixed with the deep reds of the dogwoods, along with the chill in the air, all gave him a long forgotten sense of autumn. He had never cared for cooler weather and sometimes wondered if that had influenced his desire to go to the Pacific, but this morning was alive and clear. Perhaps the reason some people enjoyed the cold so much was because their lives and hearts were warm inside.

"There's one thing I'm still uncomfortable with," Jonathan said as he broke the silence.

Michael looked over at the older man, his stomach tensing up.

"It doesn't feel right having you call me *Mr. Wright*. It's way too formal for what we actually are."

He only nodded. He had no clue what he should call him.

"It wouldn't bother me in the least if you just called me Jonathan."

He thought for a moment then shook his head and answered, "I couldn't do that. It would seem somehow dishonorable. What do the other son-in-laws call you?"

"Well, Doug has always called me *Dad*. I've known him since he was a teenager though. We got very close during those years he dated Andie. We didn't care for him too much at first. He was a bit of a rebel ... not a *bad* rebel ... one of those who just refused to conform because everyone else said it was the thing to do. He came to church because it was pretty much the only place he could be with Andie, other than our house and school. During his junior year, his parents went through an ugly divorce. His father had been unfaithful which really tore Doug up. I kind of became a surrogate father to him. As soon as he and Andie married he started calling me *Dad*. I guess you could say Doug became like a second son to me."

He absorbed the meaning in that bit of information. Perhaps Jonathan Wright was not as harsh as he had imagined. Angie talked as though he were the king of the world.

"What does Stephen Williams call you?"

Jonathan laughed. "We ran the gambit on that! He first came here as a visitor to be in Alex's wedding. He was here for only one week, and at that time I was just *Mr. Wright*. Then I began to disciple him over the phone. I quickly became *Pastor Jon*. Then once he and Annie married, it somehow changed to *Dad*. His father never cared much for him."

Michael nodded in understanding. His father had never said a single word to him that was anything other than derogatory, threatening, hateful, or bitter. In fact, he couldn't remember speaking directly to his father after the age of ten except for telling him to leave his mother alone before he shot her. Michael winced at the memory.

"No pressure," Jonathan told him. "It's just that nobody calls me *Mr. Wright* except the IRS."

Michael chuckled. Jonathan was a funny man with a hearty laugh. He was also an intimidating man, tall and strong. The fact that he had three daughters whom he adored and protected probably added to his threatening persona. Yet at the same time, he had a gentleness and approachableness that was endearing. In truth, he was very much a father figure type.

"Dad," he whispered out. "I can't remember the last time I spoke that word."

"You might grow to like it," Jonathan told him as he leaned forward to rest his elbows on his knees.

"I could try, but the word *Dad* has a few negative memories attached to it for me."

"Then perhaps," Jonathan said as he stood and stretched, "it's time to purge some of those memories. Go get dressed and put on some old clothes. We're gonna find the perfect spot for that compost box."

FORTY-THREE

Sitting on the couch watching meaningless television turned out to be the order for the afternoon. The jet lag lingered, and even though Michael's fever had finally broken, he was still drained from the flu. He found himself dozing on and off, dreaming of Padawin, then jolting back to reality when Angie would flip to a different channel. He finally gave up the couch and rolled himself back in the cushy recliner. When his body was at last prone, his dreams took him back to Padawin.

The next abrupt awakening came when a strange, loud, shrill scream sounded from outside. As his eyes came into focus, he saw that Angie had drifted off too and was now trying to discern the source of the commotion. Suddenly her eyes grew wide with recognition.

"Andie's home!" she said as she clumsily pulled herself off the couch. "That's Ashley screaming!"

"Which one is Ashley?" he asked as he considered whether he really wanted to leave his extreme comfort to greet the sister who didn't like him.

"Ashley's the three year old. She's adorable!"

"Sounds like it," he said with a grumble as he put the chair upright. "How many kids do they have again?"

"Four," Angie replied as she smoothed back her hair and headed for the front door.

When she opened the door, Ashley was standing outside of the Mason's van with a stuffed rabbit in one hand and a sippy cup in the other. She was in the midst of a heated argument with one of her brothers. Angie smiled in delight as she watched her sister begin to referee the disagreement. She well remembered camping trips. They started out with unmatchable eagerness and expectation, but always ended with exhaustion and near collapse.

Suddenly Ashley turned toward the sidewalk and caught a glimpse of Angie.

"Aunt Angie!" she screamed.

Andie looked up in confusion as Ashley ran. When she realized that it indeed was Angie, her jaw dropped. Angie picked the little girl up in delight and twirled her round and round. Andie forgot all about baby Aimee and took off for her sister.

"Good heavens, girl," Andie said in shock as she reached out to hug Angie. "What are you doing here? Trouble in paradise?"

Angie hugged her tightly and struggled to hold back tears of joy. "Yes ... literally ... trouble in paradise. A group of rebels overthrew the Padawin government last Wednesday. All Americans had to leave."

"I don't believe it!" Andie said as the horror of the situation registered. "Could you have been killed?"

"Had we not left. We're staying here until something ... well, until something changes, I guess."

"We?" Andie asked with a raised eyebrow.

"Me and Michael. He's inside."

Andie looked stunned for a moment. She took a deep breath and regained her composure. "Why is *he* here?"

"Because *he* is my husband, and he belongs here with me."

"Oh," Andie said slightly shocked. "I didn't realize we were counting this whole thing as official ... you know ... the marriage and all."

"You haven't been reading my e-mails?"

"Oh, I've read them. Let's just say I refused to read between the lines like Annie and Moms did. They think you're head over heels in love."

"I am," Angie said as Adam and Arly came running toward her. "My boys! You guys are getting so big!" Angie knelt down and snuggled them closely to her. She pulled back to look them over.

"I lost a toof," Arly said proudly as the five year-old pointed to a hole in his mouth.

"So soon? What about you Adam?" She looked over to the older brother. "You lost any yet?"

Adam shook his head. "Daddy says I'm holding out for inflation."

Angie reared her head back and laughed. Only Doug would come up with a thought like that. As she looked up, she saw Doug coming toward them with baby Aimee in hand. Angie was amazed at how Aimee's hair had grown and that she now had full-fledged curls like Ashley, Andie and Barbara.

"Hello, Dougy," Angie said as she held out her arms.

"Hello, beautiful," he replied as he embraced her. "What brings you to Alabama? Didn't care for the whole tropical island thing?"

Andie jumped in to explain, "Some group overthrew the government! She could've been killed!"

"But we weren't," Angie added quickly. "Michael and I got out safe and sound."

"How long are you home?" Doug asked.

"We still don't know. As of right now, there's no evidence of any change."

"Aunt Angie!" yelled seven year-old Adam as he ran toward the camper. "Come look at my rocks and leaves!"

"Be right there!" She looked back as she winked at Andie and Doug.

"Had no idea rocks and leaves could be so exciting."

Andie walked inside the house and was startled to find the strange man standing alone next to the couch. His short hair was disheveled, and his eyes revealed that he was either as tired as she was or had just awakened from a nap.

"I'm Michael," he said weakly as he took a step toward her and offered his hand.

"Yes," Andie said approaching him cautiously. "And I'm Andie."

She shook his hand and eyed him warily, making sure she kept her guard up and didn't let him *bewitch* her with the same charms he must have used on her once level headed sister.

"Angie speaks highly of you."

"I'll bet," Andie said sarcastically. "She *speaks highly* of Annie; she *tolerates* me."

"That's not true. She admires you very much."

"Oh, really?" Andie wondered curiously. Everyone knew that Annie and Angie were thicker than blood. Andie was definitely the *sister on the outside*. "What on earth does she admire about me?"

"She thinks you're the model of motherhood. She really admires your choice to homeschool and believes that being the first in this area to try it makes you sort of like a pioneer."

Andie just stared. Either he was a fantastic liar, or Angie actually did have some respect for her after all. "Well, you must be a good listener to have picked all that up."

"Yeah," he said avoiding eye contact, "I listen much better than I talk."

I'll bet, Andie thought to herself. "Where's Moms?"

"I think Angie said something about she was cooking for somebody … or something like that."

"Oh, yeah, it's Monday. What about Daddy?"

"I'm not sure. I would guess the church, but I honestly don't know."

Andie went into the kitchen, and Michael sorted through the strained exchange. The first thing in his mind was how beautiful she was also. He had seen pictures of her around the house and had considered her the *least* beautiful of the three sisters, but after meeting her personally, he found a fire in her deep brown eyes that was piercing and captivating. Her hair was every bit as long as Angie's and Annie's, but hers was wavy. He imagined if she were to cut it short, it would be as curly as her mother's.

"Who are you?" came a young voice bursting through the door.

"This is Michael," Andie told the boy as she stepped out of the kitchen. "This is Aunt Angie's … uh … her husband."

"Cool!" Adam yelled out. "You're my uncle then. Do I call you Uncle

Michael?"

Angie came in just at that moment with Ashley still in her arms and answered. "Absolutely!"

Doug followed close behind with Aimee and stopped short when he spied the stranger.

"This is Michael," Angie told him.

"Wow, okay," Doug said with a confused smile. "I didn't think about you being here too."

"Michael, this is Doug, Andie's husband," Angie said as she shifted the big three year old to her other arm, "and this big girl is my Ashley."

Michael shook Ashley's hand first. He felt that might be the safest. He knew Doug had been in the family many years now, and it was highly possible that he was as protective of the beautiful sisters as their father. When he did reach for Doug's hand, Doug shook it firmly and smiled.

"Nice to meet the man who tamed the wild one," Doug said with a wink.

"Doug Mason!" Andie yelled at him.

"Hey. I'm only speaking the truth! Angie had quite an untamed streak!"

"So did you," Andie shot back.

"Yeah, but I wasn't a preacher's daughter."

As the bantering began between the two sisters and Doug, Michael's heart was taken by only one sight: Angie holding the little girl. He felt himself longing for the child he thought they might have had until last night. She looked natural holding her. Before long, Ashley was out of her arms, and Angie was then reaching for the baby. She held her close and kissed her chubby little cheeks all over.

"I'd watch it if I were you, pal," Doug said for Michael's ears only. "These Wright girls breed like rabbits. We've got four, you know, and Annie hasn't even been married a year and she's already got one."

"I bet it makes for exciting family reunions."

"Yeah, that's a good way to put it. Remind yourself of that when you're in the middle of it."

Michael suddenly realized how much of life he had missed by having no family. He had visited grandparents a few times growing up, but they were as messed up as his own parents. There was always yelling and anger, and people were more miserable because of the visits than they were before, which was hard to imagine. At some point in time, the visits stopped altogether. He knew no aunts or uncles or cousins. No relatives even came to the funeral service the Lovejoys had arranged for his parents.

He enjoyed watching the dynamics of Angie and Andie, and then was amused at Doug's added antics. He was amazed at how the children ran through the house as though it were as much theirs as their grandparents. He noted how the adults seemed to have one eye on the kids, with the other fully tuned into the conversation. Every minute or so, Doug or Andie would yell out a command such as, *don't touch that* or *you know that's Mimi's favorite cup, don't mess with it*, and the kids would move on to something else. And through it all, Angie mooned and crooned over Aimee as she kissed her little hands and talked baby talk while rubbing noses.

The chaos was doubled when Barbara walked in. The kids went berserk running into her arms, and even Aimee began to squeal for *Mimi*. Barbara gave each of them a special greeting as though they were the most precious creations in her life. Then she greeted Doug and Andie with warm hugs, welcoming them back from their trip. His heart ached at the thought that this was *normal* for all of them. They took it for granted. These children had no idea there were others their ages that had never been hugged like Barbara had hugged them. Neither Angie nor Andie probably considered that there were people out there that had no one to care where they had been or what they had done. This family was blessed.

Michael helped Doug park the camper, and then everyone unloaded the camping items into the shed. Angie left with them to help unpack at home so they could all return later for a meal prepared by an insistent Barbara. Michael helped Jonathan prepare the camper for storage as it would probably not be used again until the spring when the weather was nicer. He offered to help Barbara in the kitchen, but she told him she could handle it fine alone, and for him to just relax.

Relax? How could he relax? Andie had made it clear she didn't trust him. Of course, she didn't know him, but he knew she had already made some decisions about him. He could see it in those dark eyes. They had intimidated him down to nothing, and if he could avoid seeing her again, he certainly would. However, if he were to ever feel like he was Angie's husband and part of this family, he would have to deal with Andie again and again.

In the back of his mind, though, the one he couldn't wait to meet was Annie. He had never told Angie that Stephen Williams had been his favorite artist since the very first album. When he had read about Annie on the websites, he was thrilled that Stephen had found someone with whom he could share his life and his music. In fact, he had even considered taking a week and going to Australia last autumn during their tour to see the concert. It was just too much to work out. He decided it was a selfish desire and that he could live life just fine without seeing Stephen Williams and the *mystery woman* in person. But if what Angie had said were true, Annie and Stephen would be down in a couple of weeks for a visit before their Christmas tour. He hoped that Annie was more like Barbara in her acceptance of him rather than Jonathan or Andie. From all Angie had said, Annie seemed to have no problem with the *arrangement turned genuine* situation of their marriage.

*****

The best description of supper was *organized mayhem*. There was constant talking—often with four conversations going at once. The children were thrilled with meat loaf and mashed potatoes, but by the time they had finished eating, there was as much food on their clothes, the table, and the floor as could have possibly made it to their mouths. Michael again marveled at how the adults seemed to take a child and start the cleanup process as soon as the children began to get restless and ready to leave the table. It was second nature to them. Then after an obligatory kiss to the cleaner, each child was allowed to *take off* to wherever their hearts led them.

Because of being frazzled from the camping trip, Andie's family left shortly after supper. When the last child walked out the door, it was as if a peace settled over the house. However, it wasn't a good peace, but a lonely peace. Everyone sighed and began to head in different directions. Angie and Barbara went to clean the kitchen, Jonathan left to see a family who had visited the church Sunday morning, and Michael just stood in the great room unsure of what to do. Apparently, when you were raised in this family, you understood the routines of life. He had never had any routine. All he had ever done while growing up was to try and avoid any conflict with his father and make it through one more night.

FORTY-FOUR

"Your sister's kids are really cute," Michael told Angie as they snuggled beneath the covers early that evening. "Ashley is like a little living doll."

"I know."

She curled up next to him under the cool sheets. He put his arm around her and pulled her close.

"How did you and Andie get along?" she asked.

"She was *polite* and a bit intimidating."

"She's a strong-headed lady."

"So I gathered. She seems to be a great mom though."

"The best. I couldn't believe it when she told me she was pregnant with Aimee, but adding one more to the equation seems to work fine."

He sighed and wondered what it would be like to have children around on a regular basis—laughing, crying, needing someone to care for them.

"Speaking of children," she said as she leaned up on her elbow so she could see his face, "we probably need to think about this whole *family planning* thing."

"What do you mean ... *family planning*?"

"Since I turned out not to be pregnant, it sort of gives us a chance to think about having children without being surprised into it. We need to decide how we want to go about it, you know, having children and when."

This was a conversation he had never imagined having, and after living in Podakind for ten years, he doubted this was a conversation ever among the villagers. You just married and had kids.

"What is it?" she asked about his expression.

"Oh, I don't know, I have all these mixed ideas about children."

"Like what?"

"Well, there's the fact that we hardly know each other in some ways, yet we fit so well it seems like we've been together forever. On the one hand it would only make sense for us to wait a while and settle more into this relationship before adding kids."

"I suppose."

"Then there's this other factor. We're in our thirties. Most couples our age had a head start concerning children. I'm older than Andie or Doug, yet they already have four. They still get to spend some of their youth with them. If we had kids right now, we'd be in our forties while we were raising them, and then I'd hit my fifties when they got to be teenagers."

"Forty isn't old. We could still have lots of fun."

"I know, but it's *getting there* ... getting *closer* to being old, know what I mean?"

"Sort of."

"I had nothing like what your family has. It's like I missed a whole component of life, and when I think about having kids, I want to experience so many things with them. There's stuff I want to do that I never did with my own parents. Like, I can't imagine going camping as a family. That must've been awesome. And all those pictures at the different national parks, what was that like? I want to do that. I want a family, Angie, but I don't want to sabotage anything we have. Until recently, I never imagined having a family, but now I find myself aching for one."

She leaned over and gently kissed him. "How many kids?" she asked with a grin.

"I have no idea," he said as he laced his fingers through her soft hair. "I'm still so baffled that all of this has happened. How did this happen, Angie? How did you fall in love with me? How did it happen so fast?"

"Haven't you ever heard that God works in mysterious ways?"

"This has to be one of His most mysterious."

"But isn't it wonderful?" she whispered. "No first date or having to get up the courage to seek each other out. We never had to wonder at what point we should kiss or how far was too far. No lonely goodbyes or goodnights. It's actually been a wonderful courtship. We just sort of played house for a while and then it all came together. Everyone should be as lucky as us."

"Luck had nothing to do with it. We were blessed."

She smiled down at him as she kissed him again. "Very blessed. So, what are we deciding about kids? How has this conversation ended?"

"I don't know. I don't feel I'm the one who should make this choice. You have to carry the child, and you're the one who'll pay the biggest price. What do you want?"

"I want to make you the happiest man in the world," she teased.

"Done already."

"But children is a decision we have to make together," she continued probing. "Tell me your deepest heart's desire, and then we can work back from there."

He closed his eyes as he tried to actually form an opinion. There were too many variables to just decide and let that be that.

"I didn't ask you to sort through the details," she reminded him. "I just want to know your heart's desire."

"Is this the kind of decision we make with our hearts? Shouldn't we include all the details?"

"We'll think about the details later. What's in your heart, Dr. Collins?"

He smiled again. He loved this woman. Never in a million years could he have chosen someone so perfect, someone he could love so deeply, someone to whom he could trust his life. And how did she grow to love him like this? How could she so unselfishly want to please him?

"Tell you what," he finally managed, "let's not worry about it. Let's move on, try to get through this revolution in Padawin, try to make sense of the days we have here in the States, and if it happens that you get pregnant, great—if not, then we wait."

She laughed. "Okay. So no birth control or anything."

"Not unless you want that."

"I have to tell you, it felt so good to hold those kids again tonight."

"It felt good to watch you hold them. You'll be an awesome mother."

*****

Doug and Andie were ready for an evening away from the children, so Barbara and Jonathan agreed to watch them while the two sisters and their men went out to dinner. Angie and Michael had offered to keep them, but the grandparents won out. Besides, they felt it would be a good idea for the *young* couples to spend some time visiting together. All thought it was a great idea … except Michael. He found himself miserable the rest of the day in dread of the upcoming evening. When Angie would spot him with a downcast expression, she would question why, but his response was never honest. He alluded to still being tired, which was partially true.

When the Mason clan arrived, each child was in top form and excited to be at Mimi's and Gaga's except for little Aimee. She was sound asleep and looking as cherubic as any human possibly could. Andie laid her in a small, portable sleeper in her parent's bedroom, and Michael continued to be amazed at the woman who was such a tender, understanding mother, but managed to shoot darts at him with her eyes. What exactly did she think of him?

The girls caught up on every one they knew, including their sister, Annie, during the ride to Florence. Michael listened especially close to this part of their conversation. It seemed that Annie had taken on motherhood very well, and had even refused a live-in nanny. She didn't care for the life of being famous; she missed anonymity, and she missed her family, but she loved making music, especially with Stephen.

Doug would occasionally throw in a comment or two, usually stashed with humor or sarcasm. Michael marveled at Andie's obvious love for him, but also her disdain at times. She would gently rub his shoulder one moment, then slap his arm another. He continued to banter with her, enjoying whatever attention she would give him. They had been married over ten years; he hoped he could still draw those responses from Angie after ten years. He never saw his parents show any tenderness toward each other. His mother lived in fear of his father's constant threats and intimidation. In fact, there was never communication on a deeper level. No wonder Michael struggled to express himself freely to others.

Dinner at the Japanese steakhouse turned out to be more pleasant than Michael had anticipated. For the most part, Andie ignored him. Occasionally their eyes would meet, and she would pierce him again with a glance, but the moment would always move on. He really liked being around Doug. He was funny and full of mischief, but had a good head on his shoulders. He owned his own construction business after years of working for a hard man. He was brilliant with building people's dream homes, and was personable enough to gain the trust of all who worked with him. He was an honest businessman, a good family man, and a faithful Christian. No wonder Annie and Angie had taken their times finding a husband. With Doug as the example, it would be hard to meet the standard he had set. He wondered if Angie had any second thoughts about their own marriage after spending the evening with Doug.

He also got the chance to observe Andie more. She was poised and controlled, but her laugh was as hardy as her father's and Angie's. She was more cautious and less trusting than Angie, but she put great faith in her family and in her God. In fact, the more Michael observed, the more he realized he liked her, but she wouldn't warm to him at all. After a while, he realized that she never spoke directly to him. That was fine with him. His chosen method of dealing with trouble was to simply avoid it or run away. With Andie, she seemed content to let him blend in the background.

The trip back to the Wright home found Michael struggling to stay awake. Jet lag was still dogging him, and after the huge meal with course after course being thrown on his plate by the hibachi chef, he just couldn't keep his eyes open. When Angie gently whispered they were home, he was floored. He nearly stumbled out of the van as he followed her into the house. Again, he was taken by Andie's tenderness in gathering her brood and getting them out to the van. It also created a small pang in his stomach as he thought that one day his Angie would be doing the same, only it would be guiding the children into the Land Rover after a day of visiting one of the tribes, or perhaps the Clarences in Taveren.

*****

"You were quiet tonight," Angie commented as she hung up the beautiful blue dress she had worn to dinner. Michael hadn't seen her that dressed up since their wedding in Hawaii.

"I'm scared of your sister."

She let out one of her roaring laughs as she came up to him and put her arms around his waist. "She can be very scary at times," she told him with a twinkle of laughter still in her eyes. "Give her space."

"Gladly. I wish I were one of those people who could take someone aside and say, *I know you have a problem with me, let's just get it all out in the open and get it over with,* but I'm not ... not at all."

"I know. And that's okay. Don't make this *your* problem. Andie obviously has issues, but they don't affect us. I still love you, I still want to spend the rest of my life with you, and I still want to return to Padawin with you, so whatever she's dealing with is *her* problem."

"Doesn't it bother you that your sister doesn't like me for some reason?"

"Not in the least. If I let Andie's attitudes about my life guide me, I'd still be in preschool. I don't live my life for the purpose of pleasing my very hard to please sister. We've got a good thing going, and I won't rack my brain trying to convince her of that. Patience, farm boy, patience."

"I'll try," he said still stinging from a sense of hopelessness. "I just wish I knew what to do."

She chuckled. "There's nothing *you* can do to change her mind. She's gonna have to spend some time around you, that's all."

"That's not very reassuring. I was hoping for something a little more firm."

"You're dealing with Andie. The only thing you can be firm about is that she won't change her mind until *she's* ready."

He nodded, but hated being under this magnifying glass. If anything, this would make him more nervous and more prone to do something unnatural which would only abet Andie's thoughts toward him.

Talk about your rock and a hard place, he thought.

*****

On Wednesday morning Michael awoke to a major chill in the air. He shivered his way to the bathroom and wondered how Angie managed to get up every morning without his noticing. He pulled on a pair of jeans and searched around the floor for the long-sleeved t-shirt. He hadn't worn warm clothes since leaving the States. In fact, he couldn't remember what being *cold* felt like until this week. The chill on top of Mount Sheshney was nothing compared to the frosty fall mornings and evenings in north Alabama.

He warmed his hands on the hot coffee mug and filled a small plate with two pieces of sugar toast. Edging open the door to the back porch he was surprised to find Angie out there alone.

"Good morning," she said with her typical smile. "Sleep well last night?"

"Apparently. I never know when you get up. How do you do that? Get up without my noticing?"

"I don't really try. You're just a heavy sleeper."

"I didn't realize how heavy. I'll confess, however, it's awfully hard to get up in this cold air every morning. How can you stand to sit out here and eat your breakfast?"

"I love all the seasons. It's like each one has some kind of element that

246

empowers me. The coolness sort of invigorates me—it brings this sense of newness and excitement."

"Well, I'll give you points for waxing poetic on me, but it's still just plain too cold," he continued to grumble. "I don't have any warm clothes."

"I didn't think about that. No wonder you're so grumpy. We'll go through Alex's room and see what we can come up with."

"No," he said quickly. "I don't want to wear any of your brother's things. I would feel weird."

"Why? It's no problem."

He didn't reply. He was just uncomfortable with it and he didn't know why.

"Then it looks like we need to go shopping soon," she offered instead.

"That sounds like the plan. When can we go?"

"We could go today or tomorrow. Church is tonight. If we went today, we might be pushing it to get back in time."

"What time is it now?"

"Around ten o'clock."

"How long does it take to buy clothes?"

"No, no, no, Dr. Collins," she smiled as she shook her finger at him. "That's the wrong question. The right question is *how long does it take to go shopping?*"

"Okay ... how long does it take to go shopping?"

"All day long," she smiled. "We'll go tomorrow. For now, finish your breakfast and then I've got something to tide you over."

When Michael finished eating, Angie took him up to her old bedroom and opened her closet. She reached in and pulled out a leather athletic jacket with the Atlanta Braves logo.

"Try this on."

"Very nice," he said as he put his arm through the sleeves. "Is it yours?"

"Yeah. Annie gave it to me for Christmas two years ago."

"A little big for you, isn't it?"

"Long story," she said as she adjusted the jacket. "Want to hear it?"

"Sure."

"It was my last year of residency, and I had no choice but to work the week of Christmas. One of the doctors' wives left him two days before the holidays started. He had no desire to stay home, so he told me I could leave."

She paused for a second and grimaced.

"Was he the one who made a play for you?"

"Yeah," she said regretfully. "I never encouraged him in any way, but I can't help but wonder if I was somehow responsible. I mean ... did he actually think he had a chance with me or something?"

"It wasn't your fault."

"It really wasn't, but when I think about it, the whole thing sickens me. He had a wife and three beautiful daughters, and he was willing to risk it all for some meaningless fling."

"If she left him, there was probably a lot more going on than just some beautiful resident working shifts with him."

"You're most likely right. Anyway, I called home and told my family I *would* be there for Christmas. Annie hadn't gotten me anything yet, so she rushed to the mall looking for the perfect gift. She found this jacket, but they didn't have a smaller size. She debated and labored over it, then finally decided it was too perfect to pass up. Of course, I loved it. And the fact that it hung on me was fine. It was something I felt I could hide behind for the rest of winter. I'd wrap up in it on my way to the hospital, and it felt like a warm, cuddly hug every time I put it on."

"Will Annie be upset if I'm wearing it when she sees me?"

"Annie will be honored to see you wearing this jacket," she assured him as she wrapped her arms around him beneath it. "Anyway, it kind of makes you look like a baseball hunk. When we go to the mall somebody might actually think you're one of the players."

He laughed and shook his head. "I doubt that."

"Are you a baseball fan?"

"I liked football and basketball … watching them, maybe playing a little basketball now and then. I never had a lot of time to kill watching sports."

"Doesn't matter. You still *look* like you could play, and after all, isn't image everything?"

"If you say so," he chuckled, rolling his shoulders inside the jacket. It felt good and worn in, and there was a deeper warmth knowing that it was a treasured item of Angie's. If they had to stay in Alabama through the baseball season, he promised himself he would give it a try.

I can root for Atlanta. No problem.

FORTY-FIVE

"Good morning," Angie chimed as she tugged on Michael's sleeve. "Time to get up, sleepyhead."

He slowly opened his eyes and was delighted to find her still next to him. She leaned up to kiss him good morning but wouldn't linger; she acted as one on a mission.

"Get up," she commanded as she bounced from the bed.

"What's the rush?" He attempted to pull her back down. "The stores will still be there if we decide to sleep in a little longer."

"Bite your tongue, Michael Collins!" She pulled herself away and managed to make it off the bed this time. "We're going shopping today! We need to get going!"

She disappeared inside the bathroom, and he shook his head groggily. He dreaded pulling out from beneath the blanket because the room was freezing. With a quick dash he threw off the covers and trotted to the wall heater, turning it to high. The gas bricks lit up immediately—instant heat. As he warmed himself while getting dressed, Angie emerged from the bathroom hustling about as though she were late for a major appointment. He watched in amusement as she sought out her tennis shoes beneath a pile of dirty clothes. She found one, then the other, and sat down on the couch next to the heater.

"Don't forget your jacket," she said with a wink glancing up at him.

"Wouldn't dream of it. I'm afraid I might freeze solid if I did."

"Oh, it's not *that* cold. You need to get your blood thickened up some."

"How do you suggest I do that?"

She only grinned as she stood, gave him a deep kiss, and then waved goodbye as she left the room. "Hurry up!" she yelled as she closed the door.

Michael Collins, what have you gotten yourself into today?

*****

When they finally reached the mall in Tupelo and Angie parked the blue VW, Michael remained inside as he thought about what he needed. She popped open her door immediately and climbed out. Coming around to his side, she knocked on the window. He cracked it slightly.

"What on earth are you doing?" she asked him impatiently.

"Thinking."

"About what?"

"About what I need to buy."

249

"That's not how you shop," she said firmly as she opened the door and reached her hand to him.

"No, that's not how *you* shop."

"You're right," she smiled as she took his hand and forced him out. "And since you're shopping with *me* today, I'm going to show you how it's done properly."

"Oh, boy," he mumbled as she began to pull him toward the mall. "Am I rich enough to shop with you?"

"Lesson number-one: it's not how much you *spend*; it's how much you *save*."

She pointed him to the first store and the great hunt began. She didn't remember a time that she actually had gone shopping with a man *for* a man. She had helped guy friends in the past do some shopping for other people, but she had never actually done this. At first, he was reticent about trying things on. He simply wanted to find something he liked, buy it, and leave. But after a couple of modeling sessions for her, he began to enjoy showing off the different fashions she had picked. By noon, he had tried on countless items of clothing, but had only bought one pair of pants and one sweatshirt.

"I don't think we're making very good progress," he complained as he ate his steak sandwich in the food court.

"On the contrary, we're doing great. Can you believe the deal you got on those khaki pants? You saved $25! *That* is incredible progress."

"What's next?" he asked as he slid a French fry through a mound of ketchup.

"There's this place we've got to go! They have these wonderfully soft flannel shirts."

"Flannel—sounds warm."

"Indescribably warm."

After lunch, he went to the ice cream counter and got a chocolate cone. She smiled in admiration as she watched him carefully wrap the napkin around the bottom and then lick from the top. He looked handsome in her Atlanta Braves jacket, and his baby face still had touches of pink in the cheeks and on his nose from the cold. Her heart beat a little faster when he glanced over at her and raised his cone in question. She smiled, sauntered over and took a lick.

"So, you're a chocolate man all the way?" she asked as she licked around her full lips to get all the ice cream off.

"I guess," he said as he reached up to wipe a smudge of chocolate from the corner of her mouth. "If there are options for flavors, I always choose chocolate."

"Do you ever try anything wild or new?"

He tilted his head, thought for a moment, and then grinned. "*You* are the only wild and new thing I've ever tried."

"Oooo," she cooed as she wrapped her arms around his waist inside the jacket. "And how do you like it ... this wild, new taste in your life."

"I love it. I can't imagine how I ever lived without it."

"I do believe you're almost being romantic, Dr. Collins."

His expression was one of pure contentment. That in itself melted her. She knew he had been alone for much of his life, and to realize she had filled many empty spaces gave her a sense of completion. She had always been a giver. Her nature was to meet every need she could see. Medical school had nearly drained her of that desire because it became more about *passing* and *learning* than helping and healing. Being with Michael and being in Padawin had rekindled that passion. He was a man with many wounds from a life he had not chosen. Padawin had been his escape from a painful past as well as a calling to a meaningful mission. His need for healing and her need to give had bonded the two in a way that completed them both.

As they walked down the mall hand in hand, she felt on top of the world. They went into a couple of novelty shops just for fun and had a good time laughing and wasting time. He was fascinated with the electronics shops and would stop to examine various gadgets. She was impressed at his understanding of the whole electrical process, but then she wondered why she should be. He had built an entire electrical plant in Podakind powered by the river. She sighed. The very thought of Padawin and their home there sent a pang through her heart. She was homesick.

"You okay?"

"Yeah. I was thinking about our home in Podakind. You built a wonderful place there."

"Sometimes I think I'll die, Angie, if we don't get back. I know there are needs everywhere, but for some reason the longing for Padawin soars above them all." He paused and turned to look at her. "Do you think that's wrong? Do you think I've become too narrow minded? Do you think that's why we're here instead of over there?"

"No," she said quickly as she took his hand.

She led him outside the store to a bench in the center of the mall. "Michael, your heart cries for Padawin because that's where God's called you. I feel the same. God isn't punishing the whole island because your love for the tribes there is too strong."

"Then why? Why aren't we there? Why aren't we teaching? Why aren't we helping? Why aren't you healing?"

"I don't know. I wish I did. If I could make sense of this whole mess, it would be much easier to sleep at night. I feel like all my dreams came true for those three months, then everything was ripped away."

She sat back on the bench and stared out toward the people walking by. He had a good point: all these people needed Christ too. Why did they both feel such a call toward Padawin and such a sense of hopelessness by not being there? Why were they sitting in a mall in Tupelo, Mississippi, buying winter clothes for Michael instead of doing what they knew in their hearts they were meant to do? It didn't make sense.

"You know what?" he said softly, reaching over to pull her next to him. "If I have to be away from Padawin, at least I'm with you. I do find comfort in that."

She leaned her head on his shoulder but was still struggling with the confusion. And there was one thought that continued to plague her mind, one idea that she couldn't get out of her head. "Michael, would you have left Padawin if I hadn't been there?"

"I don't know how to answer that. There are too many *what if's*."

"No," she insisted. "There's only one *what if*: what if *I* hadn't been there? What if things were as they'd always been and you were there alone? Would you have left?"

He removed a piece of lint from his jeans and then scratched his head. He was stalling.

"Just answer me, Michael."

"Why? Why does it matter? The fact is that I left. And yes, I left because of you, but I can't know for sure what I would've done if you hadn't been there."

"It matters because I dragged you back here to Alabama, and you're as miserable as mud. My family has razzed you, the weather has already turned cold, and you're dreaming of a place far away where you know you really belong. Somehow it seems like it's all my fault."

"Didn't you hear what I said? I meant it about I'd rather be *with* you and away from Padawin, than be there *without* you."

"You would've stayed, wouldn't you?" she asked him again. "You would've stayed if I'd never come."

He took a deep breath and then nodded his head slowly. "Yes."

"I didn't want to leave either. Why did you make me go?"

"I could've hidden myself. I could've erased evidence of my existence. Shoot, I could've camped in the hills and watched the village to see when the soldiers came and went."

"I could've done that with you! I could've been just as careful as you."

"I couldn't take that chance," he said as he faced her with obvious fear in his eyes. "I watched my mother die. I saw the whole thing. Sometimes I still see it in slow motion. I replay the event and imagine what would have happened had I not … or had I done something else … something different. Ultimately I know I am *not* responsible, but in the back of my mind there are always these thoughts."

"Michael …"

"No," he stopped her. "You want to know *why* I didn't stay? I couldn't see you die that way. I couldn't take that chance again. There came this moment after Chet told me we had to leave, that I imagined a gun to your head. That was my decision. It was like I had a choice with you ... a chance to change the future—I can't change the past."

"Michael, I'm so sorry."

"Why? Because you gave me something to long for other than my mundane existence?"

"But it wasn't mundane until I came along!"

"Angie! What are you saying?"

"If I'd never come along, you'd still be there doing what you love the most!"

"That's like saying if I never tasted chocolate I'd still be eating vanilla and thinking it was the greatest thing in the world! Yes, I thought Padawin was the best thing that ever happened to me ... but that was before you."

"I want you to be happy. I want to make you happy, but I feel responsible for dragging you ..."

"Stop feeling responsible for me," he said in exasperation. "I'm a big boy. I made the choice to leave Padawin with you."

"But you didn't want to come here."

"Not at first, but here we are and all is well."

"You're afraid of my sister."

"Only one of them. And your dad has warmed up to me considerably."

Time to change the subject. "Your cheeks are chapped," she said as she reached up and ran her hand across his pink face.

"Chapped here, sunburned there, what's the difference?"

"We *will* return to Padawin. We're not through there."

"And we're not through *here* either," he said as he held up the two measly packages. "Where are those wonderful flannel shirts you talked about?"

"Flannel shirts, huh," she said as she stretched her arms high above her head. "Follow me, Dr. Collins. Maybe we can get one in every color."

"Only if they're on sale, right?"

"Now see, you're learning already. And they say men don't like to shop."

She led him to a department store where they ended up in the men's section. He thought they would simply pick a shirt or two and buy them, but she had to hold up various colors to his face to determine which matched him best.

"Try this one on, and put this underneath." She handed him a black turtleneck also. "It'll add to your warmth."

He obeyed and soon returned from the fitting room with the black turtleneck beneath a green flannel shirt. Smiling in approval she insisted he turn for her.

"This is really soft. What's it made of?" he wondered.

"Who cares," she grinned putting her arms around his waist. "I love these shirts."

They stared at each other for a bit, wrapped up in the warmth of the shirt as well as the moment.

"Wow, this *is* nice," she smiled as she continued to rub the shirt.

"Yes," he grinned back at her, "it really is."

"Angie Wright!" a voice exclaimed from somewhere behind them.

Angie whipped around. "Cindy!" she yelled as she spotted Cindy Marcum and her mother, Sue.

The two girls ran to each other.

"I heard about the whole island overthrow," Cindy told her. "Mother said you were back."

"Can you believe it? I wait ten years to get there and then have to leave within three months."

Cindy eyed Michael briefly and then leaned into Angie and whispered, "He's cute. Is he yours?"

Angie laughed and nodded as she hugged Sue. "Let me introduce you all. This is Dr. Michael Collins, my husband from the glorious tropical island of Padawin. Michael, this is my best friend in the whole world, Cindy Marcum, and her mother, Sue."

"Pleased to meet you both," Michael said shyly as he offered his hand.

"I see she didn't take very long to dress you out in flannel," Cindy said as she shook his hand.

"I'm not complaining," he grinned. "I'm freezing here in Alabama."

"It's been a cold October," Cindy agreed. "Angie has a real thing for these flannel shirts. I should've guessed she would've lugged her husband down here for a few of them."

Angie then turned back to the ladies and asked, "What brings you two to Tupelo? Aren't you spoiled to the Florence area?"

Cindy looked soberly to her mother and raised her eyebrow. Sue just sighed and closed her eyes.

"What?" Angie asked, knowing that something was evidently wrong.

"You can tell her, Mom. It's Angie."

Sue's eyes began to well, and Cindy put her arm around her shoulder.

"What is it, Mrs. Marcum?" Angie asked with concern this time.

"I found a lump," Sue told her.

Angie put her hand to her mouth in shock.

"She hasn't wanted to tell anyone until we knew for sure what was happening," Cindy explained.

"Have you gotten any results back?" Angie wanted to know, now moving into doctor mode.

Cindy nodded and said softly, "Today. We have an appointment at three o'clock."

"I see," Angie said as she put her hand on Sue's shoulder. "There are many treatments and options available now. I'm sure that no matter what the results are, there'll be something adequate that can be done."

"We're hoping," Sue said with a nod. "I'd rather you didn't mention this to anyone until I'm prepared to deal with it."

"No problem. I believe, however, that if you'd share this with a few friends, you might take some comfort in knowing that prayers were being lifted up in your behalf."

Sue nodded. "I'll think about it." She tried to smile. "It's just been so hard with James dying and now this."

"That's what the family of God is all about," Angie said warmly. "Michael and I will pray for you daily. Take that comfort at least."

"Thank you."

"Will you call me with your results?" Angie asked Sue. "Maybe I can help in some way while I'm here."

"I will."

"Meanwhile," Cindy wanted to change the subject, "do you have any idea how long you'll be home?"

"Not in the least. We keep watching the news for some kind of information, but everything is the same: the rebels are still in power and ready to slaughter all American pigs."

"So, Michael," Cindy said as she turned her attention to the shy man in the background, "how do you like living with Angie?"

He smiled and squinted his eyes as he said, "She can be rather invigorating."

"Bingo!" Cindy laughed. "He pegged you right away!"

"Oh, you know I'm an open book. Besides, Padawin has to be the most beautiful place on the planet. It's hard to live there and just be blah."

"Are you capable of being blah?" Cindy wondered.

"Oh my, you missed my residency years. No sleep, long hours, little pay ... blah came rather easily."

"Glad to see she's recovered," Cindy said with a loud whisper as she leaned into Michael. "Well, we need to head out. Nice to meet you, Michael."

"Yes," he said shyly as he stared down to the floor. "I hope all goes well with the doctor today."

"Thank you," Sue said sincerely.

"Call me," Cindy said to Angie. "Let's have lunch or supper or something soon."

"Sure," Angie said as she hugged first Cindy and then Sue. "I wish you the best."

As the pair walked away, Michael noticed Angie's change in demeanor. She was concerned. From behind, he put his arms on her shoulders and leaned his head next to hers. "Are you okay?"

"Gloom, death, despair, rebellion ... cancer. Life can be miserable, can't it?"

"Sometimes," he agreed as he turned her around to face him. "It seems to have its ups and downs."

"You should know," she said as she put her hand up to caress his face, still enjoying its strange smoothness. "How did you survive all those years? How did you manage to push on through?"

"I always imagined there were better things ahead. And I was right. Look at me now. All those years I kept looking forward, hoping, dreaming. Who would've thought I'd be here ... with you ... buying soft, flannel shirts in Tupelo, Mississippi?"

She ran her hand across his shirt again. "Very soft," she said with her warmest smile.

"*You* have made all those hard times forgotten. How can I be here with you? How did you come into my life and change it all around?"

"There you go ... almost being romantic again," she said as she leaned in closer to him. "What's happening to you?"

"You are," he said as he kissed her gently.

"What do you say we buy some shirts and head home?"

"So soon? I thought we were just getting started."

"My mood has sort of changed. It's hard to shop when you're feeling gloomy."

"Actually, this may make it a little easier. We now have a simple mission in mind: buy clothes. I need some pants, and I need a new suit. We're here; let's get them. Then we go."

"But that's not any fun," she complained.

"I know. Life isn't always fun."

"Now you tell me."

FORTY-SIX

Angie let Michael drive home. She didn't say much but sat with her head leaned against the window as she stared out at the passing landscape. He knew what she was thinking: gloom, death and despair. She was seldom down like this, and he wasn't sure how to handle it. Should he be quiet? Should he be funny? Should he get her to talk with him? Should he ask her about her feelings? He had never pried into anyone's life. He assumed that if someone wanted to talk, they would talk. He found that was generally a good rule, because there were those that would start in and never shut up, and there were those that appreciated his respect of their silence. But how did he deal with Angie?

"Want to talk?" he finally asked. That seemed a safe beginning.

"I don't know how to phrase it all," she said without turning her head. "Most of it's just emotional. Thanks for asking though and trying to be helpful."

"I thought Annie was your *best friend in the whole world*."

"What?"

"You said Cindy Marcum was your best friend in the whole world, but you've always told me it was Annie."

"Oh. Outside of family, Cindy would be my best friend. Her house was practically my second home during my teenage years."

"I just wondered. She's very pretty. I bet you two were quite the duo."

"Well, actually, more like a trio. She has a twin brother named Billy. The three of us were sort of the Three Musketeers of Dockrey. Billy and I dated in high school ... on and off."

"Was he as good looking as she?"

She nodded, raised her eyebrows and said, "Oh yeah. Extremely."

Both were quiet for a bit. Michael found himself feeling slightly jealous of the good-looking twin brother even though he'd never seen him.

"Remember the news of my sort of *wild years*?" she asked.

He nodded.

"Billy was my downfall, you might say. He was very handsome and very popular. He was also very wild. While I was in the process of figuring out and questioning my faith, Billy was more than willing to help me explore the avenues that led away from the straight and narrow."

"And your dad approved of this?"

She chuckled and shook her head. "No, but he felt he had to give me enough rope to either hang myself or develop a lifeline. He had taught me what was right, and he trusted God to guide me into the right choices."

"Did He?" Michael was now wondering. "Did God guide you?"

"Funny thing about all that, even though I was doing things that I knew were directly against God, my parents, and the church, in the back of my mind was this driving call to the mission field. Bizarre, isn't it? It was like I wanted to push the limits, but not too far. I'd sneak out to dances, do a little drinking now and then, and probably made out with Billy in places I shouldn't have, but nothing ever went beyond that."

"What do you mean?"

"I never wanted any of it to be permanent; I just wanted to experiment. But even with Billy, I never let him *do* anything. And believe me, he offered to teach me *the ways of love* more times than I can remember. I knew that there were choices I could make that I could never take back, and sex was one of them, but not just sex, going too far period. He could never understand my hesitance."

"How could you hold him off?" Michael wondered. He had tried to be strong with Jenna, but she had lured him in anyway.

"I laid it on the line several times. I told him we were kids, and that I didn't want to give my virginity up because of raging hormones. I really did believe sex was meant to be special, and it was meant for love. I had no intentions of anything deeper with Billy Marcum other than some fun while in high school. I mean … he was the perfect high school sweetheart. He was a great ride for those few years, but nothing more."

He shook his head with guilt as he thought of his relationship with Jenna, his one and only relationship.

"I wasn't engaged like you, Michael," she said sympathetically. "I also knew that Billy's mind was far from *spiritual.* I always had my guard up with him. He wasn't someone I was willing to trust my life to."

"When I look back, I guess that's what confuses me the most," he confessed. "I still had my guard up with Jenna. I thought the sex would bring it down, would make me feel closer to her, would bond me to her, but it didn't. In fact, it began to alienate me from her even more. I think back so many times and wonder why I didn't believe all those Godly people who had taught me to wait until marriage. Somehow I tried to convince myself that I'd be closer to her if I rejected God's laws and standards."

"But she deceived you, Michael …"

"No, Angie, I deceived myself. I wanted to *be in love*. I wanted to really *belong* to someone. I wanted that more than I wanted to obey God in that entire situation."

"Frustrating, isn't it—the whole sin thing? God tells us what's best, but as humans we're just plain prone to thinking we know better. He never fails, but we seem to convince ourselves we need to fight for our rights no matter what, as though He were ready to pounce on us with misery at any moment, snatching away every good pleasure."

He stared silently down the road, eyes squinted and head tilted slightly downward. Had he known or even believed there was an Angie out there waiting to bounce into his life, Jenna would have never caught his eye.

"However," she decided to add, "it's almost unreal how amazing God's grace is. Just think, between the two of us, we deserved something far less than the privilege of sharing His message with others, yet He called us anyway."

He nodded, still no smile, and eyes still thinly open.

"You do know that He wipes the slate clean?" she asked him, trying to force him to respond instead of stew.

"I do know that, but when I think of what I deserve and what I've been blessed with instead, it's humbling. I didn't think about that too much … until … well until I met you."

"Why?"

"Because I could make myself believe that being alone in Padawin was a sort of penance. I wasn't miserable, and I loved my work, but I'll confess to being lonely. Many times I told myself that I felt like Adam: I was surrounded by life, but there was no one like *me*. I didn't even dream there would ever be someone for me. Then all of a sudden—wham! You walked into my life. Even when we wrote on the computer, it never occurred to me that we could … be like … like *this*."

She chuckled and shook her head.

"What's so funny?" he asked.

"This whole thing with *us*. I actually thought that seminary was my absolute last chance to find a man. For the most part, I'd given up too. Daddy told me from the beginning that if I wanted to marry and go to the mission field, I'd better find a man that carried the same call. And then when the call narrowed to Padawin, he told me I was crazy. I pushed forward with the training, preparing to be a medical missionary, and trusted God to deal with the marriage thing on His own. I can't tell you, Michael, how badly I wanted to get married, but I couldn't show that or share that with anyone. And then it was all complicated by the fact that not only could I not find a man who was called to Padawin, I couldn't find a decent Christian guy who was interested period! And seminary was even worse! As soon as someone found out I was actually a bona fide medical doctor, the walls of intimidation went up and I was put on the *rejection list* right away."

"Did you ever think things might develop between the two of us last year … while we were writing?"

"Never," she laughed. "It didn't even cross my mind. But when you asked me to marry you, you know, to solve the problem of my being appointed, a little alarm went off in my head."

"A bad alarm?"

"Every kind of alarm you could imagine! One part of me was thinking, *Yahoo! I can actually go! This man is wonderful!* Then another part was thinking, *Surely he doesn't think this is an actual proposal.* Then another part was rummaging around with *What if he really is this incredible man and I fall in love with him?*"

"Really? You thought there might be a chance?"

"Why not? Nobody else seemed to work out for me."

He smiled and shook his head.

"What about you?" she wanted to know. "Did you ever think I would be more than just your friendly local doctor to the tribes?"

"No ... not at all. In fact, I was just so excited that you were coming, the dynamics of what might happen never occurred to me, at least ... not until I left for Hawaii. I was actually scared of you for awhile."

"Scared? Of what? What did you think I would do to you?"

"Well," he tried to tell her but was too embarrassed.

"Spit it out, Dr. Collins."

He blushed and squinted again.

"Michael! What did you think I would do?"

"Oh, man," he stuttered, "well ... I thought you might ... well ... expect more from me than just a *working* situation."

She laughed and slapped her knee at the irony.

"I guess the joke really turned out to be on me, though," he continued.

"Why is that?"

"When you walked off that plane, I can't even begin to tell you *what* I was looking for. I can tell you this, though, it *wasn't* someone anything like you turned out to be. I saw you before anyone, and I was so stunned and drawn to your beauty that I was about ready to slap my own face so I would look for the *real* soon-to-be Mrs. Michael Collins."

"You went pale when I approached."

"You have *no* idea." He shook his head. "When you said you were *the* Dr. Angie, I nearly passed out. Talk about feeling guilty."

"Oh yeah? Why's that? Your feelings were completely valid. You'd never seen me or met me."

"Were you sitting around thinking, *What if this guy is the biggest dork on the planet?*"

Angie thought for a moment and then shook her head.

"See," he said. "Yet *I* did, and when you finally appeared, I wanted to run and hide. You were the most beautiful woman I'd ever seen in my entire life. I didn't deserve you."

"Thank you," she said as she reached over and took his hand. "No one could pay me a nicer compliment."

"And you still are," he managed to choke out. "And I still struggle to believe that you could love me."

She leaned over and hugged his arm as he drove.

"Michael, how could I not? How could I not love you?"

*****

After supper, Michael and Angie relaxed on the couch as she endlessly flipped through channels. Michael was relieved when the phone rang and she climbed over him to answer it. He tickled her side and forced her to push his hand away before she could reach it.

"Hello?" she giggled.

"Angie?"

"Yes," she giggled again as she sat up and slapped his hand.

"It's Cindy."

"Cindy!" she cried out as she gave her full attention.

"Having a good time, are you?"

"I think Michael just discovered I'm ticklish."

"Oh my! Sounds like you *are* having fun."

"Tell me about the appointment today."

There was immediate silence. "Not good," Cindy finally told her. "Both breasts are bad. They want to do a double mastectomy and then follow with chemo."

"Man," Angie sighed. "I'm so sorry to hear that. Did they check lymph nodes?"

"Yes, and they're clear for now."

"Thank God for that, then."

"That's what the doctor said. She says Mom's chances are good, but she's got to have the will to fight it. I'll be honest with you, Angie, I don't know if she does. She's been so down and defeated since Daddy died. It's like part of her died with him."

"I bet," Angie said as she leaned against the arm of the couch and put her feet in Michael's lap. He immediately began to massage them. She smiled and mouthed a *wonderful* to him as he continued.

"Billy and I have tried to alternate weekends with her so she won't be alone. Last weekend was Billy's; he didn't show. Typical. Something came up. If he would've called me, I would've come."

"Does he know about her cancer?"

"She won't tell him," Cindy groaned. "It's so hard to bear all this alone. Just to have *you* know is a huge relief."

"Your mother doesn't need to internalize this. It's amazing how the attitude of cancer patients affects their treatment and recovery. She needs to let this out and share it with others. She needs a support group. Cindy, *you* can't be a support group. When she goes through chemo, she's going to need more than just *you* to help out."

"I know, but getting her to agree to that has been impossible. But there's hope; she told you."

"Well, if nothing else, maybe I can be with you both during all this."

"That would be nice."

There was silence again. Angie felt a twinge of guilt as she soaked up the foot massage knowing that Cindy was struggling with her mother's condition, but it felt too good to refuse.

"I miss you, Angie," Cindy finally told her. "I've missed you through all the medical training these past years, and I missed you horribly when you left for Padawin. Who would've thought we could have grown apart like this years ago? We were inseparable."

"Life led us down different paths."

"I'll say. Very different. So, changing the subject, tell me about this *marriage* of yours. Your little husband is rather on the cute side. Did you anticipate that?"

Angie laughed as she told her, "I really don't know at this point what I thought back then. All I know is that he's wonderful, and I'm so thankful God brought us together."

"That could only happen to you. So in three months you fell madly in love?"

"Yeah, astounding, isn't it? When I think about it, I really believe it might have been love at first sight."

"First sight?"

"Let's just say, when I saw him at the airport, I was smitten. He confesses the same."

At this, Michael winked at her and nodded in agreement.

"Billy's gonna die when I tell him about this," Cindy laughed. "So … exactly *how* married are you?"

"Very … married," Angie said slowly as she pulled her feet from Michael's lap and leaned up to kiss him *thank you*.

"Hmmm," was Cindy's only response.

FORTY-SEVEN

Barbara came out to the back porch during breakfast and handed the phone to Angie.

"It's Cindy Marcum," she whispered.

Angie furrowed her brow as she spoke into the phone, "Cindy?"

"Hey, Ang. Does your morning look very busy?"

"Oh, gee, let's see, I've got three surgeries before eleven, but after that I should be free."

"Ha ha." Cindy was morose. "Seriously."

"I've got nothing. What's up?"

"Mother has decided not to take any treatments."

"What?" she yelled.

Jonathan and Michael immediately turned their attention to a panicking Angie.

"She can't do that!" Angie was upset. "You've got to talk some sense into her!"

"That's why I'm calling you. I've tried all morning and I'm out of sense. I was hoping you could be the *big gun* I could call in."

"I'll do my best, but why is she doing this? It's completely irrational."

"She started talking this way last night, and like an idiot I told her to *sleep on it*. I assumed she'd come to her senses and think better today. Instead, she only cemented in what she had decided then."

"Let me get dressed, and I'll be over as soon as I can."

"Ang?"

"Yeah?"

"Thanks," Cindy said warmly. "She loves you like a daughter."

"The feeling's mutual," Angie said sadly as she turned off the phone.

Jonathan stared at her with a questioning look as he asked, "What on earth was that about?"

"Wish I could tell you, Daddy, but for the moment, I'm bound by a gag order."

"Gag order?" he laughed. "What on earth would the Marcums not want anyone to know?"

"You'd be surprised if I told you," she said as she motioned for Michael to leave the porch with her. He followed her to the kitchen to put up their plates and mugs and then on up the stairs to the apartment.

"What's going on?" he asked when they were finally behind a closed door.

"Mrs. Marcum is refusing to take the cancer treatments."

Michael's expression turned from curiosity to concern. "Wow. What are her chances of survival without them?"

"Outside of a miracle? Zero."

They both stared silently at the enormity of what this meant.

"Cindy seems to think that maybe I can change her mind," Angie told him as she hunted for her shoes amid the clutter of the room.

"What do you think?"

"I'll certainly give it my best shot. Have you seen my tennis shoes?"

"I think they might be in the bathroom." He went in to look. "Here they are." He carried her shoes to her and sat with her on the bed as she put them on.

"You asked me not to leave you alone," she reminded him as she finished tying the last string. "You can come if you want, but I think it might be best if I go alone."

"Absolutely. I'm fine. I think I can handle your parents all right. As long as Andie doesn't come over and sabotage me into a corner, I should survive."

She chuckled." Good ole' Andie and her issues. You know, she always has issues with someone. I guess you're the lucky guy for the moment."

"I hope it's only for the *moment*."

"If you need me, the Marcums are in the phone book."

"Don't worry about me. Really, I'm fine. I mean it. Don't give it a second thought."

Angie leaned in to kiss him goodbye, and then gently caressed his face. "I love you, Dr. Collins," she said with a smile.

"Me too. And really, I'll be fine."

*****

As Angie pulled into the Marcum's driveway, she prayed for wisdom to deal with Sue. This woman had meant so much to her, and she couldn't bear the thought of watching her give up hope. The treatments would be miserable, but letting her body be eaten up by cancer would be worse. Sue needed to have hope, but she also needed a determination to live. Losing her husband had to have been unbearable, but to follow it with cancer seemed almost beyond toleration.

I suppose, God, that I really need to stop questioning what You're up to. First Padawin, now this. I understand that sometimes life doesn't make sense, but how do I deal with all of this while in the middle of it? What do I do with myself while I'm not in Padawin? Do I work or volunteer somewhere? Do I wait and believe that I'll be back there soon? And what do I say to Mrs. Marcum? How do I convince her that as long as treatments are viable, she needs to have hope?

Grant me wisdom, Lord. Grant me knowledge beyond what I meagerly have, because right now I'm as blank as can be.

She rang the doorbell and didn't have to wait long for Cindy to answer.

"Why in heaven's name are you ringing my doorbell?" Cindy greeted her.

"Just trying to be polite."

"Polite? Since when?"

"I guess it's the marriage thing. Maybe it has that affect on people."

"Yes, I'd really like to discuss this *marriage thing* with you sometime. However, Mother is the main concern right now. She's in the den watching TV."

"So, I just go on in? No forewarning or anything?"

"I'm beyond trying to play nice. Go in and straighten her out, Ang."

"You put an awful lot of confidence in me."

"You know that saying about *not putting your eggs in the same basket?* Let's just say I'm all out of eggs."

"Okie-dokie," Angie sighed as she looked toward the den. "Let's pray God makes me the proverbial chicken then."

She walked to the door of the den and stopped for a moment to observe Sue Marcum. She was sitting next to a large picture window in a small gliding rocker staring out at the yard. The television was on, but she wasn't watching. Her mind was somewhere else. She wondered if it was the best option to walk in and disrupt her, but what else could she do? She had seldom seen a person without hope, but that was the look on Sue's face, and she struggled to accept that. How could anyone totally give up and want to die?

"Mrs. Marcum," she finally managed with a smile as she walked into the room.

Sue looked up at her and returned a forced smile. "Angie, how nice to see you again so soon."

She went over to the rocker and sat on the small gliding footstool in front. "How are things?"

"Since you're here and talking with me, I'm assuming you know."

"So, it's really that bad? Do you want to talk about it?"

"Oh, Angie," she sighed, "everything is bad and horrible right now. My husband is gone. I have cancer. My children are not settled down. I have tried to see a light at the end of this long, dark tunnel, but nothing is there."

Angie nodded in understanding. She had to agree. At this moment in time, Mrs. Marcum's life seemed miserable.

"I don't really know what to say," Angie confessed. "I could try and quote all the right scriptures to you, but you know them as well as I do. I don't want to walk in here and be a cliché'. That's the last thing you need, but I do want to be a source of hope and inspiration. How can I help?"

Mrs. Marcum looked back out the window and stared again. The look in her eyes was frightening to Angie.

"Mrs. Marcum, do you *want* to die?"

Sue looked back at her with the same blank stare and said, "I don't know so much that I want to die; I just don't want to live anymore. I have nothing to live for."

"Oh, Mrs. Marcum." Angie reached out to take her hand. "That's not true. You have a purpose on this earth, and God isn't through with you yet."

"You say that with such conviction, Angie, but I don't see it. I've tried to live my life with purpose and meaning, but I sit here and wonder why I should fight to go on. What's the point?"

"Your life is far from over. You're still young and healthy and active. There are so many things you can do, so many ways you can contribute to this world."

"I am *not* healthy," Sue corrected. "I have cancer. I have a disease that will destroy me from the inside out. Why should I fight it? Why, Angie? Why go through all that time and money and suffering just to stay on this planet a few more years?"

Angie wasn't used to hopelessness. Her way had always been to find hope and cling to it. How do you deal with someone who has no hope left?

"You do it because you can," she tried to explain. "You only have to die if you choose that. God has placed wisdom and means within the reach of man to cure your cancer. Because of that, you have to believe that He still wants you here. The doctors are giving you hope, but you have to receive that and go on."

"But why?" Sue asked in frustration. "You tell me *why* I should live."

Angie tried to smile and look hopeful or comforting or something positive, but her heart was breaking inside. *Wisdom, Lord. I could use a big dose of it right now.*

"Listen," Angie began to grasp at straws, "God has given you three purposes on this earth ... at least so far. Your first was to know Him and serve Him. You've done that well, Mrs. Marcum. Your love for God was such an influence in my life for many years. You and Mr. Marcum always encouraged me to follow Christ and honor my parents. And look at all you've done in the church! Every kid that's grown up in that church has been touched by you in many ways.

"But then God gave you a husband, and you were a wonderful wife. I always wondered about some couples, if they'd make it or not. But you two had a great marriage. For the years that God gave Mr. Marcum to you, you fulfilled the purpose of being an incredible wife. That part is over for now, but that's not the only reason God put you here. You need to see that you're still a Mother too."

At this Sue winced. Her children were not the models of perfection.

"You know that your kids still need guidance."

"Some guide I've been so far."

"That's not true," Angie said quickly. "You've led them by example and by encouragement. Just because they've chosen to follow paths against your leadership doesn't make you a bad parent. But understand this: their lives aren't set in stone. You still have time and opportunity to continue to pray for them, to encourage them, and to teach them what's right."

She stared back out the window.

"What if that's part of God's purpose with your cancer?" Angie asked her.

Sue looked back with a questioning expression.

"They've lost their Dad. Maybe they're a little hardened by that. They had no warning or choice. But with you, suddenly the prospect of losing a second parent is a reality—a bad reality. You're seeing this as an opportunity to die, but perhaps God's desire is to use it as an opportunity to bring life—real life, to your children."

Mrs. Marcum didn't respond, but her expression changed slightly. Angie couldn't read it. She decided to continue the defense; it seemed to have turned on a light.

"God is known for using impossible circumstances to bring people to Him. Mr. Marcum suffered nothing. God just took him from this world because He was ready for him. The rest of us weren't ready to let him go, but God gave us no choice. Maybe with you, God is going to make your children realize that there is a bigger picture in the world."

Sue leaned forward in her chair and looked directly into Angie's eyes. It was as though she were searching for verification of what had been presented.

"I don't have the answers," Angie said weakly, "but I know that God does everything for a reason. Why He would allow you to have cancer right now, after so much loss already? I just don't know. But I do know *Him*, so I know there's a reason."

"Why did James have to die?"

"I don't know. I wish he hadn't, but that doesn't mean God blew it. All that means is that we can't understand everything about God."

"I want to know why James had to die."

"Me too, but I don't know. And your children will be asking the same thing about you if you continue to refuse treatment, only they'll have an answer: *Mother wanted to die.* That has nothing to do with God, Mrs. Marcum. That's all you. But they'll blame God for your choice."

"Why shouldn't they?" Sue said with venom in her voice. "He took James."

"Yes, and I don't know why. But He's not taking you. You have choices, and your children need to see you fight, not for your own self, but for them. You need to fight so they can understand that love suffers for the sake of others. You need to beat this, if not for yourself, then for your children, God's gifts to you."

Sue sat back and closed her eyes as tears began to line the sides of her face. Angie watched intensely hoping to see a sign of change.

"I never imagined life could be so hard," Sue told her. "I had a wonderful childhood and home growing up. I married a sweet man and lived a blessed life with him. Our children walked on the wild side, but we still enjoyed them. We had everything. I don't know how to live with this kind of void and emptiness, Angie. I don't *want* to live with it."

"Mrs. Marcum, life isn't all about you." She knew the statement sounded harsh, but it was the only truth she could come up with at the moment. The bottom line was that Sue Marcum no longer wanted to live because life was no longer perfect in her estimation.

"There are people in this world who struggle to live from day to day, not because they have cancer or have lost a loved one, but because they were unfortunate enough to be born in a country with no food, no medicine and no hygiene. They go to sleep at night and wake up each morning wondering if they'll eat that day, if their baby will live, if they can fight vultures from feeding on their relatives. Their days consist of merely surviving to stay alive. Why? Because that's what humanity does. We choose to survive until God takes us away. Mrs. Marcum, your life is empty not because there's nothing to fill it, but because you choose to keep it empty."

She was staring out the window again. Angie wondered if she had done more damage than good. She had always had a problem with just blurting out whatever was on her mind. She had meant to be compassionate, but she had ended up being condemning. She stood up to go.

"You never did care to mince words," Sue said with a chuckle.

Angie spun back around. Was that a smile? "I hate death. God made the human body incredibly resilient. To choose to die isn't part of God's plan."

"Is that why you became a doctor? To fight death?"

"That's part of it."

"I suppose I gall you, then."

She didn't know if Mrs. Marcum was baiting her or teasing her at this point, but Angie didn't want to play this game. "No, ma'am. I'm just galled by death. When you die, then I *will* be galled. Until that time, there's always hope."

"What is it in you that makes you believe you can change the world? How did you get that?"

"I believe in God, and I believe in His creative power. As long as I exist, I have a purpose. And I'll fight to fulfill that purpose until I breathe my last."

"Why did God take you away from Padawin?"

Angie sighed as the statement hit her like a bullet in the chest. Yes, she had questioned God's hand in Padawin just as Mrs. Marcum had questioned God's hand in the death of her husband and in her cancer.

"Perhaps God knew that someone needed to talk some sense into you, and I would be the only one with the guts to do it."

"Perhaps you're right," Sue said as one corner of her mouth raised a smile.

Angie nodded in acknowledgment, but she still turned to go. She'd said all she could say.

"Angie," Sue stopped her. "Tell Cindy I need to speak with her."

"Yes, ma'am."

Angie looked until she found Cindy in the laundry room.

"This is not a very glamorous look for you," she said as she sneaked up behind her.

"No, it's not, in fact, I haven't done laundry for years. I have a maid that comes in and does it all."

"You're kidding?"

"Nope. This is a bit humbling in some ways. Did you have any luck?"

"I don't know," Angie confessed as she shook her head. "She does want to talk to you, though."

"Ooo, maybe that's a good sign?"

FORTY-EIGHT

"Congratulations," Cindy said walking into the kitchen to join Angie at the breakfast nook where she was sipping coffee.

"Really?" Angie asked hopefully.

"She's gonna do it. She's not thrilled about it, but she's gonna do it."

Angie closed her eyes in release. She was worried that perhaps she had pushed too hard. "I'm relieved."

"So am I," Cindy agreed as she sat at the table with her dearest friend. "What did you say to her?"

"Religious stuff—you wouldn't be interested."

"Translation: *none of your business*, right?"

Angie nodded as she put the mug back to her lips.

"Why don't you stay for lunch?" Cindy suggested. "Maybe your being here will perk Mother up a little."

"Oh, I don't know. Michael's at home alone with my parents."

"Is that a problem? The two nicest people in the world are keeping him company, and you're worried?"

"Let me call. If all's well, I'll be glad to stay."

"What could possibly go wrong?"

Angie dialed home, and her mother answered.

"Moms, can I speak with Michael?"

"Not at the moment."

"Are you kidding? Why not?"

"He and your father are literally up to their waists in dirt. They're making one of those nasty compost things out back."

"Really? How occupied are they?"

"Extremely. I've already informed them I'll bring lunch outside."

"If that's the case, I'm gonna stay here a little longer and have lunch with Cindy and Mrs. Marcum."

Angie refilled her cup as she thought about her dad and Michael working on a project together. The idea of them spending some time alone with each other seemed good. They were both wonderful men, and Michael needed a figure in his life that could serve as a mentor in some ways. The truth was that the two had very much in common. They gardened, they did carpentry work, and they were both ministers. However, there were some major differences also. Michael was shy and quiet, a man who never spoke his mind outright. Jonathan was forward and opinionated and felt he had the right to express those opinions any time the mood hit. He generally wasn't tactless, but he wasn't the patient and withholding person that Michael was. In fact, if you ever wanted to know what Michael was thinking on a subject, you pretty much had to pry it out of him.

"Where are you?" Cindy asked Angie as she watched her stare out the window while fixing her coffee. "Is there a problem?"

"No," she smiled, coming back to reality. "Michael and Daddy are building a compost box."

"That's right. Michael's some kind of farmer, isn't he?"

"Much more than that. I assumed he was this basic agriculture guy who went over there and taught these people how to grow lettuce and cows. But I was organizing all his books one day and found his doctorate diploma lying on the floor at the bottom of a pile. He'd never even told me."

"Agriculture?"

" Environmental Engineering."

Cindy's eyes grew wide. "What does that mean?"

"It means my husband is a really smart guy but is too humble to let anyone know."

"Husband—why don't we talk about this whole marriage business? What the heck is going on?"

Angie giggled again and blew on her hot coffee. "It's a rather amazing story."

"I'm all ears."

"If I didn't know better, I'd tell you it was love at first sight."

"Yeah, you mentioned that before. Well … was it or wasn't it?"

"It's hard to say. In hindsight, I think I was taken with him right off the bat. But at that moment in time, I can't be sure."

"What was it like when you first saw him?"

Angie leaned back in the nook and tried to remember exactly. "He looked so lost and helpless standing there with this huge sign bearing my name. He had no idea who I was, so I just stared at him while he glanced back at all the passengers unloading. We'd made eye contact a couple of times, and I smiled and waved, but he thought I was some girl trying to flirt with him or something."

Cindy laughed and hit the table. "He couldn't imagine that *you* were a missionary, I bet!"

"No, he couldn't. So I just watched. He fidgeted, shuffled his feet, stared down the ramp, then looked at the floor. He'd glance back at me and start the whole process again. I was intrigued. He was shy, and I could tell right away that he was as nervous as a cat. And you know me, always the mediator, always wanting to make everybody feel good; my heart went out to him. All I wanted was to pick him up like a little boy and say *everything is gonna be just fine.*"

271

"What did he do when you finally greeted him?"

"He almost passed out."

Cindy burst with laughter.

"It's not funny," Angie told her. "I'm being serious. His face went pale, and he fell back against this column."

"I can't imagine what he must have felt," Cindy said trying to calm her laughter.

Suddenly Sue appeared in the kitchen with a smile. "I don't know what I'm missing, but I could use some laughter right about now."

"Angie's telling me about how she and Michael met at the airport. He almost passed out when she introduced herself."

Sue smiled widely this time and nodded her head. "I bet. You know Billy always said your going to the mission field was a huge waste of beauty and …"

"Mother!" Cindy stopped her quickly.

"What?" Angie wanted to know.

"Never mind," Cindy insisted. "You know Billy."

"I want to know," Angie said firmly. "A huge waste of beauty and what?"

"Body," Sue shot out before Cindy could protest.

"Mother!"

Sue went on. "It killed Billy when he found out you were just marrying this man for no other reason than to go to the mission field. He wished he could be a fly on the wall when Michael saw you the first time. So, he almost passed out? I can imagine."

"Go on." Cindy was literally on the edge of her seat with anticipation. "What happened next?"

"We got all my luggage and went back to the hotel. By the time we got married that evening, on the beach, in the sand, he had my heart. He was so gentle and shy. And then he had this look about him … almost like a child."

"Uh oh, you didn't get a mothering complex, did you?" Cindy teased.

"Actually, in some ways, yes. I wanted to take care of him; he seemed so … lost. But when we finally got to the Podakind village, I saw a completely different person. This was an accomplished man. He was smart, capable, resourceful, and much respected by the people of the tribe. And as the days went by, I began to uncover all these wonderful hidden qualities about him. In fact, he's like no man I've ever met before. And I know that our whole marriage seems bizarre in some ways … "

"In many ways …" Cindy interrupted.

"… and I can't help but believe that had I met him anywhere else, I would've been attracted for the same reasons that I am now. I used to marvel at how Moms and Daddy complemented each other. They're complete opposites, yet rather than pull each other at the seams, they give in the right places. I wondered if I'd ever find anyone like that. But that's what it's like with Michael. Where I'm strong, he isn't. I know I fill so much in his life. And where I struggle, he doesn't. And the need I have to always give and always help, he welcomes that."

"How did this happen to you?" Cindy said with a deep sigh as she leaned her head back. "I wreck my life trying to find one decent man, and you pack off to a tropical island and find one waiting!"

Angie shook her head. She didn't know. Her only explanation was God, but Cindy still wasn't ready to accept that. Angie just smiled at her and shrugged her shoulders. Mrs. Marcum, however, gave Angie a warm smile and a knowing nod. She understood.

*****

Jonathan and Michael worked the entire day on the compost project. They built the box itself, dug the hole, placed it in the ground and filled in the sides all around it. Michael went into detail about which leaves and grass and food garbage would be most beneficial. But before Barbara would let them back in the house she practically made them strip in the back yard.

"I can't thank you enough for helping me do this," Jonathan told him as they finally stepped inside the porch.

Michael grinned and with an immensely shy look replied, "My pleasure ... Dad."

*****

"I can't believe you and Daddy convinced Moms to let you build that thing," Angie said as she and Michael pulled up to the high school football stadium.

"And I can't believe you talked me into coming to a football game. Everyone will be staring at me and know that I'm *the husband*," he said with agitation.

"And I'll proudly admit to it."

The stadium was packed as the football team had been undefeated that season so far. Angie was greeted by so many people that Michael felt himself getting dizzy. He hoped he wouldn't be responsible for remembering names or faces. When they finally sat down near the band, Angie remained in constant conversation with everyone around her. However, when the game began, the attention was averted to the field. Michael sighed in reprieve.

Shortly before halftime, a tall blond man, very handsome, stood in front of Angie and said, "Hey, good lookin', I heard you were back in town."

She looked up and smiled graciously. "Billy Marcum."

"Mind if I sit down?" he asked her.

"Free country," was all she said.

Michael felt three inches tall. He believed Billy Marcum had to be the most attractive man he had ever personally seen. His hair was perfect. He had deep dimples and bright blue eyes. He was tall, very tall; a trait he imagined Angie had appreciated in high school. It had probably been hard for her to find someone taller than she.

"How was the mission field?" Billy asked in an unusually smooth voice.

"Everything I ever imagined," she replied as she stared out to the field.

"How was the whole husband thing?"

"Everything I ever imagined."

"Really?" Billy laughed. "So he was a nice guy?"

"*Is* a nice guy," Angie said soberly. "Would you like to meet him?"

"You brought him back with you?"

"Of course, he's my husband."

"Well, in name only," Billy said nonchalantly.

"Says who?" She raised an eyebrow.

Angie was looking Billy squarely in the eye now. She leaned back and gently put her arm through Michael's so Billy could see the other man sitting next to her.

"Billy Marcum, meet Michael Collins," she said proudly. "My husband."

Michael wanted to do anything but meet Billy Marcum at that moment, but he offered his right hand in greeting. Billy's face almost went white as he reached out to shake hands.

"Wo," Billy managed to utter. "So you're the … missionary dude."

Michael nodded and smiled. She wrapped her arm in his a little tighter to let him know everything was fine. He looked at her and she gave a teasing wink.

Billy was quiet for a while, but once he regained his composure, he proceeded to monopolize Angie's attention with any subject of conversation he seemed to pick out of thin air. Michael tried to focus on the game, but in truth he was straining to hear every word Billy said. She continued to hold on to him, however, as if she knew he was uncomfortable and needed assurance.

As the game neared the end, Billy finally stood and said, "Well, I really intended to visit a lot while here, but it appears you captured my attention this whole time. You always had a way of doing that."

"Good to see you, Billy," Angie said politely. "Have a good evening."

"I already have," he said smoothly. "Nice to meet you, *Mr. Missionary*."

Michael didn't speak; he just nodded at Billy and turned his attention back to the game.

As they left the stadium, Michael was quiet and withdrawn. Angie wrapped her arm in his again as they walked toward the car. He was unresponsive. He kept the pace fast and moved emotionlessly. When they were away from the crowd, she stopped him abruptly and turned him toward her.

"What is wrong?" she asked slightly perturbed.

He struggled to speak.

"Michael," she said more firmly, "talk to me. In all the months I've known you, I've never seen you like this."

He looked away and bit his bottom lip. She took a step closer to him and gazed into his eyes.

"Sweetie," she said more gently this time, "what?"

He looked up and around, trying to avoid her eyes, but finally managed to admit, "He was a very handsome man, and very tall."

Angie turned Michael's face to look at her, then said, "And he's the biggest jerk I've ever known."

"How do I compete with someone like that in your past?"

"There's no competition! It was hard for me to even *like* Billy Marcum, much less fall in *love* with him."

"Angie, I have nothing to offer you."

"Are you kidding? How can you say that?"

"He's like this model of perfection, and I'm ... well ... I'm nothing."

She took both of his hands and squeezed them. "You're wonderful," she tried to affirm him. "When I first saw you, do you know that my heart melted inside?"

He shook his head, eyes squinting.

"And I didn't even know you yet. I saw this adorable baby face that immediately made my stomach flutter. But it was more than that."

She reached up and firmly grabbed his upper arms.

"I remember especially your arms and your legs," she grinned. "They were so strong. I knew you weren't some sissy man who sat around all day. I imagined you out in the field laboring. I actually wondered if you worked out."

"Really?" He was blushing now.

"When we got to Padawin, I looked for a set of weights, but after watching you work, I knew where all that bulk came from."

"You're just being nice to me," he said, still blushing as he looked away again.

"No. If I were just being nice, I would tell you that it's not what's on the outside that matters, but what's on the inside. I love you on the inside; you're the most amazing man I've ever known. But you need to know, I very much appreciate the outside, and it's just as appealing."

He looked at her, his eyes still squinting. She found it adorable and leaned in to kiss him.

"Let's go home," she whispered in his ear. "And remember this: if I had wanted Billy Marcum, I certainly could've had him. But it's you I'm going home with tonight, and every night for the rest of my life."

FORTY-NINE

Michael was beside himself. It was the last week in October, and Annie and Stephen Williams were on their way from the Memphis airport. He tried to remain calm, but with Angie's excitement bubbling over everywhere, it only added to his own. Alex and Megan were coming too, but they were just names to him. Alex was seldom talked about in the family. But Stephen Williams ... this was his most favorite musician. And then Annie, he'd heard about her from the very first letter Angie had written him, although he had no idea whom she had married at that time. Annie was almost like a legend to him. Andie still gave him the cold shoulder, but from all Angie had told him, it appeared that Annie liked the whole setup—*Angie marries a total stranger and falls in love.*

Shortly after Stephen's jet landed, Annie called to let them know they were in the limo, and the six of them were on their way, the two couples with the two babies. Angie practically danced around the house at the thought of seeing Annie again and getting to hold baby Stevie. Michael wondered if he could bear watching her cuddle another baby.

As the hours passed miserably slow, he decided to check out the garden and the compost box again. When he walked outside, however, he was blown away by the crowd of people at the front gate. When they saw him outside, they began to yell toward him. He immediately went back into the house.

"What's wrong?" Angie wondered at his expression.

"There're a million people outside the fence," he said out of breath.

"They know Stephen and Annie are on their way."

"How do they know?"

Angie just shrugged.

Occasionally he would glance out the kitchen window at the crowd. Now police and security guards began to gather. They moved the people away from the gate and made sure there was room for the car to drive through when it arrived. The butterflies in his stomach were growing. He was going to meet Stephen Williams. He had a hard enough time meeting people in general, but how should he act when he met ... Stephen? Then there was Annie.

Angie came up behind him and put her arms around his waist. "Stephen's very easy to get to know. You guys will be like brothers before the day is over."

He doubted that. He couldn't imagine carrying on a *normal*

conversation with the man; he would be too star-struck.

"You know that you really are brothers in a way," she said as she rubbed the soft flannel shirt. "You're officially brothers-in-law."

He gave a little smile and nodded. That was true, but it still wouldn't keep him from being in awe. He glanced up at the family photo above the fireplace. Annie was a beautiful woman. He wondered how a family could produce such incredible looking children. Alex was handsome also, but he just didn't fit with the rest of them. Michael now began to panic at the thought of meeting Alex. He had never considered him. What if Alex was as disdainful as Andie? The knot in his stomach suddenly grew another notch.

A collective yell from the crowd outside the gate threw his nervousness into a whole new realm. They must have arrived. Angie leaned over his shoulder and her eyes grew wide.

"They're here!" she said with controlled exclamation. She gave him a quick kiss and then ran from the kitchen. "They're here!" she shouted this time for her mother to hear.

Barbara came running from the bedroom. She had been in New York for the birth of Alex and Megan's baby, and Annie and Stephen's, but that was the only time she had been around her new grandchildren. She nearly shook with excitement.

Michael stayed in the kitchen and gazed out the window as the white limo came slowly through the gate while security guards and police kept the crowd back. He felt another knot develop. If he didn't watch himself, he would throw up before all this was over. The limo pulled up the drive and stopped. Angie had explained that it was best to wait for them to come inside the house rather than go out to greet them because of photographers and video cameras back at the fence. The more privacy they kept, the easier it was for everyone involved.

Michael gulped when Alex stepped out from the limo. He was taller than he had imagined, and his hair was down to his shoulders. He took his baby girl and then helped his petite wife, a thin, but energetic blond from the car. The crowds screamed in delight. Alex waved slightly, but was more intent on getting his family to the front door.

When Stephen stepped out of the limo, Michael felt like a giddy girl. He couldn't believe how star struck he was. There he was, loose blond curls, dark glasses, but gentle smile. The crowd got even louder. Stephen gave them a big wave and the people responded with screams. He reached in and helped out the last two passengers, a beautiful brunette holding a tiny bundle of blond hair. When Annie stepped out, the crowd went hysterical. Stephen took the baby, and she graciously waved to the people behind the fence. She was beautiful. She took the baby back into her arms and Stephen began to gently guide them toward the house.

The opening of the front door jolted him out of his spying. The reality that these people were walking into the house now jerked the knot again in his stomach. He swallowed hard as he heard Angie squeal in delight. Walking to the entrance of the kitchen he just stood and watched for a moment. Everyone needed a chance to greet each other before he entered the scene.

Angie grabbed Megan first and they spun each other around. Barbara kissed Alex on the cheek but was obviously more interested in the baby. She took her granddaughter in her arms and nuzzled her closely. Michael now had a lump come up in his throat. Angie hugged her brother and said something warm and gentle to him; Michael could tell by her expression.

But when the door opened again, Annie walked through, and Angie nearly exploded. Annie immediately handed baby Stevie to his father, and the sisters embraced in a tight hug. Michael watched as Angie began to shake, and he knew she was crying. He could see Annie's face, but her eyes remained tightly shut. They held each other for a long time. Michael actually felt tears well up in his own eyes. He knew the bond they had was strong, and that the person Angie had missed most by being in Padawin was Annie.

"Let me see this other baby," Barbara cooed as she greeted Stephen with a gentle kiss, still holding little Ansley. "I need another set of arms!"

"You keep hold of that one," Stephen told her. "She won't be here long."

Michael continued to watch all the greetings, almost forgetting that he was there, feeling more like he was watching it on television than actually viewing it in person. He felt safe until Angie turned to find him.

"Michael," she called his name.

He was startled. He felt his knees begin to buckle. He was embarrassed that he was so unnatural around these people, but he couldn't help it.

"Come meet the rest of my family," she said with an encouraging smile.

He walked over slowly, feeling very self-conscious, but Angie reached out her hand and pulled him beside her. He found himself staring into the darkest eyes he had ever seen. Although they didn't look like Angie's, they bore the same warm and welcoming expression.

"Annie, this is Michael," Angie said proudly. "My island dreamboat."

He blushed.

"Michael," Angie continued, "this is my best friend in the whole world—for real this time."

He reached out his hand, but Annie went past the hand and embraced him. Her hug was warm and genuine. He could tell she was slightly shorter than Angie, and he wasn't prepared for the emotions that ran through him. This was Annie; this was Angie's closest confidant'. To be welcomed as he was by her gave him a huge sense of security.

When Annie pulled back, she looked deep into his eyes, a trait she obviously shared with her sister. "I can't tell you how wonderful it is to finally meet you. You're an answer to prayer."

His tongue was totally tied. Even if he had tried to speak, nothing would have come out. All he could do was smile and nod.

"And look at this little baby face," she smiled as she reached up and gently pinched his cheek. She glanced over at Angie and winked as she asked, "How did you luck out with that?"

Angie giggled as she took Michael's hand and replied, "Just an added blessing."

"This is my husband, Stephen," Annie said like it was no big deal as she reached back for Stephen's hand and pulled him toward her. "And this is my sweet little Stevie."

Michael reached out his hand, but avoided Stephen's eyes.

"Nice to finally meet you," Stephen said warmly. "You've been quite the topic of conversation around our house for the past several months."

"I can imagine," Michael managed to get out as he looked up at Stephen for only a moment. He was shaking hands with *Stephen Williams*. No one in this room knew what that meant.

"I get the baby," Angie blurted out as she took Stevie from Stephen's arms and began to snuggle it closely to her cheek. "Look at you," she began in baby talk. "You look just like your daddy. Did you know that? Poor baby."

"Hey!" Stephen protested. "I think he's very handsome."

"I'm the little brother," Alex said as he came up behind Michael and offered his hand. "I'm the quiet one in the family."

Michael grinned and shook his hand firmly. "I didn't know there was a quiet one in this family."

"Yeah, well, we're rare."

"It's nice to finally meet you."

There was nothing intimidating or pretentious about Alex. Michael liked that. They had greeted, shaken hands, and then both were content to watch the interactions between everyone else in the room. And there was a lot of interacting. When Stephen managed to nab his baby back, Angie immediately moved toward baby Ansley and pried her from Barbara. There was much protest, but Barbara simply edged her way toward Stephen, and before he knew what had happened, Barbara was waltzing around the room with her newest grandson. Annie, Angie and Megan soon engaged in lively conversation concerning the adventures of motherhood, and Stephen began to direct the driver where to drop the luggage in the great room.

"May I help?" Michael offered Stephen.

"Sure. I think these are going up to Annie's old room."

"I don't think so. You guys are supposed to be staying in the garage apartment. We'd decided to take Annie's room," Michael said a bit confused.

"Annie won't do it," Stephen said as he shook his head. "She's very sentimental about this. She wants us all in her little room."

"Well, if you can talk her out of it, we really don't mind. We even cleaned up the apartment."

"Won't happen. You obviously don't know Annie yet."

When they opened the door, everything in Annie's room was just as it had been left, including the poster of Stephen on the wall opposite her bed.

"Nice choice of decor," Michael teased.

"That's an old poster," Stephen mused as he inspected the best place for the portable baby bed. "I think she leaves it up just to taunt me. Hand me that blue bag there and see if you can help me put this thing together." Stephen pointed toward the folded baby bed bag Michael was carrying. "We bought it months ago to take on tour with us, but haven't had a need for it until now. I hope it's easier than most of the baby things I've put together lately."

By the time the two men got the bed up, Andie and Doug and their clan had made it over. Suddenly the excitement and noise went up another level. Michael even glanced out the door and down from the balcony to see what the commotion was about.

"Thanks," Stephen said as he passed Michael on the way down.

"No problem."

Michael didn't care to go down at the moment. He stared at the scene for a while and tried to imagine what it was like to be a part of this family. Andie hugged Stephen and spoke with him briefly—apparently she had no problem with *him*. The older children made pandemonium of the house while the three babies managed to get passed from one person to another. When Jonathan finally came in, the older children screamed and Alex and Annie made a special effort to speak with their father alone. At one point, Andie did glance up to see Michael, but before she had a chance to glare at him for long, he disappeared into the apartment for a small break. He needed to breathe for a moment. This type of interaction was foreign to him, and as much as he hated to admit it, he was still reeling from meeting Annie and Stephen.

He went to the restroom, combed his hair again, and then tried to think of any other excuse to remain up there. He looked around the room and smiled at its neatness; they had picked things up thinking Annie and Stephen would stay there, but that was the first time they had straightened it in three weeks.

He heard more squeals from down below and decided he had better reappear. He didn't want Angie to have to come looking for him. He was sure Andie could make a negative case out of that too. He left the room and started down the stairs. Stephen and Doug were standing off to the side now as the three sisters engaged in animated conversation. Barbara and Jonathan were talking with Alex and Megan as Barbara continued to hold little Stevie and Jonathan cradled Ansley. The two middle children were chasing a remote control car around the room as Adam tried to maneuver it away from them. Michael felt his safest bet was to join the men.

"We were wondering where you went," Doug told Michael as he joined them at the edge of the dining table. "I was afraid all the noise scared you off."

"What?" Michael asked loudly, but in jest because of the racket.

Doug smiled and slapped him on the back. "Good one."

The three of them stood there quietly watching their wives vie for control of the conversation. Michael couldn't help but smile as he saw Angie in a different light. In Padawin, she was gracious and kind always, with a tease or a joke ever lurking in the rafters of her refreshing mind. At this moment she actually put her hand to Andie's mouth and said, *Would you let me at least finish my thought before you butt in?*

"Are they always like this?" Michael asked the two men on either side of him.

Rather than respond with words, Stephen and Doug laughed out loud and nodded.

"Welcome to the brother-in-law club," Doug said rather dismally.

"Being around them all together can be sort of like culture shock," Stephen told him. "At least I got to see this part of Annie before we ever got together. I knew what I was getting myself into."

"Look at it this way, guys," Doug interrupted. "You two have a group of *us*. I did this alone for over 10 years, you know?"

"And it made you a stronger man, my friend," Stephen laughed.

Barbara and her daughters worked together in the kitchen to prepare a huge supper. Michael couldn't imagine this many in one house and then cooking enough food to feed them all. He heard yelling several times, but the loud laughter prevailed. He stayed with the men as they watched Auburn slaughter some other SEC team in football. Growing up in Kansas, the SEC teams were foreign to Michael. By the end of the first half, however, Jonathan had given him a running history on all of them. Allegiances were split among the men with their Alabama teams. Alex and Doug were staunch Auburn fans, but Jonathan pulled for Alabama. Stephen pulled for Alabama because that was Annie's team. All this made for several heated discussions among the men. They kept insisting Michael choose sides, but he would only smile and shake his head. He was definitely not ready for that yet.

Soon after dinner was over, Alex and Megan left, and then Andie and her family. The sudden decrease in people, especially *little* people, created a calm over those who remained. Annie and Angie helped their mother finish cleaning the kitchen, while the men sat around the fire talking about nothing of major importance. Michael marveled at how Stephen cuddled, talked to, and nestled his baby the entire time. He'd seldom been around people with babies, especially men. He loved watching Stevie's responses to his daddy even though he was only a few months old. He wondered if all babies were like that or if it was just a personality trait. He also wondered if his own father had ever held him when he was small.

Even though the fire was blazing, the weather was freezing and Michael was chilled. He was thankful for his turtleneck and soft flannel shirt. He thought about going upstairs to get the jacket, but then changed his mind. Annie would recognize it; what if she didn't like the idea of Michael wearing the jacket she had picked out especially for her sister? His chills were remedied, however, when the girls emerged from the kitchen suggesting an evening in the hot tub.

"I'm up for it," Stephen said immediately. "I'm freezing."

"Me too," Angie agreed.

"What?" Jonathan asked in surprise as he stood up. "Is everybody cold?"

"I am," Annie told him.

He looked at Michael with raised eyebrows and asked, "What about you?"

"I just came from a South Pacific island," he tried to reason not wanting to cause any conflict. "Anything below 80 is cold to me."

Jonathan shook his head as he went over to add another log to the fire. "You folks have got to learn to layer your clothing," he mumbled.

Barbara emerged from the kitchen drying her hands on a dishtowel oblivious to the conversation. "Jonathan, stoke that up more," she said as she walked over to the fireplace. "It's cold in here."

Jonathan sighed as the rest of the group laughed. "How 'bout I just catch the whole house on fire," he grumbled. "That ought to warm everyone up."

"Goodness!" Barbara exclaimed. "Must you be so dramatic?"

FIFTY

Michael put on a pair of cut-off jeans he used when swimming in the ocean; he had never been much for trunks. He then pulled on a t-shirt to wear out to the porch. When Angie emerged in a bikini, he whistled.

"Oh, this old thing?" she teased.

"You never wore that in Padawin."

"Of course not! I'd never wear anything like this in public."

"It wouldn't bother me one bit."

"These little things dry out so much quicker. During the cold seasons, Annie and I would practically live in the hot tub in the evenings. We got tired of trying to slip into those one pieces that were still damp and miserably cold."

"I'm *not* complaining," he reiterated.

She chuckled as she wrapped herself with a large beach towel. "No, you're not," she said as she kissed him quickly. "Now let's go get warm."

"I already am," he said more seriously than teasing.

When they came downstairs, Barbara and Jonathan were giving Stevie their full attention. Angie walked by and kissed the top of the baby's head on her way to the back porch. It was freezing outside, and Michael thought he would die if he didn't get into the water soon. Annie and Stephen were already in, and the rising steam from their arms made the tub even more inviting.

"Turn your head, Stephen," Angie commanded before she would remove her towel.

"Why?" he teased.

"Turn your head," she said more forcefully.

He obliged this time and looked toward the side of the porch. Angie slipped the towel off and got into the tub quickly. Michael eased off his shirt, and this time he was whistled at ... by Annie. He blushed.

As the evening went on, Michael found it pure pleasure to sweat. He also was at ease being around Stephen and Annie. Angie had been right: Annie had no problem with him. The four of them laughed and chatted for over an hour. Stephen was very down-to-earth, and Annie was full of mischief and fun. He was especially delighted when the girls began to walk down memory lane and share some of the shenanigans from their past. He could easily imagine Angie as one who pushed the limits in everything she did.

The conversation then moved to the Christmas album that was about to be released publicly.

"That's an awesome project," Michael spoke up.

Everyone looked at him. This was his first interjection into the conversations.

"It really is," he continued even though he felt very self-conscious. "I was amazed at the way you two seemed to mesh so well together. That *Winter Passion* song? Wow."

"Michael told me that was the *hottest* Christmas song he'd ever heard," Angie shared.

Annie burst with laughter as she nodded her head and said, "That's a good description!"

"What's it like to be able to sit down and write stuff like that?" Michael asked. "I mean, to have such a knowledge of music that you can express yourself both lyrically and musically with such ease must be incredible."

Stephen and Annie looked at each other and sort of shrugged their shoulders.

"It's second nature to them," Angie told him. "That would be like asking you how it feels to rig up a power plant in a couple of days for a medical clinic."

The conversation was interrupted when Barbara came out to the porch bearing an upset Stevie. "I think he's ready for his mama and his bed," she said sweetly as she gently rocked him back and forth.

"I'm coming," Annie said immediately getting up.

Stephen followed her out of the tub. "I'll hold him while you get dried off and dressed." He dried quickly, put on a shirt, and then took the baby in his arms. As soon as Stevie realized his father was holding him, he stopped fussing. "That's my boy," he said softly. "Daddy's got you."

Michael felt his stomach drop. What was it like to be a father? What was it like to have a father like that?

As everyone left the porch, Angie scooted next to him in the tub. "Been a nice night, don't you think?"

"Definitely."

"It would've been nicer if I could've managed to shake Sue Marcum's cancer from my head."

"When do her treatments start?"

"They've got to do surgery first. She wants to put it off until after the holidays. I keep telling her she needs to do it right away."

Michael slouched down in the tub and leaned his head back against the edge. He loved being warm again.

"So, how do you like Annie?" she asked him.

"She's an angel, just like you."

"You and Stephen seemed to get along real well."

"He's a nice guy, isn't he?"

"That he is."

"I was wondering," he said as he looked up at her, squinting slightly from self-consciousness, "were you attracted to him at all when you first met him. I mean ... he was like fair game, wasn't he, when he visited here for Alex's wedding?"

"No—no attraqction. I didn't even know who he was. And then I was so focused on getting to seminary and getting out of school, I didn't think about men."

"He's a wonderful father," Michael said softly.

"Yes, he is. He had a rough childhood. His father wasn't a very supportive or loving man."

"Really? I just assumed ... well ... with how he was with Stevie that he was just ... I don't know ... modeling how he was raised."

"Not at all."

He felt a new hope all of a sudden. When he and Angie had talked about having children, it was a deep desire of his, but he wondered if he could be a good father. One of his biggest fears was that he would somehow revert to how he was raised. He knew Angie would be wonderful, but he had doubts concerning his own abilities.

"Do you think it comes naturally?" he asked her.

"What?"

"Being a good parent. I mean, how do you know what to do and when to do it?"

"With an infant, it's not too hard. You feed them, you change them, and you love them. Seriously—it's not hard," she repeated with an added emphasis.

He nodded as he thought on that.

"You'll be a great father."

"I don't know. What if I, well ... my own father was ..."

"You are *not* your father," she said firmly. "In fact, you'll most probably be so opposite your father that I'll complain you're spoiling our children."

"You really think so?"

"Absolutely. But we'll have an advantage over everyone else."

"What's that?"

Angie put her arms around him and pulled him close as she said, "Ours will be raised in Padawin. No television, no remote controlled cars to chase around the house, no spoiled friends to influence their thinking. Their environment will be pristine, pure."

"Can you imagine growing up there?" he dreamed with her. "The ocean and the river as your back yard."

"Podakind towering out your window each morning when you wake up."

"Watching meteors at night on the beach …"

"We never did that," she halfway protested.

"There wasn't a decent shower during your brief visit there."

"Oh," she nodded quietly.

They both imagined their home on the island, and expressions of peace and longing appeared at the same time.

"Are we homesick?" she asked him.

"I'm afraid so."

"I was wondering, when we do have kids, where will they stay? Are we all gonna pile up in that room together … just get one great big bed?"

"Way ahead of you there, girl. I've already got it worked out."

"Dr. Collins, have you been dreaming without me?"

"We add on to the other side of the house just like we did with the clinic. We could knock out a door between where our bed and the closet and bathroom are. We build another connecting area just like the clinic; only this one is on the other side. We could stud it off to make four rooms too. In fact, we could actually have our own private bedroom."

"Hmmm," she sighed as she snuggled closer. "That would be nice with all the children. We could have our privacy. You *have* been thinking, haven't you?"

"Yes … and now I'm thinking we probably ought to get out of this tub. This is the warmest I've been since leaving Padawin."

"I agree. Are you sweating yet?"

"Profusely, and it's wonderful."

She stood up and reached her hand down to pull him up with her. When he came up, she pulled him close.

"This is even better," he smiled as he kissed her softly.

"Let's go upstairs," she replied with her own smile that radiated mischief.

As they left the porch and stepped into the great room, Annie was in one of the recliners nursing and rocking the baby.

"How sweet," Angie cooed as she walked over to them.

Michael smiled and nodded a greeting, but felt Annie would prefer her privacy. Before Padawin, the thought of being in the presence of a nursing mother would have embarrassed him, but the women there did it openly. He thought of Angie again. Would she nurse their children? How wonderful and natural it all was. Annie didn't seem concerned or bothered by it.

When he reached the top of the stairs, he turned back to watch for a moment. Angie was kneeling down and stroking the baby's head as Annie talked sweetly to him. He had never seen anything as tender in his life. He wondered: how did people grow up to be hard and calloused like his father? How did someone decide to reject a child when a baby was so innocent and helpless?

When Angie came in, Michael was already prepared for bed. She had gotten chilled and immediately made her way next to the heater.

"Michael?" she asked sweetly. "I know we had other plans for tonight, but would you mind terribly if I went down and talked with Annie for a while?"

He was disappointed but would never want her to know. "Of course not. Go spend some time with her. I won't even wait up."

"Are you sure?"

He nodded.

"Thanks," she said as she kissed him on the way to the bathroom. When she dropped her towel as she went through the door, he almost changed his mind.

*****

"So what's it like to be a mom?" Angie asked Annie after coming back downstairs. "I can't imagine."

"You know what? I thought being married was the most awesome thing in the world, but when Stevie came along, it's like a whole other degree of love. I don't even know if I can explain it."

"Stephen adores him," Angie noted, "and still adores you in the process."

"He's been a wonderful father—and husband. I still find myself laughing at how fast all this happened. Last year this time, I was on tour with Stephen, dreaming that he might possibly fall in love with me. And now here I am with him by my side and a baby to boot."

"You've really mellowed too."

"Mellowed?" She laughed slightly. "How can I help but not be mellow? I'm tired from strange hours with this baby, but there's absolutely nothing to complain about. Life is sweet."

"Do you wish you had waited for the baby? You know, had a few more years with Stephen to yourself?"

"Not at all. At first I was really nervous. I didn't feel like I was ready to be a mother, but as the time approached, I could hardly wait. And Stephen has been the most wonderful man through all of this. He tells me all the time it's not fair that I get to nurse the baby."

Angie giggled.

"I'm serious! In fact, when the baby wakes up at night, Stephen insists on getting him and bringing him to me, then he wants to be the one who burps him and rocks him back to sleep."

"Where is he now?"

"On the phone. The Christmas tour is going to be grueling. We're trying to hit as many cities as possible in only four weeks. Normally his tours are three months."

"Are you excited?"

"Some. It's going to be tiring having to go every single night with only Sundays off. But we won't be going abroad this time; we're staying in the States."

The baby sighed, and his head tilted back slowly as he fell into a deeper sleep.

"He's so precious," Angie said as she leaned over to get a better look.

"I know, but enough about me. I'm dying to hear about *your* life—up close and personal."

Angie sat back on the couch and smiled big. "My life is unbelievable. I'm still in awe at all that's happened."

"I really like Michael," Annie said as she shifted Stevie to her shoulder. "He seems like such a tender man."

"Annie, I've tried to tell people this: but had I met him anywhere other than Padawin, I would've been drawn to him. There are things about him that I absolutely … well, that I love. It didn't take long for me to realize that I had married someone really special."

"I want to know what it was like when you first met him," Annie said excitedly. "Were you shocked or pleased or what?"

"I think my heart went out to him first. He looked so lost and alone standing there with that sign. I hadn't expected him to look like he did; I expected someone more … I don't know, perhaps intellectual looking. Does that make sense?"

"And you saw all those muscles instead?"

Angie chuckled and nodded. "But his eyes looked so confused. The more I got to know him, the more I understood him, and the more I realized there was such emptiness in his life. He gave himself to missions so fully that it helped to fill up the void, but you know me, I was eager to do my part."

"You guys look like you were made for each other."

"We were. I still wake up some mornings and am startled to look over and see him there. Then on other mornings, I wake up and look for him immediately because I'm so scared that all of this was a dream."

"I know the feeling."

Stephen appeared from Annie's room upstairs and walked quietly down.

"Is he asleep?" he asked.

"Deeply."

"Then it's my turn," he said with a big smile. "Hand him over."

Annie stood up and they gently made the transfer. Angie marveled at how Stephen's long fingers dwarfed his little son even more.

"That's my baby boy," he whispered. "You girls keep on talking. I'll take him up and put him to bed."

"Thanks, babe," Annie said as she gently rubbed Stephen's back. "I won't be too long. I need to get some sleep before the next shift."

"By the way," Stephen said turning back toward Angie, "your Michael is one smart guy. It took him no time to figure that bed out. I was confused the moment I read the first direction. I like him."

"Me too," Angie smiled. "I was wondering, though, do you think it might be possible for me to rock little Stevie to sleep some time while you're here?"

Stephen looked up for a moment and thought. "Don't count on it," he replied with a grin. "Make your own babies."

"I intend to," Angie said flatly.

Annie's eyebrows flew up, but she waited for Stephen to leave before jumping on the comment. "Kids?" she asked. "You're thinking about kids already?"

Angie sighed and tried to explain. "Michael just turned thirty-six this month. He wants to give his children some of his youth if at all possible."

"Children? Plural?"

"Of course! Do you plan to only have one child?"

"Right now I do! I'm too exhausted to imagine another one!"

"But Padawin is different," Angie tried to help her understand. "There are no schedules or appointments or demands over there. In fact, when Michael hurt his arm and then had the flu, no one even showed up at the clinic. They just assumed I'd be taking care of him. Our time is our own."

"I can't imagine that. We've been so busy since we got married. And now with this tour coming up, I'm hoping I make it through with my sanity intact."

"Hire someone to go with you, someone who can help with the baby."

"Not on your life!" Annie snapped. "I'm not hiring a nanny to watch my kid while I perform. I'm not doing the whole celebrity routine. No way!"

"I didn't mean it that way. I just don't want to see you stressed."

"And I don't want to be one of those typical *Hollywood moms* as they call them. It'll all be over soon. It's just a part of our life. When the tour is over, we have nothing for a long time."

"What will you do with the baby while you're on stage? Are you and Stephen taking turns?"

Annie laughed and shook her head. "The other wives have offered to watch him. But I'm not gonna do the whole autograph and picture signing thing this time. When the concerts are over, I leave the building."

"Michael thinks your voice is awesome. He puts on *Winter Passion* all the time. He wants to know when you're gonna do your own album."

"You know what? I may never do one. Stephen and I have talked about doing a lullaby album, and then he wants us to do some of my songs jointly. I'm content with that. You have no idea how much work it is putting all this together. And I'll be honest, I like doing the *mom thing* very much. I wish sometimes it was all I had to do."

"Can you write lullabies?" Angie asked mischievously. "I mean ... I don't think your average baby wants to be put to sleep to *hot mama* and *passion* sing-a-longs."

Annie giggled tiredly. "It's really wonderful to be with you again."

*****

Angie tried to sneak into bed, but Michael rolled over as soon as she got snuggled beneath the sheets.

"Have a good time?" he asked sleepily.

"Yeah," she said as she slid next to him to get warmed.

"You're freezing!"

"I know. The fire had died down."

"Why doesn't your dad turn up the heat?"

"To Daddy, it is turned up."

"Come here," he said as he pulled her toward him. "Let me help you take the chill off."

She nestled into his arms and enjoyed the comfort.

"Did you fall asleep?" she asked him.

"I just drifted in and out. I guess I've gotten used to having you beside me. The bed felt *wrong*."

"Does it feel better now?"

"Much."

She moved up to his lips to simply kiss him goodnight, but as she found herself lingering again, it wasn't long before she changed her mind.

"I'm feeling warmer," she whispered. "This is much better than the hot tub."

"Excellent deduction, Dr. Angie," he said as he kissed her again.

FIFTY-ONE

Angie was beside herself with anticipation as Michael tried to open the envelope. Annie rolled her eyes at Angie's impatience and finally called out, "Settle down!" feeling sorry for Michael who couldn't open the letter from Padawin quickly enough.

"Can you tell who it's from yet?" Angie asked as she tried to pull a piece of the tape away.

"No idea," he said patiently.

Someone had written them a letter from Podakind and managed to get it to Michael and Angie. It had gone by way of someone traveling to Taveren, who in turn gave it to one of the chopper pilots, who then took it to Port Moresby and found a missionary there of another denomination, who finally managed to get it to Richmond. Fred Carson had immediately addressed it to Michael and Angie in Dockrey.

The original envelope had been taped to death, obviously from someone who wasn't in the habit of sending letters. It had been put into another envelope in order to get it to Richmond, and then the mission board had placed it into a larger packet to mail it to the Collins. When Michael finally pulled the letter from the last overly taped envelope, he checked to see who it was from. He then handed it to Angie.

"You should be the one to read this," he smiled. "This is your doing."

She took it and grinned big as she read the first sentence. "It's from Geechern," she announced to everyone. "She's the lady who helps me in the clinic."

"Angie has taught her how to read and write," Michael informed them. "For her to write this letter is no small feat. Three months—that's all Angie was there—three months." He smiled in admiration.

Angie sat on the couch and began to translate the letter to everyone in the room.

This is from Geechern. I am writing for Dr. Angie and Brother Mike.

I am wanting you to know all is good for us. We feared you would be worried for your friends here. You must know we are well. Two days after you left, soldiers came to find you. We said you were taken in the sky. They went in your house. All your things were not there, and they believed us. They wanted to scare us and threw some of your books to the floor, but we knew they would leave and not come back. We had taken all your food and things out so no one would not believe us. They said it was good for you to go because they would kill you. We were happy and celebrated that night for your lives.

I sewed a boy yesterday. He was stupid. I did the no-pain medicine first, and then I cleaned his cut well. Stupid, stupid boy. Men! Seendoo and her baby are all well. The baby is getting fat, and Seendoo walks and cooks as she always did.

You must know that Sojay and Joshua teach us each week. The ladies miss Dr. Angie and her teaching. Sometime Sojay and Joshua need help to read the Bible, but they do well. They are not like Brother Mike, but they will do until you are here again. Sojay and Joshua also travel to other tribes like you. No one there can read. They have been glad for them to come there too.

We miss you, but we are well. We do not want you to worry for us. The men have kept the fields and animals well. They clean the water in the tower and they work with the latrines. You will now know how well they all listened to you Brother Mike. Mosheed has ladies eat at her house to talk about the Truth. She says women need to be like Dr. Angie. They need to be strong and smart, but they need to love and care for their men and children. I read some of the Bible while we meet. Then we will say how we can use that today. I wish I could read better. Some of the words I can not know now.

We want you to be here. Sojay has a prayer each night that God will take away the rebels who want to steal our freedom. We pray at the meeting place. Sojay says if we pray, God will answer. God brought Dr. Angie here when everyone said she would not come. God will remove the rebels even though everyone says they will not go.

You can be having a vacation now. Rest and be with your families, but we are wanting you to come home. We need Advil. We need pink stomach medicine. We need only those. Can you get that here? If you cannot we will all be fine, but grandfather will miss the pink medicine!

We hope to see you in little bunnies! And we put all your books back. I am Geechern. Goodbye.

Angie struggled to hold back the tears. It was wonderful to hear from Podakind and to know they were all doing well.

"What's with the *bunnies*?" Annie asked as she reached to hold the letter.

Michael chuckled and explained, "Angie had trouble with some of her words in Padawin. The ones for *days* and *bunnies* are very similar. She could never seem to tell them apart."

"I still can't!" Angie said in frustration.

"Look at this writing," Annie said impressed. "I have no idea what the words mean, but whoever wrote it has impeccable penmanship. I find it hard to believe that Angie taught her; her penmanship is deplorable."

"I'm just so relieved to know everyone is okay," Angie sighed.

"… and they're keeping up with all the things I taught them," Michael added. "I was worried they might let the water and sewage systems go, as well as give up the fields."

"I could've told you that," Angie said. "They'd be foolish to live without those things again."

"And I'm pleased more than anything that they're continuing to seek God," Michael said soberly. "That's why I went there."

"And the women are meeting with Mosheed."

Jonathan interrupted their celebrating to say, "You know what that proves?"

Angie and Michael both shook their heads.

"It proves that whatever it was you did there, you did it right. Remember that old proverb about the best way to help a man? You don't give him a fish; you teach him how to fish. That's what you've done with these people. You didn't just waltz in there and change their lives in a way that made them dependent on you. Instead, you showed them how to live a higher quality of life and then showed them how to maintain it. You two need to be running our government."

Michael was shocked because what had begun as a simple explanation of Michael and Angie's work in Padawin turned into an all out discussion of the political problems in America. He was amused by the entire conversation, but the most amusing part was they all actually agreed, but they argued every point to death before finally agreeing they agreed.

He refused to add to the dialogue, but when Stevie had finally had enough of the loudness and began to whimper, Michael stood and announced, "Give me the baby. I'm his only ally in all of this. The rest of you are too loud for this little fellow."

Angie watched in admiration as he gently picked up Stevie and rested him comfortably in his arms.

"They are loud people, aren't they?" he said as he took him up the stairs to the apartment.

Angie couldn't believe that Michael had taken an initiative to do anything. She was lost to the rest of the conversation after that. All she could do was imagine what he might be doing with the baby upstairs. She finally excused herself and went up to join him.

"How are you gentlemen handling things up here?" she asked as she walked into the room.

Michael was at the window at the front of the room showing Stevie the things outside. "We are getting along just fine. Did you get tired of the political mumbo-jumbo?"

"No. I just couldn't bear the thought of you getting the baby all to yourself."

"Well don't think I'm gonna let you get your hands on him for awhile. He's mine right now."

She came to the window and stroked his little head. "He's so adorable. It's funny how much he looks like Stephen. Look at those eyes and these little curls." She curled a lock around her pinky finger.

"Who do you think our children will look like?"

"Who knows? Doug and Andie's look so different. And this little guy, I don't see a hint of Annie in there anywhere."

"The lips. They're Annie's. Look at them. He's gonna have these great kissable lips when he grows up. The girls will be fighting over him."

"Kissable lips?" she said in mock disgust. "Are you saying that my sister has *kissable lips*?"

He blushed and squinted. "I wouldn't know by experience, but *you* definitely do. And you and Annie have the same set, just on different girls."

"Oh yeah? Kissable?" She looked down at Stevie. "Did you hear that? Your Uncle Michael says I have kissable lips."

Stevie smiled and wiggled all over, and the two of them melted again.

FIFTY-TWO

The next several days were some of the best of Michael's life. He struck up a great friendship with Stephen and had the opportunity to get to know Annie well. He now understood the bond between her and Angie. He began to feel like he was genuinely a part of the Wright family. He had the opportunity to hold and rock Stevie many times, and Stephen even gave him lessons on changing diapers. He and Jonathan finished Barbara's entertainment center, and the entire family was impressed with his handiwork. Michael had begun to relax around everyone, everyone except Andie. She still wouldn't speak to him or even acknowledge his presence. It didn't bother Michael in one sense because he didn't have to be confronted by her, but it bothered him because he knew she disliked him for some reason, and for the life of him he couldn't figure out what it might be. Whatever it was, it didn't bother Doug. In fact, Doug appeared to enjoy being around him very much. It was seldom that Michael had ever felt that he had reached a genuine comfort zone anywhere, but he did now. Until ...

"You're a talented young man," Jonathan told him one afternoon as the ladies cleaned up from lunch and Stephen put Stevie down for a nap.

"Thank you, sir. I consider that a great compliment coming from you."

"Then you considered it right," Jonathan laughed, "because I certainly don't throw them around carelessly. But I'm ready to hear you preach. I think it's time."

Michael knew this day was coming, but he was hesitant. Without making eye contact, he confessed, "I don't really think I can yet."

"I assume you have a good reason. I understand that you manage to preach to four tribes each week. The way I see it, a simple Sunday morning should be a piece of cake for you. And besides, you don't even have to translate."

Michael sighed as he stared at the silent television. How did he explain this to Jonathan? "You know that scripture about when you come to the altar, but know that someone has something against you?"

"Sure. Matthew. You go to the person and make it right."

Michael squinted and looked down to the floor. "I can't preach here as long as Andie despises me."

Jonathan nodded slightly and pursed his lips as he considered the situation. "Which altar do you think Jesus was referring to?"

"What do you mean?"

"You're claiming this scripture as though the altar is the altar of preaching. Do you think that's what Jesus meant?"

He thought on it for a moment. He hadn't really considered the *altar* aspect of it. He just imagined it would appear hypocritical of him to get up and preach while someone in the congregation thought he was the devil's brother.

"What do you think ... Dad?" he finally asked hopefully, but hesitantly adding the word *Dad*.

"First, I don't know what Andie's problem is. I've confronted her about it and she acts like we're all fools about you. Whatever—that's her problem. I know it affects you, but we all seem powerless to do anything about it. But for you to say that you can't *preach* because somehow you equate that with the *altar* in the verse, it leads me to believe it's a bigger problem for you than just preaching."

Michael again quietly considered the thought. It was possible Jonathan was right. "I don't like confrontation."

"Do you feel like that's what's necessary to make this problem right?"

He only nodded.

"Well, I feel like you need to preach on Sunday. How do you think we should handle this?"

"I don't like confrontation," He repeated.

Jonathan said nothing more. He sat back on the couch and folded his arms as he stared at him. Michael could sense the pressure. As wonderful as this family had made him feel, he now found himself cowering back to that prepubescent child that was laughed at down the halls of school. He remembered the feeling of his father telling him he was a worthless brat. He recalled what it was like being back in class the first time after his parents' deaths. Everyone stared and whispered. He hadn't felt like this in many years. Why did Andie bring out his biggest fears?

"I can't do it," he said in defeat. "I can do many things, but I can't face her like that."

"I wouldn't want to either," Jonathan chuckled. "She's scary at times. But the fact remains that she has a hold on you and it's affecting you spiritually. You've got to deal with it somehow so you can be free to do what God's called you to do. I think if you're honest with yourself, you'll admit that the altar covers a little more than just preaching."

Michael rubbed his jaw and reached up to the scar on his cheek. It was another reminder of how those who hated him had treated him.

"What if there's no resolve?" he wondered.

"Then I think the monkey gets off your back and jumps to hers."

"I never have liked monkeys," he mumbled.

*****

After knocking on Andie's door, Michael took several steps back. It reminded him of witnessing while in seminary. They had stressed the importance of not crowding the door when someone answered so people wouldn't feel threatened. He definitely didn't want to crowd Andie. In fact, he would rather not see her at all.

When she finally got to the door and opened it to find Michael, she looked around as though there should be more.

"Where's Angie?" she asked without inviting him in.

"She's not with me; I'm here alone."

"Well, Doug's not here. He works all day. He should be home around five fifteen. He's working just outside of Dockrey this week."

He squinted and looked up toward the top of the door. "I'm not here to see Doug either."

"Okay," she said slowly. "Why are you here?"

He took a deep breath and tried to get the courage to look her in the eyes. He managed to look at her feet instead. His confidence was waning. "I'm here to see you."

"Really?" she replied with a chuckle. "Why on earth would you want to see me?"

"I'm not sure. I know you have a problem with me, and I'd like to do my best to fix it."

Rather than speak, Andie motioned him inside. It was the first time he had been in her house. He had driven by twice and picked up the kids once while with Angie. It was beautiful and wonderfully furnished, but it had a comfortable, homey air to it, much like Jonathan and Barbara's. The two older boys were sitting quietly on the couch doing their schoolwork while Ashley watched a movie in another part of the room wearing a small pair of headphones. The boys waved politely, but Ashley never knew he was there. Michael was impressed with the order of the children, much different than when they exploded into their grandparents' house.

"Where's little Aimee?" he wondered out loud.

"Napping," she said as she headed for a glassed in back porch. "Boys, we'll be in the sunroom. I expect your math to be finished by lunch."

"Yes ma'am," they both replied immediately as they looked back down to their workbooks.

Andie cracked open the door and then placed the small monitor for the baby on an end table beside her. She pulled her knees up beneath her in the wicker chair and folded her arms as she stared at Michael with raised eyebrows. "I'm listening," she said without emotion.

Sitting on the couch he tried to smile, but awkwardness was eating at him so badly he believed he could throw up if she pushed the right button. "No small talk then, I suppose."

"What is it that you want to say to me? My mornings are very busy."

He nodded and sighed, stared out the glass at the beautiful yard, and marveled at the mums and pansies coloring three different flowerbeds. He wanted to say, *You have your mother's touch with flowers*, but he knew it would be a useless effort to be civil. Instead, he tried to think of a way to say what he needed to say.

"Why is it that you despise me?" he finally attempted. *That was it? Those were the only words I could utter?* As soon as he said them he felt ignorant and foolish. *She must think I'm a complete idiot.*

"That's easy," she said coolly. "I think you're a deceptive man who's tricked my sister into a relationship that never should've happened."

That got his attention. He looked at her quickly and squinted again as he stared into her eyes. "Why would you think that?"

"Because it all works out just a little too perfectly to your advantage."

"I'll admit, I believe I'm the one who's benefited the most from this arrangement, but how was I deceptive?"

"Oh, come on!" she bellowed. "Out of the blue you proposed to a total stranger without having a clue as to what she looked like? Give me a break! I believe you knew way more about Angie than you're letting on? Look what you got! You got this gorgeous girl who happened to be a doctor to boot. And you act like it was all just … well … good luck."

"How would I have known what she looked like? We never exchanged or sent pictures."

"You're a clever guy," Andie said smoothly with a hint of sarcasm. "I'm sure you probably have some old buddies or teachers at the seminary you communicate with. I bet you asked about her—then someone let you know what a treat you were in for if she ever made it to Padawin."

"New Orleans seminary?" he asked.

"Yeah."

"I didn't go to New Orleans, and as far as I know, I don't know anyone there."

"Well, Facebook then!"

"Angie had no pictures on Facebook. I don't either. I only joined because she said we could live chat if we were ever online at the same time. That only happened twice."

"True … she's a computer idiot. Then you're more clever than I thought. I don't know how you did it, but I know you did. You proposed awfully fast when you found out she couldn't come because of the marriage thing."

"I was floored when I found out the reason they wouldn't let her come was because neither of us was married. I was totally hopeless. I went down to the beach to pray, trying to think if there was even one girl in any of the tribes I could marry. I had no idea what Angie looked like or even what kind of person she was! All I knew was that I had told the tribes a healer was coming. We hit obstacle after obstacle with no explanation, but when Angie wrote me to say it was because of our singleness, I immediately began to search out an answer. Marrying her seemed like the only logical solution after going through every other possibility imaginable."

"Wow, is that a backbone you're showing?" she said with mock surprise. "Are you actually defending yourself? Where is *Mr. Humility* right now?"

He felt his face go red and could sense sweat beginning to bead up on his forehead. "I'm not trying to do anything but tell you what happened."

"And I don't quite believe *your* version of the story. It's too preposterous. There's got to be more to it than that. And then this whole *super-humble-I'm-a-bad-victim-of-life* thing that you keep throwing out—it's just too much. When you picked up on Angie's heart, which is totally golden, you played it for everything you're worth. You knew exactly how to win her affections. Play the poor little lost boy and you can wrap her around your finger. I wonder how much of your story is actually true, and how much is made up."

He was now struggling to control his temper. She could accuse him of a lot of things, but to insinuate that he had lied about his past to win Angie's sympathies, and then her love, was above and beyond remaining civil. He squared his jaw and tried to hold his tongue.

"Why not tell *me* this sad little story of yours?" she suggested. "Let me see how much truth there is in it. Angie won't share it because you somehow intimidated her out of it."

"I didn't intimidate her!" he said with a voice louder than usual. "She knows ... she understands."

"Yes, I know. Precious Angie knows your pain and won't share anything without your permission. How convenient for you. However, I'm offering you the opportunity to tell me everything from the start. Let's just begin with your birth and move right on to when your parents were killed. How old were you? Oh, yes! Sixteen. What a pitifully impressionable age. I bet that was really hard for you. Did it make Angie cry?"

Michael stood up quickly and resisted the temptation to lash out at her. He wasn't as angry about her attacks on him and his character as much as he was her idea that Angie was a vulnerable fool in all this. The thought that he had duped her into the wonderful relationship they now shared was making his blood boil.

"Are you leaving me, Michael?" she asked with a laugh as she remained comfortably calm in her chair.

He bit his lip, stared toward the living room, then finally asked her, "Have you ever tried to witness to someone or share the Gospel with someone who totally rejected the Word of God as valid—someone who didn't believe the Bible was actual Scripture?"

She shook her head. "No. There's not much of a chance of that in Dockrey. We're in the Bible belt, remember? Why?"

"Because trying to tell you anything about my life would be as impossible as trying to use the scriptures as the authority for salvation. I've tried to reason with people before, trying to convince them that God loves them ... but I can't base it on anything if they refuse to accept the Scripture as from God."

"What exactly are you saying?" she asked with a bit of defense in her own voice for the first time.

"You've already accused me of being a lying deceiver. To tell you the darkest things of my life, or the brightest, would be casting my pearls before swine. You would trample them in the mud and leave them to rot."

He headed toward the porch door.

"And so what's that supposed to mean?" she called to him before he left the porch. "I think it only confirms my beliefs from the beginning: you are a trickster. You deluded, seduced and played on my sister's good nature to win over a wife, something you obviously couldn't do on your own."

He merely left. He walked through the living room without even acknowledging the boys, went out the front door and straight to the Bug. He backed out and headed for his temporary home. So many thoughts were rummaging through his mind that he couldn't think clearly. One part was screaming for him to pack and leave for Padawin. Another part told him to go to Kansas. And still another part said to turn the car around and give Andie Mason a piece of his mind. Instead, he just went home.

*****

When he walked through the door, Angie's smile was the first to greet him.

"Where have you been?" she asked warmly. When she finally recognized his grave expression, her warm smile faded to a look of concern and question. "Where *have* you been?" she asked again, but this time without the warm tone.

"Andie's," he said dryly as he took off his jacket and headed for the stairs.

"Wh-what?" she stammered in unbelief, following him up. "What on earth possessed you to go see her?"

Michael waited until they entered the apartment before he answered. "Your father wants me to preach Sunday. I can't preach knowing that Andie is out there shooting spears at me with her eyes. I just figured we could try and talk this thing out and come to some sort of truce."

She shook her head and frowned. "I wish I would've known you were going. I'd have gone with you. I could've been moral support at least."

"But the problem isn't between you and her. I'm the one she despises."

All Michael's thoughts of leaving or abandoning left as Angie edged herself closer to him. She put her forehead against his and gently smiled as she drew her arms around his waist.

"But I love you," she reminded him. "And you know what else? So does every other person in this family, including Andie's kooky husband. And every other person in this family has had the *privilege* of incurring Andie's wrath also."

"Really?" he asked as he pulled back slightly. "Even Stephen?"

"Oh, gosh, you should've seen how ticked off she was when Annie and he married in New York without anyone going. She accused him of all sorts of evil. And when Annie ended up pregnant right away, she began to make some pretty obscure accusations about their fidelity before marriage."

"Why?"

"Because she was hurt by it, or upset, or angry, or in disagreement. Who knows? It's Andie! You've noticed no one seems to be outraged at her response toward you, haven't you? Have you wondered why? Everyone else seems to think you're the greatest thing since Styrofoam."

"So what are you saying? I should just roll with it?"

"You can't change her mind. She likes Stephen now. She likes me and Annie ... again ... after many falling outs over the years. She's still married to Doug after more heart wrenching disagreements than I care to mention. There's hope for you."

"She thinks I deceived you. She thinks I somehow knew you were this incredibly beautiful woman and that I orchestrated the whole thing to get you over there and married to me."

Angie giggled this time. "If you did," she grinned as she rubbed noses with him, "then you're smarter than I ever imagined."

"She thinks I played on your emotions—I somehow tricked you into falling in love with me by gaining your sympathy and all."

"I fell in love with you because you were wonderful, not because you were pitiful."

When she began to kiss him, thoughts of Andie began to disappear. Once again he was amazed at the depth of his feelings for Angie. It scared him and excited him at the same time. Every time Andie glared at him, he felt he wasn't worthy of Angie and that he should leave her or lose her. But every time Angie looked at him, touched him, or smiled at him, he believed he would die if he had to go on without her. If Andie hated him, so be it. Angie loved him.

"Are you gonna preach on Sunday?" she asked as she moved from his lips to his ear.

"If you want," was all he could get out.

"I want."

FIFTY-THREE

The following day found the entire Wright family gathered together for the Friday evening meal. Angie noticed Michael was unusually quiet, and several times during the course of supper she asked if he was okay. He would always respond with a nod and a smile, but he continued to look stressed and uncomfortable. When the meal was finished and the kitchen cleaned, the ladies joined the men around the fireplace and immediately picked up on the topic. With the exception of the babies, the children were laid up on Jonathan and Barbara's bed watching a movie.

"I'd like to say something, if you don't mind," Michael said suddenly in the midst of what was becoming a heated discussion.

Everyone turned to look. He stood and went to the fireplace where he remained quiet for a moment, obviously contemplating what he would say.

"First," he began, eyes squinting as he searched for words, "I want to say thank-you for welcoming me into this family."

Angie's eyes grew wide and questioning. He just nodded to assure her he was fine.

"I've never really had a family, and to say I was somewhat nervous about coming here would be a major understatement, but you've been gracious to me, and I appreciate it more than you know."

Jonathan interrupted him by adding, "And we appreciate you too, Michael."

"Well, thanks, but this isn't about me tonight ... well, it is, but not for my sake. There are some things I feel you need to hear in order to really know me completely."

"I think I know you just fine," Jonathan countered him again. "I've lived with you for a month now. I've worked beside you and broken bread with you many times. I feel like I know you really well. You're the exact same man who rode home with us from the Memphis airport as you are today—with the exception of the flu. If you feel the need to tell us something, Michael, don't do it out of guilt or compulsion. You do it because you want us to know."

Angie mouthed a *thank you* to her father, but Michael went on to say, "I appreciate that, but I feel it's time to ... well ... reveal myself to everyone, sort of explain, maybe, my past a little more clearly."

"Michael ..." Angie began to protest.

"It's okay. I believe I'm ready to do this—I believe I *need* to do this."

She sat back on the couch and smiled at him for encouragement. She didn't know if *she* could bear to hear the story again. She hoped he wasn't doing this in an attempt to win Andie's approval. Like she had said before: if Andie wasn't ready, nothing would move her.

"You've welcomed me warmly," Michael continued, "which is a huge change for me. I grew up very different than you did here. My parents rented a rattrap with a leaky roof and broken windows that were taped up with plastic in the winter."

He detailed the situation of his alcoholic father and his seriously abused mother. He described the years of jeering from his peers at school and how he grew to be extremely introverted and self-conscious as a result. He then told of Mr. Lovejoy's interest in him, finally telling about the guitar and the lessons. As he got to his sixteenth birthday, Angie could feel her stomach begin to tighten. She also noticed his words were getting choppier and his brow was furrowed in frustration. He looked at her briefly, and she smiled again in encouragement, which seemed to help him move on.

As he described the last moments with his mother, her words that urged him on in his education, and their unhurried and non-stressed conversation, his expression became more intense. She couldn't believe he was able to describe what followed without breaking up emotionally, because she certainly did. Barbara and Jonathan did. Megan did, and even Doug did. Annie and Stephen both held looks of unbelief, and Alex wouldn't even glance up. Everyone struggled emotionally with the description of the scene except for Andie. She stared stone-faced as Michael talked of the Lovejoys' taking him in and his eventual conversion.

Michael went on to talk of his relationship with Jenna, which surprised Angie.

"All I wanted was to love and be loved. I know that's no excuse. I wish I could've trusted God as much as Angie did in that area. He had done so much for me, yet I chose to let Him down when it came to one of the biggest decisions in my life. When Jenna broke the engagement, I really believed that God would make me be alone for the rest of my days to pay for that sin."

He paused, then looked back at Angie and smiled a warm, tear-filled smile. "Then God did something amazing," he said emotionally now. "He brought the most incredible person into my life—the most incredible person I'd ever met in my entire existence. It makes me think of that verse where it says God gives us more than we could ever ask or imagine. I never asked God to bring anyone into my life. I didn't ask for Jenna, and I didn't have the audacity to ask for anyone after her. I thought I'd blown it. But when I say *God is good*, I don't say it lightly. Other than my salvation, Angie is the best thing that's ever happened to me. And this family has been another breath of fresh air in my life."

He paused as he took the time to look at each person in the eye, even

Andie, and then he added, "And that's all I have to say."

Alex immediately got up from his seat and hugged him. At this, Annie began to cry. If anyone in this family could come close to being able to understand the pain that Michael had lived through, it was Alex. Jonathan and Barbara also stood and went to him.

"I knew that God had to have done something above average in your life for you to be the man you are," Jonathan said as he embraced him. "How I wish you would've been here all those years; we would've added to the encouragement."

Barbara pulled him to her and softly said, "You're a part of this family now; never consider yourself alone again."

"I need to go upstairs for a moment if you all don't mind," Michael said as he excused himself and headed for the apartment. It was obvious he was about to break.

Angie jumped up to follow him.

"That's right," Andie suddenly exclaimed, "follow him out like he's a pitiful puppy!"

Everyone turned and either glared at her or stared in total unbelief.

Michael leaned into Angie's ear and whispered, "Stay here. I need to pray."

"I'll defend you," she said soberly as she looked into his eyes.

"I don't need to be defended. I did this because I believed I needed to, not to impress your sister one way or the other. I'm tired of running and hiding from my past."

"I know," Angie said as she rubbed his shoulder before he went up the stairs. She came back and sat down, glaring at Andie the entire time.

"So you all just buy into this as though it's fact," Andie started up again.

"Why would he lie about something like that?" Alex yelled.

"Because he's trying to woo all of you over with the same methods he used to reel in Angie!"

"What kind of person do you think I am?" Angie demanded to know. "Do you think me to be a complete idiot?"

"Where this man is concerned, yes!"

Alex jumped up. Everyone was shocked because he seldom showed any emotion.

"You're a real jerk!" he said to Andie. "Do you know what kind of courage it took for him to tell us that?"

"Courage?" Angie shook her head. "Do you know what kind of trust he has in this family to be able to tell you that?"

"Well, it did wonders for you!" Andie blurted. "You slept with him!"

"I slept with him, and I assume you mean *in the Biblical sense*, before he ever told me anything about his past!" Angie said defiantly.

At this statement, everyone turned their stares toward her. She sighed and bounced down onto the couch.

"Really?" Annie asked her.

"Really," Angie confirmed. "I was in love with him long before he ever opened up to me. He was this wonderful man, Godly, gentle, intelligent … I was drawn to him the moment I saw him. I'd made up my mind to wait— to wait until he could tell me all of this, but it just didn't happen that way. We were married, we were in love, and we were committed to each other."

"But you didn't even know him!" Andie began her protest again.

"Yes, I did! I knew the man that he was now. I didn't know who he was before, but I knew he was the one I would spend the rest of my life with. You haven't seen Michael like he is in Padawin. He's assured and confident. He's a leader, and the people put their total trust in him. He's transformed their lives in so many ways I couldn't even begin to tell you all he's done. Michael gave me bits and pieces of his life; he revealed his past to me slowly. But when we … when I … when things went further between us, *that* is when he opened up."

"I'll never forget," Alex started talking again, "what it was like all those years having all of you condemn me as some wimpy psycho. I can't begin to tell you how many times I thought of suicide."

"Alex!" Barbara exclaimed in shock.

"I did," he said emotionally distraught. "You all thought I had no backbone. I remember the looks you would give me when I would clam up and revert to my protective shell."

He gazed at Megan and a calm came over his face. "But Megan gave me a reason to live … and to love. It was years before I could ever tell her what had happened to me. But I did tell her, and I told her because I trusted her and her alone … nobody else."

"But she didn't have to sleep with you in order to get you to open up!" Andie declared angrily.

Alex looked back at Andie in disgust.

"Actually," Megan stood up this time and came over to where Alex was, "we had slept together."

Now the family was staring at Megan with shock.

"Look!" Angie said as she stood in frustration. "This is all beside the point! We treated Alex like an outcast. We didn't deserve his trust. Megan loved him for who he was; we judged him for who he wasn't. But back to me and Michael—we … *were* … married." She said the words slowly and deliberately. "I loved him, and he loved me. No, we didn't know everything there was to know about each other …"

"You knew nothing about each other!" Andie interrupted.

"Shut up!" Angie now yelled in anger. "I've had enough of your judgments and preconceived notions about my marriage! Whether you like it or not, I love Michael and I intend to build a life with him. I intend to have a family with him, and if we never make it back to Padawin, I intend to go wherever it is he wants to go. Your gripes and complaints aren't gonna change my mind or my heart. The sooner you deal with that, the better off you'll be 'cause I'm not budging on this. I love him ... with all that I am."

"Listen," Alex said almost pleading, "Megan saved my life because she was willing to become someone I could trust ... and eventually love. Angie is Michael's Megan, and I'm proud to know that she was willing to love the man she knew he was rather than wait for him to prove himself to be something more. Some people can see things with their hearts, Andie. But you're not one of them. If I'd listened to you, I would've left this earth long ago. But because of Megan, and her years of persistence in loving me despite my imperfections and my lack of communication, I'm a whole man today. I'm a father. I have a life, a great life. Just because Angie and I, and well, Annie for that matter, didn't do it like you did it, doesn't mean it's not real. You were ready to crucify Stephen because he married Annie on a whim in New York!"

Annie and Stephen were startled at this announcement. "That's news to me," Annie blurted out in laughter. "What was the problem?"

Angie explained, "She thought something was not *kosher* with your relationship because you married so fast and without any family present. You should've heard what she said when you ended up pregnant so soon."

Annie turned to Andie with a questioned look.

"What did you expect?" Andie said defensively. "You married at the drop of a hat, no family allowed, and ended up pregnant!"

"I expected you to believe what I said," Annie replied. "I'd never even kissed a man before Stephen!"

"Whatever," Andie finally gave up in exasperation. "I'm obviously outnumbered here. I think it's time to go."

"Wait," Jonathan said sternly as he stood and went to the front of the group. "I want to make something clear here." Everyone became quiet and gave him their full attention. "None of us are perfect. Andie, I think you need to remember what it was like to be desperately in love."

"Desperately in love, I remember," she said with a hint of sarcasm. "Foolishly in love, I don't."

"Really?" Jonathan said with a grin. "So when you told me that if I didn't approve of your marrying Doug after your first year of college that you'd marry him anyway and give up college, that wasn't foolish?"

"Come on, we had dated forever," Andie reasoned.

"Yes, you had. And if I remember correctly, you even threatened to get pregnant if I wouldn't comply."

Now the family turned their stares back to Andie.

"Wow," Annie chuckled. "That's really close to the pot calling the kettle *black*."

"Wait a minute," Doug jumped in. "For the record, Andie and I did *not* sleep together before we were married." The stares went to him now. "I just wanted to clear that up. I don't know if it was an idle threat or not—but we never ... you know ... did *it*, Dad ... Mr. Wright ... Pastor Jon ... his imminence ... sir ."

Jonathan shook his head and ran his hand through his hair. "Andie, do you remember that feeling? Do you remember that frustration of being so in love that you couldn't wait for anything to be with the one you loved?"

Andie wouldn't respond.

"Angie fell in love. Annie fell in love. When you brought Doug home that first time, I thought I could eat my socks from disappointment."

Andie stared at the fireplace now; she remembered well.

"He drove a motorcycle, had long hair, and was as cocky as anything I'd ever seen before. All I could think was that my cultured, musical, intelligent, talented daughter had fallen for the *rebel without a cause*!" Jonathan winked at Doug. "But he grew on me. All I'm asking is that you cut everyone a little slack, just like I did with you when you threatened to ruin your life if I didn't let you run off with the *man of your dreams*."

"I finished college," Andie said still trying to be somewhat defiant.

"Yes, and you held off having all those children until you had worked awhile, two stipulations I asked of you if I let you marry the scoundrel."

"Scoundrel?" Doug asked softly.

"Like I said," Jonathan grinned, "you grew on me."

Angie stood and interrupted as she said, "I'd really like to be with Michael right now. I don't care much whether Andie approves or not. But if there's any doubt about my feelings for him, I'm crazy about him. And you can etch that in stone if you want."

Doug leaned over to Stephen and whispered, "Were we crazy to marry into this family or what?"

"Crazy," Stephen agreed. "The things we do for love."

Angie went on up the stairs. It genuinely didn't matter to her how the conversation ended. She just wanted to see Michael. She knew it had to have taken a lot out of him to tell the whole family like he had. She wondered why he did it.

She opened the door slowly, fearful that perhaps he might be in a fragile state. He was standing at the window staring out toward the front yard. When she came in, he looked over at her.

"Are you okay?" she asked joining him at the window.

"I'm fine," he said with a nod and a smile.

She put her hands on his shoulder and then rested her head on them as she gazed out the window with him.

"Why did you do it?" she asked, curious to know how he gained the courage to tell practical strangers what it took him months to tell her.

"I did it because I'm tired of hiding behind my insecurities. This is my testimony; this is my God-story. I always feel like this hurt little boy deep down inside, but what I want is to be strong and stable. I want to be a man you need, not a man you feel sorry for. I want to be someone you can lean on and know that I'll be steady and sure. I want to be the kind of father my kids can look up to and believe I would take on the whole world to protect them. I look at your father, and I see two things that dominate his character: strength and love. And I'm afraid to show them both."

"I don't feel sorry for you, Michael," she said gently.

"Yes, you do, but that was okay for a while. I needed that from you. I needed to know you empathized with that part of my life. But I'm ready to move on. I felt like telling your family would give me even more strength to put my past behind me. Do you realize I never told anyone, not even the counselor, about what happened that night?"

"Why not the counselor?"

"I couldn't. I couldn't bring myself to say a word about any of it. My mind and my emotions were so muddled and unclear. He knew what had happened, and that was enough. He kept saying I needed to talk about it in order to let go of it, to remember things clearly, but he wouldn't force me. He said he would pray for me that God would bring someone into my life that I could open up to and finally release it."

Michael turned Angie to face him. "God finally answered that prayer, but not only in you, in your family also. Despite Andie, I feel like I belong here. I would've given anything to have grown up around you all and have known this kind of acceptance. I would give anything … anything except you. And all I can believe is that God knew what He was doing all along."

He leaned his head to her forehead and said with closed eyes, "If I could go back and change it, but *not* have you at the end, then I wouldn't change a thing. You've made everything I ever faced in life worth it if it brought me to you."

Angie felt tears begin to sting her eyes. This was a depth of love she had never known. "I love you, Dr. Collins," she said in a whisper as she brought her hands up to his face.

"And I adore you, Dr. Angie," he replied with a gentle kiss.

FIFTY-FOUR

Angie couldn't believe she was doing this, but if Michael could face his insecurities as boldly as he had, surely she could face her biggest: singing in public. It probably wouldn't have been near as intimidating had it just been the congregation. After all, she and Michael had sung for every meeting with the tribes in Padawin. But this was drastically different. Staring at her with expectant faces were her older sister, the music teacher, her younger sister and brother-in-law, the successful world famous musicians, her brother, a professional instrumentalist who probably made more money in a year than she would in ten, and her parents who had watched all these budding musicians grow up.

Then, as if she weren't under enough pressure already, Michael had insisted they play and sing a song they had written themselves.

"Why can't we sing 'When the Roll is Called Up Yonder' in Padawin?" she had asked him. "Everyone would eat that up, and it would be a big blessing."

"Because that song would not go with my sermon."

"Trust me on this; it would be easier for you to change your entire sermon than for me to sing that song."

He had laughed in a manner she had never seen before. "I can't believe this! You're actually nervous! I didn't think it was possible for Dr. Angie to be nervous."

"Congratulations," she responded soberly. "You've now seen a whole new part of me—and frankly, I don't like it when it comes out. It's all your fault too, by the way."

But now, Michael stood confidently before the congregation on Sunday morning as though he were back in Padawin and this were the most natural thing for them to be doing. Of course, he was an excellent musician; she was a *piddler*. He looked at her with raised eyebrows to see if she was ready to begin. She gave a weak smile and a small nod signaling him to go. He began the song with his skillful picking and she joined in with a precise rhythmic strumming. Her knees were shaking as they continued. There was one thing she was thankful for: at least she didn't have to sing a solo. She only had to harmonize with him.

I have heard the cries of those who have not heard Him
And I have seen the needs of those who've never seen His hand
I have felt the shame of those who've never known His touch
And that is why I give my life to tell them of His love.

I can hear as He speaks a gentle breeze
I can see His hand in all that now surrounds me
I can feel His image being built in me
And His love has empowered my life and made me free.

She tried to keep her eyes closed so she could focus on the song and not her family, but she still needed to look at her left hand occasionally to find some of the unusual chord structures he had taught her. She snuck a peek at Michael who was singing with all his heart and it reminded her of sitting with him on the deck with Mount Podakind in the background and the rushing river roaring beside them. Her heart ached to go back.

Without thinking, she looked out to the congregation. Since her family was front and center, she couldn't help but notice their faces. All were moved and rather surprised. When Annie caught her eye, Angie nearly broke out in laughter. Annie's expression was saying, *Why didn't I hear about any of this?* She just smiled and continued to strum, waiting for the next chorus where she would join in again and harmonize.

I have heard His words speaking of forgiveness
And I have watched him take a life that's broken and abused
I have felt Him pull me close with love and tenderness
And that is why I give my life to tell them of His truth.

I can hear as He speaks a gentle breeze
I can see His hand in all that now surrounds me
I can feel His image being built in me
And His love has empowered my life and made me free.

Without even noticing, her nerves began to calm as she remembered the night they had written the song. They had been playing silly tunes and gotten quite giddy. She told him that many people back in the States would think them foolish to find such pleasure in something so simple. They then began to think about what they might be doing if they were back in America. As the list began to wane, she had told him she would never be happy anywhere else because God had called her to minister to the people here about His love. He had smiled and said, *There's a song in there somewhere.*

She felt tears begin to well as they approached the bridge. This song was about them, about their ministry, their callings, and everything they had given their lives to. An ache had remained inside since the day they had left Padawin, and she wondered if anything would ever take it away outside of returning.

She closed her eyes, lifted her voice, and sang the bridge with him.

No one has to know why I do the things I do
All that I can say is that I trust Him through and through
Jesus gave His life, sacrificed in every way

But I choose to live that sacrifice
I choose to give a sacrifice
My life is now a sacrifice each day.

I can hear as He speaks a gentle breeze
I can see His hand in all that now surrounds me
I can feel His image being built in me
And His love has empowered my life and made me free.
I am empowered...and I am free.

The congregation applauded and came to their feet, and Angie found herself both proud and humbled at the same time. She was proud to have made it through and humbled at the response. She took Michael's guitar with her down to her seat beside Annie and tried to act as if this were all old hat, but inside the butterflies were having a hey day with her stomach. Annie didn't help by whispering in her ear, *We've come a long way from that little preview concert I got from you on your bed before you left.* Angie just smiled and gave her attention to her husband. She'd never heard him preach in English, and she was curious if his delivery would be the same. She loved to hear him expound the Word as he had a wonderful way of making it plain and clear.

"Behind our house in Padawin," he began, "stands the awesome snow-capped peak of Podakind. It's awesome because it rises nearly 15,000 feet into the air and dwarfs everything around it. As we look out our window, or sit on the back deck, it never grows mundane or inconspicuous because its sheer size and uniqueness force us to see it, to stand in awe of it, and always be aware of its presence. For Angie and me, however, there's a greater awe that accompanies the awareness of Mount Podakind: it's a volcano."

Angie smiled as his first description captured the attention of the congregation. Hearing him in English without her having to struggle with the translation was a nice change. No matter how shy or unsure he may appear, whenever he taught it was always with authority and assurance. She was glad these same qualities were shining through now.

Jonathan Wright tried never to judge a minister's delivery. If one felt called to preach, it was God's calling, and God used all types of styles and personalities and levels of intelligence to present His message. But he couldn't help being impressed with Michael. He was articulate and descriptive. He had a way of making you anticipate what was coming next. When he read a Scripture, it was as though you were hearing it for the first time because his inflections and stressing of certain words gave new emphasis to what it was saying. His thoughts were organized, and each point was built upon another. There was a flow and progression as he moved through an idea, and every concept was always punctuated with its practicality for everyday living.

As Michael began to near the end, his invitation was obvious: we are called to minister the love of God because we have experienced it in our own lives. To do anything less is sin or a confession that we don't truly know this love.

"Which is it?" Michael asked as he looked across the congregation. "Do you know the love of God? Has it invaded your life and changed your heart? Or are you dead and cold to all that God has offered? Today this altar stands open for all who need to kneel here. This altar isn't merely for those who need salvation. This altar stands ready for those who need forgiveness, those who need strength, and those who just simply need more of God than they do of themselves. Your pastor will stand here if you need his counsel, but I believe most of us know what we need to do. We need to pour our hearts out to the Father, one to One, and ask Him to renew a steadfast spirit within us. We need to remember the joy of our salvation. We need to be impressed with the presence of God in our lives simply because He is there, not because of what He is doing. Like Podakind, Angie and I never take for granted the power that this potential volcano possesses. We should never take for granted the power that our Father possesses simply because we don't see the smoke rising daily. We need to *know* that God's potential is always present, and often He's simply waiting for us to come to the end of ourselves before He releases it into our lives. Let's pray."

Jonathan didn't stand at the front of the church. He first embraced Michael and then went to the altar to pray. Behind him many followed. Angie was moved when she saw Cindy Marcum kneel. She came up behind her, put her hand on her back, and prayed silently that God would do something in Cindy's life that would cause her to take God seriously.

Andie continued to play the piano softly. As much as she had wanted to distrust Michael, she wasn't so hard-hearted that she couldn't see the Spirit of God move. The church was literally on its knees, and she knew it was because the anointing of God had been on him that morning. No matter what she may have thought about him, she had to admit that his sermon cut her heart into tiny pieces with each piece screaming spiritual lapse and lack of concern for others. Andie had built her life around her family and had come to the conclusion that all God required of her was to give to them and to meet their needs. She thought of Angie's years of selfless study for the sole purpose of giving her life to others that they might come to know Christ. And no matter what she may have thought about Michael or his motives, he had done exactly as Angie. He had even earned a doctorate and taken that knowledge to an obscure place where his entire existence was for the purpose of bringing life and Christ to others. He had left Padawin, his home and his field, not to come here and seek a name for himself or to impress people. He had come because he knew Angie's life was in danger if he didn't leave. He left only to save the life of her sister, not his own.

Andie got Annie's attention and motioned for her to come to the piano.

"Take over for me," she whispered to Annie. "I don't want to cause a scene with an abrupt stop to the playing. Just pick up so I can slip out."

Annie nodded and sat to Andie's left on the piano bench. When Andie came to the end of the chorus, Annie immediately began to play. As Andie went to the altar alone, no one noticed the sisters' switch.

Andie prayed for several minutes. She had much to confess. When Angie came up behind her and put her arm on her back, Andie turned around and embraced her.

"I'm sorry," she said softly. "I don't know why I was so hard-headed about all of this."

Angie smiled. "Because you're just hard-headed by nature."

"Do you think Michael would pray with me?"

"In a heartbeat," Angie assured her as she motioned Michael over to them.

He knelt down with them at the steps to the platform.

"I'm sorry, Michael," Andie said almost mournfully. "I can't explain all that I felt or went through where you're concerned."

"And please don't try," he said quickly. "The past is always the past unless we choose to drag it around with us. I don't want anything in the past to pull me down again. I'm ready to move on."

"You're a good man," she said sincerely. "Angie did well."

"I'm the one who's most blessed. I know Angie is a gift I didn't deserve."

"Do any of us truly deserve the blessings of God?" Andie asked.

He shook his head as they bowed to pray. Andie felt release and healing as Michael spoke to God in a trusting way. Silently she begged God for the kind of faith that Angie and Michael lived by, and prayed that she could learn from their example.

FIFTY-FIVE

After hanging his suit in the closet following the morning service, Michael turned around and saw Angie staring out the back window of the apartment. He couldn't help himself. As he walked over, he began to sing the first verse of Stephen's biggest hit, "Autumn Sunset":

Early November, gaze out my window
Watching the leaves barely hanging on

Angie turned around and smiled.

Pour me some coffee, pick up a novel
Ready to spend another evening alone.
Never thought it would be this way
I simply played it safe
And somehow I never gave my heart away.

"Why on earth are you singing such a sad, sad song?" she asked as she took his hand.

"Because it's early November and you're gazing out the window."

"Please," she said rolling her eyes. "It's so depressing."

"I know. I used to listen to that song all the time and pout because I was so lonely."

She nodded and sighed. "Don't tell anyone this, but I was never a big Stephen Williams fan."

"What?" he asked loudly from surprise.

She put her finger to her lips to hush him. "Quiet! I said don't tell anyone."

"Why don't you like Stephen's music?" he asked a little quieter.

"Because it's so sad. Even if you were a happy single person and very satisfied with life, all you had to do was listen to *Autumn Sunset* and it could throw you into a fit of melancholy and discontent."

"True. But I still love his music."

"Well, I have to admit that I love *Winter Passion*, the new Christmas album."

"Is that because of Stephen or Annie?"

"How about a little of both? Anyway, Annie's always been my favorite musician."

He grinned as he continued on singing the chorus:

So while I'm waiting for someone to love me
Someone who knows me through and through
I'll watch the Autumn Sunset from my single room apartment

And hope and pray that dreams can still come true
And long to hear the words "I love you".

"Please," she begged as she put her finger to his lips this time. "I don't need any help being depressed right now."

"What's wrong?"

"The best description I can come up with is that I'm homesick."

"Padawin?"

"Yeah. I'm beginning to wonder if we'll ever get back. And then your description of Podakind this morning made my heart ache."

"We'll get there. I know we will," he assured her as he gently kissed her forehead. "We'll raise our kids there."

"What kids?" She still wanted to pout. "I can't even seem to get pregnant."

"Angie, I thought we weren't trying to have kids—that we weren't gonna worry about it."

"I know, but everything seems large and insurmountable right now. Somehow if I were pregnant it would feel like life was actually moving forward. Instead, I feel like I could break down and cry, and that's so wrong after the awesome service we just had. You were incredible, and God used you in a wonderful way."

"Maybe we should get away for a while," he suggested. "Your dad offered the camper anytime we wanted."

"Really?" she said with a hint of hope. "Where would we go?"

"I was thinking maybe we could go visit the Lovejoys for a few days."

Angie's eyes brightened and her smile warmed. He put a mental note in his mind; he would never forget that expression.

"That would be wonderful," she said with enthusiasm. "I really wanted to visit them, but because you didn't bring it up, I didn't want to push."

"When I left ten years ago, I told them I'd probably never be back. I never intended to see them again. But … here I am."

"We could spend Thanksgiving with them."

"No, we need to be here with your family. I want to spend the holidays here."

"But not everybody will be here. We're celebrating Thanksgiving this Tuesday before Alex and Annie leave. It'd be a wonderful gift for the Lovejoys—being there then. Besides, we'll be here for Christmas."

He put his arms around and hugged her tightly. "Are you sure?"

"You're the one who suggested the trip; I'm the one suggesting the time. Let's give them a call."

He leaned in and kissed her gently. Her full lips were surprisingly warm, and as usual, Angie's response did more than just make him happy. When Barbara yelled, *Dinner's ready!* he pulled away and closed his eyes in pure delight.

"And we get to go camping too?" she asked in a suggestive tone.

"As long as it has a heater."

"Oh, I don't think we'll need a heater," she said as she kissed him once more. "What do you think?"

"I think we'll have to sleep sometime."

"You're no fun, but yes, it has a heater."

"Camping with Angie," he mulled over in his mind. "At the Lovejoys with Angie. Spending Thanksgiving with Angie. Who knew life could be so good?"

"Come on, Dr. Collins," she said taking his hand and pulling him toward the door. "Let's go eat and then look up your old friends in Kansas. I'm starving!"

"You're always starving lately."

"It's 'cause you're making me burn up so much energy," she winked as she opened the door.

*****

Michael bit a fingernail nervously as he waited for the number to connect.

"That's a nasty habit," Angie whispered to him as she ate a second piece of cake. "Do you know how many germs hide under there?"

"I've done it for thirty-six years and am still alive."

"Now I know how you got the flu."

He rolled his eyes and kept on chewing.

"Hello?" came the voice on the other end.

"Hello," Michael said taken aback. He hadn't heard a single ring. "Is this Herbert Lovejoy?"

"Yes it is," said the warm voice.

"Mr. Lovejoy, this is Michael Collins."

There was a long pause as the older man must have collected his senses.

"Michael," he finally said. "So, you're alive. We were worried when we heard about Padawin. Where are you?"

"Would you believe Alabama?"

"As long as you're not in Padawin, I'm relieved. What dragged you to the southeast?"

"A wife," Michael said with a grin at Angie.

She offered him a bite of cake. He shook his head and motioned that he was stuffed.

"You're married?" Mr. Lovejoy asked in surprise. "Is she that young lady you met at college? The two of you got back together?"

"No sir. We met in Padawin. It's a long story. How 'bout I tell you the whole thing in person?"

"Really? You're going to visit?"

317

"We would like to. We were wondering about spending Thanksgiving with you."

"Ruth and I would be honored."

"We don't want to interrupt any plans you may have already made," Michael added quickly. "We just thought it might be a good time to come knowing you would have a few days off."

"I don't care if we planned to have a hundred people over! I'd call them up or send them home, and then welcome you with open arms! We'd love to see you, Michael ... very, very much."

"We're celebrating Thanksgiving here early," Michael explained, "this Tuesday evening, in fact. Her brother and sister can't be here for the actual holiday."

"Well, bad for them, good for us, huh?"

"Yes, sir," he replied as he gave Angie a thumbs up. "We were thinking about leaving on the Saturday prior to Thanksgiving. We're going to camp on the way there—just take our time. We'd probably be in on Tuesday afternoon right before the holidays."

"Hang on, Michael," Mr. Lovejoy said, and then he yelled away from the phone. "Ruth! Michael is coming home to see us! He's coming to spend Thanksgiving with us!"

Michael heard a high-pitched yell come from Ruth Lovejoy.

"It's official," Mr. Lovejoy laughed. "Ruth just gave her *squeal* of approval."

"Wonderful. We'll see you both Thanksgiving, then."

"I can't believe it, Michael," he said softer now. "We never thought we'd see you again. We never believed you'd leave Padawin."

"Me either. I only left because of my wife. I couldn't bear the thought of ... well, losing her."

"I understand. You made the right choice, you know?"

"I think so too," he agreed as he reached over and touched Angie's face. He hung up and gave her a smile. This was going to be fun.

"Okay," Annie came waltzing in after giving Stevie over to Stephen for a nap. "I want to know how long you've been hiding all this musical talent."

"Please," Angie groaned as she cracked a pecan and began pulling out shell fragments. "I'm hiding nothing." She popped the nut into her mouth.

"I couldn't believe that was you singing and playing this morning," Barbara said shaking her head.

"Trust me; it had way more to do with Michael's singing and playing than mine."

"That's not true," he broke in. "You do very well in both areas. I love to hear you sing *and* play."

"Yeah, but the only people you ever hear sing are the tribesmen," she protested. "They are loud and bouncy. They have one volume over there:

full blast. My soft little voice is a welcomed break."

"All I can say is that I was highly impressed with the playing, the singing, and the writing," Annie told her. "That song was beautiful. Of course, after hearing you and Michael describe Padawin, how could you not write beautiful music together?"

"Well, you can't put it on your next album," Angie teased. "We're going to have to wait until we have enough songs to do an album of our own."

"That's not a bad idea," Barbara jumped in. "I would love to have music of the two of you singing and playing! It was so simple and ... well, clear. Whenever I miss you, I can put it on and feel as though you're right here with me."

"*That* ain't gonna happen," Angie said firmly. "I was only kidding, Moms. Come on, everybody—lighten up about the music, would you? So I like to sing and play with Michael. It's a *recreational* thing we do together. Nothing more."

"Hmmm," was Annie's response.

Angie knew that meant there would be more discussion to follow before Annie left on Wednesday.

"I'm serious," Angie tried to reiterate. "I'm *not* a musician. I'm a doctor. End of discussion."

"Hmmm," Annie replied again.

FIFTY-SIX

Later that afternoon, Angie felt the need to go see Mrs. Marcum and make sure everything was still on go. She knew Sue had agreed to cancer treatments, but with her initial hesitancy it was quite possible she might change her mind again. And hopefully, since Cindy was still there, it would give Angie a chance to have another talk with her. Cindy needed to understand what chemotherapy would require from all of them, not just her mother.

She didn't bother to ring the doorbell this time. She had called to let them know she was coming so she barged in unannounced like old times. She called out as she followed the television noise.

"Back here in the Florida room!" came Cindy's voice.

Angie was glad they seemed happy for the moment.

"How's everybody here?" she asked as she walked through the doorway.

"We're still basking in the glow of this morning's worship," Sue said with a smile. "Your husband preached quite a sermon."

"I didn't know he had it in him," Cindy confessed. "I mean I always thought he was cute and stuff, but I have to admit I wondered what else was there to get you so head over heels in love with him. I see it now."

"He's a wonderful man," Angie agreed as she found a seat. "He's very different over there than he is over here—very different when we're alone than in public. It doesn't bother me, though. It takes a lot of trust for Michael to open up."

"Or a lot of calling," Sue laughed. "He had no problem opening up during that sermon today."

"His description of the mountain was breathtaking," Cindy added. "I almost felt like I was sitting there with the both of you on your deck. By the way! When did you take up the guitar? What's the deal with that? The two of you were singing like you were old pros at it!"

"I don't even want to go through this discussion again," Angie sighed as she held up her hand. "I've been through it with my family already this afternoon."

"I can imagine," Sue grinned. "All this talent appearing from nowhere after all those years of protests."

"I didn't protest; I just didn't have what the others had. That didn't mean I didn't have any."

"I knew she could sing all along," Cindy said smugly as she took a sip of coffee. "I used to hear her sing at the top of her lungs with whatever was playing on the radio. You would have been a great rock star. Do you still do that head thing where you sling your hair around?"

Angie laughed as Cindy tried to demonstrate, and Sue Marcum stared in shock.

"Cindy!" Sue exclaimed. "That can't be good for your brain."

"Didn't bother Angie's," Cindy laughed. "She made it through med school."

"You haven't been here ten minutes yet, Angie," Sue said tiredly, "and you girls have already worn me out. I'm going to lie down and take a little nap before church tonight. Can I leave you two alone without fear for your health?"

"Have a nice nap, Mrs. Marcum," Angie said as she got up to hug her. "I'll make sure Cindy doesn't do anything too neck breaking while you're resting."

"I appreciate it. See you at church tonight," she waved as she went out the door.

When Sue was out of earshot, Angie grinned at Cindy and said, "I haven't done the hair slinging thing in years. I forgot all about it. It's amazing how life changes you."

"So, Missionary Mike hasn't seen the wild side of you yet?"

"Actually, he says I am the wildest thing he's ever encountered."

"Enough!" Cindy yelled as she put her fingers in her ears. "I don't want to hear about any wild encounters between missionaries. My mind can only take so much."

"Oh, come on, Cindy," Angie moaned. "I'm not a different person just because I'm a missionary. I'm the same old Angie."

"Then do the hair slinging thing," Cindy whispered.

"Do you have any more coffee?"

"If you'll do the hair thing, I'll make a fresh pot."

"Deal!" Angie laughed as she began to bob her head back and forth, slinging her hair in every direction imaginable. All Cindy could do for the moment was cackle with delight.

After a nice chat in the breakfast nook and a couple of cups of coffee, Angie began to turn the conversation toward Sue's upcoming treatments.

"Have you and Billy discussed how you're gonna care for your mom when the chemo starts?"

"No. I just assume we'll keep on doing things like we are right now."

Angie's expression became serious.

"What?" Cindy asked her. "Why the glum look?"

"I don't think you realize how harsh these treatments are on the body. They're literally destroying cells ... and not just the cancer cells. The medicine is strong—very strong. The word *chemical* is an apt description."

"The doctor explained it somewhat. I'll be able to drive her to the treatments."

"That's wonderful," Angie tried to be positive. "But I'm talking about after the treatments."

"What do you mean?"

"You can't just drop her back by the house and then tell her you'll see her on the weekend."

"Why not?"

"The treatments will make her sick."

"The doctor told us that."

"No," Angie shook her head. "Cindy, the treatments will make her miserably sick—violently sick. She'll barely be able to lift her head for a while afterward."

"I'm sorry, Angie," she said with a bit of defensiveness creeping into her voice and her expression. "That's the best I can do right now. Maybe we can hire someone to come in and take care of her until she gets over the yucky part."

Now Angie rolled her eyes and slumped down over the table. "You can't do that to her, Cindy."

"Why not? You can't expect me to miss work several days in a row! I mean, one day to take her to treatments is fine, but staying until she *feels good* is impossible."

"I know. That's why you need to think about making some life changes."

Cindy's jaw dropped, and she looked at Angie as though she'd lost her mind. "Don't tell me you expect me to come back here every day until the treatments are over. I can't do that! Drive back and forth from Florence? Sometimes I'm showing buildings at 8:00 in the evening! That's impossible! I would end up having to have some kind of treatment myself!"

"That's not what I'm suggesting. Besides, she's going to need you more than just at night. For the first couple of days, she'll be …"

"Wait … a … minute," Cindy said slowly and almost angrily as she interrupted her. "Don't tell me you think I should quit my job and move back here."

Angie stared directly into her eyes and nodded deliberately.

"No way!" Cindy almost screamed. "Are you crazy? For the first time in my life I'm enjoying who I am and what I'm doing! You can't expect me to give all this up and move in with my mother simply because she's sick."

"That's exactly what I expect you to do."

Cindy jumped up from the table, grabbed her purse, and headed out the front door. Angie followed. Once outside, Cindy dug through her purse for a cigarette and lit it up.

"*You* are the one who's crazy," Angie said as she watched Cindy take long drags and then exhale. "Your father died of heart disease, your mother has cancer, and you're out here puffing away because you're stressed! Talk about your disaster in the making."

"Leave it alone, Angie."

"Why? You say you have this great life now! You say there's no way you can leave it because it's so fulfilling. I disagree with you. I don't think you're happy or fulfilled one bit. All you've done is manage to fill the empty places in your existence with meaningless things and people so you don't have time to think about how lonely and vacant your life really is! Look how stressed you are! What happened to the free spirit you used to be?"

"I never was a *free spirit*. That was you, remember?"

"No, you're wrong. How sad that you can't even remember what it was like to have a full and meaningful life."

"What are you trying to do? Guilt me into staying with my mom? Is that it? You're here! Why don't you take care of her?"

"Because she's *not* my mother. That's the whole point! A month ago you pleaded with me to get your mother to take treatments. Do you know why she wouldn't?"

Cindy took another drag and shook her head.

"Because she felt she had nothing to live for. She feels like she's lost her husband ... and that she lost her children long ago."

Cindy closed her eyes and bit her bottom lip. Angie knew that had to sting.

"Cindy, life isn't about stuff. It's not about having great jobs or making lots of money. It's not about nice apartments or partying with friends so you can forget your worries. It's all about people, and it's all about relationships, real relationships, relationships that enrich your life and give it depth and meaning. You're all your mother has. If you aren't the one who holds her head after those treatments, who wipes her brow, who insists she eats and makes it through, she'll never go through with it and she will ... not ... survive."

Cindy was clenching her teeth and grinding her jaw. She took another puff of her cigarette and looked up toward the sky. It was cold outside, and Angie was beginning to shiver without her jacket. She wanted to suggest they go inside, but then thought against it. This moment was burning Cindy's heart, and Angie needed to keep it up until she could understand.

"Cindy," she tried to be tender, "if you could have your father back, would you do anything to get him here?"

"Stupid question. Of course I would."

"But you don't have that option."

"Obviously."

"But this is what's happening with your mother right now. I can promise you, after her first treatment, she'll plead with you not to make her go back. She'll be so sick and miserable for the first bit that she'll wish for death over another treatment. Some stranger in her house, and that includes me, isn't going to be the motivation to get her back there. But Cindy, if this had been your father, and you knew that on the other side was death, you wouldn't think twice, would you?"

Cindy bit her lip again and shook her head.

"Then hear what I'm saying to you: on the other side of this is either death or life for your mom. You have the chance to save her life, but it'll mean giving up what you're hanging on to right now. Please tell me that her life is worth that sacrifice for you."

Cindy took in a deep breath, flung her cigarette to the ground and rubbed it in with her shoe. Tears had filled her eyes, but they weren't falling. Angie couldn't imagine that anyone would actually struggle with such a decision.

"I would have to give up my apartment," Cindy said with no emotion. "There's no way I could afford to keep it without making that kind of money for very long. And there's no real estate agency in Dockrey." Cindy let out a sarcastic chuckle. "Even if there were, there's no money to be made in it here. I have to work, Angie. I can't be with her 24 hours a day. I'd go insane."

"I understand. People know your mother here. Someone would be willing to give you a job and be as flexible as necessary to see you through this time of struggling."

Cindy did the sarcastic chuckle again. "Yeah, I could go from making a six figure salary to checking out groceries at the Piggly Wiggly. This is looking better all the time."

"Cindy," Angie went over to her and gently placed her hand on her shoulder, "this isn't forever."

"It might as well be. The chances of me getting back into …"

"You've got to pray that God will work all of this out for you," Angie interrupted her. "You're acting as if all this is up to you, and it isn't. God is doing something here, Cindy, and you need to open your eyes to see what it is."

"He's killing off my parents one at a time!" she screamed in anger. "Why should I pray to Him or expect anything else from Him. He hates me!"

"You know that's not true. I understand you're hurt, but I know deep inside you know God doesn't hate you."

She sighed and looked to the ground as she fumbled the smoking cigarette butt with her toe. "I suppose I deserve all this."

"That's not it. God isn't punishing you or your parents for *your* mistakes."

"Really? Not even for adultery?"

"No. God doesn't operate like that. He accepts us all on the basis of what Christ did at the cross. Your adultery has nothing to do with what's happening to your parents. The Bible tells us that a man's days are ordained by God from the beginning. It was your father's time to go; there was no way anyone could change that, least of all you. Had you never had an affair with a married man but wedded some Godly person at 21 and had six kids by now, taught Sunday School, and helped with pre-school choir at the church, it wouldn't have changed your father's outcome. But you can change your mother's; God has offered you a way for some reason. However, you've got to accept and understand that He's giving you a chance here—a chance to make a difference."

"He might as well be punishing me if I have to leave everything I've gained just to see to it that my mother lives through the most miserable experience of her life."

"You're looking at it all wrong."

"No, I'm looking at it realistically. You're looking at it through your spiritual rose-colored glasses. Your little life is so wonderfully perfect."

"That stings, Cindy," Angie said, hurt by the insinuation. "My life *is* wonderful, I'll admit that. Why God does some things to some people and not to others, I don't know. But at this time in my life, God is choosing to bring me unmatchable happiness. In your life, He's choosing to grow you up. Deal with it."

Cindy laughed at Angie's statement. "What kind of miserable little job will I get here?" she asked shaking her head.

"You might be surprised. Remember, God's in this."

"I'll take your word for it," Cindy groaned as she headed back toward the house. "But I won't believe it until I see it." She chuckled again and shook her head. "I can't believe I'm actually gonna do this. I'm quitting my job, giving up my apartment, and moving back to Dockrey to live with my mother."

"No, you're moving back to Dockrey to save your mother's life. If you don't look at it that way, you *are* going to be miserable."

"Promise me you'll help me until you go back to the islands."

"I don't have to promise that. You know I'll be here."

"I hope so, because I expect you to hear me complain about my life every time I see you."

"Just put on a smile for your mother."

"I'll do my best."

"Cindy," Angie stopped her before going inside, "I really wish I could tell my parents about this. It'd be so much easier on your mom if she had others on her side."

"Go for it. I'm gonna need all the help I can get. If I'm willing to move back to Dockrey, you can most certainly tell her pastor she's got cancer."

"So you'll take the heat when she finds out I told them?"

"Heat?" Cindy laughed. "After losing everything I've got, a little yelling from my mother should be a piece of cake!"

FIFTY-SEVEN

"I can't believe this," Barbara said in utter devastation at the news of Sue's cancer. "Why didn't she tell me? Why didn't she tell *us*? Jonathan's her pastor; I'm a close friend. We've spent many years together doing ... everything."

"She didn't want anyone to know," Angie explained. "I couldn't figure it out either, but I honored her wishes."

"When does she have surgery?" Jonathan wondered.

"After the first of the year. The doctor did *not* want to wait that long, but Sue insisted she get through the holidays before beginning treatment."

"I don't blame her," Barbara said. "After losing her husband, and now this, it just seems too much to ask ... especially during the holidays."

"But all this will be hanging over her," Angie sighed. "Cancer isn't something you just lay low about until you're ready to deal with it. This is a wrong choice."

"In this case, I agree with your mother and Sue," Jonathan said as he shook his head. "You know I'm going to have to talk with her. I can't know all this and not insist I be there for her."

"I know. Cindy says she'll take the blame for giving me the go ahead."

The mood in the Wright house that Monday afternoon went from delightful to dull after Angie's news.

*****

"Let Michael and me take your baby out on the town," Angie asked Annie later on. "Only those who make it to church have seen him. We'll take him around and show him off."

"Isn't this pitiful," Annie groaned. "I can't even go out in my hometown for that stupid crowd at the gate."

"Yeah, but you're famous and your music is now being played around the world," Angie reminded her. "Besides that, you're the envy of many a woman out there who had sights on Stephen Williams."

"It's funny," Annie mused, "but before all this happened, it was my dream to do this. Make music, be famous ...."

"...marry Stephen Williams ..."

"Well, that too—but the point is, I never thought about all that I'd have to give up in order to have this. I have no life outside of the music business. I can't even go to the store to buy groceries or go out to a movie with my husband. For heaven's sake! I can't even take my sister and new brother-in-law out to eat somewhere in itty bitty Dockrey, Alabama! It's like this all the time. I'm penned up wherever I go, and when I go somewhere, even to church, I have to have body guards and security and clearances—it's ridiculous!"

"Would you trade it all to go back to your life before?"

"Hmmm … writing commercials, no husband, no baby—nope. I'll suffer through all this to keep them around."

"So, what about it? Can we take the baby out?"

"It's cold. You can't just expose him to …"

"Trust me, sister dear," Angie giggled. "I'll take good care of your wee one. I'm a doctor, remember?"

Angie and Michael put the baby's car seat front and center in Jonathan's pickup and took off around town. They stopped by several friends' houses and as many businesses as possible. They kept him wrapped and warm, and he showed off his best side to everyone. Never once did he fuss or fret being away from his parents or being toted from one strange place to another. By the end of the afternoon, Angie and Michael became even more attached to baby Stevie.

"I'm gonna miss him when they leave," Michael said as he wiggled Stevie's nose with his index finger.

"Yeah," Angie agreed softly. "I'm gonna miss them all."

He nodded. He had gotten close to Stephen and Annie too. "It's been fun watching your relationship with Annie. I've never seen anything quite like it before. You can be arguing one moment and embracing the next. You have a great family."

"It's your family too, you know?"

"I know, but I didn't grow up in it. I have no history with them."

"But you're building that. In time we'll look back at this particular visit with fond memories."

"Yeah," he agreed, but without much enthusiasm. "I guess the thing that hurts is that when I think of my past, I have no wonderful memories, no great stories to tell. You guys talk about your vacations and crazy antics over the years. My life was so miserable and uneventful that there's literally nothing to tell. There were no vacations except the few times we went to see relatives. And that was pitiful. Everyone was drinking and yelling. Even those times stopped. Every day was just like the one before."

He gently rubbed the top of Stevie's head as the baby drifted off to sleep. "Do you realize the love this little fellow has already known is more love than I can pull out of my memory all together? My mother was wonderful to me when we were alone, but if my father was there, I might as well not have existed. I realize now that she couldn't shower me with affection or attention while he was around. She would occasionally wink at me at the table or while riding somewhere. It let me know she cared for me, but it wasn't the same."

"I'm curious, why didn't you rebel? Why did you stay steady through all those years?"

His face grew sober and hard. "Because then I would've been like him."

She nodded. Nothing more needed to be said. Yet even though Michael was a grown man, a successful man, and a man with many fulfillments in his life, the things he missed from his childhood still haunted him and touched even the good parts of his life. She knew that no matter how much she loved him or how much she changed his life from loneliness to completeness, it would never fill the huge void and pain left from his childhood. His only hope would be to have a family of his own and for him to become to his own children everything his parents never were to him.

*****

When Tuesday's early Thanksgiving celebration arrived, it was a splendid experience for Michael. He marveled at the traditions and the amount of food spread on the table and side tables. The conversation was animated and constant, and everyone made it a genuine celebration. This was the first time Michael had spent a holiday with a family in decades. He had always refused to travel with the Lovejoys to their family gatherings because he knew he wasn't a part of their family. They had insisted it didn't matter, but to him the wounds and memories were still too fresh to try and fit in somewhere. He actually preferred being alone. He was thankful they had respected his insecurity and pain enough to never push him.

On this, *their* Thanksgiving evening, everyone sat around the fireplace and played games. He couldn't help but wonder again what it would have been like to grow up in a family where creativity and expression were encouraged. Even Alex, the shyest of the siblings, gave his share of input during the fun. Michael wondered why the brother was so different. He would never forget Alex immediately rushing up to hug him after telling the story of his past to the family. It almost made him feel like perhaps he wasn't a complete misfit.

As night began to fall, Andie and her family left, saying their goodbyes to the soon departing musicians. Angie couldn't believe tomorrow they would be gone, and it was quite possible they may not get to see each other again before returning to Padawin. Then again, it could be years before Padawin was free.

As Michael and Angie settled into bed that night, she could tell he was puzzled by his somber expression. The moon was bright again and shining through the window, illuminating the room as if a light was burning somewhere near.

"What's on your mind?" she asked as she scooted nearer in the bed. "You look mighty deep in thought."

"Why is Alex so different from the rest of you? You three girls act as though you've got the world by the tail, but he seems … I don't know … maybe unsure … a little backward. It's just odd."

"Yeah," she nodded as she leaned up on her elbow, her thoughts changing to her brother's plight. "He was abused."

"What?" Michael was jarred. He leaned up next to her, apparently not caring that the blanket fell from his shoulders exposing him to the chilly air. "Abused? How? By whom?"

"By an uncle of ours," she explained with deep regret. "Toby. He had actually tried to mess with all of us, all three of us girls, but we blew him off big time. He didn't stand a chance with us. We were smart … and tough. But he intimidated Alex. He threatened to … well, kill Annie basically, if Alex didn't comply. He even slit our cat's throat in front of him to convince him he would carry out his threats."

"No way," he gasped. "I can't believe this. Your family always seemed so perfect."

"There's no perfection this side of heaven, sweetie."

He shivered as he slid back down in the bed and pulled the cover up to his chin. She moved closer and curled up next to him.

"Would you believe we didn't find out until last winter?"

"He never told you until then?"

"We never thought Alex's problems were due to something so severe," she said with regret. "We just thought he was, you know … weird … *spineless* as one of us put it one time … and it stuck. When we found out, we could have just died—crawled under a great big rock and died."

"Man, how do you protect your children? How do you protect your family? If someone in a family like this could fall through a crack that huge, what hope is there, Angie?"

"Sweetie, there's no hope in man. Our only hope is Jesus. We do the best we can by choosing obedience to Christ, and then we trust Him to take care of everything else."

"That's not a comforting answer. If there are no guarantees, then how can you bring kids into the world? What if we have kids and something horrible happens to them? I don't think I could handle that, Angie. I think I'd literally die if something happened to a kid of mine and I couldn't stop it."

"Michael, there *are* no guarantees, but you don't stop living your life because of that. You can't worry about things that haven't happened. With each new person you love, you also open yourself up to loss. That's life, sweetie. The only assurance against hurt is isolation. And Michael, isolation isn't what God designed us for."

He was silent a long time. Angie knew he was struggling to process the story, and she had learned to give him time rather than push or even attempt to help him work through it.

"I don't know if I can do this, Angie," he whispered fearfully.

"Do what?" she asked, leaning over his chest, her hair falling down over him.

"Do this," he said barely able to breathe. "Live with ... with love ... again. You, children, family. I'd die, Angie, if I lost anyone else."

She could hear his fear. She knew he was overwhelmed by the information. She leaned down and gently kissed his forehead, then his nose, then his scar, and then his lips. "We have no need to fear, Michael, because we're not in control. God brought me to you, not to destroy you, but to fulfill you. If He gives us children, they're His gifts to us, not His burdens. Don't become confused about what is from God and what isn't."

"But why Alex?"

"I don't know," she said as her face was right next to his. "Why not me? Why didn't Toby drag me into the woods and slit the cat's throat and threaten me?"

"I couldn't bear it if it had been you."

"But it wasn't me, and instead I'm here with you. I'm a part of your life. God has granted us this time together. Who knows what the future holds? But if you fear the future, it'll destroy your present. You lived through your childhood. You lived through your sixteenth birthday. You lived through Jenna. Each of those periods could've destroyed you ... and they tried to destroy you, but look where you are now."

"I adore you, Angie," he said as a tear streaked the side of his face. "I couldn't bear to lose you."

"Michael, I'm not lost to you. I'm here with you right now. I am with you, sweetie. Okay?"

He pulled her down and kissed her tenderly as his eyes flooded with tears. She knew no one had ever touched his life the way she had, and she wanted him to thrive each moment they had together.

*****

When the limo was loaded the following morning, Michael knew Angie was struggling to keep her emotions in check. There were moments when she seemed completely out of control. In fact, she acted downright irrational. Annie was leaving to go on tour. This was what Annie did. This couldn't be as hard as when she left for Padawin.

"Are you okay?" he asked her as Annie hugged her parents goodbye.

"I'm an emotional wreck," she confessed to him. "It's like I'm in a near panic."

He had noticed her becoming more and more emotional the past week. When he had talked of going to Kansas to visit the Lovejoys, she'd perked up a bit. Perhaps she just needed a change. The fact that she was home in Dockrey was another reminder that she was *not* in Padawin.

When Annie came to hug her, Angie literally began to sob.

"Pull yourself together," Annie told her as she patted her back. "We'll be here for Christmas if you're not back in Padawin by then. And if you are, you really won't care one way or the other what I'm doing."

"I know," Angie said as she wiped her eyes. "It's just been so wonderful to see you again, and your baby, and see how happy you are."

"And I feel the same, except for the baby part."

Angie laughed. Annie was her soul sister for certain, her kindred spirit.

"Have a great tour." Angie was trying to sound upbeat. "Knock their socks off with that voice of yours."

"I intend to. It's the one consolation I have in this life I've chosen. The applause is a great pay off."

Annie then turned to Michael and gave him a tight hug. "You take care of her. She's been acting like a fruit loop lately. She's totally in love with you, you know?"

He nodded and blushed. "I'll care for her as if my life depended on it, because frankly, sometimes I feel like it does."

"Good. That tells me you're totally in love with her too."

"More than you could ever know."

"Trust me; I know."

Angie took the baby and snuggled him closely as everyone began to walk out the front door. As soon as Annie and Stephen stepped outside, the crowd at the gate began to scream and yell. They walked quickly to the limo and stooped inside. Angie leaned down and handed Stevie to Annie.

"God bless you all," she said tearfully.

"You too," Annie smiled back. "We'll see you soon."

Angie nodded, stood back from the car, and put her hand to her mouth as the driver closed the door. When the limo pulled through the gate, she fell into Michael's shoulder and wept. Then, feeling overwhelmed, she went inside to lie down.

FIFTY-EIGHT

Saturday morning found Angie back on top of the world. This was the girl Michael remembered. She had been miserably moody since Annie left, not hard to get along with, but emotions always brimming at the surface. It was hard to get through a television program without her crying. As they packed up the last of their things in the camper, they said their goodbyes to Jonathan and Barbara and loaded up in Jonathan's pickup for a little adventurous trip to Kansas. She sidled up beside him on the bench seat, stuck in the CD of Annie and Stephen's Christmas album and began to sing at the top of her lungs.

When they found the campground for the first night, he hooked up the camper while she prepared supper. In his opinion, it was a bit elaborate for a campout meal, but he made no complaints. She had prepared a wonderful chicken dish and set the table with candles and soft music in the background. This was better than any restaurant anywhere in the world. As she cleaned up from supper, he built a fire outside. The night air was cold, and as the fire began to blaze, he stuck out his hands to warm them.

"Beautiful fire," Angie beamed as she came out of the camper to join him.

"Beautiful lady," he replied in adoration as he leaned over to kiss her.

"Thank you," she grinned.

They sat next to each other in the folding chairs and took a moment to enjoy the quiet of the evening, the crackling of the fire, and the warmth of being alone together for the first time in over a month.

"I still regret not ever having built a fire for you on the beach in Podakind," he bemoaned. "You would've loved it. And then you dig up a few clams and throw them in there until they pop open. Delicious. Wonderful."

"Those moments aren't gone for us, Michael," she said as she reached for his hand. "Those are things we have to look forward to."

"There are so many things I would've done if I'd known we had so little time. I didn't realize ..."

"Michael," she interrupted him, "first of all, we didn't know. Second, our time there isn't over; it's merely stalled. Daddy was talking to me one evening, and he kept telling me that God has reasons for what He does. Nothing happens by accident; everything is on purpose, His purpose."

"I wish I knew what that purpose was," he grumbled as he took a stick and stoked up the fire again.

"We may never know fully what God was doing, is still doing. But there are some things we *can* know that He did."

"Like what?" he asked as he sat back in his chair and took her hand.

"You got to meet my family. They got to meet you. You became a part of us. That's all good stuff."

He nodded in agreement.

"I was able to talk Sue Marcum into chemo treatments and surgery. Somebody else could've possibly done that, but God used me because I was at the right place at the right time."

"Then there's the Padawin tribes," he joined in with the list. "Sojay and Joshua took on the yoke of leadership, whether they were ready or not."

"Geechern was thrust into medicine."

"And then Mosheed along with Geechern began to take some leadership with the women."

"Plus," Angie looked at him with a grin, "we had some awesome time off. We sort of had this extended honeymoon in a way. We were able to get away from life there and get a chance to know each other in ways that may have never happened had we stayed in Padawin."

"And it's been a pleasure," he grinned watching the firelight dance across her face. Again he was swept away by her beauty.

"What are you thinking?" she asked at his expression.

"How beautiful you are."

"It's funny. I used to hate it when someone would call me beautiful. It was almost always included with some suggestive comment or insinuation. I used to dress down so badly because I didn't want anyone to notice me. I would wear slouchy clothes, no makeup, pull my hair up tight in a ponytail, anything to detract attention."

"It didn't work, did it?"

"No."

"Face it, lady: you're beautiful … even in slouchy clothes, no makeup, and a ponytail."

She giggled as she placed his hand over her heart. "For the first time in my life, Michael, I'm actually proud to be beautiful. For you to think I'm attractive means the world to me. I feel like it's a gift to you—something I saved all these years."

"I have to confess, I'm a bit proud myself. When I got gas the last time, the two guys working at the counter made a comment about how *hot* you looked. Then one of them said something about you wearing a ring. The other one asked if he'd seen who she was with. The guy pointed me out. I waved and smiled. One of them gave me a thumb up. I feel like when people see me with you, they think I've got more going on than I probably look like. If they only knew how we met."

"Michael, I still swear to you that if we'd met anywhere else, I would've been drawn to you immediately. It's probably a good thing we never did. You would've been so insecure you would've never even talked to me!"

"I imagine you're right."

"So you see," she said as if the discussion had reiterated her point altogether, "God certainly had a plan and purpose in waiting to put us together in Padawin. Therefore, God has a plan and purpose for taking us away from there for a while."

"Signed, sealed, delivered! I won't argue this point anymore."

"Good boy. Are you ready to move this party inside?"

"But my fire is just getting cranked up," he protested.

"Yeah, but so am I," she said with a grin.

Michael picked up his chair, folded it right away, and then reached down for her hand. "Partying inside sounds much more interesting."

"Dr. Collins," Angie said in a refined Southern accent, "I believe I'm training you well."

"You must be," he said with a gentle kiss, "because I'm ready to follow you anywhere, particularly into the camper."

"Good boy," she said kissing him back.

*****

Michael and Angie spent three nights and days camping, hiking and exploring various state parks in Arkansas before making the drive to Olin, Kansas late Tuesday afternoon. The terrain had gone from hilly to just plain flat. She didn't want to complain about his old stomping grounds, but for a girl raised in northwest Alabama, central Kansas appeared downright dull. She did enjoy the various barns and family dwellings that spotted the landscape, but other than that, one mile looked exactly like the last.

When they finally entered the Olin city limits, she was a bit amazed. Somehow, this wasn't what she had expected.

"I used to think Dockrey was the middle of nowhere," she said as they passed a gas station and then the only grocery store in what could barely be called a town. "Now I realize I was wrong. Dockrey is simply *next to nowhere*; this place is the middle of nowhere."

"Tell me about it," he chuckled turning left and driving past the school.

"What a huge school for such a tiny town," she said in surprise as she stared at the impressive facilities.

"It's not just for Olin. Kids are bused in from little settlements all around here. Some come from as far as forty miles."

"You're kidding. What a long bus ride."

"A lot of farmers are all over the place. That's our economy."

"Well, except for the one grocery store and a gas station."

FIFTY-NINE

Ruth and Herbert Lovejoy sat quietly in their living room anticipating Michael's arrival. When he had left for Padawin ten years ago, he told them he would never be back. His intention was to leave the States, set up his life in the Pacific, and stay there until he had to retire, at which point he would probably remain in Padawin anyway. He had never fit in over here ... never.

"What do you suppose she's like?" Ruth asked breaking the silence.

"I would suppose she's wonderful," Herbert replied as he continued to peruse the newspaper.

"I don't know, Herbert. What about that young lady he almost married in college. I never did like her. She wasn't good to him."

"And he didn't marry her either, did he?"

"No, but he would have. She was beautiful—at least on the outside." She remembered Michael bringing the girl home a couple of times, and she had never been impressed with Jenna. She had been snooty, uppity, and constantly telling Michael how to improve himself. She had made it clear to Ruth that it would be a waste of talent for Michael to traipse off to some island to do mission work. He was much better suited to pastoring here in the States. When Ruth had said that she should take that up with the Lord because Michael felt called to the Pacific islands, the girl merely laughed and said that callings changed all the time.

"Where'd he meet her?" Ruth asked.

"He said in Padawin."

Her jaw dropped with a gasp. "Do you think she's one of those tribal women? That'd be just like Michael! Go off and marry some woman from a different culture."

"Would you blame him?" he retorted, beginning to get agitated with her meddling. "She's probably some island beauty who waits on him hand and foot."

"Herbert Lovejoy! That would be terrible! Michael is an intelligent and sensitive young man! He needs more than a maid for a wife!"

"I have a wonderful idea," he suggested as he pulled down the paper for a moment and glared over the top, "why don't you stop speculating about her and just wait until they get here? Then all your questions will be answered."

"Humph," she mumbled as she got up to clean something, anything, to help take her mind off of Michael's bride and the impending arrival.

Within five minutes, however, their curiosities were settled when the faded red pickup and camper pulled into the driveway of the two-story farmhouse.

"This is utterly picturesque," Angie said in delight as she took in the view. The house was old, but well kept. White vinyl siding had obviously been added recently, and a red barn behind it looked freshly painted. There were chickens and guineas poking around the yard and a huge field that apparently was gardened during the warmer months. Then to top off the country setting was a windmill standing out in the middle of the pasture with a large herd of cattle.

"I love this place," Angie breathed in sheer pleasure.

"There's Mr. Lovejoy," Michael said with excitement as an older man came out the front door and onto the wraparound porch. He must have been in his early sixties, but his hair was still dark and his body slim. Following behind him was his wife, a shorter woman, slim also, but with gray hair cropped just beneath her neck. She wore an apron and was drying her hands on a dishtowel. Angie grinned at the sight; it completed the scenario with the house and the barn.

Michael jumped from the truck and walked quickly to Mr. Lovejoy, embracing him for a long time. Angie got out of her side and made her way toward the two. When Mrs. Lovejoy got a good look at her, her hands came up to her mouth. Angie wasn't sure if it was in delight, surprise, or disgust, but she reached out her hand in greeting anyway.

"Mrs. Lovejoy, I presume?" Angie said with her nicest smile.

"My goodness, dear, yes," the lady beamed back at her. "I'm so relieved to meet you. I was scared to death Michael had gone and married one of those island women!"

At this, Michael laughed and broke away from Mr. Lovejoy. He reached over and hugged the lady's neck. Herbert went to Angie and embraced her also.

"Nice to meet, young lady," he said sweetly.

"You too, sir."

"Mr. and Mrs. Lovejoy," Michael began introductions, "this is my wife, Angie. And Angie, these are my surrogate parents."

She smiled. "I'm so glad to meet the people who had a hand in making Michael the wonderful man he is today."

Ruth's face grew bright as her grin spread from one side to the other. "Well, come on inside! It's freezing out here!"

"Let me help Michael get their things," Herbert offered, so the two ladies went toward the house together as the men went back to the camper.

Ruth led Angie up the steps to the porch and then inside to a comfortable living area with nine-foot walls and expansive rooms. The furniture was definitely old, but impeccably kept like everything else in the house. When Angie saw the television, it looked so ancient she wondered if it was possibly black and white. Ruth offered her a seat on the couch, and Angie reclined continuing to smile the entire time.

"We're so pleased to have you visiting with us," Ruth began cordially. "How did you end up in Padawin with our Michael?"

"I'm a doctor. I wanted to go to the tribal communities in Padawin and bring medicine there."

"Oh, my goodness," Ruth exclaimed with an even larger grin. "You're a medical doctor?"

"Yes, ma'am."

"And so you and Michael met there?"

"Actually, it's a long and confusing story," Angie said, wondering if she should spill it out now or wait until everyone was together and then let Michael do the talking.

"As much as I'd love to hear it, if it's long, we'd better wait. I hope you don't mind us taking you out to dinner tonight. Most everything will be closed up the rest of the week for the holidays."

"No problem at all."

The men came in with two bags and set them near the door.

"We'd better head on out," Herbert said. "It'll start to get packed in another thirty minutes or so. You ladies ready?"

"Absolutely," Angie said popping up. She went over to Michael and took his hand as she whispered in his ear, "Is there actually a restaurant in this town?"

"It's a few miles out. Steak house."

"Yum," she said licking her lips. "I'm starving."

The four piled into the Lovejoy's quad cab pickup. Angie had never ridden in the back of one before and was very pleased with the room. She wasn't one for conventional, cute, or tiny cars. In fact, had she not gone into missions, her dream was to own a Jeep and a big dog. The Land Rover was an apt substitute, and Michael sufficed much better than the dog. She chuckled at her own thoughts.

They drove approximately ten miles out of town to a rather large barn-turned-restaurant building, complete with a walk-though silo at the doorway. Cars were everywhere. Angie couldn't imagine there were actually this many people in or around Olin. After parking, they walked through the silo and into a delicious smelling, homey looking atmosphere where every man present was in a cap and overalls or dirty dungarees. Michael and Herbert stuck out like sore thumbs.

As the waitress led them to their seats, Angie found herself getting several stares and nods. Along the way many greeted Mr. and Mrs. Lovejoy. Once they were seated, a younger man in overalls came over to the table.

"Michael Collins?" he asked as he looked in wonder at Michael.

"Johnny Turbyville!" Michael exclaimed as he jumped up from the table. The two embraced and laughed at each other.

"You look like a hick!" Michael told him as he sprung one of the straps on the overalls.

"I am!" Johnny laughed back. "And look at you, all dignified in your flannel shirt and turtle neck—look like a darned professor."

"That's my wife's doing," Michael told him, moving aside so he could introduce Angie. "This is Angie, my better half."

"Better half indeed," Johnny said more gently as he stuck out his hand to her. "Man, they don't make girls like this in Olin. Where'd you find her?"

"Alabama," Michael said a little shyly.

"What makes you think *he* found *me*?" Angie offered as she stood to shake Johnny's hand, while Ruth Lovejoy beamed at Angie's response. "I really think I got the best end of this deal. Michael Collins is a whiz kid."

"If you say so," Johnny said shaking his head. "She got any sisters?"

"Two," Angie told him, "but they're both married."

"Good" Johnny bellowed. "Then I don't have to think about cheating on my wife!"

"These girls are out of your league anyway," Michael told him. "One of them is married to Stephen Williams."

"Stephen Williams! *The* Stephen Williams? *Autumn Sunset* boy?"

Michael nodded.

"Oh, man!" Johnny exclaimed. "I just bought that Christmas CD for my wife! So that's her sister?"

"Annie, yep," Angie said proudly. "She's my little sister."

"Unreal!" Johnny crooned. "I can see the resemblance now. Long dark hair … full, sexy …" he stopped as he motioned toward his mouth.

Angie blushed slightly and rolled her eyes.

"Anyway, good to see you, Michael," Johnny went on. "How long are you in town?"

"Not for long. We're staying with the Lovejoys if you want to get in touch with me."

"Sure thing," Johnny smiled. He then turned to Angie and said, "Nice to meet you."

Herbert leaned over to Angie and asked, "Your sister is actually married to Stephen Williams?"

"Almost a year now. You're familiar with Stephen's music?"

"For nearly ten years our FFA band insisted on playing *Autumn Sunset* and *I Knew it Was Love*. One year for Christmas someone gave me one of his albums with just piano music and his singing."

"*That's* who you're talking about?" Ruth suddenly joined in. "I love that album. He's a masterful musician."

"You ought to hear her sister," Michael told them. "We have the Christmas CD in the truck. And you know how incredibly Stephen plays piano? Wait until you hear her playing. The first time I heard her on the album, I swore it was Stephen. Angie insisted it was her sister. I never really believed it until I heard her play it for myself last week."

"My goodness," Ruth exclaimed. "Are you musical too, Angie?"

Michael jumped in to answer first. "Yes, she is, although she won't admit it. She plays a little guitar and sings like a bird."

"And I stress *little* guitar," Angie said firmly.

"I'm anxious to hear how you two met," Ruth decided to change the subject. "This sounds really interesting."

"Tell you what," Michael offered, "do they still let you choose how you want your steaks here?"

"You bet," Herbert told him.

"Let's order first then we'll get down to details."

"Sounds like a plan." Herbert rubbed his hands together in anticipation.

Before long, a man appeared at their table with a cart containing a large slab of beef. They showed the man how thick they wanted their steaks, and he cut them right at the table. Angie was a little shocked when Michael chose a very thick cut and ordered it medium. She preferred hers thin and well done, and that was how she had always prepared them in Padawin. She smiled to herself as she thought about the fact that Michael had never said a word about it. He always acted like it was the best thing he'd ever tasted. Soon the man wheeled away to another table, and Michael began his story.

"About two years ago, I got an e-mail from this med student in Alabama," Michael began. "You do know what e-mail is, Mrs. Ruth."

"I know," she told him, "but we don't have it in the house. I'm too old to learn computers."

"I have one at school," Herbert chimed in. "I'm considerably more advanced than my wife."

Ruth slapped his arm and then motioned for Michael to continue.

"This med student said she felt a calling to the tribal areas of Padawin and wondered if there was any need where I was working. I was thrilled! I'd been there for eight years all by myself and had managed to bring many innovations to the tribes, but they still turned to the witch doctors for their health issues. It was horrible because these guys would do the most bizarre things to cure diseases. Many people died because of their stupidity.

"As the months went by, we continued to write. She finally finished her medical training and was preparing for seminary. I suggested she go ahead and apply for an appointment to Padawin. She did, but was rejected."

"Oh, my," Ruth mused. "Why?"

"They didn't say," Angie interjected. "It was rather disheartening. I'd gone through all this education, and with one simple *no* my entire future was erased."

"She went on to seminary, assuming all would turn out well, but by the end of her seminary year, she'd sent a total of four applications, all of which were flatly denied, no explanation. We were both really discouraged and confused."

"I can imagine," Herbert said slightly shocked. "You'd think they'd be thrilled to send someone over there."

"I did my best," Michael went on, "contacting them regularly, explaining the horrific situation I was dealing with concerning the witch doctors. All they would say was that it wasn't possible to appoint Dr. Wright to the Padawin tribes. They'd gladly send her to Taveren, the capital city, but not to the tribes."

"My cows and grasshoppers!" Ruth spat out in disgust. "What on God's good earth were they thinking?"

"That's what my Daddy wondered," Angie told them.

"Her father is a pastor in Dockrey, Alabama, a small town in the northwest section of the state. When Angie was sent a letter saying she shouldn't attempt another application to the island, once again without explanation, he told Angie to pack a bag, and they headed to Richmond."

"Good for him!" Ruth said with heart.

Angie grinned at the lady's response. Ruth Lovejoy was a spirited woman, and Angie enjoyed watching her take in all the details as though she were directly affected by the story.

"He comes to find out, after interrupting a meeting of the mission board …"

"Way to go!" Ruth interjected.

"… that they were uncomfortable with assigning two single people to the same location."

"Well, I never!" Ruth put in again.

"They said it showed a lack of propriety, and even though they trusted us implicitly, if anyone ever wanted to make a case against us, it could destroy the reputation of the board."

Angie picked up here by adding, "They said had either one of us been married there would've been no problem."

"Wait a minute," Herbert said as the lights began to come on inside his mind. "Are you telling me you two got married just so she could go to Padawin?"

"Eventually," Michael said as he put up a hand to stop Herbert's train of thought. "At first, Angie and I both tried to think of people we could possibly marry to see this thing work out."

"Good heavens!" Ruth said in unbelief again. "You two were mighty committed to getting her there!"

"I knew I was called to Padawin," Angie told her. "There was no doubt about that. But I can tell you my dreams were greatly deflated after my trip to Richmond."

"I should say so," Ruth agreed.

"I tried to imagine taking a wife from among the Padawin people," Michael said.

"My stars, Michael!" Ruth exclaimed again. "You must have been out of your mind!"

"I was!" he said trying to share his frustration. "I went through a mental list and then realized how unfair it would be for that woman ... especially after Angie arrived. I mean, here would be this intelligent American woman who I'd work with shoulder to shoulder, fulfilling our dreams together, and my tribal wife would all but be ignored. In fact, my relationship to the doctor would be more like a marriage than my one to my wife. That's when it hit me!"

"Ahhh," Herbert sighed and nodded. "Just marry the doctor."

"And I don't suppose it mattered that she was beautiful to boot," Ruth added.

Angie quickly told them, "We'd never exchanged pictures."

Herbert's eyebrows shot up. "You're kidding?"

Michael continued, "All I knew was that I wasn't getting married to anyone anytime soon, and Angie obviously wasn't either, so I suggested we marry each other. She agreed, the board agreed, so we met in Hawaii, tied the knot, and moved back to Padawin to live happily ever after."

"... until the rebellion," Angie threw in.

"I don't believe it," Herbert said shaking his head again.

"But you two ... well ... seem so right together," Ruth told them in confusion. "I mean, you act as though..."

"... as though we're in love?" Angie helped to clarify Ruth's obvious puzzlement over the entire situation.

Ruth nodded.

"We are," Angie told her with a warm smile. "I don't exactly know if it was love at first sight, but it sure didn't take long for me to realize what a jewel I'd found in Michael."

"It was definitely love at first sight for me," Michael grinned.

"I bet," Herbert grinned back.

*****

That night Angie crawled beneath the electric blanket and snuggled up close to Michael. "It gets way too cold in Kansas for my liking," she said as she shivered next to him. "This blanket is wonderful."

"Now you know why I love Padawin so much."

"And you complained about the cold in *Dockrey*," she pouted. "Piece of cake compared to this."

"Cold is cold. It doesn't matter how much or how little."

"I have a question for you."

"Shoot."

"Why didn't you ever tell me you liked your steaks thick and pink? It was probably all you could do to down the ones I cooked for you in Padawin."

"I'm a steak lover. There's no way to ruin a steak."

"But you *prefer* them thick and less cooked than I prepared them."

"I'm an Angie lover too," he said as he pulled her even closer. "You could've burned them and served them with spiders, and I would've eaten them up with no complaints."

"You're a sweetheart," she said as she reached up to kiss him. "But at least I'll know how to cook your steaks now. And for the record, I like the Lovejoys."

*****

As Ruth climbed into bed beside her husband, vigorously rubbing lotion into her hands and arms, she asked, "So what do you think of Michael's wife?"

"Gorgeous," was his first response. "A doctor too. Can you imagine that?"

"I'll tell you this, she's wonderful, and she's good to him. Did you see how she treated him? She acts like he hung the moon and the stars."

"Quite a gal."

"I was worried, I'll tell you," Ruth went on, her voice shaking as she continued working the lotion into her skin. "That girl at college was no good for him. She would've ruined him, torn him apart piece by piece, chewed him up and then spit him out."

"Funny, isn't it? They married for the sake of the gospel, never knowing they'd be the perfect match for each other."

"Hmph," Ruth said with a chuckle. "Hard to believe there are people out there who don't believe in God."

SIXTY

Michael and Angie were awakened the next morning by an abrupt knock on their upstairs bedroom door. It took them a few moments to register where they were and what was going on as it was still dark outside.

"Michael?" Herbert's voice called from the other side of the door. "The gate is down and several cows are out. Could you give me a hand? I'll saddle Trixie for you. There's a pair of coveralls hanging on the back porch."

"Sure," Michael said groggily as he sat up in bed. "Give me a minute."

"Hate to do this, it being your first morning here, but I'll be honest with you; I'm glad you're so you can help me."

"No problem. I'll be right out."

Michael turned on the bedside lamp, and Angie sat up next to him giving him one of her mischievous grins.

"What?" he asked as he shivered in the cold of the room.

"You're gonna be a cowboy this morning?"

"Yee haw," he said unenthusiastically. "Welcome to Olin."

"How does he know the cows are out? Its pitch black outside."

"I haven't seen this early of the morning in years," Michael groaned as he climbed out of bed. "I hate cold weather."

"This is *really* cold," Angie complained with him as she tossed his bag over. "I hope you packed long johns."

"I won't need them with those coveralls."

"Do I get to watch you round up the cattle?"

"Suit yourself. But if you think it's cold in here, it's unbearable out there."

"So what do I do while you're playing cowboy?"

"Watch Ruth cook," he said as he pulled on a pair of jeans. "The work may be hard, but the breakfasts are always awesome."

It took them nearly an hour to locate all the cows and get them back inside the fence. An old wooden post by the gate had given way to a cow's shoving and knocked the entire gate to the ground.

"When are you gonna replace these things?" Michael asked as he helped him pull the gate back up. "Why don't you put metal stakes out here instead? It's a wonder the whole fence hasn't fallen apart."

"Ach, I don't like metal. It seems so unfriendly and unnatural."

"Perhaps, but metal doesn't rot."

"That's a lot of work, though … having to replace every single post in this pasture. I'll just do it one at a time as they continue to fall."

"What if you lose some cows in the process?"

"You don't *lose* cows out here; they just get misplaced for the moment. You eventually get them all back."

Angie sat with Ruth in the kitchen as the older woman prepared a huge breakfast. She cooked bacon *and* ham, fresh biscuits, gravy, coffee, and was waiting on the men to cook the eggs so they would be hot. The sun was beginning to peek over the horizon when they finally made it in. She watched Michael as he took in a deep breath and smiled at the smell of a large breakfast. Angie had to admit that she was rather hungry for it herself. She felt a little inadequate, however, because she had never cooked a big breakfast for Michael, at least not *for* breakfast.

*****

Thanksgiving at the Lovejoys came and went quickly. It was a small celebration, something Angie had never experienced for a holiday in a home, but she was happy for Michael that he was back at *his* home during this particular Thanksgiving. She enjoyed watching him interact with the Lovejoys and their family. There was *almost* a sense of belonging about him, but never completely. There were moments when he loosened up, but they faded quickly when the discussion moved to things from the past. The only times that Michael appeared free were when he described life in Padawin.

She struggled with her own emotions often during the visit. She couldn't understand why he hadn't kept in touch with them when he left the States. He had made such a deliberate decision to cut off everything from his past, that he was willing to remove the good along with the bad. However, as much as he hated his past, it would always be a part of him. And if they ever had children of their own, he would have to somehow make peace with it in order to fully share his life with his kids. When his children would ask someday about what he did as a boy, he couldn't pretend that part of his life never existed.

Michael preached on Sunday morning, and he and Angie sang again. She couldn't believe how much easier it was to sing in front of strangers than it had been at her home church. Michael did a wonderful job, as usual. Ruth and Herbert were proud of him and the man he had grown to be. The church was warm and welcoming and encouraged him greatly as most of them were very familiar with his life.

On Sunday afternoon, as Michael and Herbert walked over the land, Ruth took some time to talk with Angie and ask a few questions that had been plaguing her mind for years.

"Do you think he's really happy over there?" Ruth asked as she swayed nervously in an old wooden rocker.

"He seems to be. He fits over there, Mrs. Lovejoy. He's a different person. He has authority and confidence ... like when he preaches."

"It was hard to believe that was Michael this morning. He was so eloquent and clear-minded. As a teenager, he often stuttered and seldom said anything. Days would go by that he didn't utter a single word."

"He was rather shy when I first met him too. But once we got past the initial meeting and the awkwardness of what we were facing, he began to loosen up. When we got to Padawin, he was a different man altogether."

"Well, I guess I'm glad to hear it," she said somewhat unsure. "I just wish he didn't feel the need to isolate himself from everything back here. The people today were so pleased to see him and hear him speak."

"Michael's a complex individual. I know he has so many hurts from his past ..."

"It was awful," Ruth interrupted. "You should've seen him the first few days after his parents died. He was pale and troubled, always on the verge of tears, but never able to let them fall. He never said anything except *thank-you* for us taking him in. He moved through the rest of that year like a zombie—the walking dead. We tried to pull him out of it, but he kept struggling with the whole thing being his fault."

"It still haunts him, you know? After twenty years, it would seem like something would ease up, but I guess a situation *that* horrific never truly leaves you."

"I suppose," Ruth sighed. "The counselor said he'd never open up about it. He said until Michael was willing to face the truth, he'd never be rid of the demons."

"So, why was he released from counseling? Why didn't the counselor make him stick with it until he finally dealt with it properly?"

"It's like the old saying about leading a horse to water but being unable to make him drink. He said only Michael could force the truth out. All the counselor could do was *give him the tools*, as he put it, to move on with his future. I guess it worked out all right."

"I guess," Angie half-heartedly agreed.

As wonderful as Michael was, and as much as he had seemed to overcome his past, he was still timid and unsure about himself in many ways. Angie wished there was a key to unlock the fears and the pain so he could step out of whatever the chains were that held him and finally be free to be the man she knew God had created him to be.

"You know that old house still stands today, untouched and unmoved?" Ruth told her.

"You're kidding?" Angie responded almost out of horror. "Michael described it as being old and rickety when he lived there."

"It was and is. No one had the nerve to mess with it after the horrible incident took place. The owner hired some men to go in and clean it out, then he just left it there—wouldn't rent it but wouldn't tear it down either. The *blight of Olin* it's been called all these years."

SIXTY-ONE

On Monday morning, they decided to stay one more day with the Lovejoys. The visit had been mostly wonderful, but there were moments of melancholy when Michael would pull away to himself and be almost untouchable. Had Angie not known his past, she would have been offended by his apparent rejections, but she understood how difficult it must be for him to be here and to face all these memories again.

Later that afternoon, the two of them took a walk out on the grounds while waiting for Mr. Lovejoy to return home from school. He explained the different facets of the farm and told of the animals he had raised there for various FFA projects. She tried to pay attention to his descriptions, realizing that this was where the only pleasant memories of his youth took place, but all she could think about was the counselor insisting that Michael needed to face the truth of his parents' deaths. He had told her that she had been the only one he had shared the story with until he had told her family also. Maybe that was all he needed to face. Maybe that was enough for his healing to take place. But if so, why was he still so withdrawn about things ... and about himself.

"What on *earth* are you thinking about?" he finally asked in exasperation. "I might as well be talking to the cows out there."

"I'm sorry," she said trying to shake the thoughts. "I keep thinking about ... aah ... never mind."

"No," he said with a little assertiveness. "Obviously it's upsetting you, whatever it is."

She cocked her head to the side and grimaced. Was this something she really wanted to get into?

"What is it, Angie? I want to know."

She took a deep breath and blew her hair up. She hated frustration. "Take me to the house where you grew up," she said hesitantly.

"No," was all he said as he turned to walk in a different direction.

She stood still for a moment, surprised at his reaction, and then ran to catch up with him.

"That's it? No? Nothing more?"

"That's it," he said firmly.

He continued to walk at a fairly fast pace, but she matched him stride for stride.

"I think you should take me there," she told him.

"I'm not going back."

"You said you'd never come back to the States either, but here you are."

His expression began to grow agitated. She didn't want to press him, but she felt it was time for him to deal with this issue once and for all.

"I'll be with you," she said gently.

"Stop it!" he yelled at her. "I'm *never* going back there again! I'm not going with you! I'm not going with anybody!"

She was startled. She had never seen him angry. He had raised his voice for the first time, and the fury in his eyes was almost fearful to her. Obviously she had hit a bigger nerve than she was aware of.

"Why won't you go?" she asked calmly.

He swung on his heels toward her, his face red from both the cold and his ire. "You figure it out, doctor!" he said sarcastically. "I watched my parents blow their brains out there! I don't want to remember it; I don't want to relive the scene yet again! Enough is enough!"

"Michael," Angie still tried to remain serene, "you never faced this with the counselor. You even told me that yourself. We have a future together, but I can only get in so deep with you before I'm shut out. There are things you need to face so that we can be complete."

"Complete?" he shouted. "What more do you want of me? I've given you everything I am!"

"No, you still hide parts of yourself from me. Michael, I want to know everything there is to know about you. I don't want anything hidden between us."

"What do you think I'm hiding?" he threw his hands up in desperation.

"Take me to that house, and let's find out!"

"Fine!" he yelled out. "Fine! Fine! Fine!"

He turned back toward the house and began to walk even quicker. She ran to catch up with him again.

"Why are you doing this?" he yelled out again. "Why can't we leave it alone?"

She grabbed his arm and pulled him to a stop. Getting directly in front of his face she made him look at her. "Because I love you," she said more forcefully than tenderly. "And I've committed my life to you for better or for worse. I'm ready for us to move on in this relationship."

"Move on? I thought our relationship was fine! What's the problem that's so grave it requires me being dragged back to the biggest horror of my life?"

"Michael, we're honeymooners. Everything right now is wonderful and perfect. All we do is drool over each other. When I look at you, everything within me goes warm, and when you touch me, it's like nothing I've ever experienced before. But I've seen marriages, Michael; it won't always be like this. It's easy to feel close when every moment we're together feels like an electrical charge. But there's more to marriage. I'm in for the long haul, and I don't want to wake up one morning and find a stranger in the place of the man I once was so intimate with—a man I gave myself to so willingly. I want to wake up ten years from now and know more about you than I do at this moment ... and not because I had to figure it out by watching your reactions to life situations but because you *told* me one night sitting on the beach, or out on the deck, or lying in bed."

She moved in closer to him, but he pulled back. "I'll take you to the house," he said bitterly.

"Michael!" she said urgently. "Don't you understand what I'm saying? I think you're this incredible man with so much ability and talent, yet you lay low and move like a snake in the background of everybody's life. You hide in Padawin because you can accomplish so much there, but no one has to see it. It's a *safe* place to run away. You have all this potential brimming beneath the surface, God given potential, but it lies dormant because of your fears and insecurities about ..." she gestured her arms wide around her, "...about this ... this place."

He turned away and began walking toward the truck.

"Can you not even answer me?" she screamed at him.

He turned back, and she could see the tension in his jaw. "If you want to go, you'd better go with me now," he said tersely. "I'm moving like a blind man, not knowing what I'm doing. If you give me a moment to think this through, to give you some kind of intelligent answer, I'll come to my senses and not take you there."

He climbed into the cab of the truck and slammed his door, immediately cranking the engine. She decided not to question it. She opened the passenger's side and got in. Her nerves were on edge, and her stomach was churning. For the first time in days she wasn't the least bit hungry. She wanted to talk to Michael, to tell him everything would be okay, that this was something *he* needed to do, but she thought it better to keep her mouth shut. The answers to his problems were locked away inside that house, and she was ready to see him freed from his prison of hurt and fear. Even if it meant losing him because she pushed too hard, she loved him too much to watch him continue to be less than he was created to be.

The drive was as tense as the previous conversation. Neither said anything, and for a brief moment Angie wondered if she was doing the right thing. She had studied psychology, she had been raised by a father who was a wise counselor, and everything within her told her this was what Michael needed to do. When he turned down a barren, gravel road, she could see the house looming down at the end. He didn't need to tell her which one had been his. They passed a nice house on the left and two on the right before dead-ending at the shack that looked as though it could barely stand on its own. Michael turned off the ignition and just sat there.

He wouldn't look up.

She reached over and took his hand. He pulled it back with a jerk, but she grabbed it again and held on to it tightly.

"You can try to read anything you want into this, but all I want is for you to face this once and for all, and finally put it behind you," she told him frankly. "You can even hate me for it if that's what you want to do … I don't care. I'd rather see you healed of all of this junk and leave me, than watch you wallow in it for the rest of our lives together."

With that said she squeezed his hand, opened her door, and jumped from the cab. The tension must have gotten to her more than she realized because as soon as her feet hit the ground, she felt the world begin to grow black. She turned around immediately and braced herself with her hands on the seat.

Michael didn't notice. He had stepped out of his own side and walked around to the front of the truck with his hands in his pockets. "You coming?" he asked bitterly. "I'm not doing this alone."

She took several deep breaths and tried to gain her momentum. Things were still spinning inside her head.

"Just a minute," she said as she leaned down toward the seat for a second.

He never looked back. He just stared at the house, hands in his pockets, and waited for her to join him. When she finally felt stable enough to walk, she shut her door and stepped up to his side.

"It's as bad as you described it," she said forlornly.

"Did you doubt?" he asked sarcastically.

She rolled her eyes as they stepped toward the front door. If he wanted to continue to play this bitter game, she would let him. She knew it was a defense mechanism to protect himself from all he must face again. Let him yell; let him scream—it had probably been pent up inside him for so many years that it was bound to explode.

They stepped up one step onto a narrow, broken porch, and Michael eased open the screen door. It fell down in his hands and dropped to the porch.

"Do all the doors and gates in Kansas do this eventually?" she asked in a teasing mode as she thought of Herbert's gate falling apart too.

He didn't answer. He reached for the doorknob and cautiously opened the front door. It creaked and moaned as he anxiously slid it open, and the smell of age and mustiness began to seep all around them. He motioned her to go in first so she crept inside. The house was tiny. The kitchen could barely fit a stove and refrigerator, both of which were gone, but she could see where they had stood. In fact, the house was completely bare now. There were two rooms off of the main area, and a small living room sat off to the side.

She looked back at Michael; he seemed frozen in the doorway. His expression, however, hadn't changed. He was still feeling anger and frustration at having been made to come.

*****

Herbert Lovejoy pulled into his drive and noticed the absence of Angie and Michael's truck. He got his briefcase and walked slowly up to the house. When he went in, he was about to ask his wife where the young couple was, but the distraught look on her face stopped him.

"I don't know where they went," she started, "but Michael was mad—downright mad, Herbert. I heard yelling and screaming and just thought maybe they were teasing or something. I looked out the window, and lo and behold, they were in each other's faces going at it!"

"Michael and Angie?" he asked not being able to really believe it.

"I've never seen him mad in all the years I've known him, but he was raving mad."

"Michael? Mad? And you have no idea where they went?"

"No idea, but the doors slammed as they got in."

"Michael has no temper," he said as he rubbed his chin. "He's never been mad ... except ...'' Suddenly a realization struck Herbert Lovejoy that sent chills throughout his body. "No, Ruth," he said in fear. "Please, no." He turned back toward the door.

"Now where in the tarnation are you going?" she asked in frustration.

"How long have they been gone?"

"About ten or fifteen minutes."

He now ran out the door and she ran after him. "For mercy's sake, where are you headed to?"

"Call Sully Roberts!" Herbert shouted back. "Tell him to meet me at Michael's old home ... and fast!"

"The police chief?" she asked even more confused than before.

"Just do it, Ruth!" he yelled. "For once in your life could you just do something without barraging me with a million questions?"

*****

"We were eating here," Michael said as he showed Angie where the table had been. "I was on this side and Mama was over here. When Dad came through the door, we both had a perfect view of his brooding, bloodshot eyes."

She nodded. "What happened next?"

He leaned against the wall where he had sat that night and looked toward the door. "He came staggering in, walked over to the table and grabbed Mama by the hair," Michael described as he pointed out where everything took place. "He threw her to the floor ... right about there. He wanted to know what was going on, and Mama told him it was my birthday. He ranted a little bit then saw my necklace. He ripped it off and started cursing like crazy."

Michael moved to where his father had been standing and told her, "I knew he was really drunk, so I took a little of that *backbone* and *initiative* that you seem to think I can't express anymore ... and told him to leave her alone. *Come back when you're sober*, I told him."

He moved back a step or two.

"He then started laughing this really evil laugh, and Mama began to beg him to let it go. She was pleading with him not to *do anything*. I remember being confused. I didn't know what he might do. He let go of her and then came after me. He grabbed me by the hair this time and dragged me into here," he explained walking into the space that had been his bedroom.

"He threw me against the wall ... and ... and ... my guitar was over there ... next to the window ... it was still in its case. He grabbed it out and started bashing it all over. Mama came running in then. She tried to grab what was left of the guitar ... and ... man ... I think he threw her against that wall."

The wall he pointed to was still covered in blood and debris, though significantly faded.

"She pleaded for him to stop, begging him not to do anything that would hurt me. That's when he left the room. She looked at me and sighed in relief. I kind of smiled at her, thinking he was gonna leave. I thought he was so drunk that he was about to drop anyway."

"I was trying to get off the floor so I could help Mom up when he came back into the room ... carrying the pistol."

He sighed deeply as he sat down on the floor where he had been thrown. He glanced around the room as though he were trying to remember every detail of that evening. Angie felt herself growing faint again. She tried to find a wall to lean against, and made it a point to avoid the blood stained one. She knew which part of the story was coming next, and she doubted seriously if she could stomach it again.

"He pointed the pistol at my head and Mama went berserk. She started pleading with him not to hurt me. She was going crazy. He turned around and aimed the gun at her. I got really mad then. I jumped up and ... it seems like I actually jumped on his back. Yeah ... and then he threw me against that wall."

He got up and walked over to another wall and ran his hand down the surface. "That's when he hit me with the remains of my guitar." Michael reached up and touched the scar on his cheek. "I remember the taste of the blood trickling into my mouth. Mama was pleading again, and he took ... like maybe two strides," Michael took the steps, "and he aimed the gun at her head. I told him *no*, and he started laughing at me again ... calling me a little wimp."

He stopped for a moment as he pulled out the memories. His face was contorting, and his eyes were squinting. He turned his head to the side for a moment.

"He shot her. It ... her blood ... and stuff ...," he pointed to the stained wall, "went all back there."

Angie walked over to him, but he jerked away from her and gazed nervously around the room.

"Then he took the gun and pointed it at me," he said more from confusion than conviction. He paused and began to shake his head as he looked back around the room. "No ... I don't think ... wait a minute." He was very confused now.

"He pointed the gun at you ..." she said trying to help.

"No!" He yelled.

She jumped.

"No," he whispered this time. "No, he didn't."

"What happened then, Michael? What happened after he ... shot your mother?"

He walked over to the stained wall and held out his hand.

"He handed me the gun," he said with wide eyes as he turned back to her.

"You're confused now, sweetie," she said as she tried to redirect him back to the story she had heard twice.

He shook his head as he closed his eyes and re-imagined the scene once again. Angie watched as he traced through all the steps silently. When he got back to the wall, he held out his hand once again.

"No—no, no, no, no," he said as he turned back to her, his face white and ashen. "He gave *me* the pistol."

"Then what happened?" she asked as she came over to him. "Did you drop it? Give it back?"

He slowly shook his head as he lifted up his hand. He formed it into the shape of a gun and then stuck it out toward the wall.

"Bang," he said in an audible whisper.

"Michael?" she said softly as she put her hand on his shoulder. "What are you saying? This isn't how you told the story before ... you always ..."

"Angie," he said as he began to gasp for breath, "I can't believe this. Angie, do you know what I did?"

He was now breathing heavily. She felt her body grow faint again. She immediately pulled them both to the floor and tried to get Michael to slow down.

"Sweetie," she said gently as she stroked his hair. "Calm down. Calm down. Breathe, Michael. Take slow, deep breaths."

He shook his head as his body began to shake. Suddenly Herbert Lovejoy appeared in the doorway. He stared at Angie with a questioning look.

"Why are you here?" Herbert asked her.

"To bury some ghosts ... or at least that's what I thought," she replied as she cradled Michael's head against her shoulder. "Do you have any idea what's going on here?"

Herbert closed his eyes and leaned his head down. He rubbed the back of his neck as he glanced at Michael. "Does Michael know what's going on?"

"I'm not sure either of us knows what's going on," Angie breathed out in frustration. "I've heard Michael tell this story before, but something has changed all of a sudden. I'm not sure what happened."

Herbert leaned down next to them and asked, "Michael, why did you come back?"

"I made him," Angie said quickly. "There are so many things about Michael that are still wrapped up deep inside this whole situation ..."

"... and they should've stayed there," Herbert said resolutely as he stood back up and began to pace. "I admire you, Angie, and you're a wonderful wife to Michael, but you should've left this alone. You should've left *this* alone."

Another man entered the room. He was in a police uniform and looked to be near the same age as Herbert.

"What's going on, Herb?" asked the officer.

"Michael," Herbert said as he pointed to the shivering man on the floor. "His wife, Angie."

The man nodded at her and then looked back at Herbert. "Does he know?"

"Angie?" Herbert went back to her. "What did he remember?"

Angie started to speak, but Michael screamed out instead, "I killed my father! *I* did it! I'm a murderer! Oh, no ... why didn't you tell me that?"

Angie felt the faintness growing again, and the darkness was about to overtake her, but the officer quickly came down on his knees next to her and gently slapped her out of it.

"You knew!" Michael screamed at both of the men as he tried to come to his feet. He staggered under the emotional load of what he had just remembered. Angie found the strength to support him with her shoulder, but rather than lean, he fell onto her, his body still shaking. She screamed out in pain as her ankle caught his full weight.

"Michael, you're hurting her!" Herbert yelled as he tried to pull him up. "Get off of her!"

"You knew I was a murderer," Michael began to weep as Herbert and the officer pulled him away from Angie. "You both knew. I remember it now."

Angie moved herself back and leaned against the blood stained wall.

She maneuvered her leg around so she could examine her ankle. The pain was excruciating, and she once again felt darkness begin to surround her. Michael's sobs were the only things that kept her coming back to consciousness.

"Michael, it wasn't your fault," the officer was explaining. "You were provoked. He killed your mother and then he taunted you with the gun. He would've killed you had you not stopped him."

"You don't know that!" Michael cried out. "I don't know that! He handed me the gun … and he laughed at me … he laughed so loud that it … it … it reverberated inside my whole head. I can't believe this! I can't believe this! Why didn't I remember this? How did this happen?"

"You were in shock when Miss Annabelle got here," Herbert explained. "The gun was next to your father's body, and you were holding your mother. When I got here, you couldn't say a thing. We weren't sure what had happened. But when Officer Roberts came, he knew immediately what had transpired by the setting of the scene."

"So everybody just lied?" Michael said through his sobs. "And you all led me to believe something else?"

"I wasn't going to let you take the blame for what was legitimately a self-defense issue!" Sully Roberts said forcefully. "You listen to me, Michael! You were a good boy! Your dad was a rotten, no good, low down piece of human flesh. He had already killed your mother!"

"But where did I come up with this elaborate story of his shooting himself? That's just a lie! It's a plain lie! And I believed it … but somewhere down deep I knew the truth!" Michael was now rocking back and forth.

Angie wasn't sure which hurt more: her ankle or her heart. She wanted to yell for these men to leave her alone with Michael, but she couldn't move; she couldn't even get to him.

"Michael!" she yelled. "Please, come here! Please!"

He looked over at her, and his face was soaked with tears. Her stomach almost heaved as she reached out her hand to him. The reality of all that had happened was about to overtake her too, but she needed to stay strong for him. He slowly crawled over to her and laid his head in her lap. He knocked her ankle, but she bit her lip and managed not to scream.

"Miss Annabelle came up with the story," Sully went on to explain. "She was telling me what she *believed* had happened when you finally decided to speak up."

"You told us that after he shot your mother, he gave you the gun and dared you to pull the trigger," Herbert told him.

"We thought," Sully hesitated, " since there was no real evidence …"

"… and no one else was at the scene yet …" Herbert added.

"… that we could doctor everything up, do a little rearranging, and no one would be the wiser."

"Sully cleaned the gun powder from your hand and erased your fingerprints from the pistol. He then ran it all through your father's hand again."

"Then I placed it in an ideal position for a suicide victim," Sully confessed.

"Miss Annabelle sat next to you and pounded into your head that your father killed your mother and then turned the gun on himself," Herbert tried to help Michael realize *why* he had believed that fabrication all these years.

"By the time the other officers came, we had an ideal situation set up. I took your statement, feeding you Miss Annabelle's lines again … and you managed to eek it out."

Michael leaned his head back in Angie's lap and looked up into her face. This isn't what she had imagined when she decided to help Michael face his past. She was now wondering if things would have been better off had she, nor he, never known. She gently caressed his cheek and ran her finger across the scar he had received in this very room.

"I'm sorry," she said weakly, still feeling as though she could faint any moment. "I should've never done this."

"Oh, Angie," he said in utter defeat, "at least I know the truth. I always had this underlying feeling that I was a horrible person, but I never knew why."

"Michael!" she exclaimed as she put both hands to his face. "You're *not* a horrible person! You were a child who was the victim of extreme abuse! You could've put any other person in your position and have expected the same result!"

"Listen, Michael," Sully said as he knelt down next to them, "you would've been let off. All charges would've been dropped. There wasn't a judge or jury in this county who didn't know what a suck-egg hound your sorry father was. All we did was save your reputation and dignity a little bit in the process."

"You didn't need to walk out of your parents' death with a murder rap to boot," Herbert told him. "We were only thinking of you, son."

He slowly sat up, nudging her ankle again in the process. This time she cried out. Michael turned back immediately and discovered how heinously swollen it was.

"Oh, no," he said as he began to sob again. "Did I hurt you? Oh, Angie … I'm so sorry."

"It's fine, Michael," she tried to reassure him as the pain became unbearable again.

This time, however, she didn't know which would happen first. Would she pass out, or would she throw up? Everything went black before she knew what was happening.

SIXTY-TWO

Angie came to in the back seat of Herbert's truck. Michael was holding her, and they had her ankle propped up on a pile of unopened FFA jackets still encased in their plastic packaging. Her ankle was throbbing beyond any pain she had ever known before. She had been unable to tell if it was actually broken or just sprained. She knew from experience that a sprain could hurt just as bad. Michael was trying to speak soothing words to her, but she could tell that he was still in emotional shock over remembering his father's death.

When they arrived at the hospital, she was in and out of consciousness. The team bustled around her taking vital readings and trying to determine the condition of her ankle. "Michael!" she managed to yell out at one point.

No one paid any attention to her as they kept shuffling all around. She was getting agitated. She felt nauseous again, and then passed out. When she came to, several nurses were over her, busily trying to get an IV going. She looked for Michael and finally found his gaze. He looked pitiful. She tried to reach out her hand.

"Hang on a second, honey," one of the nurses said. "You can have loverboy back in just a minute, but we gotta get you down to x-ray pronto."

"No!" Angie yelled out again.

This time Michael pushed his way over to her. The nurse was rather put out, but he told her to lay off and let him find out what his wife, the *doctor*, was trying to say. He took her hand.

"What is it, Angie?" he asked as he leaned down to her lips.

"I'm so sorry," she said weakly. She knew she was about to lose it again.

"It's okay, honey. Everything's okay now."

"Okay, Mister," the gruff nurse said harshly as she pushed Michael aside. "Enough of the chit chat. We've got to get your wife's blood pressure stabilized and get this ankle x-rayed."

Angie was waning again. Nausea was overtaking her, but so was the black. *Don't leave me, Michael.* She heard him fighting for her as she went out again. *He called me honey. I'm so sorry. Why did I do it? I don't know. Honey. He called me honey. He called ... honey ... I'm so sorry. I love you, Michael.*

*****

When Angie opened her eyes, she was in a strange bed with no light anywhere and was surrounded by unusual, yet familiar, noises. As she

358

forced her eyes to open, it was then she remembered her ankle. It was tightly wound. She tried to move her arm, but it was taped up with an IV. She looked around to see if she was alone. Michael immediately ran to her side, turned on a light and took her free hand.

"Angie!" he whispered with excitement. "Are you okay?"

She rolled her eyes around as she tried to focus. She wasn't sure what it was they were giving her, but it was working well.

"I don't know," she managed to say. "What's the verdict? Am I broken or sprained?"

"Sprained," he grinned as he leaned down to kiss her forehead. "Extremely sprained. How do you feel?"

"Like a blown volcano," she said faintly. "There's nothing left inside me. Weak. Drained."

"You apparently had no idea, but there's something great inside of you."

She tried to focus on his eyes, his smile.

"You're pregnant, Angie," he said gently. "As they were taking you down to x-ray they asked if there was a chance you might be pregnant. It nearly slammed me against the wall! I told them it was possible. They took precautions for the x-ray then tested your blood for pregnancy along with everything else."

She could feel herself begin to swoon again. She closed her eyes and tried to process that fact. But slowly everything else began to come back to her memory. The house, the revelation, the lies. She looked back up at Michael immediately.

"How are *you*?" she wanted to know first.

"I'm thrilled," he told her with a smile. "We're really gonna have a baby."

"I don't mean about the baby," she said as she shook her head. "I mean about everything else. Are you okay?"

He stood up straight and squinted his eyes in that unsure way. He fiddled with her fingers as he tried to get his thoughts to make sense. *Just spit it out, Michael,* she thought.

"I'm okay," he said as he nodded his head in definite affirmation. "I'm okay. I'm not ... wonderful by any stretch of means, but I'm okay."

She sighed deeply. She didn't know how he could be okay, but she was too weary to pry.

"By the way," he smiled as he sat down on the bed next to her, "did you hear the part about we're going to have a baby?"

Now she began to grin. She reached up and gently ran her hand over his scar, then down his chin. She could feel tears begin to well up behind her eyes, and she wasn't sure if they were from joy, exhaustion or confusion.

"Is this good timing?" she asked him as she was very unsure of their future.

"Impeccable," he said kissing her hand. "I ... I ... still don't know how to handle all that I learned today, but I know that it was something I should have remembered long ago. And you were right, Angie. Subconsciously I *knew* the truth, and I needed to face it."

"You're not a bad person, Michael," she said with deep conviction. "You're truly wonderful, and I still love you with all my heart. Please don't think that any of this changes anything between us."

He looked at her strangely, shook his head and asked, "Did you think I would ever leave you?"

"I didn't know. You got really angry with me today. I actually thought for a while there that you were ready to kick me out of your life forever."

He sighed in desperation as he looked up to the ceiling and shook his head again. "How could you think I could ever live without you? You're my life, Angie. You're my *Spring Dawn*." His song ... the one he had never completed. "I can finish writing it now, and we can go home now."

"What do you mean *go home*?"

"Remember you said God had to have a purpose for making us leave Padawin?"

She nodded and sat up slowly in the bed.

"I had to face this," he told her honestly. "I had to understand the truth. It's one thing, Angie, to ask forgiveness and get forgiveness. It's another thing to hold it inside and never face it at all. I honestly don't remember when I drew the line and crossed over into the pretend version of the story, but I've carried it with me all these years. And you were right: it affected me ... deeply. I couldn't be the minister God needed, I couldn't be the husband you needed, and I certainly couldn't be the father this baby will need without getting this out and off of my conscience."

"Oh, my heavens!" she suddenly exclaimed. "I'm pregnant?"

He looked back down at her and gave her the most unusual expression. "What are they giving you? Haven't we been through this?"

"Oh, man," she said as she felt herself go weak again. "I'm really pregnant?"

"Your blood pressure's been doing wacky things. That's why you kept passing out. They think it's related to the pregnancy."

"I'm pregnant?" she asked again in unbelief.

"Yes, dear," he began to laugh. "You're really pregnant!"

She took a moment to let the reality register and simply shook her head in disbelief. She was pregnant. "Wow, Michael, wow."

"Is that okay?"

"Ooooh, it's absolutely wonderful. Will you think I'm a complete idiot if I start crying again?"

He chuckled as he shook his head. "If so, then I'm one too. When they told me you had tested positive for pregnancy, I burst into tears. It was almost too much, Angie."

"I guess the timing *was* rotten."

"Don't ever say that. Today, I regained a part of myself that had been missing all these years. I can't tell you how scared and unsure I was about being with you or having children. But now … I feel like I'm a real person. I'm not on the outside looking in. I'm not this spectator in life anymore. It's okay; I can really live now. I have nothing left to protect. I know the truth. And what's more, you know the truth. Your wish came true: you *really* know me now."

"No regrets?"

"Oh, plenty! But I can't do the *what if's*. I've got you, I've got a baby, I've got a family, I've got a ministry, and I've got an incredible life. *Those things* I will never regret, nor will I ever take them for granted."

She gazed at him in admiration and wonder. How did God manage to bring two people together who had started out so far apart in many, many ways?

"You do know that I love you, Dr. Collins?"

"I'm counting on it, Dr. Angie," he whispered back as he kissed her softly. "Did I mention that I adore you also? And that I think you're the sexiest missionary I've ever laid eyes on?"

She kissed him back and ran her hand through his hair. "Please tell me I don't have to stay in here overnight."

"Okay. How 'bout I tell you that you already stayed here overnight, and that the sun will be rising in about ten minutes?"

"I missed our first night apart since we've been married," she said sadly.

"Trust me, it was miserable."

"Can I leave today?"

"If your blood pressure is back down. The truck and camper are in the parking lot waiting to go."

"Where am I anyway? I know this isn't Olin, Kansas."

"Salina."

She looked up at him again. Things would never be the same between them, but that was good. No barriers, no hidden secrets, and nothing to hide behind or from. She pulled him closer and kissed him again. It felt right for her to be with this man, and she couldn't help but look forward to their future together, no matter what it held.

SIXTY-THREE

The trip back to Alabama was quiet and thoughtful. Angie's ankle hurt miserably, but she refused any pain medicine for fear of harming the baby. She propped her leg up on the seat as best she could and shifted her body often in an attempt to find a comfortable position. The later the day became, the harder it was to find any ease.

Michael refused to picnic. He drove through a fast food place and ordered burgers and fries for them to eat while on the road. He had planned to drive straight through to Dockrey, but when he realized the pain and discomfort she was having, he decided it would be best to stop early. He wanted to get a hotel, but she insisted they camp. She wanted a fire to sit by and a familiar place to sleep. He wouldn't let her cook, however, even amidst much protesting on her part, knowing she would have to stand on the ankle. He stopped by a nice restaurant and ordered two dinners to go.

At the campsite, he carried her from the truck to the door of the camper. She eased her way to the bed and let her body stretch out. Relief! He then brought in their dinners and set out the candles and soft music just as she had done on their first night camping together.

"You should've let me cook," she complained, though with not much energy.

"Not on your life. It's my turn to spoil and care for you a little bit."

"Spoil? I don't think I've ever been *spoiled* before."

"Get used to it then," he said handing her a fork. "I plan to do an awful lot of it the next few months."

"Why is that?"

"Because I'll have you all to myself for only a short while now. In a little bit, we'll have a wee one who will demand a lot of our attention. I want you to always remember how much I loved you *before* the baby came into our lives."

"You don't have to spoil me for me to understand that," she said as she reached over and took his hand.

"Well, that's how you've treated me. From the first moment I met you, you've spoiled me, catered to me, and met my every need. Now, it's my turn."

She relocated her ankle, trying to get it up somehow so the throbbing would stop. Michael jumped immediately and grabbed one of the folding chairs, placed it next to the table, and then gently lifted her foot to rest on it.

"You're serious about this spoiling bit, aren't you?"

"Very serious," he told her eye-to-eye.

The following two days, the drive was mostly quiet. Angie managed to sleep some because of the lack during the nights. It had been near impossible for her to get comfortable in bed with the pain of her ankle. When she did awaken one time on Wednesday night, she noticed Michael had a distraught look on his face. As they were riding the next day, she noticed the look again.

"What are you thinking?" she asked, then teased him by adding, "I hope it's not about me with that sour expression."

"Never," he said as the grimace turned to a grin. He looked back at the road, and did his meditative look again. "I was wondering what we should tell your family about all this—you know, all we've learned about my story."

"Nothing. What happened is the past. That's where it needs to stay."

"But they know an altered version of the past. It's kind of like lying to just leave it."

She shook her head as she shifted her body around again. This was one time that she wished she were five-four instead of five-eleven. "If you feel like you have to say something, just tell them we learned more things about your past, that it was difficult to face, but we want to leave it there."

"And what about your ankle?" he raised his eyebrows. "Do you blame that on me? It was my fault, remember."

"I remember. How much do you weigh anyway?"

"It's all muscle, you know?"

"I know—believe me, I know."

"Seriously," he said trying to get her back to the subject. "I mean … I fell on you. Do we tell them that? How do we explain it?"

"We don't have to go into great detail. We just tell them we had a little accident and you tumbled onto my ankle."

"What if they ask for details?"

"Michael!" she was getting exasperated. "My parents aren't drill sergeants! It will suffice."

"If you say so," he said doubtfully.

They pulled into the Wright driveway on Thursday evening just before suppertime. They hadn't mentioned any of the happenings in Olin to Jonathan or Barbara, so they were both shocked when Angie hobbled out with a wrapped ankle.

"What in heaven's name happened to you?" Barbara asked with alarm as she moved quickly to Angie.

"A silly accident," Angie mumbled out. "We were doing a little sightseeing and Michael sort of fell on my ankle."

"My goodness!" Barbara exclaimed.

Angie looked over at Michael and gave him a wink as if to say *all's well* and *I told you so.* He gave a look of relief.

"Does it hurt badly?" Barbara asked as she let Angie lean on her shoulder.

"Like the dickens," she moaned as she put weight upon her mother.

"Is it a bad break?" Jonathan asked while surveying the injured leg.

"It's just a sprain," Angie explained, "but it's definitely a bad sprain."

Michael watched her hobble on her mother's shoulder and could take no more of it. He came up next to her, turned her sideways, and then lifted her up in his arms. Angie giggled.

"There you go!" Barbara laughed in glee. "That's what you call modern day chivalry."

"I'd be careful if I were you," Jonathan warned. "She may start expecting that kind of treatment even when her ankle's better."

Michael held her close to his chest and laughed. "You need to eat more," he said as he effortlessly carried her into the house.

"Tell me that in another six months," she grinned.

"I can't wait."

They enjoyed a delicious dinner of Barbara's famous Beef Stroganoff, and Michael insisted on taking Angie's place in the kitchen helping clean. Barbara raised an eyebrow at Jonathan.

"You're going to end up ruining my reputation," Jonathan mumbled to Michael as he walked by him to carry his plate into the kitchen. "Carrying wives, cleaning kitchens—boy, am I gonna have a hard time around here when you leave."

Barbara raised her hand toward Jonathan and said, "You'd better leave him alone. Michael is a nice, polite man. We don't get those around here often."

"I think I'll join Angie in the living room," Jonathan grumbled as he placed down his plate. "*She's* not in a bossy mood tonight."

He stepped out of the kitchen and found his daughter struggling to get to the great room. Stepping up beside her, he put an arm around her waist.

"Thanks, Daddy," she said as she leaned into him.

He helped her toward the couch, but she opted for the recliner instead. When she finally got her feet up, she gave a sigh of relief.

"How was Kansas?" Jonathan asked her.

"The state? Big and flat. The town of Olin? Tiny and tinier."

He smiled. Like the rest of his daughters she didn't mince words often.

"In fact, it was probably a lot like Dockrey ... only minus the really deep, Southern accents."

"Have a good time?"

"Pretty good. It was odd being with Michael's *almost family*. But it was good for people there to see how he turned out."

"I bet they were quite impressed with his bride too."

"Oh, Daddy," Angie rolled her eyes. "They didn't even know I was there."

"I doubt that. You turn heads wherever you go."

"You would've loved this restaurant we went to," she changed the subject. "They bring this massive slab of beef out and then ask you how big of a chunk you want."

"Were they able to shave yours off?" he teased knowing she liked her steaks thin.

"Believe it or not, I took one about a half an inch."

"Bravo!" he clapped as studied her tired face for a moment. "Are you all right? You look a little pale. Do you have some pain medicine for the ankle?"

"I'm fine, and no, no pain medicine. It's not that bad."

"You wouldn't know it by watching you. I'd be willing to bet it's the worst injury you've ever incurred. You never were accident prone."

"Unlike Andie," she giggled a little. "How many broken bones did she have *before* she left home?"

"Three before, two after."

"Want some Advil?"

"Nope, I'm fine."

"Tylenol?"

"Daddy!"

"Don't get irritated," he said gently. "I'm concerned. I'm not used to seeing you disabled. You're my strong girl."

"The only thing disabled is my ankle, and it's *mildly* disabled."

"Yes, and it apparently had no affect on your tongue, I see."

He turned on the television, and before long, she was dozing in her chair. He watched her for a moment and felt a twinge of pride swell his heart. This was a girl who had come a long way. In many areas, she had been his *difficult* child. She was the only one who had been openly rebellious during her teenage years. She was the only one who had refused to continue with music lessons, even though it was now obvious that she had ample enough talent to have validated the lessons. She had been as smart as a whip in school, but didn't care much for completing assignments. She had always been the gripe of many a teacher who couldn't give her an "A" in class even though her test grades were straight "A's". *If only she would have turned in her report! If she would have given a little more time to her project. Why won't she read the assignments? Do you not make your children do their homework?* When she finally committed her life to missions, it was as though the light went on in her life and everything changed for the better. Her grades skyrocketed. Her attitude improved drastically. And suddenly she had this purpose driving her. Everything she did began to move her toward missions and medicine. She gave herself to learning as much as she could that would grant her knowledge in that direction. And as for being a daughter, she went from black to white.

"You have a beautiful daughter," Michael said as he joined Jonathan on the couch. "In fact, you have three. How did you manage that?"

"Probably all my genes," Jonathan sighed. "I come from good stock."

"And Barbara?"

"She's lucky to have me," Jonathan winked at him.

SIXTY-FOUR

After a long nap, Angie awoke in the recliner and opened her eyes slowly. Her father and Michael were deeply engrossed in a carpentry show. Her ankle was throbbing beyond tolerance and when she shifted slightly she winced in pain.

"Are you okay?" Michael asked quickly as he jumped up and came next to her.

"Honestly? My ankle is killing me."

"I'm getting some Tylenol," he said insistently.

"No," she blurted out. "I'll be fine."

"It'll take the edge off of your pain, Angie. Besides, the doctor said Tylenol was completely safe."

"Don't tell me what the doctor said," she said curtly. "I've seen the studies, read them all myself. It's best to avoid anything if at all possible."

"And I'm saying that we've reached beyond the point of what is *at all possible.*"

"Excuse me," Jonathan butted in. "First, I'd like to know why you have no pain medicine period."

"I don't need it. It's an unnecessary luxury."

"Okay, doctor, whatever you say," Jonathan nodded although he was unconvinced. "Now explain to me why you won't even take Tylenol."

"Because the pain isn't that bad."

Jonathan made a noise like the sound of a buzzer and told her, "Wrong answer. You're talking about seeing studies, Michael is talking about Tylenol being safe, and none of this is making sense. I watched you pour Advil and Tylenol down his throat the first several days you were here."

Angie and Michael just stared at him. He stared back, raised his eyebrows, and then held his arms up in question.

"Go get Moms?" Angie said. "She should be here for this one."

"Barbara!" Jonathan yelled without delay. "Could you come in here for a moment, please?"

"I could've done that," Angie griped at him.

"Then you should have," he offered back.

Barbara came in and wanted to know what the yelling was about.

"Sit, dear," Jonathan told her. "Your daughter is about to face us with something serious, I think."

"Oh, my," Barbara said with concern as she sat slowly beside her husband on the couch. "How serious?"

"Angie?" Jonathan replied as he patted Barbara's knee.

"Well … okay …," she began, her eyebrows down in concentration while she bit her lip. "I'm pregnant, but not *very* pregnant."

"Not very?" Jonathan asked weakly. "What on earth does that mean? You can't be *somewhat* pregnant!"

"What she means," Michael came to the rescue, "is that she's barely even a month. We didn't know she was having a baby until they wanted to x-ray her foot, and because we haven't been trying to *prevent* pregnancy, I told the hospital it was a possibility. They tested her."

"The hurt ankle sort of stressed out my blood pressure a little, and they were concerned about that too," Angie continued explaining. "Anyway, I'm pregnant."

Barbara just continued to stare as Jonathan sat back on the couch.

"I'm tickled pink," Michael nearly giggled as a silly grin spread across his face. "I know this is probably a huge shock for you guys, but, what can I say—I'm tickled pink."

"And how are you with this, Angie?" Barbara wanted to know before she would give any response.

"When I think of everything I've accomplished in my life, this has to be the most awesome thing that's ever happened to me," she said honestly as she took Michael's hand.

Her mother now smiled, stood up, and went over to hug her. "Then I'm happy for you." She released Angie and turned her attention to Michael. "And as for you, I'm tickled pink."

"Thank you," he smiled as he returned the hug. "I can hardly breathe sometimes when I think about it all."

"You'll be an excellent father … as you are an excellent husband," Barbara affirmed.

Jonathan, however, was still taken aback by the announcement. Angie was a grown woman, an intelligent woman, and a levelheaded woman, but when it came to matters of the heart, it appeared she threw common sense out the window. And when it came to Michael Collins, it appeared she would do anything to make him happy. However, he remembered and understood newfound love. He had to agree they were older than most new couples. As he glanced over at Angie, she was beaming while watching Barbara and Michael discuss the baby. He knew there was nothing more fulfilling in life than a wonderful spouse and family—not even a successful ministry could compete with that. And he had often worried that Angie would never find someone who could share her life's calling and raise a family with her, yet here it all had happened, fulfilled and moving on, and who was he to pass judgment on their timing or their methods?

"I have one question," Jonathan finally said soberly.

Everyone turned to him.

"What is the deal with my younger children?" he asked them all. "Andie and Doug married, waited several years, then started a family. The rest of you seem to be in a race as to who can have kids the quickest. Is there a reason for this?" He had a slight twinkle in his eye which indicated he was halfway teasing and halfway serious.

Angie grinned and said, "Because we want to be as happy as you and Moms. Besides, Andie was only nineteen when she married. I'm thirty, Daddy."

"Yes," he sighed as he finally came to his feet. "And I suppose there's something magical about being thirty and pregnant."

"But I'm thirty-six," Michael put in. "Nothing magical about that. I'm just plain getting old."

Jonathan laughed heartily as he extended his hand to Michael first. "Old indeed," Jonathan continued to laugh as he pulled Michael up from the arm of the recliner and embraced him tightly in his arms. "You don't know the meaning of *old* until you've been up with a baby every night for six weeks in a row!"

"I'm looking forward to it," Michael told him.

"Yeah, you e-mail me from Padawin and repeat that when it's all a reality."

"You can count on it."

"And as for you," he said as he leaned down to his daughter, "you have certainly been full of surprises this past year." He stopped, stood back up, and added, "This past year? Shoot—your whole life! You've never done anything conventional or halfway, Angie Wright. Why should I expect you to start now?"

"That ... uh ... would be *Angie Collins*," Michael reminded him.

"Of course," Jonathan chuckled as he leaned back down to hug his daughter. "You definitely belong to this man, don't you?"

"Hook, line and sinker, Daddy," she whispered into his ear.

"If I didn't believe it before, I certainly do now."

He went back to his seat and simply smiled at them. Yes, he was happy for them. As little common sense as it made, this whole relationship had been born out of uncommon sense, thus he would leave it at that.

"Now," Jonathan said, "I have a little bit of news for you."

"Goody," Angie grinned, wondering if her mood could get any better. "Is it good news?"

"Hmmm," he replied.

"Hmmm?" Angie mocked him. "That doesn't sound good."

"It's a little bittersweet. You know that Kay Thornton is retiring at the end of this year."

"Right," she nodded. "Hard to believe. She's been the church secretary longer than you've been the pastor."

"You make that sound *really* long," Jonathan glared over at her.

"It is *really* long, Daddy."

"Anyway, we've known all year that this would be her last, but last Friday, day after Thanksgiving, Joe came over and had a little talk with me. Another church has called him, a larger church in a much larger city."

"Joe? Our music minister?" Angie asked in unbelief.

"He's really good," Michael added.

"Yes, he is. And I always knew that Dockrey was merely a stepping stone for him. He needs something bigger and better, a chance to put all his abilities and talents to work. We're peanuts compared to where he needs to be."

"What a bummer," Angie groaned.

"But there's a little silver lining in all of this," Jonathan said with a smile. "Rather than try and have two committees working at the same time, I felt we should just focus on one for the moment. Joe's last Sunday will be the first Sunday in January. Kay leaves December 31st. I'd rather get the church to work on a music guy to begin with, but we can't function without a secretary. So, I offered the position temporarily to Cindy Marcum."

Angie's hand came to her mouth and her eyes popped open. "Cindy Marcum is going to work in a church?" Angie asked in shock.

"She's not *that* deplorable," Barbara said.

"Cindy's come a long way," Jonathan agreed. "The fact that she's willing to sacrifice everything to stay with her mother during the cancer treatments says a lot about the changes that are taking place in her life."

"I didn't mean it as bad as it came out," Angie apologized. "I agree that Cindy has had to make some hard choices, and she's chosen the right ones for a change."

"Since she's only a fill-in secretary, she'll have the freedom to be off when she needs to so she can take her mom to treatments and tend to her when necessary."

"And I can be in the office to answer phones when she has to be away," Barbara told them. "She still has to do all the bulletin business and finances; I can do nothing on a computer. But she can even work at home if she needs."

"And the church is okay with this?" Angie wondered.

"The deacons voted *almost* unanimously last night to do it," Jonathan smiled knowing Angie understood two particular deacons always voted against him. "They feel like this can be a huge ministry of the church to the Marcum family. James and Sue put in a lot of time, money and service here over the years."

"Wow," Angie said thoughtfully, "I actually think this is kind of neat. Cindy's probably gonna need as much support during all this as her mother will. You can bet Billy will be absent for most of it."

At the mention of Billy, Michael winced. Angie reached over and took his hand. "No competition, Dr. Collins."

Jonathan wanted to laugh, but instead gave a knowing smile.

SIXTY-FIVE

On Friday evening, Andie's family came over for dinner. Doug was in top form, his wit and charm oozing from every pore. Andie, however, was noticeably sullen. Angie tried to make several jokes directed her way, but they all fell flat. Doug found them funny, and the rest of her family seemed to be enjoying the evening. Angie tried to find a moment alone with her, but it was impossible. The kids were demanding a lot of attention, and since Angie couldn't stand for long to help in the kitchen she wound up in the recliner waiting for the ladies to finish.

After a while, the older children decided to watch a movie, and Barbara began to walk baby Aimee around in her arms to get her to sleep. When the men went out to look at the compost box, Andie found a spare moment and sat on the couch to chat with Angie who was lounging back and relaxed.

"Is everything all right?" Angie asked her carefully, not wanting to add to the blues.

Andie smiled and gave a slight chuckle as she said, "I suppose so. Who knows?"

"Well, that's a vague answer. I don't know any more now than before I asked."

"It's no big deal," Andie sighed as she lay out on the couch. "Life changes again. It's always a little hard to prepare for another big step."

"Tell me about it," Angie nodded, almost giving in to the blues herself. Andie's mood was contagious. "So, what's happening with you?"

"You wouldn't believe me if I told you."

"Of course I would, especially with that gloomy cloud that's been following you all evening."

Andie closed her eyes and laid her head back against the arm of the couch.

"Is it that big of a deal?" Angie asked her.

"You wouldn't think it would be by this time."

"For crying out loud, Andie! Spit it out, would you?"

"Sure ... just like that," Andie nearly sounded mournful. "I just found out last night I'm pregnant again."

"What?" Angie sat up in complete surprise. "That makes five kids!"

"Believe it or not, Angie, I've figured that out already. Trust me, that reality has hit me hard."

"I didn't mean it was *bad*, I just meant ... well ..."

"That it's a lot of kids," Andie finished the sentence.

"Who cares?" Angie began to laugh. "Have as many as you want!"

"I didn't know I *wanted* anymore."

"You do know there are ways to prevent all these kids from happening?"

"Yes, yes, yes," Andie sighed again. "It was just one of those nights. We weren't being very careful. Things just happened … and … well …"

"I understand," Angie nodded slowly.

Suddenly Andie began to laugh.

"What's so funny?"

"This conversation!" Andie said still laughing. "Anytime I've ever come close to talking about mine and Doug's *personal* life, you and Annie would freak out on me. Suddenly now you're agreeing with me! There's another one of those life changes for you!"

"I wasn't married before. I couldn't relate—and didn't want to relate. I understand a little better now."

"Oh, heavens," Andie said as she went back to her original mood. "I can't figure out what I feel about this. Aimee is just getting to the stage where life is beginning to be *normal* again. She's sleeping through the night, eating real food, and can entertain herself while I work on school with the boys. I wasn't prepared to start over again. I was actually looking forward to having older children for a change."

"Stop fretting about it. This baby will simply be blessing number five in an already incredibly blessed household."

"That's easy for you to say. You don't have a parcel of kids running circles around you all day long!"

"But I will very soon," Angie said softly.

Andie jumped up to a sitting position and stared at her in complete astonishment. "Are you telling me …?" She stopped before she could even get it out.

"I found out while in the hospital," Angie smiled. "I'm right around a month."

"Me too! Well, somewhere around that—a little more maybe. Our kids will be almost exactly the same age! I can't get over all of you! Annie, Alex, now you, getting married and having kids right off the bat. What is with this?"

"We all admire you so much. We want to be just like you and have everything that you've got."

"Yeah, right," Andie said as she rolled her eyes and picked out a strand of hair to twirl.

"Actually, I'm being halfway serious. I always envied what you and Doug had. It was this ideal life."

"Really?" Andie was laughing again. "Funny way of pursuing all that envy. You picked a career, a life and a place that made it almost impossible to have a husband and a family."

"I didn't *pick* anything; I was called."

"See, I don't get the whole *calling* thing. I never felt *called* to do anything."

"You're kidding, right?"

"No, not at all. I've never done anything out of compulsion. I've always just done things."

"You sure felt *called* to marry Doug," Angie chuckled. "You would've moved heaven and earth to spend the rest of your life with him."

"That's *not* a calling. That's more like a … a … for crying out loud, I don't know! I think it was more hormones than anything else."

"Hormones wouldn't have lasted thirteen years and five kids later."

"Don't be surprised," Andie answered quickly. "That's why number five is on the way."

Angie giggled at her sister's response, and soon Andie was feeling giddy with her.

"You have this calling to do something today that not a whole lot of people feel called to do," Angie told her seriously.

"What? Change diapers? Again and again and again?"

"You've given yourself to being a wife and a mother completely. You've made Doug an incredibly happy man. I watched him tonight; he practically floated around the room. I had no idea why. Here's a thirty-two-year-old guy with a stressful business, a stay-at-home wife, four kids, and yet he's acting as though the world had just made him king. Why? Because you've let him become that."

"Oh, please," Andie groaned. "I can promise you I'm not that noble."

"And I can promise you that you are. In ten years, I hope I'm half the woman you are. I may have an impressive education, and it may sound *important* that I've given myself to missions, but if I mess up the family part, I mess it all up."

She paused then added one more statement: "I truly admire you and what you've done with your life. I pray that my calling as a wife and a mother will be as strong as my calling to the mission field … and as strong as yours has been."

Andie smiled and wiped a tear before it fell. She chuckled a little again and then went over to the recliner and hugged her. "Thank-you," she said as she actually joined Angie in the chair. "You almost make me feel like I'm doing something splendid and decent by having this child."

"That's because you are." Angie scooted over more to the edge to make room for her sister. "Do you think we'll still be able to share this chair in another six months?"

"I don't actually think we're sharing it very well right now, but for a moment, it did seem like old times, didn't it?"

"Watching scary movies and eating popcorn until the wee hours of the morning?"

"Yeah, and waiting for Annie to fall asleep so we could put shaving cream in her hair."

"Telling Alex that the horror movie wasn't pretend but was a documentary of a place just down the street from here."

"I would kill my kids if I ever found them doing that to each other. It's a wonder we're not still grounded."

"Actually," Angie reflected, "I think I still am grounded. They just let me off for med school."

Andie laughed again. "You were a bad girl for quite a while there. I'll be honest with you; I never thought you'd turn out so well."

"I guess I'm just full of surprises."

The phone rang and brought them back from memory lane. Andie struggled to get out of the recliner so she could get to the phone before it woke the baby up. She tripped on her way to the table and fell to the couch as she reached the phone.

"Hello?"

"Yes, I'm trying to reach Michael Collins," said a man's voice urgently.

"Then you reached the right place," Andie told him. "Hang on just a second and I'll hunt him down."

At that moment the men came in through the back porch door.

"It's downright cold out there!" Doug exclaimed as he trotted to the fireplace.

"Telephone, Michael," Andie said as she held the phone out to him.

Michael took the phone and plopped down onto the couch beside her. "Hello?"

"Michael!" yelled an excited voice. "This is Chet! Turn on the FOX News channel right now!"

"I'm fine, Chet, and how are you this chilly November evening?"

"No time to chat, partner. Turn on the TV now! I'll call you back when it's all over! Bye!"

The phone clicked.

"That was Chet," Michael said to Angie. "He was a bit ... uh ... I don't know ... flustered? Excited? He said to turn on the FOX News channel."

"Got it," Andie said as she picked up the remote, turned on the television, and then changed the channel to the station.

There was a reporter talking about some facts, but then the scene changed.

"That's Arisha!" Michael yelled in unbelief.

"Who?" Andie wondered.

"President Arisha," Angie clarified. "He's the president of Padawin. He was captured by the terrorists that first day."

"Turn it up, Andie," Michael said as he knelt in front of the TV.

The reporter was saying: "Arisha was actually rescued six days after the overthrow. One of the Special Forces units of the Padawin military easily penetrated the room where he was being held, and he was relocated to a safe place until the military could depose of the terrorists. It seems that indeed that is now the case. Apparently, the military has been involved in covert operations from day one of this measly attempt at a government takeover. Sources say that several intelligence agents easily penetrated the organization from the start and were able to be drawn into its confidence where they obtained inside information. General Kinpost said not a single day went by that the military was not aware of the plans and strategies of the rebels. The reason for taking so long? They wanted to do a thorough job.

"President Arisha stated that before they led an all out raid against the insurgents, they needed to make sure no one was waiting in the wings to attack or lead another rebellion. It appears their job was indeed thorough, and to quote Arisha, they have '… exterminated the vile bugs that sought to decay the freedoms of democracy under which this nation has lived peacefully for over two decades.'

"The biggest damage that has been done has been to the morale and health of the Padawin people, especially those in the larger metropolitan areas. Because of the threat of national security, there has been no trade for nearly two months, and people have been living off of whatever supplies were available. Surprisingly, though, there was no rioting or plundering among the Padawin citizens, even though the rebels did their share. Market managers actually began storing and rationing food and supplies under the belief that if they could survive for a short while, their military would remove the terrorists."

"Meendoksu Kalleela, a market manager in Taveren explained it like this:"

A clip of the Padawin store manager came on the screen. He began speaking in Padawin, and an interpreter was heard over him.

"We would take no payment for the foods and medicines that our people needed. All consumerism was stopped. We believed if we banned together as a nation, we could stay strong to the end. These rebels were idiots. Why would they think the Padawin people would follow them? We are a free nation ruled by men who are educated and trustworthy. We knew only time was needed to find their stupidity and their weakness, and then they would be flushed like a toilet. They are sewage, and that is what we knew all along."

The reporter appeared back on the screen. "I think he pretty much summed up the feelings of the citizens in this small series of peaceful Pacific islands. Although many are hungry and sick, there is still celebration today on the streets of the Padawin cities. The faith of this nation in their government is astounding. And as is obvious, it was not a blind faith. These people knew who the true leaders were."

The reporter signed off and the news went directly to a snowstorm heading to the Midwest. Andie punched off the television, and everyone sat quietly for just a moment. But Michael couldn't stand it. He jumped to his feet and began to holler at the top of his lungs. He ran to Angie's chair, lifted her out, and began to swing her around.

"It's over!" he finally yelled something understandable. "Angie! Honey! We're going home! We're going *home*!"

Angie threw her arms around his neck and began to cry uncontrollably. Michael sat down with her on his lap, buried his face in her hair, and began to cry also. They were oblivious to anyone around them. The kids had come running into the room to see what the commotion was about. Barbara came in with baby Aimee, and Doug and Andie had embraced, emotional themselves at the Collins' reactions.

Jonathan went behind the weeping couple at the couch, leaned down, and put his arms around them both. Tears came into his eyes. He knew that this was all they lived for. This was their dream and their hearts' desire. But he also knew that the time he had spent with them, these past two months, would be something that wouldn't occur again for a long time. He had let go of Angie once, and now he knew he had to let her go again. This time, however, he would be sending her with a man that he had come to know and love as a son. He respected Michael as much as any man he had ever known, and there was a sense of relief knowing that his daughter would be under his care, protection and love. It stung to realize that he wouldn't see this grandchild until it was several years old, but he had given Angie and her call to missions to the Lord many, many years ago; doing it again would just be the next step of faith in his life.

*****

"I can't believe we're going back," Angie said softly to Michael that night as they buried themselves beneath the covers trying to get warm. "It almost seems like a dream."

"No," Michael pulled her closer to him, "this is no dream."

"You know what?" she asked him as she gently moved her ankle in a position where she could lean up to see his face. "We get to have that fire on the beach … roast clams … gaze at the constellations. We get to do all those things you regretted."

"You were right. You said there should be no regrets because we'd go back and do it all someday anyway. I tried to believe you, Angie, but sometimes it was hard."

She smiled in the moonlight and gently shook her head. "You'd think after all the miracles God worked out just to get us together, we could certainly trust Him for something as minor as a little government overthrow."

He laughed lightly as he caressed her hair through his fingers. "Hindsight is always twenty-twenty, they say. Maybe we can learn now to trust God in everything."

She leaned down and kissed him softly, still full of emotion from the evening. He pulled her closer and let himself melt in the sense of her presence.

"I've got to get in a different position," she said as she caught her breath. "My ankle will never last like this."

He helped her to lie back, and then an impish smile began to grow on his face.

"What *are* you thinking?" she asked at his expression.

"When the baby begins to grow, you'll have to retire this Braves jersey for a while."

"Are you complaining about my pajamas?"

"I liked the purple thing you wore that night shortly after we got here. Whatever happened to it anyway?"

"It was itchy. I don't like lace."

"Yeah, but I do," he grinned again. "Can't we pack it up and take it back with us?"

"I'm not gonna be able to wear that either when the baby gets big— when I get big."

"I know, but until then …" he teased her as he picked at her jersey.

She smiled as she thought about this wonderful man she was married to. If he liked purple lace, she could try it once in a while.

"I'll pack it," she whispered.

"Yea … that's one part of Western culture I don't mind bringing back with us."

"I won't miss television."

"I won't miss the cold."

"Besides, everything that's good in life, we already have … you and I."

"Amen to that, Dr. Angie," he breathed as he kissed her again.

"And amen, Dr. Collins."

SIXTY-SIX

After a discussion with Chet, Vicki, and Fred Carson, it was decided they would wait until after Christmas and New Year's to return to Padawin. As anxious as Angie was to return, she was thankful for the extra time to spend with her sister. The tour would be over December twentieth, and then Annie and her new little family would return to Dockrey for the holidays.

Angie's ankle was taking its time healing which made her miserable from sitting all day long. Michael and her father spent most of their hours accomplishing as many projects as occasion and money would allow. She was thankful when Cindy Marcum came over to visit.

"If it isn't the new church secretary," Angie grinned.

"Yeah, can you believe that?" Cindy laughed. "Who would've ever thought? But you know what? I'm really humbled they even offered me this. I could just see myself going from selling million dollar commercial buildings to stocking groceries at the Pig."

"Million dollar commercial buildings? I thought you were selling homes."

"At first," Cindy said as she stood to warm herself by the fire. "But they said I had this *classy air* about me, so they started putting me in on their commercial dealings. Way more commission."

"I bet. You weren't kidding when you said you were making a ton of money."

"Yeah, but that's all behind me ... at least for now. I gave up the apartment and am officially moved in with Mother again."

"I bet you had to give up that tiny little sports car of yours too," Angie assumed, remembering how completely cramped she had been in it when they had gone out last summer.

"Oh, no, I paid it off the first year."

"Promise me you won't drag your mother to her treatments in that itty bitty thing."

"If I didn't know better, I'd think you were complaining about my car. Now *there's* a surprise: Angie Wright complaining."

She grinned. "Want to know a real surprise?"

"Sure! Who's it about? Wait ... is this actual truth or just a piece of juicy gossip? If I'm gonna be the church secretary, I've got to curb the gossip thing."

"It's about me, silly. I don't gossip anyway."

"True," Cindy nodded as she moved to the couch. "You were always a stick in the mud when it came to that—unless it had to do with Kelly McCall."

"Yes, Miss America. Would you believe she and Annie are friends now?"

"No way!" Cindy exclaimed in shock. "I guess since they're both of celebrity status, there's nothing left to fight about."

"I suppose."

"So, tell me your news. I could go for a big surprise."

"You gotta keep it a secret, though," Angie warned her first.

"Yeah, okay," Cindy closed her eyes and held out her pinky.

"I don't need a pinky promise. You word is good enough, *Miss church secretary*."

Cindy laughed and then gave Angie her full attention as she pulled off her shoes and curled up on the couch.

"I'm pregnant," Angie told her.

"Get out of here! You are not."

"I really am. Just a little over a month."

"Well, you guys certainly didn't waste any time starting a family, did you? Are you excited or just scared to death?"

"Mostly excited, but I've had some blood pressure problems. That means I'm gonna have to keep it in check."

"Well, as a doctor, you should understand the symptoms pretty much. So, you're gonna go back to Padawin anyway? You're gonna have the baby there?"

"That's the plan. If there are any complications, I can go to Taveren."

"I have to admit, I was really hoping you'd be here for mother during all of this—what she's about to go through."

"No," Angie shook her head, "that's your job."

"At least you got her to go through with it."

"But you're gonna have to make her stick with it. This won't be a piece of cake."

Cindy nodded. Smiling at her friend, she said, "You probably could've given me some good tips on church secretarying too. I vote you stay around a little longer and keep me on the right page."

"Oh, I can do that now," Angie laughed. "Pay attention: never tell anyone anything. You'll know everything the pastor knows, but part of your job is keeping it secret. Also, never tell anyone where the pastor is. Protect him at all times. If he went home for lunch, he's simply *out*. If he went to the hospital to visit, he's *out* again. Make peace among the staff. When they gripe about each other, just nod and smile and say, *my goodness, how horrible for you*, but never actually make a comment in agreement."

"Does that include your father?"

"That *especially* includes my father," Angie said soberly. "He can get on a big pity party if he finds a listening ear. Let him gripe to Moms. She knows when to give him sympathy and when to slap him out of it."

"Really? She slaps him?"

"Figuratively. She can put him in his place when it's necessary."

"Should I write all this down?"

"No. It'll come back to you when the occasion arises."

"I hope so," Cindy sighed nervously.

*****

"Can I talk to you about something?" Michael asked Jonathan as they sanded the new shelves for the master bedroom.

"Absolutely. What's on your mind?"

It took him a few moments to actually begin. "Angie and I did a little more in Olin than we owned up to."

Jonathan's eyes popped wide open. He was thankful to be bent down and hidden behind a shelf. Wanting to keep Michael at ease, he made no comment but kept on sanding. If he felt the need to approach him with something, it must either be severe or bothering him considerably.

"She pushed me to go back to the house where I grew up … where my parents died. Angie's never pushed me to do anything. She's made *suggestions* now and then, but she's never been forceful … until then."

Jonathan wanted to say, *Then consider yourself lucky because Angie can be very forceful when the mood hits her which used to be quite often.* But he still remained quiet.

"I got a little forceful myself," Michael chuckled slightly.

Jonathan smiled and thought, *Good for you!*

"She kept insisting that I perhaps *hid* behind some of my past. I didn't know one way or the other. I knew I hid behind a lot of stuff, or at least that I *hid* a lot … period, but she seemed to think I needed to face my past again so I could put some things to rest. She felt like it would be good for our relationship if I could somehow go through it all again … at the scene of the crime, so to speak."

"So Angie's a shrink now?"

"I guess she knew what she was doing, so I won't question her methods."

"I take it something happened there."

"Oh yeah," Michael said as he now leaned back against a wall. "I was pretty rude to her, having no desire to go back to that place whatsoever. And then when I began to go through the events of the night of my sixteenth birthday, I was rather … oh … I guess cold and indifferent toward her. I didn't think I could ever treat Angie like that, but there I was … consumed and bitter.

"Then we got to my bedroom; that's where everything took place. As I began to remember the events, just as I had told Angie, and then later, your family ... something happened."

Jonathan now sat up. He found it curious that Michael had been short with Angie, although, if he could admit it, he would have loved to have seen it. Michael was just a little too perfect where Angie was concerned.

"I remembered things differently when I actually started going through the scene." He began to become hesitant.

"Go ahead," Jonathan urged, sensing his tentativeness.

"I remembered my father getting the gun and threatening to shoot Mama. I really believed at that point that he was too drunk to do much of anything. I jumped on his back hoping I could throw him off balance, but he tossed me aside like a pillow. That's when he went over to her and made good on his threat." Michael paused here, obviously struggling to relive the scene yet again, but he seemed to really need to get something off his heart. "I always thought that he turned the gun on me then."

"That's what you told us."

"Yeah ... and that's what I always believed ... until I was there and began to go through it." He paused again. "It wasn't like that. He handed the gun to me. Then he laughed and started his big spill about how he never wanted children and certainly didn't want me. He cackled in his drunken stupor and went on and on, digging at me deeper and deeper. Then he told me that either he was going to kill me and then kill himself, or I could have the privilege of taking him out first, but since I was such a huge wimp, he knew I'd never follow through. He made some smart remarks about Mama, looking over at her, and then he started laughing again and began the name-calling. My blood began to boil at how flippant he was about her. She'd sacrificed everything in life to keep him happy and to keep me happy. She didn't deserve an end like that."

He stopped talking and stared out the open garage door. Jonathan was afraid to hear what happened next.

"So," Jonathan cautiously asked, "did you pull the trigger?"

"Yes, sir," he admitted as he winced.

The elder man nodded in understanding. No wonder this had been hard to talk about, and no wonder he and Angie had agreed to keep it hidden. "How does that make you feel, Michael?"

"See ... that's what bothers me," he said with a little more emotion now. "I know that I should feel this horrible sense of guilt about it, but I don't. In fact, I almost feel vindicated somehow. All these years I've beat myself up because I believed I just sat there and did nothing while my mother died. But when I realized that I actually *did* avenge her death ... I feel, man, like it was *right* in some morbid way. I feel guilty about not feeling guilty. I mean, what kind of man can commit murder and not feel guilty, not feel completely condemned because of it?"

Jonathan took a moment to sigh deeply and collect his thoughts. This was quite a revelation. Michael, the most humble and gentle man he had ever met, turned out to have shot his own father. But it wasn't so cut and dry as that.

"First of all, I don't know if *murder* is the proper term for what you did," he tried to help him make sense of the situation. "Yes, you *killed* him, but not as though you *hunted him down* or *lost it* and suddenly blew him away. I also think you need to keep in mind the fact that somewhere during all this he shot your mother and then threatened your own life. But even if he didn't threaten you, this situation is not necessarily *murderous*. What he did to your mother? That was murder. What you did to him? That was self-protection or even justifiable vengeance. But I think you need to pull the *murder* word from your mind. That's the reason you can't feel guilty."

"I'll be honest with you, I don't exactly know *how* to feel about it. I can tell you this, though, for all those years, I felt like a spineless wimp. I felt like I was this worthless, pathetic kid … always … no matter how old I was. I always felt responsible for her death. But somehow this changes things in my mind. I feel like I *did* do something—in fact, I feel like I did the only thing I could've done."

"Then I think you're on the right track."

They sat quietly for a while. Jonathan hadn't been prepared for such a morose discussion, but the fact that Michael had been willing to trust him with this made him feel honored. But had his advice been correct? Did Michael *murder* his father, or was it legitimately self-defense? To know Michael was to know pure humility. Whatever the crime, Michael had more than paid for it these past twenty years.

Jonathan reached over and patted his back in support. "You've had one unusual life, my boy, and I hope you realize that with Angie along now, you may never get to experience *normal*."

"Who wants *normal*," Michael smiled. "How could life with her ever be anything but incredible?"

"Just remember, as the years roll by, that *incredible* doesn't always mean *wonderful*," he semi-warned him. "You guys are such newlyweds right now that you can't imagine hard times will come someday, but they will. And when they do, always remember the strength and inner beauty that attracted you to each other. Always remember love is a *commitment* that's sometimes accompanied by feelings, and sometimes not."

"You're right. I can't imagine ever thinking that Angie isn't the greatest creature in the world."

"Well, I'll agree with you that Angie is an *incredible* young lady, but she's got a hard-headed side that is one tough monster if you ever hit against it. All my girls are like that."

Michael chuckled.

"You think it's funny?"
"Well, sir, they all say they're just like you."

SIXTY-SEVEN

Stephen and Annie deliberately scheduled their final concert in Birmingham so when it was over they could head directly for Dockrey. Michael was thrilled to be attending his first Stephen Williams concert, and was even more thrilled knowing he was a brother-in-law. Stephen had arranged for a huge touring coach to pick up Jonathan, Barbara, Andie, Doug, Angie and Michael in Dockrey, transport them to the concert, and then Stephen, Annie, and Stevie, along with Alex and his family, would all return to Dockrey together.

Backstage passes had been sent so when they arrived at the auditorium, the bus was ushered to the back door. Everyone took their turn getting out, and then a guard checked their passes, radioed someone inside, and waited for the door to open. It was freezing, and Michael thought his fingers would fall off from frostbite if he didn't get inside the building soon. He ran his hands quickly up and down Angie's arms under the guise of warming her up.

"Thank you," she whispered as she looked back at him. "I'm about to freeze to death. One thing I'm so looking forward to in Padawin is the warmth. What was it you said about the seasons there?"

He leaned into her hair and reminded her, "We have two seasons: summer and wetter."

"That's it," she smiled as she turned around and embraced him. "And I promise to never complain even when it seems too warm or too wet."

"Me too."

The back door finally opened and the group was escorted in and led to the wings area of the stage.

"I'll notify the Williams that you're here," said another man with a walkie-talkie. Angie recognized him from the year before.

"Aren't you one of the Rockys?" she asked, referring to the nicknames Annie had given to all of the bodyguards.

The man smiled and extended his hand. "Yes, I am. I'm Guy. I remember you well also. You're the sister, the single one."

"Not anymore," Angie smiled as she held up her left hand.

"Congratulations," he told her. "Who's the lucky guy?"

Angie pulled Michael over and introduced him. "This is Michael, my wonderful husband."

Guy shook his hand, and Michael could tell he was looking on him with admiration. Apparently Angie had made quite an impression on the young, muscular Guy. She began to tell the man all about her life since the tour last year, but Michael stared at the wedding ring she had shown proudly to indicate she was indeed married now. His heart panged a little because in truth, when that ring had been given, it represented nothing more than a necessary convenience to get her to Padawin. He hadn't thought much about it until now. He had often looked at his own ring, turning it around on his finger, and felt proud to be wearing it. But as he watched her hand, moving back in forth in animation, it looked bare and simple. That wasn't a true representation of how he viewed her, their marriage, or their life together. She meant everything to him, and she should know that.

Within a couple of minutes Stephen and Annie appeared with Annie carrying little Stevie. He was yawning and looking as though he could drop off to sleep any moment. Angie squealed in delight as she hugged Annie desperately, and then immediately took Stevie in her arms. Michael felt the lump grow in his throat again as he watched her cuddle the little boy, and then when Stevie smiled back at her, her response was priceless. Within a few months, she would have her own child to share her life with, and he would be a part of that.

He couldn't stand watching Angie with the baby without getting in on it. "My turn," he said gently as he took Stevie from her.

"He's a natural," Annie laughed as she patted Angie's shoulder. "You guys need to have a half-a-dozen or so yourselves one day."

They had decided not to tell Annie about the baby until she was home for Christmas, so they only smiled at each other. Barbara then came up and managed to steal Stevie away from Michael. As everyone continued to greet each other, he actually found himself feeling as though he were truly a part of this family. Stephen talked with him for a while and told him a few of the high points that had occurred on tour.

Another man with a radio came up and announced, "Five minutes, Mr. and Mrs. Williams."

"Okay," Stephen said as he thanked the man with a nod. "You need to escort my family to their seats. Let me have Stevie."

As Stephen reached out his arms to take the baby, Barbara pulled back and said, "Not on your life, Stephen Williams! No offense, but I would rather spend this time out here tending to my grandchildren than sitting in there listening to the music. I have all the CD's already."

Stephen laughed and nodded and then motioned for Bull, another of Annie's bodyguards, to come over.

"This is my mother-in-law, Barbara Wright," Stephen told him. "She'll be watching Stevie tonight. Could you take her to where the wives are?"

"I'll just sit here if you don't mind, unless he starts getting fussy," Barbara said cooing at the baby.

Stephen nodded. "If she needs to leave, take her then."

Bull nodded and then stood next to Barbara as was his habit when assigned to watch over someone.

"You don't have to guard her, Bull," Stephen said. "Just make sure she finds everything she needs."

"Right," Bull nodded immediately as he took three steps back.

Guy escorted the rest of the family out to their seats, front and center. Michael hadn't been to a concert since his college days. He was excited, not only to be seeing Stephen Williams but also Annie. When he had first heard her sing and play on the Christmas album, to have said he was impressed would have been an understatement. Then when Angie had made her play the piano interlude during their visit to Dockrey to prove that it indeed had been *her* playing on the album, he had been beyond impressed.

The lights began to dim, and the crowd behind them began to go wild. Michael could make out figures finding their positions on stage with penlights. The band started playing long slow tones that only added to the anticipation of the crowd. As the music built, so did the screaming level. Michael now understood why Barbara had kept Stevie backstage rather than bring him inside the auditorium.

An announcer now spoke over the music and the crowd, "Ladies and gentlemen, Stephen and Annie Williams would like to wish you a Merry Christmas—their way."

The crowd jumped to its feet and the lights burst onstage, red and green. The band went into the album's arrangement of *We Wish You a Merry Christmas*, and Stephen and Annie appeared onstage. The cheering became even louder. Michael laughed when he saw Angie stick her fingers in her ears. Stephen and Annie held hands as they approached the front of the stage, they kissed and then went to their separate keyboards where they began dueling with each other right away on who could play the wildest rendition of the old Christmas classic.

By the time the concert was finished, Michael had never felt more inferior as a musician. He now understood why Angie downplayed her talent so quickly. He loved playing his guitar and singing, but had he grown up with the same musical proficiency that Angie had around her, chances are he would prefer to hide it in the closet also.

The family was immediately escorted to the backstage area again where they found Stephen holding his son and Annie giving directions to have their luggage taken to the bus. They had agreed to sign autographs and meet fans for fifteen minutes tonight, so after hugging their baby, they were whisked off to a secure area where they could greet eager folks awaiting a closer glimpse of the stars. The family was escorted back to the warm bus where they would wait for the stars.

*****

"That had to be one of the highlights of my entire life," Michael told Angie late that night, actually early the next morning, as they climbed into bed. "I apologize, by the way, for forcing all this music stuff on you around your family. I had no idea your sister was so … well …."

"Incredible?" she offered.

"Yeah. But that doesn't mean I don't love your music too. I love to hear you sing … especially when you sing with me. We'll never be Stephen and Annie, but what we do is just fine."

"We can be the *Stephen and Annie Williams* of the Padawin tribes," she chuckled.

"We'll never make any money doing that, you know?"

"We'll never make any money doing anything. That's not why we do what we do."

He pulled her close to him and found comfort in her nearness. He was exhausted from such a long day, and it felt wonderful to just lie next to her and begin to doze. She laid her head on his chest after a gentle goodnight kiss, and all he could think of was how amazing his life was now.

"You know what?" she asked as she roused him from drifting. "There's only one way this moment could be any better."

"How's that?"

"If it were warm, if we were back in Padawin, and if the moon were reflecting off the snow on Podakind."

"That's three things."

"Nope, because if we were in Padawin, they'd all be true."

He pulled her closer and rubbed her arm to help her warm up. She was right: the only thing that could be better than this right now would be Padawin. It wouldn't be long.

SIXTY-EIGHT

Michael had never seen anything like Christmas time at the Wright house. He had only *thought* Thanksgiving was full of family traditions. On Monday, the entire day was given to decorating the house; Andie was the only one not there, but she was busy with her own crew. Jonathan put Stephen and Michael to work hanging various lights and fixtures around the yard and near the fence. The crowd outside was thrilled that Stephen was out and bantered with him the entire time. Michael admired his ability to talk with them and tease without feeling invaded or violated. One lady began to get a little out of line, and the crowd, realizing their incredible advantage at the moment might be lost, managed to move her out of the way.

Inside, Angie and Annie and Barbara fussed over who held the baby and who hung the garland. Barbara finally won Stevie, so the girls were stuck with the rest. Neither of them cared much for decorating, so most of their time was spent arguing about how it had been done last year. In truth, they couldn't remember.

"You stand on the ladder and do the high part over the fireplace," Angie told Annie.

"No way. I do *not* like heights."

"I don't really care. I'm not climbing a ladder. My ankle still hurts."

"Well, I'm not getting up there either. I don't do ladders."

"Apparently *one* of us is going to have to climb up there, and it ain't gonna be me."

"Why are you being so ornery about this? Just climb the ladder and hang the garland."

"Hello?" Angie said as she stuck out her leg. "Bad ankle. Are you not paying attention to me?"

"Yes, I hear all your whining." Annie rolled her eyes. "But if we're gonna start talking about *delicate* conditions, I'm afraid I have you beat."

"I doubt that. Try me." She was resolute because no matter what was said, she could top it with being pregnant; Annie didn't know yet.

"Okay." Annie folded her arms. "I understand about your pitiful little ankle, but I happened to discover last week that Stevie is gonna have a little brother or sister this next year. Now ... *you* top that."

Angie screamed at the revelation. "No way! Moms! Come here! You're not gonna believe this!"

Barbara came running into the room much to the delight of little

Stevie who cackled as he bounced up and down.

"What's wrong?" she wondered breathlessly.

"Annie's pregnant!" Angie blurted out.

"Oh, my heavens!" Barbara said in shock as she plopped down onto the couch. Stevie cackled again, assuming all the bouncing was for his benefit alone.

"For crying out loud," Annie exclaimed. "You guys are sure making a lot out of this."

"You have no idea!" Angie said as she broke into laughter.

"You're right! What's the problem?"

"You're never gonna believe this," Angie said as she took Annie's hand and led her to the couch.

"What's going on?"

"Andie's pregnant too," Angie told her.

Annie's eyes grew wide as she took in the information. "You're kidding?" She began to smile. "When did she find out?"

"Not long ago."

"Five kids?" Annie breathed out. "Don't they know what causes this?"

"Them? What about you?"

"Wait," Barbara said as she put up her hand. "There's still more. Go on, Angie."

Annie looked at Angie and shrugged her shoulders.

"So am I," Angie told her.

"No way!" Annie screamed.

Stevie was startled and looked over at his mother.

"I don't believe this! We're all three pregnant at the same time?" Annie was dumbfounded.

Angie nodded and started laughing again.

"Do you realize what this does to me?" Barbara asked them.

"Ages you?" Angie teased. "I mean, three grandbabies in one year?"

"Three in one year?" Annie exclaimed. "Try six in two years!"

They both laughed now.

"I could care less how *many* I have," Barbara told them. "It's just that one will be born here while another one's being born up in New York and then a third one is off somewhere in the South Pacific! Do you realize the mental mess I'll be in trying to coordinate all of this? None of these babies had better be born on the same day! I'll ground all of you if that happens!"

Angie won the most *delicate* condition since she was both pregnant and down in the leg. After the decorations were finished, Barbara made some tuna salad for lunch and everyone had a great laugh at all three sisters being pregnant at the same time. Annie and Angie decided to pay Andie a visit and break the news together.

As the girls bundled themselves up, Michael and Stephen sipped hot cider by the fireplace.

"You ready to be a dad?" Stephen asked Michael.

"Very."

"It's great, you know?"

"I'm looking forward to it. How about you having a second kid already? Does it seem overwhelming?"

"Not yet. It can be overwhelming now at times, having a baby around, but it's also incredibly rewarding … and, well, just plain fun. Like, when he smiled the first time? That was awesome. We both nearly cried. And guys like you and me? We have this advantage that other dads don't: we get to be around most days with our kids. We're a team, and not tag team, a together team."

Michael nodded and sipped more of his cider. "I can stay with the baby while Angie works in the clinic, unless it's during the planting season." Then he thought for a moment and added, "That should be fun."

*****

After a carefully thought out plan to get Annie out of the Wright compound and beyond the fence of fans, the two sisters didn't bother knocking when they heard the commotion inside Andie's house. They walked on in to complete chaos. Loud children's Christmas music was playing while baby Aimee bounced in the doorway on some kind of bungee contraption with a seat. Ashley was doing her best to string popcorn with a needle and thread as Andie looked over to coach her now and then. The biggest mess, however, was the boys' attempts at making Christmas decorations with Styrofoam balls, glitter, colored ribbon, and glue—lots of glue. Andie was in the middle of it all with glitter and glue in her hair, on her hands, and on her sweatshirt.

"Aunt Annie and Aunt Angie!" Arly yelled out when he caught sight of them.

Andie looked up and rolled her eyes. "Wonderful timing, girls," she said as she stood and wiped her hands on her sweatshirt. "Just a second."

Andie went over to the stereo and turned off the music.

"Mommy!" yelled Ashley. "We can't do Chwistmas wifout da music!"

"We can for a little while," Andie told her. "Adam! Do not glue ribbon to Arly's hair!"

"Yes, Mama," Adam groaned as he gave Arly a sly look.

Andie picked Aimee up from the bouncing bungee and motioned for her sisters to follow her to the glassed-in porch. She collapsed on the wicker couch and kissed Aimee a few times while talking baby talk.

"Not enough torture at Moms'?" Andie asked sarcastically.

"Oh, we just wanted to see how the other half lives," Angie told her. "This is rather educational. Is this what I have to look forward to on down the road?"

"Depends," Andie sighed. "If you have just the one, I imagine life would be much different. If, however, you choose the multiple route just get it in your mind that life is never going to be simple, peaceful or completely orderly for some time."

"That sounds so defeatist," Annie said mournfully.

"I didn't say it was bad."

"No simplicity? No peace? No order?" Annie questioned with raised eyebrows. "That doesn't sound very pleasant."

Andie pulled Aimee up to her face and snuggled her cheeks with her own again. "I suppose Annie knows your news by now," Andie said to Angie. "And mine too, I'm sure."

"Yeah, but we have even more news," Angie told her excitedly.

"Really?" Andie said as she pulled Aimee aside. "Give it to me, then."

Angie looked at Annie and nodded for her to bear the glad tidings of great joy.

"Stephen and I are gonna have another baby too."

Andie pulled Aimee down quickly as her jaw dropped. "No way," she said slowly in complete disbelief.

"Way. From the best I can figure, I'm due sometime around June."

"Me too," Andie laughed.

"I'm guessing July for me ... missed you guys by a month," Angie said.

The three sisters stared at each other for a moment and then burst into laughter. Over the years, many bizarre things had happened to them, but this one took the cake. Even Aimee joined in the laughter as it continued on and on.

"Maybe they'll all be boys ... or girls," Andie suggested. "When they get together, they'll have a ball."

"They'll almost be like sisters ..." Annie added.

"Except without all the fighting," Angie put in.

"But we won't get to see yours until forever," Andie said to Angie. "When will you be back again?"

"In a few years ... don't know for sure."

"You won't have a baby then; it'll be a full-fledged child," Andie told her. "Okay, you and your computer illiterate self must learn how to download pictures to the computer and upload them to Facebook. Videos too. Get that brainiac husband of yours to figure it out. We'll have to settle for watching it grow up on the internet."

"Good heavens!" Annie sighed loudly. "This all sounds so depressing! Can't we talk about the positive things instead of the negative? I don't *even* want to think about Angie going back to Padawin and being gone for who knows how many years!"

"Look at it this way," Angie said as she took Annie's hand, "I'll be as happy as any person could ever be. And you will too. So what? We've all grown, gotten married, and our lives have changed drastically, but that's what life is supposed to be about. Just imagine, this time next year, you'll be chasing two kids. Andie will be chasing five. I'll be toting one on my hip while I check out all the people in the clinic. And we'll miss each other, but it won't be a *bad* missing. It'll be ... well, it'll be *our* versions of *normal.* And then when we do get these moments together, it won't be the same anyway. It'll be like when Andie went away to college that first month. I thought I would die."

"I did die when *you* left for college," Annie groaned. "I was left here with Alex, who happened to hate me at the time."

"But you made it through, and look at you now," Angie smiled at her. "Married to Stephen Williams!"

"Talk about your lucky breaks," Andie grinned. "Who would've ever thunk that?"

"But here we are," Angie kept moving toward her point. "And as much as we'd like to stay together and be connected always, the truth is, we've all moved on in our real directions. Growing up, life at home with Moms and Dad, that was all preparation for real life. And now here it is."

"I'll be honest with you," Andie said in her typical no-nonsense manner, "having you guys around is nice, but it messes up my schedule big time. I'm glad when you're here, and I'm glad when you leave."

"Thanks a lot," Annie glared at her. "Love you too."

"I *do* love you," Andie emphasized, "but it's like Angie said, my life is now *this* family. What I do *here* is what I do. What I do when you're here is *not* what I do. Life is so much easier when things are normal. And stop looking at me like I just cut your throat, Annie. You'll know what I mean in a little while. You've got a newborn for the most part. It's fun visiting family and such right now. Everybody fights for the baby who's innocent and cuddly. Wait until he turns two and three and then you spend your moments at Moms' house telling him not to touch the TV or the stereo, to leave the plants alone, not to drop his food on the floor, and to stay out of rooms with closed doors. Then add three more..."

"Four more soon, remember, you've got another one coming," Angie added.

"Exactly!" Andie slapped her knee, startling baby Aimee. "You enjoy the visits, and you enjoy it when it's over."

"I just miss you guys so much," Annie tried to convince them.

"Ditto!" Andie exclaimed. "I miss you all too, but at this time in my life, I enjoy the reprieves as much as the non-reprieves."

"Look, we should make a deal," Angie decided. "Any time the three of us happen to be here at the same time, we need to get away, just the three of us, and spend an afternoon or an evening together."

"So we can have this same *encouraging* discussion?" Annie asked sarcastically.

"No, grumpy bottoms," Angie replied. "So we can catch up, share, remember, and move on. That's what *this* part of our family is for right now. You need to put on your positive panties and get a grip, sister."

SIXTY-NINE

On Christmas Eve, the family gathered around the fireplace for its annual *Wright Christmas Night*, as it was always called. In previous years, each family member had been required to do something creative in celebration of the holiday. This year, however, since the family had grown to encompass *families*, it was decided that each family could share its own presentation. Starting with youngest to the oldest, Alex and Megan did a silly reading of *'Twas the Night before Christmas*. Obviously, Megan had put a lot of time and thought into making it extremely entertaining. The family was nearly rolling with laughter, including the children, by the time they bid *all a good night*.

Next came Annie and Stephen, complete with Stevie dressed in a Santa suit, sans the beard. Everyone had expected them to do something spectacular musically seeing that every year all Annie ever did was play a Christmas song on the rickety piano in the great room. However, they opted for a rather silly skit and then finished by singing something a-cappella.

When it came time for Angie and Michael, they hadn't even considered silliness, as that had never been accomplished successfully before during a Wright Christmas Night. If anyone ever got too out of hand, Jonathan would always clear his throat and remind the group that this was a time of serious reflection and celebration of the birth of Christ. Angie made the mistake once, after a particular inane incident, of asking exactly how the words *celebrate* and *somber* could go together. What ensued was a long dissertation by her father on the depth of the Christmas story and its effect on the eternal outcome of each individual's life. By the time he had finished, no one really cared and all were ready for bed.

Angie and Michael got their guitars and sat together on the edge of the hearth.

"Well, this is a switch, isn't it?" she grinned as they settled in. "I should get special marks, Daddy, for being totally serious this time."

"I think all the marks go to Michael," Jonathan said with raised eyebrows. "Is this a year you'll actually do something appropriate."

"Very appropriate," she continued smiling. "Michael and I have worked up a carol to sing for you in Padawin. As usual, Michael will be doing all the good stuff; I'll just be following along behind him. If it happens to sound nice, he gets the credit."

Michael began by gently picking his guitar, creating a soft rhythm that easily allowed Angie to join in with a soothing strum. As the instruments went on, Michael began to sing:

Quiet night, holy night
All is peace, all is bright
See the maiden, mother and Son
Holy baby, so gentle and calm
Sleep in heavenly peace—sleep in heavenly peace.

Next was Angie's verse:

Quiet night, holy night
Son of God give us light
Shining beams from Your holy face
Rising dawn of Your paying grace
Jesus this is Your birth—Jesus this is Your birth.

Michael played a beautiful interlude before they sang the last verse together in harmony.

At first, the family sat in silence when the song was finished. Then Barbara began clapping with tears in her eyes. The rest joined. Everyone was still shocked by Angie's newfound expression of music. In fact, it was downright startling to watch her actually play an instrument and then sing along.

"I'm glad to see that the investment in the Ibanez wasn't wasted," Annie teased as the two stood with their guitars.

Next up was Andie's family, and they sang as well, several songs, and did motions to a few of them. Andie played the piano as Doug tried to remember the words. He was almost as entertaining as the children seeing that he was clueless for most of it. Ashley, along with Arly and Adam gave the performance their all and more than made up for Doug's confusion.

Jonathan then got up, a little teary, and proceeded to bring the evening to an end.

"This has been exceptionally nice," he said, a bit choked, "for many reasons. First, I didn't plan on having the whole family here this year. This is a first, four children, four spouses, all the grandchildren, and let me get this straight: there are three more on the way? Is that correct?"

Everyone nodded.

He narrowed his eyes toward Alex. "Son, you don't have any surprise baby announcement, do you?"

"No, sir," Alex replied immediately. "We're still trying to juggle just one."

"That's not juggling," Andie quipped. "That's coasting, little brother."

"We may have to build a bigger house if we keep this up," Jonathan grinned. "But this will be the last year we'll do this for awhile. Next year, Angie and Michael will most definitely be in Padawin. Alex and Megan, along with Stephen and Annie, who knows? But we're here together like this right now.

"I want to say to my daughters and my son, well done. Mine and your mother's wish for each of you was to live happily ever after and responsibly ever after. You're there. And as far as the spouses go, well, I was a little concerned with Doug at first." Doug's eyebrows flew up and the rest of the family chuckled. "A little bit of a rebel, he was," Jonathan laughed slightly. "I was highly concerned when he drove up here that first Sunday afternoon on his beat-up Suzuki asking if he could take Andie for a ride ... my sweet, innocent fifteen-year-old. Needless to say, Andie was *not* allowed to ride, but Doug did come to church with us. And after his willingness to follow her to church for months, I finally let her ride on the back of that loud jalopy. But Doug, you're a true son to this family, and I'm proud of the husband you've been to Andie and the father you've been to these children.

"But it doesn't stop there," Jonathan continued. "Megan, you've been around this family nearly as long as Doug. We wondered if Alex would ever marry you. But here you are, an integral part of his healing. If it hadn't been for you, I doubt seriously he'd even be with us today. But look at you both—happy, content, with an adorable baby girl. Thanks, Megan, for your love and commitment to my son. I owe so much more to you than I could ever say."

Megan mouthed a *thank-you* through her tears as she took Alex's hand. The rest of the family nodded.

"Now Stephen," Jonathan said slowly. Stephen grinned big as Annie slipped her arm through his. "What on earth can I say about you? Annie had been in love with you from the time she was sixteen. When you walked into our house that day, I knew the rest of the story. I mean, who could resist Annie's talent and beauty combined. Had she been only one or the other ... possibly? But she was a double whammy on you, old boy, and I fear you had no choice in the matter."

"You got that right," Stephen admitted. "She cast her spell on me that first morning when she broke her coffee mug on the floor."

"I'm just thankful she came to her senses before she lost you!" Angie added.

"Me too," Annie crooned.

Jonathan sighed deeply as he looked around the room at his family. His gaze stopped on Michael and Angie.

"Now, what do I say about you two?" Jonathan shook his head. "This has got to be the most bizarre thing I've ever seen in my life, but it's taught me something very important. I've always looked for God in the normal things, in the common things, in the things that *should* happen. Not that I didn't believe God stepped outside of my box sometimes, but what you two accomplished? The only explanation for that is God."

There were giggles from the room, but Angie and Michael took it seriously. They knew this wouldn't happen again for several years, and they wanted to take in every word he had to say.

"Michael," he said looking him in the eye, "you're an exceptional man. I wish I had known you years ago and could've been someone more important in your life. I'm so thankful for the Lovejoys and how they chose to take you in and move you past the struggles you were forced to face. I always knew that if Angie married, it would have to be someone extremely unique, someone out of the norm. I had no idea how *out of the norm*!"

More giggles ensued, but Angie took Michael's hand and continued to listen.

"The thing that amazes me about all of this is that from the outside looking in, we would've all thought Angie would've changed you. She's outgoing, outspoken, and extremely giving. And I confess that most of our first impressions, not all, were that you got a really good deal out of this marriage situation."

"I did," Michael spoke quickly.

"I know," Jonathan agreed, "but what you don't see is what you've given to Angie, what you've added to her life. I told her long ago that with her goals, or as she referred to them, her *callings*, it would be highly unlikely that she would ever find someone to share her life with. And the thing about Angie was she was so committed to those callings that she threw aside any hope for a husband and a family. I was impressed, but I was a bit sad … because all of this …," he motioned around the room at his family, "… this is what has given more meaning to my life on earth than anything else.

"Look at what this farm boy from Kansas did for my doctor," Jonathan said with a bit of emotion now. "You gave her love, a deep love, in ways no one else could give her because of your past. And that kind of love is the kind that makes Angie thrive. And you share her dreams with her. Who else in the entire world desired to go to the islands of Padawin and work with the tribes there? No one! Only the two of you. Your lives together could only be completed in each other.

"And now you're going to have a family. I always knew Angie would make a wonderful mother because she was the most nurturing of my four children. *What a waste*, I used to think, because if anyone needed to be a mother, it was she. But her call to missions was so strong that she was willing to sacrifice the joys of motherhood and family to see it happen.

"Michael," Jonathan addressed him personally now, "it could've been easy for you to have refused to open your heart to her. You've been through enough hurt in your life to last twenty lifetimes. I don't know if I could've given my heart away so easily."

"It wasn't that easy," Angie finally put in. "I wondered if he'd ever come around."

"How could I not?" Michael said to everyone. "Look, I fell for Angie the moment I saw her, but I spent the rest of my time telling myself I wasn't worthy of her."

"Well, you're worthy," Jonathan nodded. "Very worthy. And you also managed to accomplish something that none of the rest of us could: you got her to sing and play an instrument … in public!"

The family clapped in agreement.

"But I guess I stand most amazed at the love you two have developed and the complete admiration you have for each other. If I could've picked two people more perfect for a relationship, I couldn't have done better. Michael, thank-you for being the only possible man Angie could ever love. And Angie, thank-you for bringing this man into our lives. He's meant more to me than any of you will ever know. I look forward to watching you grow together over the years to come. I anticipate great things from your ministry, great things from your marriage, and great things from your family. However, I would like to add one thought here: don't feel like you have to compete with your sisters on child bearing—take your time."

"Oh, I intend to outdo them all!" Angie exclaimed, a bit teary from her father's proclamations. "We're gonna have at least ten, and try to get them here within nine years!"

"Let's hear her say that after the first one comes!" Doug called out.

The rest of the family expressed some thoughts and then Alex, Megan and Ansley left for Megan's home where they would be spending Christmas, and Andie and her family left for their home. Only Annie and Angie would be here the next morning. They had exchanged gifts that evening with those who would be elsewhere, but now everyone was leaving slowly and moving to their rooms for the night.

SEVENTY

After preparing to turn in for the night, Angie snuck a small gift from one of the drawers and waited patiently on the bed for Michael to emerge from the bathroom. When he did, she patted the bed next to her, hiding the gift behind her back. But Michael held up a finger as he went to one of the little apartment cabinets and produced a smaller gift himself.

"What are you doing?" she asked.

"I wanted to give you one special thing tonight ... with just the two of us," he told her.

"You're kidding? Me too." She pulled the gift from behind her.

He smiled as he sat down next to her and showed her his gift. "Wow," he sighed nervously. "I didn't expect a secret one from you."

"Ditto," Angie said excited, but then her expression became hesitant.

"What is it?"

"I'm a little nervous about whether my gift is appropriate or not."

"How could you give anything that would be inappropriate?"

"Well, as you learned tonight, I can be *very* inappropriate at times. But when I first thought of this, I imagined it would be perfect. I bought it off the Internet without even giving it a second thought, but then when it came, and I looked at it for awhile, I started thinking maybe I had done a bad thing."

"Angie," he said softly as he leaned over to kiss her cheek, "you could never do a *bad thing* to me."

"Well, we'll see," she said as she held it out to him.

He took it and shook it gently, then grinned as he carefully tore the paper from the package. "Other than the monkey, this will be the first Christmas gift I've gotten in ten years."

"You're way too slow at this."

"I'm making it last a long time."

When the paper was removed, a small, white box lay beneath. Michael glanced up at her curiously, and she bit her lip in anxiety. He opened it slowly and found another, velvety-covered jewelry box beneath.

"Hmmm," he smiled. "What have you done, Dr. Angie?"

He opened it at last and then stared at its contents. She shot a look at his face to see if she could read his expression. There was none, however; he just stared.

"I shouldn't have done it," she said with a sad sigh.

"No, it's wonderful," he reassured her. "It's totally wonderful."

"It's taken you back; I can tell," she countered now wishing she'd thought differently when she had bought it.

"Angie," he reached over and took her hand. "It really is wonderful. It's an incredible gift, a very thoughtful gift."

He reached into the box and removed the golden chain with the small, golden acoustic guitar attached. He held it up to the light and examined it more closely. "This is much nicer than the one my mother got me."

"It holds a two-fold meaning, Michael," she said to him as she slid over closer. "Part of it has to do with your mother. Knowing that I'm about to be a mom myself leaves me with this empty feeling when I think about the fact that there's nothing you have in your life to remind you of her. I understand completely why you put the necklace in her casket, but if I'd been your mother, I would've wanted you to keep something to remember me by. So, as one mother thinking about another, I did this for her ... and for you. Your mother represented the ultimate sacrifice of parental love. Your memories of her are only goodness and kindness. You need to hold those close when our baby comes so you can remember how right it felt as a child to receive those things from her."

"Thank you," he said softly as he leaned up and kissed her forehead tenderly. "I'll treasure this always. I mean it. You couldn't have given me a more thoughtful or *appropriate* gift."

"The other meaning," she smiled from relief that he seemed genuinely appreciative of the necklace, "has to do with me."

"Okay, I like the sound of that too. Explain," he said as he offered her the necklace to put around his neck.

As she opened the clasp and attached the ends of the sparkling chain, she told him, "When we were married, I gave you a ring. At that time I had no idea how I'd fall for you so deeply. It was just a ring, oh, I don't know, of *commitment* I guess. It was really nothing more than that."

She turned him toward her and adjusted the chain and the charm. She smiled at the result, and then looked at his face. "I wanted you to have something personal with you that would remind you of *me*," she said as she reached up and touched the charm again. "I know that in your mind you see me as this person who came in and sort of whisked you off your feet and changed your fate for the better, but you need to know what you've done for me. I mean ... I always imagined somewhere out there was someone I could love, care for, and raise a family with, but as the years went by, I felt more and more alienated from that dream. Few men treated me with any respect; they were always so crude and suggestive. Even one guy in seminary acted like the first date was a sign up for a make-out session. I was frustrated, humiliated, and as time went on, and no one shared my call to Padawin, I felt even more hopeless.

"When we met that first day in Hawaii, I never dreamed that all of *this* would actually happen. I was just hoping that we would get along and become great friends. But as each day went by, and you treated me like a queen, like I was special and worthy of respect, not because I was a doctor, but because I was a woman—no one had ever done that before. You appreciated me for being exactly who I was. You made me feel like I not only belonged in Padawin, but also like I belonged with you. When you told me you loved me that first time on Mount Sheshney, my heart nearly exploded. I couldn't believe we had found each other."

"Me either," he admitted as he reached up and moved a strand of hair from her face. "You were like a breath of life that blew into my arid, dried-up existence."

"And even *that*, Michael, is wonderful to me ... that I'm more than just some girl who happened upon you. I'm someone whom you can trust and love, and you're someone that I can help heal in so many ways."

"And you have healed me, Angie."

"I know, and you can't imagine how much that means to me. My heart was drawn to you the moment I saw you in the airport holding that silly sign."

He grinned and shook his head in embarrassment.

"But I didn't know how far it would go," she explained. "So, now, I wanted to give you something that meant more than just *I'm committing myself to you so I can go to Padawin*. I thought about another ring, or a watch, or a bracelet, but then, I thought about how many nights we spent out on the deck playing our guitars and singing, writing songs and talking in between, and suddenly I knew what I wanted for you. This," she reached up to touch the charm again, "represents a part of my life that I hid in many ways because I had this incredibly talented family. I didn't *hate* music or even music lessons. I just got tired of hearing, *You're not quite as gifted as your sisters, are you?*"

"No one said that," he said in disbelief.

"Oh, yes. Our piano teacher," she replied. "She accused me of not practicing, but when everyone affirmed to her that I indeed did practice, that's when she told me I just didn't have it like the others. That hurt. My best defense was to push it aside, bury it down, and move in another direction."

"But you're very talented," he assured her. "You've learned so much on the guitar, and your voice is almost angelic."

"I agree," she admitted for the first time in her life. "But, the truth is, I'm not on the same level as my sisters nor my brother. I think we can agree on that."

"Somewhat, but neither am I."

"But look what you've done with me," she said softly. "You actually had me playing and singing before my family. No one could've ever done that. You bring out the very best in me, Michael, and I want a part of me to be with you always. Thus … the necklace."

He took her hand and gently rubbed it inside his own. He kissed her tenderly and then pulled out his gift. "Your turn," he told her. "I don't know if I can give as flowery a description of why I'm giving you this as you did for mine. I hope the gift itself says it all."

Angie grinned and took the smaller box from him. She didn't take her time as Michael had. She ripped off the paper to find a small box.

"Jewelry also," she grinned bigger. She lifted the lid, and this time she was the one staring in shock. "Oh, heavens … Michael … it's so beautiful … so elaborate," she said as she stared at the diamond engagement ring.

He slid from the bed to the floor and took her hand.

"I never want to have any regrets with you," he told her. "But I do wonder sometimes what might've happened had we met somewhere other than Padawin. I would want to believe that we would have fallen in love, as deeply as we are now, but I can't know that. Yet it's like you said, our wedding rings, though symbols of commitment, they don't really symbolize what developed between us. This ring is my way of saying that I love you, that I would've wanted to marry you at some other time or some other place, and that if I had to do it all over again, I would in a minute. So," he stayed on one knee, "I want to ask you to be my wife forever, officially, and give you this ring as a symbol of that."

She couldn't help it; tears were filling her eyes and beginning to roll down the sides of her face. She couldn't decide whether to take out the ring and place it on her finger or take him in her arms and hold him close. She finally joined him on her knees, holding him tight with her head on his shoulder.

"My answer is *yes*," she said tenderly in his ear. "I would marry you anytime, anywhere, even on the moon if I had to."

She pulled back and reached into the box to take out the ring. She carefully placed it on her finger and then held it up for him to see. He smiled then leaned in to kiss her again. She moved her arms around his neck and pulled her body close.

"Merry Christmas, Dr. Collins," she whispered.

"Indeed, Dr. Angie."

*****

Christmas morning was laid back and easy without Andie and the kids, but Angie missed the noise and clamor that was the norm. This was the first year Andie and Doug had asked to stay home on Christmas morning with their own family. Angie understood. She would want that also if she had four kids. But Christmas without children was somehow not the same. As they exchanged gifts, everyone taking their individual turn, Angie couldn't help but tell everyone it was horribly boring.

"Well then," Annie responded, "since you're feeling so *grumpy*, I suggest we spice things up a bit. What do you think, Stephen?"

"Absolutely," he grinned. "Be right back."

"What *are* you two up to?" Angie wondered. "I smell a plan here."

"Exactly," Annie told her. "Sit back and relax, sister dear. Or better yet, how 'bout you put on *your* positive panties?"

Stephen went up to Annie's bedroom and returned with a guitar case. Angie and Michael watched as he came down the stairs, and were shocked when Stephen handed it to Michael.

"For me?" Michael asked.

"Open it up and take a peek inside," Stephen told him.

Michael unbuckled the hard shell case and discovered an Ibanez guitar, exactly like Angie's, except it was blue.

"Unreal," Michael breathed in complete dismay. "Are you serious? This is for me?"

"Angie told us how you salivated over hers," Annie explained. "We couldn't resist. Besides, you deserve it. Anyone who could get Angie to play and sing in public should get some kind of major reward."

"It wasn't *that* hard," Michael insisted. "At least not *Ibanez guitar* hard."

Jonathan cleared his throat and added, "I beg to differ. I don't know what that thing cost, but it's worth it for what you managed to accomplish."

Michael looked at Angie sitting next to him and winked. She smiled adoringly and let him know she understood his thoughts. No one else knew about the critical piano teacher that had destroyed her confidence in music. He actually felt honored that she had shared something with him that she had never shared with anyone else. She trusted him, like she trusted Annie, and that was a huge thing.

"Isn't there something more?" Annie asked as she stood up and handed Stevie to Barbara who had been begging for him all morning.

"Oh, yeah," Stephen said as he grinned again. "You gonna help me, Annie?"

"Absolutely!"

When they returned they literally wheeled in several Gateway boxes stacked on top of a red wagon.

"Computer?" Angie asked. "We have computers."

"Not like this, you don't, sister."

Stephen explained, "This is a top of the line media processing unit. You can put pictures and videos on here and edit them any way you want. Plus, and this is so cool, it has a multi track recording studio, recording equipment included, so you can record your songs while sitting out on that big back deck you talk about all the time. We've included high quality cameras, both video and still, so when Junior comes along we get to see his life chronicled on a regular basis via the internet."

Angie frowned. "And you think we're gonna know how to run this stuff?"

"I've got several days left here with the engineering genius," Stephen reminded her. "I guarantee you he can start his own TV station by the time I finish with him."

Barbara applauded with excitement. "This is wonderful! We can see your life over there and your baby and all those marvelous people you've told us about!"

"Michael?" Angie asked dubiously. "Do you think you can do this? I don't even want to try."

"No problem," he assured her. "I never attempted it before because I had no reason to. I have many reasons now." He turned to Stephen. "Thank you ... sincerely. I wish I had something comparable to give in return."

"Just make sure Angie keeps in touch with Annie. They're like lifelines for each other. Annie starts panicking when she doesn't hear from her. Make her contact her at least once a week."

"Will do," Michael told him.

*****

Michael collapsed into bed that night, not sure if it was from exhaustion or from eating so much turkey that he actually had to undo his belt.

"I think you've put on a little weight since we've been here," Angie said as she snuggled up in the bed next to him.

"If I didn't before, I can guarantee I did today. Am I getting pudgy down there?"

Angie felt his tummy and then tickled him slightly. "I believe I feel the beginnings of a *love handle*," she teased.

"Good. I'll be matched for when you start getting there. It wouldn't be fair for you to gain all the weight with this baby."

"I feel sorry for you. I probably starved you those months I fed you in Padawin."

"Are you kidding?" he exclaimed. "I ate better than I had in years! Shoot—than in my whole life!"

"But I didn't cook in large amounts. You've eaten here like I've never seen anyone eat before."

"Trust me, you cooked just fine, amounts and all. Besides, your mother always cooks so much food. I just assumed she meant for it all to be eaten."

"Are you telling me that if I cook a ton of food you'll eat a ton of food?" She got up and leaned over him, her hair falling down onto his face.

"I'll do anything you want me to do," he said as he reached up and pulled her to him.

"We ought to get along just fine then Dr. Collins."
"Agreed, Dr. Angie."

SEVENTY-ONE

"So, Stephen Williams' wife, Annie, is *your* sister?" Vicki Clarence asked Angie again as they loaded the helicopter in Taveren.

"Yep," she said out of breath from walking back and forth with various boxes of medicines and personal items.

"Do you sing too?" Vicki wondered.

She smiled to herself and answered, "Yep."

"Play piano?"

"Barely. I took a few lessons. I'm more of a guitar person."

Michael loaded the last of the larger boxes and secured the computer equipment to ensure it wouldn't slide around during the final leg of their return to Podakind.

"Will they make it safely?" Angie asked him as she wiped a drop of sweat from his brow.

"The odds are in our favor," he winked at her. "Feels good to sweat again."

"Tell me about it," Chet said as he walked by with another box. "Ya'll didn't even get snow. Try dealing with two kids and a bunch of wet snow."

"Our turn's coming," Michael said as he grabbed another box from the ground and followed behind Chet.

"Take your time. Enjoy some years alone together first. Watching you two tends to make Vicki and I long for the old days a little bit."

"Too late," Michael grinned.

"Too late for what?" Chet asked as he set the box down in the helicopter.

"Angie's pregnant."

Chet turned around quickly and dropped his jaw. "No way," he said with a slight laugh.

"Due in July."

"You're serious! Well, I'm in complete shock! You guys didn't waste any time. Stephen and Angie's sister had a baby pretty quickly too, didn't they? They talked about their baby at the concert, but I thought they only got married last Christmas."

"Nine months later, here came little Stevie," Michael told him as they walked back to where the boxes were stacked. "He's adorable."

They continued loading until the chopper was packed full. Angie expressed concern that perhaps it was too weighted down, but the pilot assured her that this particular vehicle was used for transporting ammunition and that her few boxes of meager medicines wouldn't cause it to even bobble. After an excited farewell to the Clarences, Angie and Michael boarded and buckled themselves in. As they took off, she felt her stomach flop in the quick ascension.

"You okay?" Michael yelled into the helmet's microphone as he took her hand.

"Little queasy."

"Your blood pressure okay? Still monitoring it?"

"Yes, doctor," she said with a smile. "But this whole flying thing is still new to me."

"I want you to see something as soon as we clear this big hill," he told her pointing to her side window. "Keep your eyes peeled right over there."

She stared out as her stomach continued to churn. When they finally rose above the hill, her stomach flipped this time from awe. "Is that Podakind?" she asked nearly breathless from the sight.

"Yes. Awesome, isn't it?"

"I had no idea you could see it from this far."

"It's nearly 15,000 feet. You could see it from anywhere on the islands if it weren't for all the mountains, hills and trees … well, and the almost ever-present clouds."

"Heavens, Michael, I think I'm gonna throw up."

"Really?" he asked again in concern. "Should I get something for you? A bag or something?"

"Let me sit back and close my eyes for a moment."

She leaned back in the seat and continued to squeeze his hand. The view of Podakind was so overwhelming, coupled with the quickness of the ascent that she was struggling to keep her balance emotionally and physically.

"Do you have a cold drink in that cooler?" Michael asked the pilots.

"Yes, Brother Mike. Several."

"May I take one for Angie? She's not feeling well."

"Of course. Take as many as you like."

He reached into the cooler and pulled out a Sprite. Rubbing it around her face and neck first to help cool her off, he then opened it for her to drink.

"Thanks," she smiled. "I'm feeling a little better now."

She opened her eyes and glanced around Padawin again. She marveled at all the peaks beneath her. "How many volcanoes are out here? I obviously paid no attention to any of this when we left the island."

"We didn't leave this way," he reminded her. "We headed straight out over the ocean toward Port Moresby."

"Volcanoes do worry me a little bit."

"Didn't we already have this discussion about living amidst the *Ring of Fire?*"

408

"That whole name is a bit foreboding. Couldn't they come up with something less ominous?"

He laughed and grabbed her hand again. She was feeling better.

"This is very different," he said as he glanced around the familiar sights of his home for ten years.

"What is?"

"Coming home with you here," he told her as he looked back. "I've made this trip countless times, always alone, always going back to dig in for more of the same. But everything feels so different this time."

"That's because everything *is* so different."

"Tell me about it. Incredible wife, baby on the way, said goodbye to a family back home; it's almost too good to be true."

"It's different for me too. When I came here last time, via the Land Rover, of course, I was so nervous. I didn't know what you thought of me, what the people would think of me, if I would fit in, if things would work out. I was just going on faith that the God who called me here would be the God who would settle me here."

"And settle you, He most certainly did. In my heart first of all."

"Ditto."

The six-hour trip by Land Rover was hard to remember as they approached Podakind by air in only thirty minutes. As the helicopter came nearer to the village, they grew more excited at the familiar sites.

"There's Sheshney," he pointed out.

"Fond memories there," she winked.

"Ditto," he laughed. "Look at the fields! Good heavens! They've kept them in perfect shape."

"I guess you taught them well."

"I guess. And with Sojay and Joshua leading the Bible studies and the rest of the men keeping the fields up like that, they don't even need me anymore."

"Ah, but they still need me. You can watch the baby while I work."

"Yeah, I'll be known now as *Brother Mom* instead of *Brother Mike.*"

She laughed hard at that statement. He was a completely different man than when she had come here with him the first time. Six months had changed both their lives in ways they could never have imagined.

"Oh, man!" he exclaimed. "Look at the people!"

"They're coming to greet us! Look how pretty the colors are."

"They knew we were coming. They're dressed in their celebration clothes."

"They couldn't know. They must be celebrating something else."

"No, that's for us," he said firmly. "They've been waiting out there for us."

"Did someone tell the people we would be coming back today?"

Michael asked the pilots.

"Most certainly," one responded. *"When the rebellion was over, your board sent many supplies that Doctor Angie had ordered. We came and brought them and spoke of your return."*

"So they knew we got Geechern's letter," Angie smiled. "And her grandfather got his Pepto-Bismol."

The helicopter began to descend, and the people were waving like crazy. Some of the children even danced around. As it came to a stop and the blades shut down, everyone surrounded it. Angie and Michael removed their helmets, unbuckled themselves and stepped out to a cheering crowd. They both waved, and immediately the children approached and hugged them as a group. Angie spotted Geechern and motioned her over.

"How has your medicine gone?" Angie asked her as she hugged her tightly.

"Very well," Geechern smiled at her. *"There are so many things I still do not know how to help. People would come and I would tell them, 'You will have to wait for Dr. Angie. I just do not know.'"*

"We will have many bunnies to learn by," Angie told her. *"In time you will know more than you could have ... hmmm ... I don't know the word I'm searching for."*

Geechern laughed heartily and said, *"And maybe I will give you lessons on speaking some!"*

Sojay and Joshua approached. They first embraced Michael and then Angie. She felt her heart would burst with joy. Her stomach was churning again at all the excitement. The pregnancy was obviously beginning to have some effect on her. She would need to check her blood pressure as soon as she could get into the clinic.

Sojay's wife, Mosheed, made her way to Angie and just held her and cried a few moments. *"We have needed you back so badly. Our women are hungry to know God now and His freedom, but Geechern and I know so little. Sometimes Geechern just reads from the Word because we know nothing else to do."*

"You have honored God with your obedience," Angie told her. *"You have planted many seeds while we have been away. God will bless you for what you have done."*

Angie spotted Seendoo and Kartushah with their baby. Both mom and babe were definitely healthy. She walked over to them and took the little one.

"We have so wanted to thank you for saving Seendoo's life and the life of our child," Kartushah said humbly. *"We are indebted to you. Please always ask us for anything you need."*

"You are not indebted to me," Angie said gently. *"God brought me here. He prepared me to come here for many years. You owe Him."*

"Then we will honor Him," Kartushah vowed.

The men of the village began to help unload the supplies as Michael directed which went to the clinic and which went to the house.

When they finally walked inside their house, they were warmed by the welcome the people had prepared. The ladies had woven a new spread for their bed. The refrigerator was stocked with many foods, and fresh flowers had been placed on every single table around the room. As people brought in their boxes and bags, they insisted Michael and Angie sit and relax. She obliged, but he couldn't remain still.

Geechern came over to Angie at one point and asked, *"You look pale. Can I get something to help you?"*

"Some juice might be needful for now," Angie told her, thankful for the offer.

She returned with a glass of juice and sat next to her. *"You are not right,"* Geechern said to her. *"Have you been sick?"*

"Not really, at least not until today. I'm ... uh ... there I go again. I don't know the right word. I'm going to have a baby."

Geechern squealed in delight and hugged her again. *"You are pregnant then!"* She exclaimed as she gave the proper Padawin term.

"Pregnant?" Angie asked as she rolled her eyes. *"Oh, no—that sounds too much like cows. Does it come from that word?"*

"Actually, yes. Please try and learn the right word so you do not tell people here that you are a herd of cows!"

"I will try!"

As the day moved on, the villagers began to gather at the pavilion with many foods and presents to celebrate the return. Angie could tell the excitement was getting to her so she sneaked inside the clinic to take her blood pressure. It was slightly elevated. She didn't want to take the medicine, but high blood pressure was more dangerous to both she and the baby than the medicine itself. She walked back into the house and began to rummage through boxes to find it.

"Are you okay?" Michael asked as he came inside looking for her. "I wondered where you went."

"I felt weird again, so I checked my blood pressure. It's a little high."

He rushed to her and insisted she sit down. "Tell me what you need and I'll find it," he insisted. "Don't push yourself here, Angie. Let me tell the people that you're pregnant and that you're having a little trouble. They'll understand."

"No way! I'll be fine. I think the excitement, the flying, as well as the time changes have contributed. Apparently, I'm going to need to take it easy during the next few months. It may calm down too as the pregnancy progresses."

"Listen to me, Angie," he said seriously as he sat beside her, "don't do anything to risk your life or the baby's. If you need to stay inside and lie down for the whole nine months, that's fine. Please take it easy."

She reached up and caressed his cheek. "I'll be fine, Michael. I'll be careful too. I promise."

*****

Later in the evening, after everyone had eaten and danced and sang, Michael and Angie were about to excuse themselves so she could go inside and rest, but Sojay stopped them and asked them to stay a while longer.

"I must tell of something that we want you to know," Sojay said to them. *"You came here to share Christ with us, but you have become much more than that. When you were gone for so long, we came to know that you were not separate from us, but part of us. You belong to our village. We are glad you went to see your old families, but your family is here now. We can farm without you, Brother Mike, but we still need to know so much about our God. We missed your teaching, but more than that, we missed your spirit.*

"I would also like to say that Dr. Angie became a part of us so quickly, that when she left, we grieved in our hearts for her. Her medicine is good, but her life is better. Dr. Angie, you gave us a new spirit here, and you were badly missed. If you could not even heal, we would still love you and need you. But we are glad for your medicine too!"

Everyone clapped at this proclamation.

"We also are thankful to God for Dr. Angie being Brother Mike's partner. We were so sad for him because like Adam, there was not a helper made for him. But when Dr. Angie came, Brother Mike was made complete. Brother Mike did much for our village, but when you two came together, you completed our village. This celebration is more than just to welcome you home; it is to officially make you a part of our tribe."

The people now stood to their feet and began to chant, *"You with us and us with you, we are one,"* over and over again.

Michael was moved to tears. He had been here for ten years but had always been an outsider. When teenage girls and boys were old enough, they went through this very chant and ritual to be considered official members of the Podakind tribe. Now the tribe was performing this for them. He took her hand and pulled her next to him as the tribe surrounded them both. They danced, sang and chanted more. Michael interpreted the various symbolisms that were being expressed.

"Are you doing okay?" he asked as he leaned into her ear so she could hear him.

She nodded. He didn't look convinced, so she pulled his ear to her lips and said, "The medicine worked. Everything is fine."

He gently kissed her and went back to clapping with the singing.

When all was through and they were officially citizens of the tribe,

Michael asked if he could speak. Sojay got everyone's attention.

"Our Brother Mike wants to speak to us, but I have a question I must ask him on behalf of the tribe," Sojay said with a mischievous grin. *"We cannot help but see that you have lost the brown of your skin, but also gained weight in your middle. Did you not do any work in America? Did you just eat over there? And even Dr. Angie is looking pale. You should not leave us again like this! It is not good for you!"*

The tribe laughed again as Michael nodded his head slightly in embarrassment. Angie laughed also as he squinted his eyes in self-consciousness, something he hadn't done for quite some time.

"I see what you are saying here," Michael began as he patted his slightly bulging tummy. *"First, it was way too cold to work outside over there. You cannot grow food when there is ice in the ground. Instead, I sat in a warm house by a fire and ate, ate, ate."*

Everyone laughed again.

"The sun hardly shines there," he continued. *"It would get dark early in the afternoon. Nothing could keep my skin brown. But as for Dr. Angie, you must all know something."*

He reached out his hand and motioned for her to join him. She came up and put her arm around his waist.

"She did not get fat, but she will very soon," Michael told them all. *"We are having a baby."*

At this the crowd began to scream as it came to its feet again. She leaned into him and rested her head on his shoulder. He knew she had gone her limit. He put up his hand to quiet the wild group. Slowly they settled down to listen to his final words.

"Angie is having a little trouble with her pregnancy," he explained to them. *"She will need to rest more than she did before."*

The people nodded.

"She has good medicine to take, but there will be times that she needs to lie down and take it easy. It is not good for her to get too excited."

"And you are telling us this now?" Mosheed said in disgust. *"We would not have gone on so long if we had known this! Shame on you, Brother Mike!"*

"I did not realize ..." he began, but Angie cut him off.

"I am okay," she said strongly. *"I have only moments of not being good. I have traveled a long time, and right now is my morning from where I came from. It is like I have been awake all night and not had any sleep. When I finally do rest, and my nights and bunnies are back to normal, I will be much better."*

Michael smiled at her continued misuse of the word *day*. He had now begun to hope that she would never actually learn the difference. It was just one of the many things about her that he found endearing.

"Then you must go and sleep," Joshua said as he approached the couple. **"And we will not line up at your clinic until you have rested enough to help yourself."**

"Thank you, Joshua," Michael said as he extended his arm in a handshake.

Joshua offered up a final prayer of thanksgiving for their safe return, and then he prayed for the health of Angie and the baby to come. She was so tired that she struggled to stay on her feet. Michael held her tightly as she leaned on him, and as soon as the prayer was finished, he escorted her home.

Back in the house, he helped her prepare for bed and then tucked her in, lying beside her and smiling at her beauty. She smiled back but closed her eyes wearily.

"It's nice to be home," she murmured as she took in the comfort and familiarity of their own bed.

"I've got a question for you," he said.

"Will I have to think very hard?"

"I doubt it. How long before you start showing? You know, when will we begin to see the baby growing?"

"A long time—probably around five months. Why?"

"I was just wondering," he grinned as he moved a strand of hair from her face. "I don't want to be fat all by myself."

She laughed and rolled to her side. "You're not fat. Besides, once you get back out in those fields, plowing and working cattle, you'll take those few extra pounds right off."

"Put me on a diet," he told her instead. "No more fried chicken."

"You're not fat, Michael. You're healthy."

"I'll tell *you* that when you're rolling out of bed at nine months."

"Please do," she said as she reached up and gently ran her hand down the side of his face.

Within minutes she was asleep. Michael cuddled up next to her and marveled at his life at this moment. It was more than he could have ever asked or imagined. And yet, in one sense, this was all only the beginning. He couldn't help as tears begin to brim in his eyes while watching her sleep. His own body was tired, but his heart was full. He began to pray and thank God for all He had done, and as he did, he was able to finally release his past to the Lord. It felt good to let go of the grudges, the regrets, the misery and the pain. God was indeed good, and he felt a twinge of guilt at having waited all these years to admit it fully.

SEVENTY-TWO

It took Angie several more days than before to get her body back on schedule from the time change. She struggled a little with morning sickness, but it was never debilitating. She didn't consider it necessary to mention to Michael. Her blood pressure did stabilize, and she felt she could probably stay off of the medication as long as she didn't over exert herself or get too excited about anything. She and Geechern stocked the clinic, but she spent most of her time sitting on the deck taking in the view of Podakind, the river, and the ocean, while picking her guitar, reading a book, or translating the book of Joshua into Padawin.

Michael jumped back in full force. He worked on weeding the ground with the men and then began to prepare another section for a new crop. They harvested several of the fields and vaccinated the cattle and chickens. By the end of their first week, he had a fairly severe sunburn, and Angie felt like they had settled into the old routine: she was taking care of him again rather than the other way around.

Neither did she stop with the fried chicken. On Friday evening she prepared two of the tiny birds for them to eat: one for the evening and one for a trip up Mount Sheshney on Saturday. Michael didn't complain about the food as he was starving by the time evening rolled around. And when she pulled out a hidden chocolate cake from the cupboard, he didn't hesitate on the large piece she brought him out on the deck. When they had finished their cake, he suggested they get out their guitars and play. She agreed wholeheartedly and they spent nearly two hours making their own kind of music, laughing and talking about how wonderful it was to be where they belonged.

"You seem to be much better than the first day," he said as he took her guitar and locked it up inside the case.

"I am. The rest did me some good, but I'm looking forward to getting back to the clinic on Monday."

"You *will* take it easy, won't you? Promise me."

"Promise," she smiled.

He left with the guitars, placed them in the corner of the room, and then returned to the deck to join her in the swing.

"Does the swinging make you nauseous?" he wondered.

"No."

"So, only mornings do?"

She looked at him in surprise. "What makes you think I'm nauseous in the mornings?"

"I can tell," he said putting his arm around her and pulling her beside him. "You're pale, you don't eat much at all, and I've seen you several times prop yourself beside the counter with your hand on your tummy."

"Very observant, you are." She sighed in contentment. "I can't believe I don't miss my family. I almost feel guilty about it."

"You shouldn't. This is your family now. Remember? That's what they told us when they inducted us into the tribe."

"I'll miss my family when the baby comes."

"Me too. I really grew to love your family."

"It was mutual," she smiled as she took his free hand and held it to her belly. "I can't wait to feel it move."

"Me either. Whenever it happens, you'd better stop whatever you're doing and call me right away. I'll die if I'm not there."

"You got it."

They sat in silence, gently swinging back and forth for a while. The moon was bright, the night was warm, and the river was rushing by. Michael gently rubbed her shoulder as she snuggled her head deeper into his neck. This had to be paradise, or at least as close to it as one could get on planet Earth.

*****

The hike up Mount Sheshney was slow and easy. Michael had been concerned it might be too much for her now, but she insisted all would be well if they took their time and remained hydrated. When they finally reached the summit, he tried to make her sit and rest immediately.

"Not yet. Let's get a picture of the two of us up here. We can set the camera up on a rock and then do the timer. I want to frame this."

"Why?" he asked as he ran his hand through his sweaty hair. "We look rough." He then looked over at her as she removed her ponytail and shook out her long hair. "*I* look rough, that is. You look incredible."

"This is where we first declared our love for each other. Remember?"

"Do I ever," he grinned as he pulled her over to him briskly. "That is a day that will go down in Collins history. Do we tell our kids about that when they ask how we fell in love?"

"Goodness, I don't know *what* we'll tell our kids about our unique romance. But right now, let's get a picture."

They took the shot and then set up the picnic. He dug into the fried chicken, potato salad and fruit salad. She laughed as he commented about getting fatter and fatter if she didn't stop.

"If you cook it, I'm going to eat it," he insisted. "Look at you! You're pregnant and gorgeous! By the time you start showing, you're going to have to roll *me* out of bed!"

She laughed and leaned over to kiss him. "I don't care. You're still adorable! Your cheeks are even getting chubby. I just want to pinch them sometimes."

"I'd prefer kisses."

She wiped her hands on a towel and crawled next to him. "I'll gladly oblige that, Dr. Collins," she teased as she planted a long one on his lips.

"There you go," he grinned as he pulled her down to the ground with him. "You've just hit on the one thing I'd rather do than eat."

*****

When the clinic opened on Monday, the line was enormous. Apparently the other tribes knew Angie would be back in business this day. Michael was concerned she might overdo it and get overworked or overstressed causing her blood pressure to shoot up again.

"Don't worry, Dr. Collins," she said sweetly as she kissed him goodbye. "If our *workout* on the top of Sheshney didn't faze me, I'm guessing I can handle today just fine."

He blushed as he shook his head and opened the door to leave for the fields.

"See you at lunch," she called out.

"Yes, doctor."

Angie and Geechern worked nonstop until lunch. Michael had to insist she take a break and eat something. She agreed, knowing now that her habits affected the baby also. He made grilled cheese sandwiches for them while she lay down to rest. He was glad he had insisted because by the time lunch was ready, she was asleep. He brought a sandwich and a glass of milk to the couch and gently roused her.

"I thought you said you wouldn't take it too hard," he said as he helped her sit up.

"I didn't think I had. Apparently I worked harder than I thought."

"Should you call it a day?"

"Not today. Let me see everybody. Then, if it looks like a whole day will be too much, I can start setting some stricter hours. This probably won't last past the first trimester anyway."

"But what if it does?"

"Then we'll deal with it one day at a time."

Angie was right. Within the next couple of weeks her strength and stamina returned. She was tired at night and complained about having to get up so much to go to the restroom, but her body seemed to have settled into the pregnancy fine. Her blood pressure hadn't surged since their first week back, and the morning sickness left also. She was free to live as she had before they left.

*****

One evening as they sat on the back deck, thunder rolling in the distance, he told her he had something special for her. He went inside and got his guitar. Pulling up a chair in front of her on the swing, he smiled his sheepish smile.

"What are you doing, Dr. Collins," she asked curiously.

"Finishing something I started years ago."

He began gently picking the blue Ibanez, and Angie immediately recognized the song: *Spring Dawn*. He had played it for her one of their first nights together. It was the song he had written about Padawin and how it had changed his life. She thought it beautiful, but every time he sang it he complained about it not being finished.

"Did you finish it?" she whispered to him.

He nodded and began to sing.

The bitter cold is painful
The winter seems so long
For all my life I've shivered
I've always been alone
But suddenly the sun has come and opened wide my heart
And suddenly the cold I've known is melting all apart

I can almost see the dawn as I watch the sun arise
And the mountain calls my name as this place makes me alive
And the winter that has chained my restless soul for much too long
Has suddenly begun to fade as I see the new spring dawn

My heart has always wanted
To simply just belong
But no one ever held me
I sang my songs alone
But suddenly the sun has come and warmed this side of life
And suddenly the cold I've known has vanished with the night

I can almost see the dawn as I watch the sun arise
And the mountain calls my name as this place makes me alive
And the winter that has chained my restless soul for much too long
Has suddenly begun to fade as I see the new spring dawn

I waited as I waded through what seemed like wasted years
But when your eyes found mine I left behind the painful tears
You held me and you healed me, you breathed life into my soul
And the story that is now my life would never have been told
Had you not opened up your own

I can almost see the dawn as I watch the sun arise
And the mountain calls my name as this place makes me alive
And the winter that has chained my restless soul for much too long
Has suddenly begun to fade as I see the new spring dawn
You have touched my heart and you are my new spring dawn.

He finished the last few bars and then glanced up at her in his shy way. She was tearful again because she knew this song was now about her. She moved his guitar to the deck floor and then straddled his lap. She held his head to her chest for a long time as she let herself cry. This was one part of the pregnancy that she was struggling with: the emotions. When they surfaced, they were strong, and right now she felt overwhelmed.

"Are you okay?" he asked softly.

"I'm wonderful," she choked out. "I just can't believe you turned that song around to be about me."

"It was always about you," he whispered, "I just never knew it."

"It was about Podakind."

"No, it was about moving beyond my past. I moved beyond it in some ways, but never completely, not until you came into my life. Angie, I sometimes wonder how I ever made it without you. How did I find the strength to get up every morning and face the day not having you here?"

"I'm here now," she breathed out as she began to calm down, "and I always will be."

"I'm banking on that, but you know what? As hard as it would be to lose you, my life has been so much richer having had you in it. If something did happen, I could still go on, Angie. You've changed me ... forever."

"I don't know if I could, Michael," she said getting emotional again. "I couldn't lose you ... I just couldn't."

"Honey," he pulled himself into her chest again, "let's not go there. We've been through so much just to get here. We take one day at a time ... okay? We wake up glad simply for another day together."

She nodded and calmed her thoughts as she held on to him. As hard as it had been to leave her family that first time to come to Padawin, she had left eagerly this last time. She felt connected to him in a way that she never had with her own family. She considered the scripture that talked of a woman leaving her home to become one flesh with her husband. She understood it now. Michael was a part of her as no one ever had been. Being with him made her feel complete in a way that she could never have imagined before. And the realization that she carried their child drew her even deeper into his world.

"Better?" he asked as he pulled away again.

She nodded and stood up, pulling him up with her. She put her arms around his waist and drew him close again. "I made cake," she said with a smile as she leaned back to catch his response.

"Did you now?" he grinned.

"Want some?"

"Are you eating with me?"

"It seems I'm always eating lately."

"Me too," he sighed.

"Have a seat and I'll bring some out."

Thunder rolled again, a little closer.

"Maybe we should go in," he suggested.

She nodded, took his hand as he picked up the guitar, and dragged him inside. As she cut two slices of chocolate cake, he put on a Stephen Williams CD. "I can't wait for their next album to come out," he said as he shoved a huge bite of cake inside his mouth.

"Me either. Wait until you hear some of the songs she's written."

"Do they compare to *Winter Passion*?"

"Oh, yeah."

"You preacher's daughters are something else," he chuckled. "All this hidden passion oozing from everywhere."

She raised her eyebrows and asked, "Are you complaining?"

He laughed and shook his head. "Not for *one* minute. I rather like the passion!"

"Just checking," she grinned as she slid over next to him on the couch.

Autumn Sunset began to play on the stereo, and Michael sat down his cake along with Angie's. He pulled her up from the couch.

"What are we doing?" she asked as he moved her into his arms.

"Dancing again. We need to practice for the next tour."

Rather than dance to *Autumn Sunset*, she went over and turned off the stereo, but she came back and took him in her arms again.

"Depressing song," she told him. "You sing to me instead. I move much better to your music anyway. Stephen can sing his songs for Annie; you sing your songs for me."

Michael pulled her down into a dip and began to hum as he pulled her back up. He then began to gently sing.

I can almost see the dawn as I watch the sun arise
And the mountain calls my name as this place makes me alive
And the winter that has chained my restless soul for much too long
Has suddenly begun to fade as I see the new spring dawn
You have touched my heart and you are my new spring dawn.

"Nice song," she whispered as they swayed around the room with rain beginning to fall outside. "Sing it to me every night."

"No problem," he said with a gentle smile as he twirled her around.

"I love you, Dr. Collins," she said warmly leaning back to catch his eyes.

"I *adore* you, Dr. Angie. Absolutely … positively … adore you."

WINTER MIDNIGHT
(Book #3 in the Autumn Sunset Series)

Cindy Marcum is doing her best to change her life both for her mother's sake as well as her own. As Sue Marcum begins cancer treatments and Cindy starts work as the temporary church secretary, they only imagined that their lives had become complicated. But when recently divorced Kyle Sarkos steps into the picture, they become entangled with a mysterious murder and a displaced child. As their search for the truth takes them across the U.S., they learn to deal with the deep regrets of their pasts and come to understand that God truly can work all things for the good of those who love Him.

SUMMER SUNRISE
(Book #4 in the Autumn Sunset Series)

Deception, whether accidental or deliberate, always carries a price. Annie Williams has held a secret from her husband for years, but can the well-meaning intentions of her heart erase the hurt such a secret could bring? Billy Marcum has almost pulled his life together, but the lies of his past seem to dog his heels at every turn. Can he possibly turn the page at last and build a life that is no longer self-centered and no longer destructive towards those he loves the most? The church in Dockrey has grown too large for Jonathan and Kyle to handle. As a new staff member comes on board, will he be a team player in the ministry or a tool of deception and divisiveness? When the truth is interwoven with lies, each life will be affected in some way.